Sin Bin

I0694580

CHELSEA CURTO

Copyright © 2025 by Chelsea Curto

Proofreading by April Editorial

Copy editing by Britt Tayler at Paperback Proofreader

Cover by Chloe Friedlein

All rights reserved.

No part of this book may be reproduced in any form or by any electronic or mechanical means, including information storage and retrieval systems, without written permission from the author, except for the use of brief quotations in a book review.

This is a work of fiction. Any resemblance to actual persons, living or dead, businesses, companies, or events is entirely coincidental.

*For the ones still trying to figure everything out.
You're not behind. There's so much time, and something even better is
waiting for you on the other side.*

*(And for the readers who love when the six six grumpy hockey coach gets
on his knees and begs. Brody Saunders is for you.)*

AUTHOR'S NOTE

When I sat down to write Sin Bin, I wasn't sure where I wanted Hannah and Brody's story to go, to be honest. I knew I wanted the two of them to start their relationship with a one-night stand, but after? I was clueless.

Then I started thinking about ways the two of them would be forced to spend time together. With Hannah being a figure skater, having her coach Brody's daughter felt natural. But I wanted her to go through a journey of her own as well.

That's when it hit me: burnout.

An athlete who was successful and competitive for many years reaches their breaking point and just wants to fall back in love with the sport they've spent their whole life doing. A bit of a stretch? Sure. Then I found a couple U.S. figure skaters who retired at an early age, only to come back a few years later with renewed determination.

The number of elite athletes in the world is small, but the feelings Hannah experiences toward skating—dread, dislike, loathing, disinterest—are things any of us can feel doing *anything* in life.

While this book shifts away from the previous books in the DC Stars series as far as the female main character being a dynamic figure on a sports team, Hannah is no less powerful just because she's an athlete… and Brody recognizes that power. She's just as capable, just as smart, just as sarcastic and sure of herself and what she wants out of life.

The themes remain the same: a man uplifts the woman he's in a relationship with. He supports her, he listens to her, and he shows her her worth.

Please note some instances of hockey game play, figure skating programs and scoring etc have been altered for readability and enjoyment.

I love Brody and Hannah dearly, and I hope you enjoy Sin Bin.

Xoxo,
Chelsea

CHARACTER CATCH UP

I always do my best to write my books as standalone novels even though they're part of a series, but many of the characters mentioned in Sin Bin have their own books. I never want anyone to feel confused while reading, so I created a quick character catch up so you can know who is who before diving in.

If this is your first book of mine, welcome! I'm so glad you're here.

If you're a big DC Stars fan, I hope you're excited to be back with the boys.

For timeline purposes, the first chapters of Sin Bin takes place at the ***same time*** as the Hat Trick prologue. When we time jump to sixteen months later, we're in the season ***after*** Hat Trick. Hat Trick's epilogue takes place in chapter twenty of Sin Bin.

Maverick Miller and **Emmy Hartwell** have their own book, **Face Off,** which is book one in the DC Stars series. It's a dislike to lovers, rivals with benefits, black cat x golden retriever story full of banter and spice.

Piper Mitchell and **Liam Sullivan** have their own book, **Power Play,** which is book two in the DC Stars series.

It's a grumpy x sunshine, goalie x rinkside reporter, teach me, accidental marriage story.

Hudson Hayes and **Madeline Galloway** have their own book, **<u>Slap Shot</u>**, which is book three in the DC Stars series. It's a single mom x hockey player, sunshine x sunshine, slow burn story.

Riley Mitchell and **Lexi Armstrong** have their own book, **<u>Hat Trick</u>**, which is book four in the DC Stars series. It's a former sunshine x sunshine, hockey player x athletic trainer, friends with benefits story.

As always, I've left lots of clues about upcoming books. I can't wait to see if you find them!

DC Stars Roster

Maverick (Mavvy) Miller - right winger
Liam (Sully) Sullivan - goalie
Hudson (Huddy Boy) Hayes - defenseman
Ethan (Easy E) Richardson - center
Grant (G-Money) Everett - left winger

Brody Saunders - head coach
Riley Mitchell - honorary Stars player

Sin Bin is a romantic comedy full of laughs, spice, and swoon, but I want to share a few content warnings that some readers might want to be aware of.

-explicit language
-alcohol consumption
-multiple explicit sex scenes
-mention of infertility (brief)
-loss of a limb by a side character (brief, off page)
-mention of a skating accident
-mention of burnout
-mention of postpartum depression (brief)
-mention of a parental death (brief, off page)

As always, take care of yourselves and protect your heart. If you have any questions about any of the things listed above, please know my DMs are always open (@authorchelseacurto on IG).

ONE
BRODY

THIS CLUB IS TOO FUCKING loud, or I'm too fucking old.

Both are probably true.

My daughter would be the first to remind me I'm too geriatric to be out this late, and she's right. The pounding headache and my wavering patience that's growing thinner by the second is far from enjoyable, but the blonde who's been taunting me all night from across the club almost makes it tolerable.

I take another sip of my beer to stop myself from doing something stupid like going up to her and asking her name.

As if I don't already know it.

Hannah Everett.

The younger sister of my second line left winger, Grant Everett, and someone I shouldn't be within ten feet of.

That hasn't stopped me from looking at her.

I drag my eyes away from her bare shoulders. I force myself to focus on something other than the flush on her skin when she lifts her arms above her head and sways to the beat of the music pulsing through the speakers.

When was the last time I was with a woman? Two years ago? Maybe three? The months blur together when the NHL season gets underway. Training camp late in September bleeds into the regular season then the post season, and now that I'm thinking about it, it might be closer to four years since my last rendezvous with someone other than my hand.

Christ.

I'm pathetic.

"You want another round?"

I glance at the bartender who's pointing at my beer bottle. I strain to hear him over someone screaming into a microphone about being world champions and the answering round of applause and cheers. If it's one of my players, they're going to be in so much trouble. I'll bang on their door at six in the morning as punishment for acting like a showboating dickbag.

I don't give a damn about their hangover.

They might have won the Stanley Cup earlier tonight and brought the trophy back to DC for the second year in a row, but I'm not afraid to call them out if they do something stupid that embarrasses the franchise.

My headache is going to last all day tomorrow. Spending the start of my offseason in the DC Stars' governors' office while they lecture me about getting my players under control sounds like my idea of hell.

Coaching responsibilities and all of that.

"Nah. I'm good." I pull out my wallet and find my credit card. "I'm going to close my tab."

"It's on the house tonight."

"No the fuck it isn't."

"Yeah, it is." The bartender laughs. "You're the youngest coach in NHL history to win two Cups. Your money is no good here."

"I don't like when people argue with me." I shrug off the praise and rifle through my wallet. Dropping five twenties on the counter, I shove the bills his way. "Take it."

"Between the tips your players have left and the publicity they've generated from tagging us on social media, I'm going to be able to pay my rent for the rest of the year with tonight's earnings. It means a lot." He scoops up the money and shoves it in the overflowing tip jar. I spot plenty of hundred-dollar bills. Tons of twenties and fifties, and pride races through me. My guys might be menaces half the damn time, but they have good heads on their shoulders. "You want a water to go?"

"That would be—"

"Leaving already? You can't be that bored."

A voice from behind me carries over the music and interrupts us. I glance over my shoulder and find Hannah smiling my way.

Suddenly I'm hot all over.

And in need of another drink.

"Yeah," I say. "This place isn't my scene."

"What is your scene?" she asks.

"I don't know." I gesture to Maverick Miller, the team's captain and star player, standing on top of a bar without his shirt on. My gaze cuts over to Ethan Richardson, our center, lifting the Cup over his head. "Somewhere I can hear myself think."

"I know a place that's quieter."

"Doubt that's possible. Everyone in this city recognizes me."

"That's a bold assumption. Not everyone loves hockey." She leans an elbow on the bar and swirls her drink around. Her lips clamp down on her straw, taking a long sip of what looks and smells like whiskey and ginger ale while her eyes never leave mine. "Do you always walk around thinking you're important?"

Her sarcasm makes my cheeks heat. I'm too warm. She's too close. "Important is the last thing I am," I grumble. "I'm the most boring person on the planet."

Her eyes flick to the collection of friendship bracelets on my wrist. Olivia, my thirteen-year-old, made them for me to wear to tonight's game, a good luck memento she thought I needed. Hannah's attention moves to the tattoos that span from my hand to my biceps. Her gaze lingers on the ones hiding under my shirt, barely visible at the dip of my collar, before letting out a hum.

"My apartment is free."

"You don't know anything about me. I could be a serial killer," I say.

"I could probably fix you if you were." She lifts an eyebrow, voice dropping low. "Are you a serial killer, Brody?"

Hearing my name makes me pause. It's rare anyone in my life uses it, often going with Coach or Dad or Saunders, but I like how it sounds coming from her. I also like the grin she's trying to fight off. Her whole face lights up, and I don't know if I've ever seen someone so happy.

"If the rumors about me are true, I could be," I say. "I come with a warning label."

"Even better." Her smile widens. She stands up straight, and I shouldn't be noticing how short her skirt is. The way it barely reaches the tops of her thighs and how it hugs her hips. "I have some knives you can use."

A sound whooshes out of me. It might be a laugh. I'm pretty sure it is, but I cover it up with a cough.

Having her think she's funny is dangerous. It's going to give her the wrong idea. A sense of power, and that's not going to end well for anyone.

Especially me.

"Are you old enough to drink?" I ask, even though I know the answer.

She is.

I'm well aware of everything about her, and bringing up her age is the easiest way to draw a line between us.

If only she would take the fucking bait.

"I'm old enough to do a lot of things." Hannah tips her head to the side. Her ponytail is held together by a white ribbon, and the sight of it jumbles my brain. "Are you young enough to be out this late? I thought there were laws against senior citizens driving after a certain time of night. We have to be close to your curfew, old man."

"Brat," I mumble. It's a bad sign when all she does is laugh. "That's not how you should talk to your elders."

"You have to be, what? Close to fifty?"

"I wish I was close to fifty. Then I'd be close to death, and it would get me out of having to talk to anyone ever again."

"What a lovely way to look at life."

My lips quirk. I scrub a hand over my jaw and look around, hoping Grant hasn't noticed us talking. Gossip is the last thing I need, but no one is paying attention to us.

All the guys are celebrating. They're enjoying their victory in their own ways, and hanging out with Hannah can't be the worst thing in the world.

Something tells me she would be a lot of fucking fun.

"I'm thirty-seven," I say. "Almost thirty-eight. Tomorrow is my birthday."

"Really?" Her teeth sink into her bottom lip. It's entirely too distracting. "What are we doing to celebrate?"

I'm severely out of practice. Absolutely clueless when it comes to dating and women and relationships, but it almost feels like she's flirting with me.

My throat bobs around a swallow. A hundred wicked thoughts run through my head, and each of them would get me in a shitload of trouble.

Fucking you against a wall would be a great way to start another year.

For a minute, I can't bring myself to care about the repercussions the daydream would bring, because I'm leaning into her space. I'm listening to her sharp inhale and testing the waters to see how she plans to play this.

"I don't know," I answer. "What did you have in mind?"

"I did say my apartment was free." Hannah wets her lips. I follow the path of her tongue, imagining what it would feel like licking down my stomach and up my cock. I have to squeeze my eyes shut. "Do you want to take a walk?"

"You're too young for us to—"

"To, what? Be friends? Get some fresh air? I'm twenty-four, Brody. I can drink. I can vote. I can hang out with other adults. You can save the lecture."

My eyes open and meet hers. They're a pretty shade of blue. Big and wide and watching me, and the rational part of my brain is screaming at me to walk away. To shut this down before it goes too far, and I sort through the list of all the reasons why this is a bad idea.

There are thirteen years between us. She's related to one of my players which automatically makes her off-limits. Hanging around is a recipe for disaster. An invitation to get my ass kicked, but I can't force myself to leave.

I've been looking at her for a while now, and one wide smile and the tilt of her head tells me I don't stand a chance.

I'm weak as shit.

"A walk," I repeat, firm in the declaration. Maybe the louder I am, the more I'll believe it. "That's it."

"Calm down, Daddy," she teases with a smirk and the flip of her ponytail. My fingers curl around the edge of the bar to stop myself from reaching over and wrapping the long strands around my wrist. From giving a sharp tug and pulling her into my lap. "I know how to behave myself."

It's not her I'm worried about.

It's me.

She turns and saunters for the door, not bothering to check if I'm following. I shuffle behind her, aware I might be making the biggest mistake of my life.

I can't bring myself to care.

TWO
HANNAH

GRANT

Hannahhhhhhhhhhhhh!!

Where did you gooooooooooooooo?

ME

My head started to hurt, so I left early.

GRANT

Are you okayyyyy? Meds? You need medz?

ME

No meds. I'm in good hands :)

GRANT

You're the best sister everrrrrr.

ME

And you're so wasted! Be safe, have fun, and
call me later this week! Proud of you, G.

THE RUMORS about Brody Saunders are true. He doesn't talk much. He communicates in grunts and scowls. He's tall as hell.

And he's hot as sin.

I'm not afraid to admit I did a deep dive on him when Grant was drafted by the DC Stars a couple of years ago. Everyone kept talking about what a young team they had, led by a fantastic new coach, and curiosity got the best of me.

A pass through his (very limited) social media later, concluding that Brody is *really fucking fine* would be an understatement. He's a man in every sense of the word with broad, wide shoulders and a neatly-trimmed beard. Dark hair, dark eyes. Tattoos decorating his arms and the back of his massive palm.

I've always been drawn to people who would burn the world down for me if given the chance, and I have a feeling Brody fits that characteristic to a tee.

How I ended up next to him on the sidewalk is still a mystery, but I'm not going to question it. Not when he sees me shiver at the gust of wind that rips through the June air, pulls off his sweatshirt, and hands it to me without a word.

"You don't want it?" The scent of his cologne tickles my nose when I slip the hoodie on. "Thank you."

"I'm six six and two hundred pounds. The dead of winter is my favorite time of year," he answers.

"I spend almost every day on the ice, but I still prefer warmer temperatures. Guess it's my Florida blood. It dips below sixty degrees, and I'm miserable."

"How long have you been skating?"

"For many years. How long have you been playing hockey?"

"Longer than you've been alive." The muscles in his jaw tighten like he's mad about his history with the sport. Maybe he's mad at me. "Where are we going?"

"For a walk. If we happen to pass my apartment, we can

go up." When he eyes me, I hold up my hands. "This isn't some plan to jump your bones. If I wanted to do that, I could've left with anyone else."

"All the single guys at the club sucked. Trust me. I interact with them on a daily basis."

"Who said I was limiting myself to men?"

"What does that mean?"

"I'm bisexual," I say. "And, no. My brother doesn't know."

"Your brother doesn't know?" Brody stops walking and steps toward me. I shuffle back, having to tip my chin up to look at him towering above me. Liquid heat pools in my stomach when his palm rests against the brick wall behind me, gaze unreadable. "Would he have a problem with your sexual preferences? If so, I'll rip his throat—"

"Thank you, but you can save the hero speech and threats of violence." I put a hand on his chest and he yanks away from me like he's been burned. "Grant wouldn't care. I think on some level, he already knows. We're best friends and tell each other almost everything. I just... I don't want my personal life to be part of his professional life. The media is ruthless. He shouldn't have to field questions about who I'm sleeping with when he's getting ready for the most important games of his career, so I'm keeping it to myself for now."

"If he ever gives you any shit..." Brody trails off, running a hand through his hair. "You tell me, and I'll take care of it."

"I'll keep that in mind."

"Do you live with him?"

"God, no." I laugh. "We didn't have a lot of money growing up, and we shared a room until Grant was eleven. The day he got his own space was the best day of my life. For as much as I love my brother, we do not function well as roommates."

"Is your apartment close?" he asks.

"It is. Interested in coming up?"

"Only for a few minutes, then I'm leaving."

"I'm not forcing you to spend time with me. You can go whenever you want."

"Someone might give me an earful if they saw me leaving your place."

I sidestep past him and start in the direction of my building. "Good thing I'm just the lowly sibling of an NHL player."

"Lowly?" Brody's footsteps echo behind me, his voice almost a growl. "Not sure that's true. You're a world champion figure skater."

His observation catches me off guard. The toe of my shoe hits a dip in the concrete. I stumble over my feet, but before I can fall, his hand is around my waist. His fingers dig into my hip, and I'm completely safe.

"How do you know that?" I breathe out, a palm on his bicep to steady myself.

"My daughter is also a figure skater. I listen when she talks."

I remember reading an article about him having a kid, but it never mentioned anything about a wife. I wrangle myself free from his hold.

"Please don't tell me you're married."

"No. Amicably separated from Olivia's mother after we realized the only place we were compatible was in the bedroom after a night of drinking. We co-parent well. We don't do relationships well."

"How old is your daughter?"

"Thirteen." Brody smiles when he says it. His face comes to life in a way I haven't seen from him all night. "She's full of energy and keeps me on my toes."

"Clearly she doesn't get that from you."

"No." A gentle laugh. Humor in the shake of his head. "She does not."

Comfortable silence settles between us for the next few blocks. He walks on the side closest to the street, and when we make it to my apartment complex, I smile.

"This is me. Still want to come up?" I ask.

"Sure." His eyes darken when I tug on the hem of my skirt. "But only to make sure you get inside safely."

"I heard you the first ten times." I tap my key fob against the door and push the glass open with my hip. "I'm on the eighth floor."

Brody looks around the lobby, nodding hello to the security guard sitting behind the concierge desk. "Is this a safe area?"

"Yeah. There are families in the neighborhood, and it's nicer than what I could afford by myself. Grant helps pay for it," I say when he gives me a questioning look. "Figure skating is a very expensive sport, which I'm sure you know all about with your daughter. People assume we make millions of dollars, but we don't. A win at the World Championships brings in sixty-four thousand. Which, yeah, isn't terrible, but the unfortunate side of being an athlete is not making money unless you're winning. When you've had a rough couple of years like I have, it's even harder."

"What do you mean?" He hits the button for the elevator and brings his hand to the small of my back as he ushers me inside when it reaches the ground floor. "Are you injured?"

"I can't find my groove." The elevator doors close, and I realize this is the first time I've acknowledged the sensation that's gripped me every time I've laced up my skates the last few months. "My late teens and early twenties were really good placement wise, but that success has fizzled out. I had a rough showing at an event in March. Since then, motivating myself to train has been difficult."

"Is that the last time you competed?" The elevator rises. Brody's palm is still on my back, and I swear his thumb grazes along the line of my spine. "That was a while ago."

"It is, but I'm sure this feeling will pass. It's all an ebb and flow, right?" The elevator doors open, and I lead the way down the hall. When we get to my apartment, I slip my key in the lock, turning the knob. "Here we are."

"Shoes on or off?"

"Whatever you're comfortable with." I kick off the heels I've been wearing for hours and groan at the relief of freeing my toes. "Want some food?"

"My last meal was lunch before the game, and that feels like days ago," Brody says.

"Congratulations on being back-to-back champions, by the way. The guys played really well in a tough series."

"They did. They're going to be the reason my hair turns gray, but I couldn't ask for a better group." He pauses, huffing out a laugh. "Don't tell anyone I said that. It would only inflate their egos, and I like knowing I scare them."

"Grant is terrified of you, but you're also his idol. He alternates between excitement when you acknowledge him and fear he's going to piss you off." I round the corner to the kitchen, motioning for him to follow. A quick check of my fridge shows limited food options, and I move a bottle of salad dressing out of the way. "Do you want the bad news or the good news first?"

"Bad. I thrive off negativity."

"I don't have anything to eat."

"And the good news?"

"The pizza place down the road is still open, and they make the best pineapple and ham pizza in the city."

"You're joking." Brody leans against the counter, arms folded over his chest. The move shows off the veins in his forearms and more of his tattoos, and it's unfair how goddamn attractive he is. "You like pineapple on your pizza?"

"Let me guess. You only like cheese and sauce. How boring."

"You say boring, I say classic. We don't need to reinvent things that have nothing wrong with them."

"I bet you aren't spontaneous."

"What gives you that impression?"

"Just a hunch. Half cheese, half pineapple coming right up." I laugh and grab my phone from my purse, putting in an order. "Should be ready in twenty minutes."

"You're making me live life on the edge tonight."

"You can't be too bothered. You're still hanging around." I head for the liquor cabinet in the living room. "Do you want a drink?"

"Are you going to have anything?"

"I could go for two fingers," I murmur, looking at him over my shoulder. When I do, I catch his eyes moving away from my ass. There's a guilty expression pulling at his lips. "Maybe three. I bet I could take it."

THREE

HANNAH

"HANNAH."

Brody stares at me, my name a warning.

"What?" I feign innocence and stand on my toes to grab two glasses from the cabinet. Heat engulfs me from behind, his presence known before I can see him. His firm chest presses against my back. Our hands brush when we both reach for the decanter of liquor. "I'm talking about whiskey. What are *you* talking about?"

"You know what you're doing."

"I'm not doing anything." I pour us each a drink. There's barely any distance between us when I spin, facing him, and his fingers graze mine when he takes the glass from me. "Lighten up, birthday boy."

"Cheers," he says, a deep and rumbly tone I feel all over my body. We knock the drinks together and take a sip in unison. His eyes never leave mine while I swallow, and when I bring the glass away from my lips, Brody lifts his free hand. He brushes his thumb against the corner of my mouth where a drop of liquid sits. "That's better."

Holy hell.

I wonder if it's scientifically possible to combust from a single touch, because I'm on the precipice of imploding.

I knew he was a large specimen of a man, but seeing his palm up close and knowing it could easily wrap around my throat nearly sends me into a tailspin.

I let out a laugh and move for the couch, sitting on the cushions. I pat the open space next to me, watching him drop his head back and stare at the ceiling.

"I shouldn't."

"Then don't." I shrug and sip my drink, turning to look out the window at the city lights twinkling below. "Makes no difference to me."

Out of my peripheral vision, I notice him shift on his feet. He downs the rest of his whiskey in one swallow and sets the empty glass on a table before walking my way.

Brody sits beside me and lifts my legs so there's room for him. He drapes my calves over his thighs, slings an arm over the back of the couch, then sighs. I giggle.

"What?" he asks.

I hide my smile when he rests his hand on my shin. "Nothing."

"I don't like secrets."

"For a guy who was reluctant to come up, you sure look comfortable." I laugh when he scowls. "It's okay to have fun, Brody."

"I have plenty of fun."

"Let me guess: You play chess. Wait. No. You do the cross-word puzzle in the morning. With a *pen*."

"Both are good for keeping your brain sharp."

"Which is important at your advanced age."

"Fucking brat."

He strokes his thumb up my calf, stopping when he gets to my knee. I shiver, embarrassed to admit the effect he has on me. It's a blessing when my phone chimes to let me know the pizza is here.

"I'll be back," I say, standing.

The weight of his gaze is heavy on the walk down the hall. I smile at the doorman who hands over the cardboard box, and a pitstop in the kitchen has me rummaging through my junk drawer until I find what I'm looking for.

In the living room, Brody is in the same spot where I left him. He glances up as I approach with a burning candle placed in the middle of the pizza.

"What's that?" he asks.

"Your cake." I hold it out to him. "Make a wish."

"A wish." His eyes stay on me when he leans forward, blowing out the candle. He pulls it out of the pizza, licking it clean, and I squeeze my thighs together at the sight of his tongue. "Done."

"I hope it comes true."

"So do I."

"Happy birthday, Brody."

"I don't need any of this." He takes the box from me and puts it on the coffee table. He reaches for my hand, tugging me back to the couch. "And it's not going to get me to eat pineapple pizza."

"I would say my plan has been thwarted, but not everything is about you." I grab a slice and take a bite, moaning at the melted cheese. "You should have some."

"*Fuck*. That sound." Brody scrubs a hand over his face and closes his eyes. "You've been distracting me all night."

"Me? I didn't do anything."

"You don't get it, do you?"

"What is there to get, Brody?"

"We shouldn't be having this conversation."

"Did I do something wrong?" I set the slice of pizza down, dusting off my hands. The shift in his mood is confusing. "I'm sorry if I'm making you uncomfortable, but I—"

"Uncomfortable? You could never make me uncomfortable." His eyes blink open, and they're darker than before.

"You asked me what I do for fun, Hannah, and tonight it was thinking about all the ways I'd fuck you if I had the chance."

"You want to *fuck* me?" I whisper. The world tilts on its axis. "Is this a joke? You don't talk to me at team events. You don't even look my way. I thought you hated me."

I tried to not let it bother me when he didn't acknowledge me at the team's Friends and Family night last fall. I pretended not to notice when he walked past me earlier tonight during the on-ice celebrations and shook everyone else's hand. He's never been mean about it, but it still stings.

I've been operating under the assumption Brody Saunders couldn't care less about my existence this year.

I guess I was wrong.

"I don't hate you. This season has made it painfully obvious I'm attracted to you," he says. "And I can't do anything about it no matter how badly I want to."

"What?" This is too much information to process after a couple of drinks. After his gaze shifts and he stares at me with white-hot intensity. The temperature in the room swells to unbelievably warm, and I'm a little lightheaded. "You like me?"

"I shouldn't have told you any of that." Brody shakes his head. "I should go."

"Or you could stay and tell me more about the ways you would fuck me," I blurt, emboldened by the way his eyes rake down my thighs. Hungry, aching. "If that's what you want, you should do it."

"It is my birthday," he murmurs. A justification for why he should give in. The reasoning behind his decision.

"It is."

"And I've been so fucking good this year."

"I bet you have."

Time stops.

I'm no longer breathing.

One minute, neither of us are moving. The next, I'm on

top of him, straddling his thighs. Brody meets me halfway, a hand on the plane between my shoulders, the other under my ass. His fingers fan out over my backside, twisting the fabric of my skirt and giving it a tug.

"Hannah," he growls, mouth inches away from mine. His teeth nip at my bottom lip, and warmth overtakes me. "Are you sure?"

"Pretty fucking sure," I breathe out, lowering myself onto his lap.

He pulls back and scans my face, searching for any sign of hesitancy. When I give him a small nod, I swear he growls.

"Fuck it," he says, losing the war with himself. A battle I'm glad to win. "I don't give a shit anymore," he adds, and his lips crash against mine.

FOUR

HANNAH

BRODY'S MOUTH IS HEAVENLY.

His lips make me dizzy. Sparks of color burst behind my eyes with every swipe of his tongue, and I have to wrap my arms around his neck to anchor myself to him.

I've kissed a lot of people in my life, but it's never been like this: all-consuming. Rough and possessive. *Desperate.*

A moan rattles out of me when I feel the strain of his hard cock through the denim of his jeans, and I need *more.*

"You've been taunting me all night with this goddamn skirt." His palms slip under the leather and move up my legs. He runs his fingers over my thighs, pausing when he reaches my underwear. "I couldn't look away from you."

His hands move, pulling my—his—sweatshirt over my head and yanking down the front of my shirt, exposing my breasts. It's the most determined I've ever seen someone to get my clothes off, and I feel wanted in a way I never have before.

"Is that why you were scowling at me?" I ask, a sigh stuck in my throat when he pinches my nipple. "You looked like you had a stick up your ass."

Brody's laugh is a rough exhale in the crook of my neck.

"I was trying not to imagine what your cunt felt like, but I couldn't help it," he says, pressing his lips to the line of my throat. He sucks on my skin, leaving behind a mark. When he pulls my hair free from its ponytail, he puts the ribbon holding it together somewhere I can't see. "Would you be tight? Would I have to work for it? Or would you take me so well because you're as desperate for me as I am for you?"

There's not a rational thought left in my brain, and when he leans forward, biting the soft part of my breast, I swear I see stars.

"Take my skirt off and find out."

"What do you want from this?" he asks.

I look down at him, finding flushed cheeks and messy hair. There's a small drop of saliva on the corner of his lips. I wipe it away, mimicking his move from earlier, and the last fragments of my rationality splinter when Brody turns his head and sucks my finger into his mouth.

"You," I blurt, adrenaline-fueled. My hands move to his chest. I try to memorize every divot, every hard slope of his body under my fingertips. I peel his shirt over his head, marveling at his sculpted physique. "Jesus Christ."

"My name is Brody, sweetheart. Try to get it right next time." He cups my cheek with the hint of a smile. "Tell me, Hannah. Was this your plan all along? Bag the coach, get him to reveal his deep, dark secret about his crush on you, and have some fun?"

"Fuck you," I say, embarrassed when he shoves my skirt up my waist and traces his fingers over my underwear. There's a damp spot on the cotton already, and he groans when he finds it. "My only plan was to attempt to be your friend, but from the way you were eye-fucking me all night, it seems like *you're* the one with a plan. You're conflicted, aren't you? You want me, but you're trying to justify why you should stay away from me. You think I'm too young." I take his hands and pin them against the curve of the couch. Mischief gleams behind his eyes. "Too off-limits." His pulse jumps when I kiss his cheek, his throat. "Guess what, Brody? I'm a woman who knows what she wants, and tonight, I want you."

"Where is your room?"

"Down the hall, but we can—"

Brody stands and lifts me in his arms. He carries me, each step purposeful as he opens the doors on his right and his left. I hide my giggle in his bare chest when he finds the bathroom and curses under his breath.

"It's a goddamn maze in here."

"Walk straight." A full laugh bursts free when he tries the linen closet. "*Straight*, Brody."

He finally opens the door to my room and stomps across the rug. He deposits me on the bed and steps back, a hand on his belt and his beautiful body bathed in moonlight.

"You should know something about me, Hannah."

"What's that?"

"I like to fuck my women where I can enjoy them." His fingers work the zipper on his jeans, pulling down the fly before popping open the silver button keeping them on his hips. "Where I can eat them out until they come."

My heart nearly flatlines when he steps out of his pants, leaving him in only a pair of gray briefs that show off strong legs from years of playing hockey.

Brody kneels on the edge of the mattress and crawls toward me. He eases me onto my back. Strokes his fingers across my stomach in the cruelest form of torture I've ever experienced. He bends, whispering, "Let me take care of you."

"Beg," I say, and his nostrils flare. He grips my knee, fingers digging into my skin. I lift my chin, realizing the power I have, and my mouth curls in a smile. "Show me how badly you want to take care of me, Brody. How attracted you are to me."

"Please," he croaks. He shoves a hand in his briefs, giving

himself a slow stroke. The other palm moves higher, to the inside of my thigh. "I'll make it so good for you. Let me get you out of my fucking head. I want—I *need* to make you come."

"That was very good." I grab his chin, my thumb dancing along his jaw. "Go ahead, Coach. Get me off."

"*Hannah.*" My name is a rasp. The hand in his briefs moves faster, a sharp twist of his wrist. "Are you sure?"

I take off my shirt. Brody groans when I push my breasts together. "I'm practically naked. I'm wet. You tell me if you think I'm sure."

"You're so hot." Some of his confidence wavers. He blows out a breath. "And your tits…" He tips his head back, staring at the ceiling. "*Fuck.* You're making it very difficult to behave."

"I think the point is to *not* behave. What if I do it first?" My hands move down my body, stopping at my skirt. His eyes are on me again, his pupils blown wide as he follows the path of my palms. "And you watched?"

Brody's shoulders rise and fall when I bring my skirt over my thighs and take it off. He stops breathing altogether when I twist the waistband of my underwear around my fingers and wiggle the cotton down my hips. When I go to toss the piece of fabric on the floor, he puts a hand on my wrist.

"I want them," he rasps, taking the underwear from me. He brings them to his nose, inhaling deeply before he runs his tongue along the inside seam. "You taste sweet as hell."

"Yeah?" I tip my thighs open. My feet slide across the sheets so he has a perfect view between my legs, and Brody wraps the underwear around his wrist. "After you watch, you can have another taste."

"*Fuck,*" he groans again, and I don't think he's capable of saying anything else. He inches toward me, cock still thick and hard in his briefs. "I want to see."

I've never performed in front of an audience, but his desperation spurs me on. I push a finger inside myself, back arching off the bed at the stretch. "That feels so good," I whisper, savoring the sensation settling low in my belly.

Brody moves at lightning speed, lying flat on his stomach. His eyes are level with the hand touching myself, attention unnerving while he watches me intently. "How many fingers does it take to get you off, Hannah?"

"Three of mine." I gasp when I add a second finger, squirming on the sheets and chasing the high I'm craving. "I'd probably only need two of yours."

"You'd take them so well, wouldn't you? I'd get you warmed up. I'd make you come on my hand, then I'd fuck you nice and slow."

Who would've thought Brody Saunders would be the most talkative when he's half naked and in bed with a woman? Who knew the man who scowls more than he smiles would have a filthy mouth, narrating everything he wants to do to me?

It's the best kind of surprise.

"I've never come from penetration." I curl my fingers at the admission, hitting a spot that feels particularly delicious. "Only from foreplay. And never with a guy. Only with a woman."

"Women are significantly smarter than men. But I'd be able to do it," he says, and there's a smugness behind it. Arrogance that's extremely hot. "I could get you to come on my cock, and you'd thank me after."

Hell.

His confidence is intoxicating, and I wonder if it's because he's the oldest person I've been with. There's something so appealing in his assuredness. In fantasizing about the things he'd whisper in my ear while he plucked me apart until I was nothing but a mess of limbs and sweat and satisfaction.

"I would," I tell him, bracing myself to add a third finger. When I do, Brody wraps his hand around my wrist. He guides me, and this might be the most intimate moment of my life.

He can see *everything*, and his eyes spark with patient agony. "It would be so good with you."

"Hannah," he croaks, and it's a plea. Like he's begging me to put him out of his misery. He presses a hot kiss to my knee, the scruff of his beard burning my skin, and he grinds into the mattress. None of this feels real. "I want—"

"*Yes.*" I close my eyes, sinking into the exquisite pleasure that comes from touching myself and knowing exactly what it takes to have a mind-altering orgasm. There's no faking. I can get there and rejoice, all while Brody watches. "Whatever it is, the answer is yes."

He slows my movements. He's gentle as he eases my hand away. I groan at the loss of contact, of feeling full and then empty, but he kisses my knee again. "Bring your legs to your chest. Hold yourself open for me. Let me touch you."

My eyes flutter open. The authority in his voice makes me want to do anything he asks. I'm practically panting, but there's no time to wonder how I might look or sound because his broad chest is nudging my legs wider. I watch with awe as he puts my feet on his shoulders and blows a warm puff of air against me.

With shaky hands, I reach between my legs and spread myself for him. What follows is a string of crude expletives. A murmur of all the places he wants to put his tongue and another rut against the mattress.

Desire is written on his face when he places a large, warm palm on my stomach and uses his other hand to push a single finger inside me.

I gasp.

It's the most wonderful thing I've ever experienced. He gets to his second knuckle, and I'm groaning. Tightening around him, and he rumbles out my name.

"Okay?" he slurs. I don't know if it's from the alcohol he's been sipping all night or the electric current buzzing between us, but I don't care. Not when he presses a thumb to my clit and rubs a slow circle, the movement simultaneous with the easy way he fucks me. "Is that okay, Hannah?"

Brody brings his finger all the way out, then presses it back inside me. It's quicker, more determined, and I can hear how wet I am. How needy I sound, and I almost lose it entirely when he spits on my pussy and wipes his saliva on me.

"No," I say, and he stops immediately. He props himself up on an elbow before I'm pulling his hair. Urging his face lower, frantic as I give him a shove. "It's so fucking good. Don't you dare stop."

"You're so pretty. Perfect tits. Perfect body and perfect strong legs." He grinds his hips into the mattress, and I love that he's not hiding his enthusiasm for me. I love that he's enjoying this as much as I am even though I'm not touching him. "I've been dreaming about you for goddamn *months*."

"Really?" He adds a second finger, the stretch just at the point of uncomfortable. I grip the sheets, reveling in how *good* he makes me feel. I'm on top of the world, and I never want to come down. "You should've done something about it."

"It's better this way. One time. I'll get my fill of you, then I'll walk away. I'll get you out of my head."

One time doesn't seem like it could ever be enough, but I'm not going to argue. There's no world where the two of us exist as something other than a mindless hookup in the dead of night no one will ever know about.

We're too different. We live opposite lives, him with a career and a kid, and me seconds away from an existential crisis. We want different things, have different priorities, but tonight?

Tonight I'm going to enjoy the hell out of him.

"*Brody*. I need more. I'm close, but I—" I jolt forward when he puts his mouth on me, making circles with his tongue. "Yes. *That*. More of that, please."

"Now who's the one begging?" He nips at the underside of my thigh, then puts his mouth back on me. His tongue and fingers work in tandem to drive me wild, and I've never been this turned on before. "Look how wet you are. This isn't going to take long, is it?"

It's not, but I'm not ashamed of how my body responds to him. How can I be when Brody holds himself above me, long fingers sliding in and out? There's a thumb on my clit. A whisper of how good I am, of how beautiful I look, and a rough kiss that tips me over the edge in a fit of pleasure.

"It's too much." I squeeze my eyes shut when the orgasm hits me, but Brody doesn't relent. He keeps his fingers inside me, letting out the ghost of a groan when a second orgasm surprises me with trembling aftershocks. "I can't. It's—"

"Look at you grinding on my fingers because you're so needy. No one's taken care of you like this before, have they, Hannah?"

No, I think. *No, they haven't.*

I'm thoroughly worn out. Perfectly sated, and it takes several minutes for me to calm down. My skin is sticky with sweat that Brody bends to lick away from between my breasts. His movements slow and he pulls his fingers out of me, running them along the inside of my thighs.

"Condoms are in the bedside table." I gesture to the drawer on my left. My arm feels like it weighs a thousand pounds. "Whenever you're ready."

"Not yet. Move up the bed," he says. I squint and shift across the mattress, every movement grueling and exhausting. Brody pushes up on his knees and pulls his briefs down. "Open your mouth."

I part my lips. He moves to me, a hand wrapped around his length while he gives himself a rough stroke. I whimper when he rests the head of his cock on my tongue, the taste of pre-cum greeting me.

I close my mouth and he rocks forward. I moan around his shaft and he puts a hand on the wall, grunting when I lick him from base to tip.

"What do I have to do to get you to fuck me, Brody?" I say when he pulls all the way out. "Tell you that you're the best I've ever had?" I reach for his balls and cup them in my palm. He almost topples over, his groan echoing around us. I smirk. "Because you are."

FIVE
BRODY

I'VE DIED and gone to heaven.

Maybe it's hell, because I'm sure there will be consequences to all of this, but I really don't give a shit.

I can't bring myself to care when Hannah is blinking up at me with pretty eyes and asking me to fuck her.

I put a hand on the back of her head, tracing her jaw with my knuckles. "Glad to know having my cock in your mouth is the way to keep you from insulting my age."

Her grin is coy when she tilts her head to the side and swirls her tongue over the head. I groan, my restraint splitting in half when she scratches her nails down the front of my thighs.

I'd love to finish in her mouth. I'd love to see my cum on her lips and watch her swallow it down. Or maybe on her chest, decorating her tits. I blow out a breath knowing there's no way in hell I'm going to be satisfied with having her just one time.

"There are other ways to keep me quiet." Hannah touches my balls again, and my groan turns wild. I grip her hair so tightly I'm sure I'm hurting her, but she doesn't complain. "I want you inside me, Brody."

"Last time you were tested?" I ask, trying to be responsible. We need to have this conversation before we do anything else. Before she obliterates all of my brain cells.

"Recently, and everything came back negative. I haven't been with anyone since. I'm also on birth control."

"Me too. Negative. No one since." I pull out of her mouth and reach for the bedside table. I almost knock over a glass of water when I tug on the drawer, grabbing the box of condoms she mentioned and ripping it open. Foil packets go everywhere. I hold one up, my eyes meeting hers. "I need to hear you say you want me to fuck you, Hannah."

"Brody." She sits up, legs open wide, and I can't miss the wet spot on her sheets she left behind after her orgasm. I swear I'm going to think about the sounds she makes when she comes for the rest of my life. "I want you so badly. Don't you want me?"

"Yeah." My voice cracks. "What—how—" I swallow. "Tell me your favorite position."

"I like being on top," Hannah says. She pats the pillows, switching places with me. "For round two, maybe you can fuck me from behind."

"A second round is optimistic. I have a feeling you're going to be the death of me." I adjust my position, stretching out on her bed and reaching for her. "Come here."

She moves, straddling me. Her thighs press against mine, and I sigh. Her body is warm and soft and *perfect*. I put a hand on her waist, my thumb running over her hip bone. Hannah hovers above me, then lowers herself slightly, the ultimate tease.

"It's, ah, been a while for me." My grip on her tightens when she leans forward to kiss my cheek. One lift of my hips and I'd be buried in her. *How fucking reckless.* "No judging."

"I'd never judge my elders. That's disrespectful," she whispers, gasping when I give her clit a light tap. "*Brody.*"

"I might need to take you over my knee." My hands move

to her ass, cupping both round cheeks. Her muscles are solid from years of being an athlete, and she has the most beautiful body I've ever seen. "Would you like that?"

"Maybe I would, *Daddy*," she teases, whining when I give her ass a hard smack.

"You can't say that to me."

"Why? Because you like it too much?"

I grind my teeth when she lowers herself another inch. There's almost no space between us. "*Hannah.*"

"I want to feel you."

"You can't feel me?" I give in to temptation and lift my hips, close to losing myself entirely when the head of my cock pushes past her pussy lips. "Do you feel me now?"

"You're so big, Brody. I want you to fuck me and—" Hannah pulls her mouth away from my neck. I rub a hand up her back, grabbing some of her hair. "Is that your phone?"

I blink, yanked out of the trance she's put me in by the sound of my ringtone echoing down the hall. "*Shit.* Yeah. I think it is. I'm sorry. I hate to be the dickbag who pays more attention to his phone than to you, but I need to check it. It could be Olivia or her mom letting me know—"

"Don't apologize. Family first." She smiles and climbs off me. My eyes rake down her body, and I have to stroke myself when she holds up a foil square. "I'll be here when you're ready."

"Two seconds."

I kiss her forehead and almost sprint down the hall, ignoring the twinge in my knee. My daughter left the arena with Kali, my ex, after the game, but they both know my phone is always on. I never consider the days I don't have custody a childfree time, and if Olivia needs me, she has my full attention.

I grab the phone off the table where I left it in the living room and roll my eyes at the name on the screen. I silence the noise and walk back to Hannah's room, tossing it on the pile with my clothes.

"Not important. Just my drunk captain calling me."

"You're not going to answer it?"

"Why? So I can hear him sing some terrible karaoke song?" I climb back on the bed. Run a hand up her leg, squeezing when I get to her hip. "He called five other times, which tells me he's plastered. I'm not dealing with that."

"What would be your karaoke song?" Hannah hisses when I push a finger inside her. "Something dark and gloomy, I bet."

"You'd never catch me doing karaoke." My phone rings again. I look over my shoulder and Maverick's name flashes across the screen a second time. "You know what? I'm not going to wait to kick Miller's ass. I'm going by his house first thing in the morning with a marching band."

"Just answer it, Brody. You can tell them to fuck off, then you can fuck me."

I can't help but smile when she sticks out her bottom lip in a pout. Another call comes through. This time, it's Hudson.

"That's a tempting argument," I say.

"Here. I'll do it for you. They're probably so drunk they won't recognize my voice."

"Be my guest."

I hand over my phone and Hannah answers it, just as I push another finger inside her.

"Brody's phone." She gasps, a hand on my wrist. "Can I help you?"

I don't hear what's being said on the other end of the line, but I can tell something is wrong. Hannah freezes. She moves her hand to my shoulder, tapping me. I look at her, watching her palm shake as she shoves the phone in my direction.

"What?" I ask.

"This sounds important."

The thing they don't tell you about being a coach is how

you assume the role of big brother or father figure to the guys on your team. There is glitz and glamour and all the good stuff that comes with winning, but you're also the one they turn to when something goes wrong.

I've been there for the death of parents. Divorce announcements and guy's wives miscarrying.

There's no manual or guide for empathy, and you figure out how to navigate the heavy shit as you go. Balancing being a human while also being a professional athlete is hard, and I know firsthand it never ends up how you want.

I sit on the edge of the bed and take the phone, pressing it to my ear.

"This better be really fucking good," I bark out.

"Coach?" Hudson croaks, and my spine straightens. "Is that you?"

"Hayes. What's wrong?"

There's a long pause, and I'm fearing the worst.

He's the most responsible one on the team. I count on him to keep the guys in line when I'm not around, but I remember the day I found him in the locker room when his mom passed away. The blank stare he gave me when I helped him to his feet and the way he crumbled in my arms.

I hope to god nothing happened to his dad.

"Riley," he says.

"Riley? Riley Mitchell?" I ask, mentioning my star defenseman.

"He was in an accident."

"What do you mean an accident?"

"A car accident," Hudson says, and my knees buckle.

"What?" I collapse to the ground, a hand over my mouth. My heart stops beating. "When? How?"

"In his Uber on the way home from the club. The driver called Maverick and—" There's a wail from his side of the phone, and my body moves without me directing it. I stand

and fumble with my clothes, grabbing anything I can find. "They aren't sure he's going to make it."

"Where are you?" I put on my shirt and yank my jeans up my legs. I'm trying not to panic, but bile creeps its way up my throat. My head pounds, excruciating pain radiating across my temples. "I need a hospital name, Hudson."

"MedStar. Georgetown. We just got here and—"

"Be there in twenty."

I hang up. Silence hangs in the room, and I press the heels of my palms into my eyes.

"Brody?" Hannah touches my shoulder. "What's going on?"

"Riley was in an accident." My voice is flat, monotone. I lift my chin to look at her, the hazy outline of her shape blurred by my tears. "They aren't sure if he's going to make it."

"Oh my god." She scrambles to grab a blanket, wrapping it around her body. "Is he—of course he's not okay. I'm so sorry."

Guilt grips me so tight, I struggle to breathe.

I want to ask how the fuck I missed their earlier calls. I want to figure out why I didn't hear the phone ring the other five times, but the answer is obvious. I was too distracted. Too caught up in Hannah and ignoring my responsibilities when I should've stayed at the club. I should've been the one to make sure all my guys got home safe, but I left the second a beautiful woman gave me her attention.

I gave in too quickly. I acted too stupidly, and now one of my players is in a hospital fighting for his life.

I should've been there to answer the fucking phone.

I could've stopped it. I could've told Riley to wait and take a different car. I could've fucking driven him.

"I need to get to the hospital."

"Do you want me to go with you?"

"It's better if you don't." I'm numb. The room is spinning.

"There would be questions about why we're there together. Questions I don't want to answer."

"Can I do anything to help?" she whispers.

"No." I force myself to put one foot in front of the other, only stopping to look back at her when I reach her bedroom door. The pain magnifies when I notice the hurt on her face, the twist of her lips from my rejection. I'm not a believer in divine intervention or fate or any of that other cosmic bullshit, but this seems like a big fucking sign from the universe that I need to stay the hell away from her. My guilt turns to regret, to disappointment in myself when I shake my head. When I roll my shoulders back and say, "I got caught up in the moment tonight, and we need to forget it ever happened. I was never here. We never spent any time together. We left the club separately, and I didn't—"

"Get me off and have your first night of fun in months?"

"Yes." I blow out a breath. I hate how easily she can read me. "That."

"Is that really what you want?" she asks, her tone softening.

No.

It's not what I fucking want at all, but it's what has to happen. She's too good. Too *perfect*, and I don't want her brought into the hell I know is going to greet me the second I leave her apartment and head for the hospital.

Nothing in my life—and her brother's life—is ever going to be the same. I can't give her the attention she deserves. Not when every time my phone rings, I'm going to wonder if it's another one of my players calling because they're hurt and they need me and I'm letting them down.

"It has to be." My throat is on fire, and I hate myself. "There's no world where this could ever be anything more than sex."

"Okay." Hannah lifts her chin and brushes her hair away from her face. "It's already forgotten."

It stings.

It shouldn't, since I'm the one with my head up my ass and *ruining* this, but it fucking hurts.

"I'm sorry," I mumble.

"So am I."

There's probably something else I should say, but it's not about me right now. I turn down the hall, taking off in a sprint. My lungs protest. My knee aches, but I need to get to Riley. I need to get away from the hurt in her eyes so I don't solidify myself as the meanest motherfucker to walk this planet.

There are footsteps behind me, but I don't stop until I'm outside on the street, both hands on my thighs and holding back vomit. I should turn around. I need to look back and see if I can find her window so I can apologize, but I physically can't. I can't bring myself to do it, and I know I'll hate myself from now until the end of time.

THE HOSPITAL WAITING room is crowded when I get there. Not a single one of my players is talking, and it's the quietest I've ever heard them. I heave a deep breath and walk up to Liam Sullivan, my goalie, who is pacing the hardwood floor.

"Hey." I put a hand on his shoulder. "I'm here."

He deflates when he sees me and points to a woman sitting behind a large desk. She has a phone pressed to her ear, unintimidated by the six-foot-three goalie towering over her with a scowl. "She won't tell us what's going on. And my patience is about to run out," Liam says.

I elbow him out of the way, and he doesn't put up a fight. "Excuse me." I lean over and press the button on the phone, ending the call the receptionist is on. "I'm Riley Mitchell's coach. Have his parents been notified? They live out of state."

"I was in the middle of doing that before someone decided to hang up on them," she draws out with a pointed glare. "If you don't get back on that side of the desk, I'm going to have security escort you out. I don't give a hoot who you are."

"I tried that already." Liam glares at the woman again. She doesn't relent. "It's bullshit."

"Come here." I lead him to a corner, not arguing when Maverick joins us. I glance between them and push away the fear that's threatening to choke me. They're looking to me for guidance, and I need to get my shit together. I need to be strong when this is the weakest I've ever felt. "Tell me everything that happened."

"Riley left the club early." Maverick gulps down a breath. "Most of us were still celebrating, and the next thing I know, my phone's ringing. The guy calling told me there was an accident, and Riley was being taken to the hospital."

"Have they given any indication of what happened to him? Where he was hurt?"

"No." Liam grunts. "Just that he lost a lot of blood, and they—"

The doors to the emergency room open. A doctor walks out, and everyone rushes over to him.

"I'm guessing you all are here for Riley Mitchell?" he asks.

"We're his teammates." Maverick pushes his way to the front of the group. "Is he—"

"He's breathing," the doctor tells us. "That's the good news."

My blood turns ice cold. No one is moving, and everyone's attention rests on me.

I'm the one in charge. I'm the one who has to ask this next question, and my stomach drops to my feet.

"And the bad news?" I manage to get out. "Please?"

"He suffered very serious injuries to his right leg which resulted in major blood loss. Surgery to repair the leg… well, it's impossible. We're going to have to do a transfemoral amputation, and after, he'll—"

"What the fuck does that mean?" Maverick snaps. "You're going to have to dumb it down for us."

"He's going to lose his leg above the knee," Lexi Armstrong, the team's athletic trainer, tells us, and hell breaks loose.

"Jesus fuck," Ethan yells, kicking a wall. Grant is quick to wrap his arms around his best friend's stomach before he does something stupid. He tosses a look my way, apologizing on Ethan's behalf, but all I can see is Hannah. The same eyes, the same mouth, and my hands curl into fists at my sides. "This is the best fucking hospital in the city and you can't fix his fucking leg? What the fuck do they pay you for?"

There's a conversation about Riley's surgery and recovery time. I screw my eyes shut, transported back to my days as a player when I suffered a career-ending injury: a blade slicing above my knee. The stitches, the pain, and the discussions that happened after, trying to figure out how quickly I could get back on the ice.

The team rushed me. I wasn't completely healed when they put me back in the lineup, and I wasn't the same player. My days of professional hockey were over.

If there's any chance of salvaging Riley's career, I'm going to make sure we take his recovery slow.

I want to give him the chance I never had.

"Will he be able to skate again?" Maverick asks.

The doctor gives us a smile that tells me everything I need to know.

No.

He won't.

Everything he's ever known about himself is gone, and none of us will be able to help him get it back.

I should've answered the fucking phone.

The guys disperse after hearing that news to grieve in their own ways. I drift off to the side, taking a seat in a hard plastic chair. I stare at the floor, wondering what the fuck I do now when a phone rings.

"Hello?" Grant's voice. Shaky. Broken. "Hey, Han."

Of course she's calling to check on him because she's good and wonderful and the bright light in pitch-black dark.

I want to scream. I want to move far away from him, but I find myself leaning back. Trying to catch parts of their conversations while still feeling like a piece of shit.

"You heard? I'm not surprised. The internet is already picking up the story and publishing photos. I'm doing okay. Riley is breathing, but he's going to lose his leg." Grant pauses, a sob rushing out of him. "This is the worst night of my life."

Mine too, I want to say. *Tell your sister I'm sorry.*

"I'll call when I leave the hospital. Yeah. Sure. Love you too."

There's a long stretch of silence. I put my elbows on my knees, burying my face in my hands. I'm not equipped to handle this. A situation like this one was never talked about in any of the personal development books I read, and I don't know how the hell we go forward from here.

A tap on my shoulder stops me from spiraling. I lift my chin, wiping my eyes.

"Coach?"

Grant's voice wobbles again. I look over my shoulder and find him sitting in the chair behind me. Curled shoulders. Tear-stained cheeks and red-rimmed eyes, and he doesn't look like the kid we drafted five years ago. He looks like a man that's been through hell.

"Hey, Everett," I say. "Want me to grab you a water?"

"No. Not thirsty." He points to my chest. "Your shirt is on inside out."

"Oh." I glance down. There's a smudge of Hannah's lipstick on the collar, and I want to burn the thing to ash. "Thanks."

"I'm worried about Riley." His bottom lip quivers. A new wave of tears hit him, and I'm out of my seat in an instant. Making my way over to his side and sitting next to him. "I want him to be okay."

"I worried about him too." I put a hand on his shoulder. "The doctors are going to do a good job taking care of him."

"He's one of my best friends. All the guys are, but Riley is special. Yeah, he's good on the ice, but he listens when I need to vent. He gives me advice. He's a nice guy." A quiet laugh followed by a sniff. "Even when I flirted with Lexi. He has such a crush on her." His chuckle fades away. "Guess this is a reminder we should tell people how we feel about them. Things can change in the blink of an eye."

"That's true." I roll my lips together. I can't believe I walked away from Hannah like that. I'll never forgive myself. "We're going to get through this."

"Are we?" Grant stands. He paces, hands in his pockets. "What's the point in playing when he's not part of the team? I'm never going to be able to look at this championship without thinking about tonight. About Riley."

"I don't have the answer to that." I avoid looking at him. All I see is *her*. "Hockey has been there for me in my darkest moments, and sometimes, we're not playing for ourselves. We're playing for those who can't. But I'll tell you the thing I *do* know: you're not in this alone."

"I'm not?"

I finally let myself look at him, but I wish I hadn't. He's as distraught as I feel.

"No," I say. "I'm here. Your brothers are here. We're going to figure out the next steps together."

"Do you promise?" he asks.

"Yeah." I nod. Maybe I'll start to believe it. "I promise."

SIX

HANNAH

Sixteen months later

"THAT WAS WEAK, Hannah. Your posture is collapsing." Justine, my coach, gives me a pointed look from across the ice, and I acknowledge it with a sharp nod. "Engage your core and fix it."

"Got it," I say, bending to tighten the laces on my right skate. It's easier than being the focus of her displeasure. "The next one will be better."

"Hey." Tierney Barnes skates up to me. My best friend tosses one of her box braids over her shoulder and puts a hand on her hip. "You normally land that part of your program perfectly."

"Not today." I roll my shoulders back. Anxiety sits in the pit of my stomach. I take a deep breath, but it feels like I'm swallowing knives. "My entry sucks this afternoon."

"Want me to take a look and give you a different perspective?"

"And interrupt your day? Nope."

"It's not interrupting when I want to help. Do it again."

Tierney gestures at my spot on the ice. "Let's see if we can figure out what's throwing you off."

I fight back a smile. She's invested now, and her persistence is one of my favorite things about her. "Fine, but only if you don't make fun of my weak core."

"Says the girl whose skating resume includes a gold medal at the World Championships and two silvers at the U.S. Championships."

"That was years ago. I haven't medaled since."

"We both know a weak core is the last thing you have." She snaps. "Do an upright spin, please."

I don't want to give all my attention to a move that feels impossible, but she's giving up her time to help me get my shit together. It would be stupid to not take advantage of it, and I give her a nod.

I begin the program at the top, nailing all of the early elements. My double Axel is perfect, and my triple Lutz is even better. I push into my layback, the upright spin I prefer the most, but my right ankle wobbles. I lose control of my edge, and I can't stop myself from collapsing on the ice.

A little girl in a pink tutu and pigtails passes me, wrinkling her nose when she sees me on my ass with a knee that's not nearly as bruised as my ego.

"Well. This is a new level of embarrassing." I blink up at the fluorescent lights above me. "That's one of the first technical components I ever mastered, which means I'm falling apart."

"You're not falling apart." Tierney offers me a hand and I take it, letting her pull me up. "The good news is it's an easy fix. Your calf isn't parallel to the ice and your knee is angled when it shouldn't be."

"I'm in my head." I fix the pink ribbon tied in my hair and hook my thumb over my shoulder. "Which means I need to tap out early. The last thing I want is a broken bone."

"Want to grab lunch and get your mind off things?"

"Please, but we should hurry. Coach is shooting daggers at me, and I don't like being on the receiving end of her anger."

Tierney giggles. "At least she's nicer than Coach Bellamy was. Remember when she made us do MITF testing for an entire three-hour practice? Everyone else had dropped out, and we were the only two who survived all those turns, steps, and edges."

I smile.

I could never forget.

We're both from Florida, and we became fast friends as the youngest ones in our first skating class twenty years ago. After Grant was drafted by the Stars, I moved to DC with him. I knew the training in the area was significantly tougher than down South, and I had big dreams I wouldn't be able to accomplish unless I broadened my horizons. There's almost always a skater from the Atlantic region on the podium at the U.S. Figure Skating Championships, and since I've been here, I've kept that tradition alive.

When I told Tierney about the caliber of talent in my club, she moved to DC too. I quickly learned grueling training is more tolerable when your best friend is on the ice with you.

"The good ole days." I skate to my bag on the bleachers. "She told us we were the only people she deemed worthy enough to continue training with her."

"If she wasn't good at her job, I would've stopped skating years ago."

"Same. Now look at us: you're one of the best skaters in the world, and I'm a has-been happy to cheer you on."

"Stop." She laughs and pinches my cheek. "That's enough self-deprecation for today."

"Fine. I'll go back to being optimistic." I smile and drop on the bench, stretching out my legs. I wipe the smudge away from the toe of my skates and slip soakers over the blades. "Where do you want to eat?"

"How about that Thai restaurant near your apartment? They make the best Tom Yum Goong in the city."

"You're speaking my love language. Did you drive today?"

"Yeah." Tierney adjusts the bag slung over her shoulder. "Do you need a ride?"

"I drove too. Meet you there in twenty?"

"Last one there has to pay the bill," she says, but I know she's kidding.

Her brother, Jamal, is an NBA player who was traded to the DC Bullets two seasons ago. Having siblings who are professional athletes means they cover a lot of our expenses, even when we try to fight them on it. Every other week I have a Venmo notification letting me know Grant sent money I didn't ask for.

Payback for all the nights you sat in that shitty college arena that smelled like death and cheered me on, he said when I refused the first check he handed me. *I have more than enough money. Take it so I know you're looking after yourself.*

I do my best to think about the long-term instead of the things I want to buy right now. After paying my coaches, I put Grant's contributions in a savings account where most of my earlier competition earnings sit. The content I create for social media performs well; the short clips I film of myself skating rake in a couple thousand dollars a month. The sponsorships with Edea and Gatorade bring in money too, but from a competitive standpoint, it's been a rough stretch of time.

"You don't stand a chance, T." I grin, popping to my feet. "I've always been a sore loser."

THIRTY MINUTES LATER, I slide into the booth across from Tierney with a scowl.

"I had to park two blocks over because of construction *and*

I got catcalled by a group of douchebag finance bros. Today blows."

"Men." She shakes her head. "Always such a disappointment."

"Cheers to that." I reach for the water waiting for me and take a sip. "Thanks for giving up some of your afternoon so you can commiserate with me about my shitty skating skills."

"I wasn't going to bring it up, but since you did..." Tierney rests her elbows on the table. "Are you ready to tell me what's really going on with you? And don't try to bullshit me. I know when you're lying."

I hesitate. It would be easy to blame the way I've been out of sync on a sore ankle or a situation happening in my personal life, but Tierney is the most supportive person I know. She's been there for me through everything; a friend before I made it big and a friend who sees me as someone she loves, not as her competition, and lying about how shitty I've felt lately isn't fair.

"I'm going to tell you something that's scary to admit, but the more I consider it, the more I think it might be true."

"You're freaking me out, Han."

"I'm... I'm pretty sure I'm suffering from burnout." I pause and rub my thumb across my bottom lip. "Skating has been my entire life for as long as I can remember. I love it more than I've ever loved anything else, but lately..." My exhale is heavy. There's an ache behind my ribs that's been persistent for weeks. Dread down in the brittle of my bones. "Lately, it feels like a chore. I don't look forward to practice. I'm drained all the time. When Coach tells me the things that are wrong in my program, I'm overwhelmed by trying to figure out how to fix them. And honestly? I just don't *care* like I used to."

"Oh, sweetie." Tierney stares at me. "How long has this been going on?"

"This time around? About four months."

"It's happened before?"

"Unfortunately. But I broke out of the funk."

"What helped stop it last time?"

My mouth snaps closed.

Last time the cure was Brody Saunders and the orgasms he gave me, but that will not, under any circumstances, be happening again.

That night is locked away inside a vault. Ironclad, impenetrable. I don't play it back. I don't daydream about it. I don't let myself wonder how differently it could've gone if Riley hadn't gotten hurt.

It's sealed off. Closed up and finished.

Lately, though, I've found myself thinking about Brody when I'm lonely and confused and debating what the hell happens next in my life.

It's not because I miss him. *God*, no.

I've never relied on another person to be my source of happiness, and he's not going to be the first.

I just... I can't help but hope he's okay.

I've seen him from a distance at games and he's *looked* fine. Intense in his coaching. Meticulous in the way he studies his whiteboard before giving his players orders. A playoff run last season despite the challenges the Stars faced.

That night... the way he left... it wasn't him. At least, it wasn't the him that I saw for the hour prior. The one who knew I skated and told me he had been thinking about fucking me for *months*.

His departure hurt at first. I took it personally. I'm not justifying his shitty behavior and the ask for me to pretend like the whole thing didn't happen, but the more time that's passed, the more I *get it*. He was scared. Grieving preemptively for a loss he thought was coming, and it was never about me.

I would've bolted too.

The flowers he sent the next day helped soothe the sting. A big bouquet. Dozens and dozens of roses that match the tattoo on the back of his hand. No note, but I knew who they were from. An apology, an acceptance he can't change what's done, but he can better about not being a total dick going forward.

Brody was right that night, all those months ago. There *isn't* a world out there where a thing between the two of us could ever mean more than sex, but I can't deny the impact he had on my skating.

I was doing well in the aftermath of our hookup.

A silver medal at the Eastern Sectional. A pewter medal finish at the U.S. Figure Skating Championships after a weak program, but the excitement has faded. That same discomfort creeps up when I lace my skates, and this time, I don't know how to fix it.

"Something that's impossible to replicate." I shove away the thought of his palms exploring my body. The brush of his fingers against my jaw. "I've been tossing around the idea of stepping away from skating."

"You're going to retire?"

"Maybe temporarily? This sport is all I know, and the longer I go through a rough patch where my technical work is shit and I'm unmotivated, the more obvious it's becoming I need to figure out who I am away from the medals and pressure of constantly performing at such a high level." I sigh. "I need to fall back in love with skating, and that's not going to happen if I keep pushing my body to do things it doesn't want to do."

"Okay." Tierney scoots her chair closer, taking my hand. "How are we going to do that?"

"Ah. Another question I don't have the answer to." I laugh and lace our fingers together, grateful for her. The knot of tension I've been carrying with me for weeks starts to unravel the more I share, and I'm glad I was honest. "The first order of business is dropping out of Skate America. After that? We'll see."

"*Drop out?* You're projected to place in the top spot for the women's singles. Everyone is saying it's your comeback, and—"

"I'm not happy, T. What good is an attempt at another medal if I'm miserable trying to earn it?"

"Fuck. You're right. I'm sorry for suggesting otherwise. Forget about the medals and rankings. Other than the burnout, are you doing okay mentally? Being an athlete is such a fucking trip, I swear to god. And the comments on social media? It's a hellhole."

I swallow. I'm not ready for the backlash I'm going to get from fans when I announce my decision to pull out of next month's competition. The rumors will fly. There will be speculation. I'll have unwanted attention on me, but disappearing into oblivion without so much of a word about my absence isn't fair to the people who like to watch me skate.

"I might need to disable comments on all my Instagram posts," I say weakly.

"I did that years ago, and I'm much happier. Do you want to take a weekend away? Jamal has a game in New York on Saturday. We could get courtside seats. Find a hotel room overlooking Central Park and order room service."

"I'll take you up on that offer when things slow down in the new year. As for being okay... I'm not okay, but I'm also not *not* okay. Does that make sense? I'm a work in progress."

"A work in progress is still something to be so proud of." She glances at me. "You should tell Grant what's going on. I know their season just started so you think your shit isn't as important, but it is. Promise me you'll give him a head's-up?"

"Fine," I relent. "I will. But I know how it's going to go: he'll try to fix the problem because he's a people-pleaser who doesn't like when his loved ones aren't happy. Which is unfortunate, since I'm not sure I can be fixed."

"You're unbreakable, Hannah Everett. We're going to figure this out."

I fumble with my water glass in an attempt to stop the tears that are threatening to fall.

Unbreakable is the last thing I am. Cracked and fragile and absolutely clueless about where I go from here is a more accurate description of my current life. I'm so far from the girl I was five years ago, back when magazines wanted to take my picture and people packed into arenas to watch me perform, but deep down, I feel it. The glimmer of hope. The flicker of optimism, and maybe there's a solution out there I haven't considered yet.

I just have to find it.

SEVEN

BRODY

THE DOOR to my penthouse condo slams shut. Heavy footsteps stomp down the hall. I look up from my laptop just as Olivia charges into the kitchen like a bat out of hell.

She drops her backpack on the floor and rips open the pantry, grumbling under her breath. I blink, wondering when I should intervene, and decide it's best if I keep my mouth shut.

Fourteen years of being a parent, and I still can't figure shit out.

Add in a teenage girl going through body changes and her first year in high school while I'm starting the hockey season and about to be on the road the majority of the next eight and a half months? I'm out of my element.

I learned a long time ago that Olivia takes after me. She's stubborn. Hard-headed and fiercely determined. The more I push her to do something, the less likely she is to do it, so I keep my mouth shut. I press play on my laptop, watching video from last night's game that resulted in us giving up two goals to a team significantly less talented than us.

I slow the speed on the footage and jot down some notes on the piece of paper in front of me, keeping an eye on Olivia as she pours herself a glass of orange juice and lays out a stack of crackers.

"Dad," she says.

"Hm? What?" I pretend like I didn't notice she was there. "Oh. Hi, sweetie. What's up?"

"Everything fucking sucks."

"What did I tell you about cursing?"

"You curse all the time." She drops in the chair across the table from me and sighs. "And you turned out just fine."

"Thanks, kid." I shut my computer so I can give her my full attention. I love my job. I put a lot of time into it, but being a parent—even one who is still clueless—will always come first. Especially when my daughter seems like she's on the verge of a crisis. "Why does everything suck?"

"Practice was horrible."

"Did you get hurt?" I assess her knees and feet, checking for a brace or a wrapped ankle. I'm relieved to find pink leg warmers and no bandages. "I don't see any injuries."

"No, I didn't get hurt." Olivia groans and buries her face in her hands. "Coach Susannah is having a baby."

"Uh. Okay? How does that have anything to do with your figure skating?"

"Because she's taking a leave of absence and I won't have a coach anymore!" Her shoulders shake, but I resist reaching out so I can give her space. "With only ten months until the Potomac Memorial Open, which is my shot at a national qualifying series, I can't not have a coach!"

"Ten months? That's a long way away, isn't it?"

"Says the guy who is planning for the Stanley Cup even though it's October."

"Fair point." I rub my jaw. "Okay. I'll pay someone a shit ton of money, and they won't be able to say no."

"It doesn't work like that, Dad. People don't care that you're a millionaire." She lifts her head, and I'm surprised she's crying. I know skating means the world to her, but this feels easily solvable. "There are regimented schedules. Designated time we can use the ice, and I'm a solo skater. I don't have a partner, so I have no one to join. Everything I've worked so hard for is going to shit."

"Language, Livvy." I sigh. "Have you told your mother what's going on? She's good with these kinds of things—talking to people. Social interaction. It's not exactly my forte."

"I know. Everyone annoys you." She rolls her eyes. "Mom said to talk to you because you're the one with the checkbook and resources. But I'm telling you, we can't buy our way into a new training schedule, Dad."

I snort, knowing it's exactly what Kali would say.

I love Olivia more than anything else in my life, but she's the result of a drunken one-night stand. The details are hazy, but the weeks leading up to the moment I invited Kali back to my place are as clear as day: the conversation with my head coach and the athletic trainer after the pain in my knee plagued me when I returned to the lineup post-surgery. The meeting with the team's president and general manager who assessed my performance and said I was taking up a roster spot from someone healthier than me. Officially announcing my retirement from the NHL and the black hole I spiraled into, refusing to leave my apartment.

I saw myself as a failure. I didn't know who I was without hockey, and I shut down. I cut out friends, family. The only time I ventured out was to go to a bar down the road from my place. I was wasted and met a woman who didn't give a shit about my last name or the jersey I would never wear again.

One thing led to another. I panicked when Kali tracked me down on social media and told me she was pregnant. We talked about options, but at the end of the day, I knew the decision was hers.

Nine months later, Liv was born.

Kali and I tried dating. In the beginning, things were good between us. With no hockey, I was always home, and we were happy. Then, the disagreements started. We were exhausted all the time. We fought about everything: her wanting to go out for dinner. Me wanting to stay in. After six months, we decided we were much better as friends who co-parented their rambunctious as hell daughter than a couple who'd found their happily ever after.

We're present in each other's lives. We show up for Liv, and Kali still doesn't care about my last name or the money I have. She's never asked for anything. Never threatened to take me to court, and now she's happily married to a dude named Bryant who collects Christmas ornaments and thinks I coach lacrosse.

He's not a big sports guy.

"I'll talk to some people at the arena who have daughters. And Liam. He takes skating lessons in the summer. Someone has to know something. I'll make some calls."

"Wait." Liv giggles and wipes her eyes. "Liam figure skates?"

"Yup. Helps with improving edge control and agility."

"I wonder if Coach Susannah has worked with him."

"No way. She's too nice to put up with him." I scoop my phone off the table and stand, grateful for the break in work. "Let me see what I can do, kid. Hope is not lost."

"Thanks, Dad. You're the best."

Olivia smiles up at me. There's a pang in my chest when I look at her, and I'm hit with the terrible realization that she's not four years old anymore. She's a young adult going after her dreams, and I remember what I was like at her age: relentless. Spending every waking hour on the ice perfecting my skills so I would be the best college recruit the country had ever seen.

I know what my parents sacrificed to make that happen. The hours they put in shuttling me to and from practice, which somehow led me here, but I wouldn't change a thing. It's why I'm going to scour this city from high to low until I find the best coach for my daughter. I don't care what I have to offer them. If it makes Olivia happy, I'll do it.

"Start on your homework. I know you have an algebra test tomorrow," I say, heading for my bedroom.

"It got canceled," she yells after me.

"Study anyway," I call back, shutting my door and sitting on my bed.

I know what I have to do, but I'm not excited about it. I've always kept my interactions with players to a minimum. I don't spend a lot of time with them off the ice. I don't text them like they're my best friends, but in the time that's passed since Riley's accident, I've let myself be more accessible to them.

I've eased up on shutting them down so quickly when they ask me to hang out away from practice and games because they're my family. And family is really fucking important, especially after going through a tragedy that nearly ripped us apart.

Riley is doing well. There are good days and there are bad days, but overall, we're treading toward more good days. He spent some time last season coaching next to me, and the kid has a talent for paying attention to detail.

I'm still holding out hope he'll be able to play again one day. It would be a goddamn dream to see him put on a jersey back on.

I drum my fingers against my phone and groan, typing out a text to the team.

ME

Have a favor to ask. Does anyone know any figure skating coaches? Sullivan, who is the person you're with in the offseason?

RICHARDSON

No fucking WAY. Did Coach create a group chat? This is the best day of my LIFE.

ME

> This is for research purposes only. When I get the answer I need, I'm blocking all of your numbers so I can't be added to anything else.

MILLER

> I knew he liked us off the ice. One day apart, and he can't bear the thought of us not being around.

HAYES

> Hey, Coach. I know Lucy just started lessons, so I'll check with Madeline and see who she's with. Is this for a beginner? A rookie you're trying to book some more time on the ice for?

ME

> It's for my daughter, who is very talented and has dreams of making the Olympics. Her coach is taking a leave of absence, and she's panicking.

RICHARDSON

> Dude. G-Money. Your sister is a figure skater. Does she coach kids?

I stare at Ethan's message and promptly throw my phone into the pillows. It buzzes twice, answering a question I want nothing to do with, and I'm about to change my goddamn number.

Reaching out to Hannah Everett is *not* part of the plan.

The last time I saw her, I was six seconds away from fucking her before I stormed out of her apartment and never looked back.

I've purposely avoided every team gathering where she might be in attendance.

Friends and Family night at the rink where everyone's parents, significant others, kids, and partners joined for food and fun? I said I was sick.

The party the guys put together to celebrate Riley's one-year anniversary of surviving his accident? I didn't have to pretend I had food poisoning when I overheard Grant mention she wouldn't be there.

It's better this way. There aren't complicated feelings or getting involved with someone who has a life completely opposite from mine.

If she even *wanted* to be involved with me after the way I left that night.

There's no way in hell she would.

I wake up. I coach hockey. I review game footage and make lineup changes. Eat a meal or two and hang out with my kid. After all of that, I go to sleep, and I do *not* fucking think about the blonde-haired, long-legged woman with a ribbon in her hair who seems to haunt me.

Yeah fucking right.

My phone vibrates again, and I know it's not going to stop anytime soon. I reach over, scowling at the messages that have come in.

EVERETT

Oh, yeah. Hannah skates, and she's damn good.

She told me she's been going through some things lately. I bet she wouldn't mind the extra cash. I'll text her.

I reread Grant's message and want to scream.

What the hell is she going through? Is she okay? Is she safe?

More importantly, why the fuck do I care?

RICHARDSON

Tell her I think she's hot and I'll make her feel better.

EVERETT

Shut the fuck up, Ethan. I'll kick your ass if you touch her.

RICHARDSON

Who says I haven't already?

SULLIVAN

Congratulations, Coach. You've unleashed a monster. I'm blaming you when I play like shit at morning skate.

I work with Belinda Powers in the summer, but she's busy. Been coaching an NCAA girl taking a gap year who's the best skater I've seen in decades.

MILLER

Rude. I'm right here.

SULLIVAN

You're old and slow.

MILLER

Goddamn, Goalie Daddy. That wasn't very nice.

ME

We're finished here. Morning skate is at 9 tomorrow. Last person on the ice is doing laps.

RICHARDSON

9?? I thought it was 11!!

ME

You all are pissing me off. Now it's 9.

EVERETT

Dammit, Ethan.

I delete the group chat, but I can't get a moment of peace because a minute later, my phone rings. Grant's name is on the screen, and my pulse jumps with anticipation.

Based on his reaction to Ethan's comment, there's no way he knows about me and his sister. If he did, he would've decked me in the face by now. I'm still on edge when I answer his call, doing a lap around my room to calm myself down.

"Hello?"

"Coach." I can hear him grinning on the other end of the line. "What's up?"

"You're calling me, Everett."

"Right." He laughs, and there's a muffled voice behind him asking a question I can't make out. "I texted my sister and asked if she would ever consider coaching. Not to brag or be an obnoxious big brother, but she really is one of the best skaters in the country."

"You didn't need to do that," I say.

"She said she's interested in hearing more. I'm going to give you her number."

"That's not—"

"If you want your daughter to be the best, you're going to need Hannah," he says, and I sigh.

He's not wrong.

After the night at her apartment, I went down the rabbit hole of watching her old skating routines. She's better than good. She's *fantastic*. I've never seen someone move so effortlessly on the ice, and my job is to literally get people to skate like that. There's fluidity in her movements. A lightness to the way she glides, and she's graceful on top of all of it.

It's the most beautiful thing in the world.

I'm not keeping track of her successes. Just… researching. For Olivia.

"Fine," I grumble. "Give me her number. I'll reach out."

"Sweet. I'll text you in a few." There's a soft giggle on his end of the phone followed by a sigh. "Gotta run, Coach. See ya in the morning."

"Everett," I bark out, and he clears his throat.

"Yes sir?"

"Are you behaving yourself?"

"Of course I am." He laughs, and I'm not convinced. "Later, Coach."

We hang up, and he texts me her number. Hannah's information is right there in the middle of my screen, and I take a deep breath.

Tomorrow, I tell myself.

I'll message her tomorrow.

EIGHT

BRODY

I DON'T MESSAGE Hannah the next day, or the day after.

I don't reach out to her at all because I'm a pathetic excuse for a man, and when my assistant coach stares at me from center ice, I scowl back at him.

"You look like shit." Mikal Reynolds tips his head to the side. "Did you get any sleep last night?"

"Do I look like I got any sleep last night?" I grunt, watching the third line guys finish running a drill. "Stop asking me questions you know the answer to."

"Noted." He smirks and blows his whistle. Everyone comes to a halt, looking my way. "You're up, Coach."

"Our game the other night against San Fran wasn't pretty. We got beat down the ice on almost every play." I throw a glance at my first line players, glad when they dip their heads in agreement. I'm all for celebrating victories, but owning up to mistakes and shitty skating is just as important. "I know it's early in the season. Our stamina isn't where it was in the play-offs last year, but we're better than that. It's our second season of adjusting to our lineup without Mitchell in it." I turn to look at Riley leaning against the boards. "Our rookie slotted in well last year, but we can't make excuses about chemistry anymore. You all know how to play the game. I want you giving your all when you're on the ice, no matter how long you're on it. If I see anyone giving a half-assed effort, I'll switch you out with someone who wants to be there. Any questions?"

There are murmurs of agreement, and I give the boys a nod.

"Good. Let's wrap up our ice time with some stationary puck control drills, then we'll head to the weight room for sled pushes and box jumps. Sullivan and Davenport," I say to my goalies, "I want you two working on net deflections with Trevor." I point to our goalie coach on the opposite side of the rink. "Focusing on overlap, not RVH."

"Fucking cruel, Coach," Liam mumbles, fixing his mask.

"You rely on it too much." I shrug. "Don't give up two goals to a shitty team, and we'll talk."

"Ouch."

He glares at me, but he knows it's all tough love. Sullivan has been the best goaltender in the league the last four seasons, and his preferred feedback style doesn't include having his ass kissed. He wants to know what he's doing wrong, which is why he dips his chin in a nod. Gently bumps my shin with his stick and heads toward Trevor with Richie Davenport, his backup.

"Coach." Grant skates up to me and fixes his helmet. "Have you talked to my sister yet?"

"Nope." I bite my tongue so hard I swear I taste blood. I gesture for him to follow me to the guys forming two lines. "I'm busy with you all and trying to be a present parent on top of everything else."

"Oh, yeah. Makes sense." He grins and takes the spot behind Maverick, glancing my way. It's really fucking unfair how much he and his sister look alike, down to the way he cocks his hip to the side. "I told Hannah you were going to reach out, and it's been a week. Don't make me look bad, Coach."

"Thanks, Everett," I say, painfully aware of how many days it's been since he passed along her number.

I've typed and deleted a hundred messages to her. Each one has gotten progressively worse, and I stayed up all night last night wondering how the hell I'm going to ask her to do something for me when the last time I saw her, I was telling her to forget I ever had my head buried between her legs.

Fuck.

Those goddamn thighs have haunted me. So has her creamy, smooth skin and the smell of her perfume.

I hear her moans when I'm alone in my hotel room during away games. I see her hair scattered on the pillows and her knees opened wide when I try to fall asleep, and, come to think of it, I'm not sure I've been right in the head since I left her apartment.

Who could be after being in the presence of someone who is so perfect, it makes you feel so goddamn unworthy?

I pinch the bridge of my nose to clear the memory and crouch low, lining up a puck.

"You're first, Miller," I call out, happy for the distraction.

"Huh?" He blinks, pushing himself to a standing position from where he's leaning against his stick. "Sorry. Did you say something to me?"

"Where's your head?" I pass the puck to him, narrowing my eyes when it bounces off his skate. "If you showed up to practice under the influence, I'm going to be pissed."

"What? No. I'm not *drunk*. I haven't had alcohol in—shit. Weeks? Months?"

"Makes book club way less fun," Ethan chimes in.

"Care to share why you're off in your own world then?" I ask. "I hope it's for a good reason, otherwise we're ditching the drills and your teammates will skate laps while you watch."

He taps the puck with the blade of his stick and gives it a lazy hit. "It's Emmy."

Grant gasps. "I swear to god, if you're divorcing my second favorite woman in the world, you're going to get an earful from me, Miller. And probably a fist to the face."

"You better not have fucked up," Ethan warns. "You can't do better than her, but she can do *way* better than you."

"I'm not as fast as I used to be, but I can still kick your ass," Riley says.

"Mav. Why didn't you tell us the two of you were having problems?" Hudson asks.

"Will all of you calm down? We're fine, and no one needs to kick my ass. My wife could do that just fine on her own." Maverick's lips twitch. "It's the baby. Emmy isn't due until December, but she woke up this morning in pain. I'm worried about her."

I know Emerson Hartwell, his pregnant wife, well. I was the one who scouted her from the ECHL and signed her to the Stars' roster a few years ago, marking the first time a woman has ever suited up for a regular season NHL game.

She's a complete badass who played with us before an end-of-season trade sent her to Toronto. She wound up in Baltimore as their starting left winger after another move, but she's not expected to play this season after finding out she was pregnant earlier in the year.

Maverick has mentioned her struggle with infertility during our player-coach meetings in the past, but it never interfered with the effort he gave on the ice. His distractedness is new, and when I take a second look at him, I notice the exhaustion lining his face. The sunken cheeks and unshaved jaw he runs his knuckles over.

He looks like shit, and my chest pinches tight.

"Is Emmy okay?" Grant demands. "Has she been to the doctor?"

"The *doctor?* Something like that warrants a trip to the hospital," Ethan says.

"Never thought I'd see the day when Richardson was right about something involving a woman's health." Hudson chuckles. "But he's right, Mav."

"I'm listing you as a healthy scratch for tomorrow," I say, and Maverick's mouth opens in protest. I hold up my hand, stopping him from interrupting. "You're not in trouble. It's so you and Emmy can make sure everything is okay with the baby."

"I've never missed a game before," he says.

"You've also never been up all night with a screaming newborn, but things are about to change for you, Miller. Take the next three days off. See who you need to see, and come back ready to work. Sound fair?"

"Yeah." Maverick nods. His shoulders drop away from his ears. "Sounds fair. Thanks, Coach."

"Wow. I never knew Coach had a heart," Ethan whispers to Grant, and I blow my whistle.

"Forget the drills. Fifteen laps for everyone. Last five need to be explosive, and you can thank Richardson when your ankles start to hurt." I grin when everyone groans. "Begin."

AN HOUR AND A HALF LATER, I open the door to my office in our practice facility and glare at my cell phone sitting on the desk.

I'm going to send Hannah that text message even if it's my fucking demise.

It's not as good as a phone call, but I don't know what I'm supposed to say.

Watching you get off that night was the hottest thing of my life. I've replayed it over and over again. Or, *Hey, I know we haven't spoken in almost a year and a half, but do you think I could convince you to give my daughter figure skating lessons? Thanks so much.* Maybe, *I'm so fucking sorry for what I did and how I did it. How can I make it up to you?*

I groan and collapse in the desk chair, putting my forehead against the wood.

I can fucking *do* this.

I'm a thirty-nine-year-old man, for fuck's sake.

I'm the best coach in the NHL.

I've had my leg sliced up. I've been through hell and back.

A text message about figure skating won't be my biggest fear.

I stare at the number Grant gave me and copy it. My fingers hover over the keys, clueless how I'm supposed to start, before my thumbs move on their own.

ME

> Hey. Grant gave me your number. I'm not sure if he mentioned it, but my daughter, Olivia, needs a figure skating coach. Are you interested? I'll pay.

I hit send before I have a chance to double-check what I've typed, and when I read it back, I groan again.

"Get it together, Saunders," I mutter, typing out another text.

ME

> It's Brody. Brody Saunders. The DC Stars coach.

That's not any better. There needs to be a way to unsend texts because two incoherent thoughts in a row is unhinged behavior. Something I would've pulled back in my early twenties, and I shake my head, disappointed in myself.

ME

Sorry. Let me try this one more time. Hi, Hannah. It's Brody. Grant gave me your number, and I hope it's okay that I'm reaching out. My daughter needs a figure skating coach, and you come highly recommended. Let me know if that's something you'd like to discuss further.

I hope you're doing well, I type after a beat, adding the last thought before I hit send.

I stare at my phone for the next fifteen minutes, waiting for an answer that doesn't come.

NINE
HANNAH

GRANT

Did Coach text you yet?

ME

He did.

GRANT

Thank god. He created a group chat with all of us and seemed pretty panicked about finding someone to help his daughter.

Glad he finally reached out. Do you think you're going to take the coaching gig?

ME

TBD. I don't know shit about children and even less about coaching them. Remember that summer I was a camp counselor and the girls in my cabin bullied me? Traumatizing.

GRANT

Weren't they 8? And spoiled brats?

ME

Traumatizing!

GRANT

No way Coach's kid is like that. Dude probably runs a tight ship haha.

Saw your post about withdrawing from Skate America.

ME

Did you see some of the comments asking if I was pregnant and that's why I was dropping out? Or if I failed a drug test?

GRANT

Oof. Sorry, Han. People suck. Everyone wants to have an opinion, but not everyone with a platform deserves a microphone.

Want to meet up this week so you can tell me about your decision? I'm in town until Thursday, then it's off to Canada, eh!!!!

ME

Sounds great, G.

GRANT

I'm here for you, sis.

ME

I know you are, and I appreciate you.

I HAVE to give Brody credit for being so ballsy.

Sixteen months without any communication—just like he wanted—and he pops up out of the blue, asking if I'll coach his daughter. Grant gave me a heads up the text was coming, but it still caught me off guard.

It's been forty-eight hours since his bombardment of messages—three of them, which is hysterical to me—and I haven't answered him. It's kind of fun picturing him walking around his living room and wondering if he'll ever get a response.

"Sorry I'm late." Grant sits across from me at the tiny table I scored when I got to the bar ten minutes ago. He pulls the bill of his hat low on his head, covering his shaggy brown hair that's in desperate need of a cut. "I was playing video games with the guys. Kicked Liam's ass to high heaven in *Halo*."

"It's cute how codependent you all are. Can't even spend a night apart." I squint at the feeble attempt of facial hair lining his cheeks and below his nose, the start of a hideous mustache that makes me cringe. "What the hell is on your face? It looks like an inchworm."

"*Whoa*. That's uncalled for, Han. I'm getting ready for when the team does Movember. We don't shave for a month so we can raise awareness for men's mental health, prostate cancer, and testicular cancer."

"God." I groan. "Now I feel like a bitch for making fun of you."

"You could never be a bitch." He flashes me a grin and flags down a server, asking for a seltzer water with lime while I put in an order for a white wine. "Good to see you, sis. What's new in your life?"

"Besides pulling out of one of the biggest competitions of the year, getting trolled on social media, reading subreddits about myself that aren't even close to true and contemplating what the hell I'm going to do with my future? I'm great."

"Fuck. That's heavy. Cheers." He knocks his glass with mine when our drinks arrive. "You want to talk about any of that? You know I'll listen."

"I do know that, but I've given my therapist an earful these past two weeks. I'm fine. I promise. I've been…" I cross my legs, taking a beat to finish my answer. "I think I'm going to tell Bro—Coach Saunders that I want to work with his daughter."

"Yeah?" Grant smiles my way. "That's great news, Han."

"I know I have zero coaching experience, but I'm wondering if I approach skating from a different perspective, I might be able to fall in love with it again. I'm sure there's some psychological reasoning behind my recent dislike of the sport. Why I'm anxious every time I get on the ice, and coaching could be rewarding in a different way."

"That's some philosophical shit right there. I know I'm clueless about figure skating—"

"That's not true. Mom still has that picture of you wearing that full-body costume of mine you put on when you were younger."

"If that *ever* gets published anywhere, I'm burning the city down."

"But you were so cute in all those sequins." I laugh. "What do you know about Coach Saunders' daughter?"

"Olivia? She's been to a few practices and I've seen her at games. More outgoing than Coach, but so is a wall."

Except when he's in bed. Then he won't shut up.

I sip on my wine to keep myself from blurting out the intimate thought. "How old is she?"

"Uh. Fourteen? Thirteen? Old enough to have a cell phone. Young enough to not have a car."

"Hm."

"Hey." He gives my shin a gentle kick under the table. "You're contemplative over there."

"I know how much skating meant to me when I was her age, and it's brought me so many wonderful things in life—current athletic slump notwithstanding." I set my glass down and sigh. "I'm going to have to step away from the sport one of these days. What good has my career been if I'm not inspiring the next generation?"

"You want to talk about inspiring? You're already doing that, Han. When I was at your last competition, girls everywhere had ribbons in their hair like you wear. You don't need gold medals to prove your worth."

"Will people still respect me if I walk away? It's not like I'm injured. I'm just unhappy."

"Fuck what other people think. You want to retire? You can retire. You want to coach? You can coach. You want to go to beginner Learn to Skate classes and relearn basic moves? You can do that too. People love to talk shit, but until they know the burden you're carrying, they shouldn't be allowed to have an opinion. You don't need a reason to walk away. Your happiness is enough."

"Thanks, G." I smile and reach across the table to knock the brim of his hat. "And beginner Learn to Skate classes? What the hell would I do there?"

"If that's where you first fell in love with skating, maybe it's where you could fall in love with it again."

"That's not a bad idea. Something to consider in my temporary hiatus."

"How long of a break are you going to take?"

"Not sure yet. I told my coach I needed a couple of months off to find my focus. She agreed, but only because I wasn't setting a good example for the younger skaters." I snort. "And now I'm going to try and coach one? I'm in over my head."

"No way. You're going to do this, Hannah, and you're going to do it well. Besides. Coach might be the king of hockey, but I bet he knows jack shit about figure skating. He'll probably say all of your moves are perfect tens, even when you mess up."

"Probably." I smile. Interacting with Brody again so I can give his daughter skating lessons? There's a plot twist I never saw coming. "Guess we'll find out."

GRANT OFFERS to drive me home, but I decide to walk. The late autumn air is nice, even when a breeze ripples past and I pull my jacket tighter around my body. At a red light, I fish my phone out of my pocket.

I find Brody's messages buried under a dozen other notifications have come through the last two days and take a deep breath. I tap his number, reading through what he sent me one more time.

UNKNOWN NUMBER

> Hey. Grant gave me your number. I'm not sure if he mentioned it, but my daughter, Olivia, needs a figure skating coach. Are you interested? I'll pay.

> It's Brody. Brody Saunders. The DC Stars coach.

> Sorry. Let me try this one more time. Hi, Hannah. It's Brody. Grant gave me your number, and I hope it's okay I'm reaching out to you. My daughter needs a figure skating coach, and you come highly recommended. Let me know if that's something you'd like to discuss further. I hope you're doing well.

Brody Saunders. The DC Stars coach.

As if I don't remember every detail about him—his fingers pushing inside me. The hot, wet press of his mouth on my neck and how hard he was. The way we almost fucked and his threat of putting me over his knee.

We were so close.

Inches.

That's all that separated us.

Heat inundates my body. I fan my face, begging my brain to not latch on to the rough husk of his voice when he asked if I could feel him.

It's the hardest task of my life.

I swipe away from his message and pull up the internet instead, typing in his name and adding + *daughter* to the end of the search. Google loads, and I can't find photos of her anywhere.

I'm not surprised. I bet he keeps her out of the public eye to protect their privacy. He's not the most famous athlete in the world, but he's still someone people know. And in a city that's obsessed with hockey, I'm sure trying to keep your kids safe without leaving a digital footprint is harder than it sounds.

I hope she's never had people offer to coach her for selfish reasons: they want access to her dad. A firsthand glimpse into a life of someone they could take to publications and sell for an exuberant amount of money. General creepiness.

Brody lit up when he talked about his daughter. His whole face changed, and it's obvious she's the best part of his life. Watching her end up with a coach who only cares about themselves and boosting their resume without having Olivia's best interests at heart makes my chest hurt.

It happened to me years ago. One of my first coaches saw my potential. She saw Olympics and Championships and how my success could benefit her, so she pushed me to my limits then well past. My body ached. I was reprimanded in front of the other skaters at my rink when I didn't place as high as she wanted. My spirit was crushed. I thought that was how intense every coach was… until I found the right one.

I want the same experience for Olivia.

Not for Brody's sake, but in honor of the little girl I used to be who had big dreams and a big heart.

I can get past whatever brief relationship Brody and I had in favor of a young skater with the world out in front of her. I pull up his messages again, my thumbs typing out an answer I've already decided on.

ME

Thanks for your offer. Full disclosure, I don't have any coaching experience, which is important for younger figure skaters so they'll be trained correctly. Totally understand if you want to go a different route after learning that.

I push open the door to my apartment building, and his response comes seconds later. It's like he's been waiting for me to message him.

UNKNOWN NUMBER

My daughter told me how good you are. I watched videos of you, and she's right. You're terrific. As someone who was also thrust into a coaching role somewhat unexpectedly, trust me when I say you learn as you go.

ME

Okay, yeah. I'd be open to talking more about a potential partnership.

UNKNOWN NUMBER

Are you free tomorrow? Guys have an off day.

I unlock my door and slip inside, kicking off my shoes. I'm free for the foreseeable future thanks to my self-imposed break to do some soul searching, but I take a beat before answering so he doesn't think I'm too eager. Dropping onto the couch, I drum my fingers against the side of my phone.

ME

Tomorrow should work. Where's a place that's convenient for you?

UNKNOWN NUMBER

The arena, if you're okay with it. I have meetings all morning.

ME

Sure. Noon?

UNKNOWN NUMBER

I'll be here. Check in at the security window and they'll get you a visitor's pass. Text me if you have any issues.

ME

Sounds good.

I rub a hand over my chest. Nerves sit at the base of my spine, but it's a different feeling from what I've been grappling with as of late. Is this this hope I feel? The excitement I've been looking for? My way to jumpstart my passion for skating again?

God, I hope so.

My phone buzzes one more time. I don't look at it until later, after I shower and climb into bed for the night. When I do, the message I read makes my belly swoop low. It makes those nerves melt to something secretive I've tried to forget.

UNKNOWN NUMBER

Looking forward to seeing you.

TEN

BRODY

I'M A FUCKING WRECK.

I check the clock every five minutes throughout the morning. I sweat through my T-shirt and have to change after a meeting with my coaching staff. I can't stop pacing around my office, and when Lexi pops her head in at ten minutes to noon, she smirks.

"Why are you ruining the carpet?" she asks, a clipboard tucked under her arm.

"I'm not doing anything to the carpet."

"Not yet. But if you keep walking in circles, you're going to put a hole in the brand-new flooring the arena operations team spent all summer working on."

"Maybe the carpet is the problem," I grunt. "Did you need something?"

"You're in a mood. What pissed you off today?"

"The sun came up."

"Hopefully this helps." Lexi smiles and walks into my office, setting a stack of papers on my desk. "Riley's monthly injury update. He's cleared to start practicing with our AHL affiliate."

I stop in my tracks and stare at her. She's been working

75

with him relentlessly since his accident last summer. She's learned every component of his prosthetic leg. Put him through intense physical therapy exercises and has him skating again.

She fell in love with him too.

Almost everyone on this team has found a significant other. Four years ago, I wouldn't have believed that was possible, but I'm glad for it. It makes my job easier. The press wants to hear about our game play these days, not what supermodel someone is sleeping with.

Even Liam, our resident asshole, isn't as grumpy and bent out of shape as he used to be. Last week he did an interview with ESPN after a shutout, and he didn't drop a single curse word during the conversation. I was shocked.

Riley's rehab has been the most important item on my agenda, and I see the effort he's putting in. I know how much time Lexi has dedicated to individualized therapy and research on athletes with prosthetics. I hear them leaving the training room long after the other guys have gone home, and it's evident why she's one of the best athletic trainers in the league. She gives a shit, and it's a huge part of why he's been able to get to this point.

"Are you serious?" I grab the top paper off the stack, reading through it. The words *cleared* and *vigorous physical activity* pop out at me, and I let out a disbelieving laugh. "Holy shit, Armstrong. You did it."

"Riley did it, but it was a collaborative effort. I hope this is the start of a new era in professional hockey. One that's inclusive to all athletes, no matter what their bodies might look like." She turns her head at the knock on the door and offers a smile to Darcy, the team's intern. "Hey, Darce. Who is the pizza for?"

"Coach." She hands the cardboard box my way. "It just got here, and it's very hot."

"Since when do you order pizza to the arena?" Lexi asks.

"I have an afternoon meeting, and I'm not sure how long it's going to last," I explain. "I wanted to make sure the person joining me has a chance to eat."

"A meeting, huh?" Lexi grins. "That's very accommodating of you."

"Out, Armstrong," I bark, ignoring the girls' laughter when I shut the door behind them.

I stare at the box, positive this is way too fucking much. Asking Hannah to come here is a business meeting. We're not two friends catching up—I ruined any chance of that being a possibility—and I'm tempted to hand off the food to the custodial crew cleaning up the locker room down the hall.

There's no time to stew over it though, because there's another knock and the turn of the doorknob. I blink and Hannah is standing in front of me wearing dark jeans, white sneakers, and a sweater that slips off her right shoulder.

Sixteen months without seeing her, and my first look at her has me forgetting where the fuck I am.

"Brody." Her voice is smooth. Rich with a touch of heat. It's just like the whiskey we drank at her house, and I have to blink again to stop my vision from turning fuzzy. "Sorry I'm a few minutes early. If you're busy, I can wait out in the hall." Her attention flicks to the pizza I'm still holding. "Or if you want to finish your lunch."

"No. Come in." I gesture her inside, making sure to give her a wide berth. She closes the door behind her. "It's pizza."

"I'd be concerned if it wasn't. It is pizza-shaped."

"I ordered it in case you were hungry." The tips of my ears burn. "Since it's lunchtime."

Hannah lifts an eyebrow but doesn't miss a beat. "Let me guess. Boring cheese?"

"Only half of it. The other half has pineapple and ham. Extra pineapple, in fact." I set the box on my desk and grab a stack of napkins from one of the drawers. "Rumor is it's not half bad."

She snorts and sits in the chair across from me. I hand her one of the slices, careful not to brush her fingers with mine when I pass over the pizza.

"I—"

"Tell—"

We talk at the same time, and I almost choke on my bite of food. She tips her head to the side, assessing me while I pound my chest and swallow.

"Go ahead," I rasp, wondering why the fuck I don't have any water in here.

"It's your office." Hannah motions to the jerseys in frames hanging from the walls. "You first."

"I know we're here to talk about my daughter, but I need to say something else first. About that night at your place."

Her inhale is sharp. "We had fun. You left. I'm a big girl, and I'm not sitting around writing your name in my diary, Brody."

"I wanted to apologize for acting like a piece of shit," I say in a rush of words, and she pauses mid-bite. This is *not* how I practiced this earlier, but I roll with it. "For how I left. For the things I said. I was panicking, if we're being honest. I had tunnel vision, which lead me to being selfish. Running out of there was inconsiderate. Telling you to forget it ever happened was even shittier. I don't expect you to forgive me, but I need you to know I understand how my behavior was… really fucking lame. I've never cared what other people think about me, and I don't know why I cared then. Deep down, maybe I thought that if I pretended *that* didn't happen, the rest of the night didn't happen too. It wasn't fair to you."

"You sent me flowers." Hannah sets her pizza down on the napkin in her lap. She adjusts the sleeve of her sweater, pushing it back over her shoulder. "Right?"

"I did." I tear off a piece of crust and pop it in my mouth, not mentioning the hours I spent researching different floral arrangements from the hospital waiting room. The websites I read until my eyes burned with tears. Until I found a bouquet I thought would maybe, *maybe* convey a sliver of how sorry I was. "I recognize it's a cop out from an actual apology, but I needed you to know I was thinking about you even when my actions proved differently."

"I appreciate the apology, Brody. We're both mature enough to recognize there was a lot happening that night. Emotions are always magnified when intimacy is involved. I know we didn't have sex but——"

"We may as well have," I finish for her. A faint blush sits on her cheeks, and she gives me a nod.

"Exactly. Tensions were high. You were worried about your player. It sucked in the moment, but I'm not mad. Not anymore. That was a lifetime ago."

"It was." I nod. "But you can still be mad at me. For what it's worth, I'm still mad at myself. And I'm going to work to earn your trust back."

Hannah's lips twitch. She leans back, getting comfortable with one leg draped over the other. "Tell me about your daughter."

A switch in conversation. Good. This is good. Easier to process, easier to talk about.

"Olivia. She's fourteen, and she skates every day but Wednesdays, Thursdays, and Sundays." I pause, wanting to ask Hannah how she's been. If she came to any of the games last season and if I could've spotted her when I glanced out in the crowd. I never let myself look. "Two hours every afternoon, except for Fridays and Saturdays when she puts in four hours." I rub my hands over my joggers and clear my throat. "You don't have to agree to this. Spending hours skating with a teenager is——"

"I spend hours skating as it is. Adding someone else to the mix would make it more fun. Does Olivia do the short program? Pairs?"

"Short program. She has the Potomac Memorial Open on her calendar, which is in—"

"Virginia, next August. This is a regional event. The next level is sectional championships, then the U.S. Championships." She takes a bite of her pizza. "I'm guessing she's a Novice? A Junior? Wait. Maybe she's an Intermediate? Is the Potomac Memorial her first big event?"

"No. She's done…" I fumble with my phone, scrolling through the photos I have of Olivia in her skating outfits. Her on the ice, head dropped back and caught mid-spin. There are so many questions. "She did the Cranberry Open last year as an Intermediate."

"Good for her. I like people who are ambitious and not afraid to dream big." She smiles and takes my phone from me, zooming in on the photo. "She has good footwork."

"You can tell that from a picture?"

"I've been doing this for twenty years, Brody. Could you tell if a guy has good footwork from a photo?"

"Yeah," I admit, and her smile grows. "Easily."

"Look at us. We're two peas in a pod." Hannah hands back my phone and finishes her pizza. "I'm more than happy to coach Olivia. It'll be a learning curve as far as instructional foundations go, but I'm willing to put in the work to get it right."

"I've been coaching for over a decade. Sometimes I still can't get it right."

"That's reassuring."

"Life is bleak, then you die."

Her laugh is loud and bright. It's a full-body thing, with a scrunched nose and little wrinkles around her eyes. Whatever higher power I've been bartering with to make sure I'm not still attracted to her really said *fuck you*, because even with the snort she lets out, she's absolutely fucking beautiful.

"One way to look at it." She chuckles again. "Since we're on the topic of coaching, I wanted to run an idea by you."

"Okay." I lean forward. "What's up?"

"Skating has lost its magic for me." Her smile fades. Her unhappiness is a punch to the gut. "It's a chore these days, not something I love. I met up with Grant the other night, and he threw out a suggestion I think might help me. I was wondering if you would help me approach skating in a new way."

"I'm not following."

"Could *you* coach *me*? Run drills with me? I want to spend less time on Axels and jumps and more time going back to the basics of skating. The Stars are consistently one of the best teams in the league. Their fundamentals are good, and that's because you're the one coaching them."

"Wait a second." I frown, confused as hell. "I don't know shit about figure skating. That's why I'm hiring you to work with Olivia."

"You know everything about *skating*. I've seen your old tapes. You used to fly across the ice. Your edge work was incredible."

"Not so much now. I'm old and slow." I touch the collection of friendship bracelets on my wrist. I wear them all the time, liking that I have Olivia with me wherever I go. Making her happy is my biggest priority. It's my *only* priority, and while I'm not sure how I'm supposed to help Hannah, I'll do it if it means Olivia gets what she wants. "I'm not sure what kind of coaching I can give you. Between practices and traveling for games and different time zones and being a parent, my free time is extremely limited."

"Could you do two hours a week?"

I don't know if I have two hours anywhere in my days to add in more to my workload, but all I can hear is the plea in Hannah's voice. The desperate weight of her gaze and how she scoots to the edge of her chair, waiting with anticipation.

Agreeing to help her doesn't fix what happened in the past, but it's a start. The first step of the two of us getting along, and it's why I'm nodding. Why I'm opening my laptop so I can look at my schedule.

"Yes," I say, and the way she beams at me makes me feel like I won the goddamn lottery. "Two hours is doable."

"Thank you. If nothing changes after the first couple of weeks, I'll stop taking up so much of your time and try something else." She claps. "Now I need to scout out a location to work with Olivia. I have a few connections, but I'm not sure what rink can get us on their calendar right away."

"Use the Stars training facility. It's brand new. There are women's locker rooms, so you'll have somewhere to put your stuff."

"Women's locker rooms? Do you open the rink up for public skate?"

"No. But if we ever have another woman on the team, she needs a spot where she feels comfortable getting dressed."

"*Oh.*" Hannah's face softens. "Because of Emerson Hartwell."

"Exactly."

"I forgot you brought her to DC. You changed her life."

"She's the one who proved herself in the league."

"You're not a fan of compliments, I see." She tosses her used napkin in the trash can next to my desk, and I'm grateful for the shift in conversation. "Let's get back to Olivia. I like the schedule she's currently on, but she's still growing. I don't want to put an extreme amount of strain on her muscles off the bat. As we get closer to her competitions, we'll start slotting in more ice time. Are you comfortable with her participating in light strength training? Mainly balance drills and stability focused exercises."

"As long as she's not turning into a bodybuilder before she can drive, whatever strength training you have planned is fine. We have a weight room you all can utilize here. If there's a piece of equipment you need but don't have, ask. I'll get it."

"You're a powerful man, Brody Saunders."

"Just a dad who cares about his kid."

"Do you have a day of the week that would work for when you and I meet up?"

"It's going to have to be flexible. Since you'll be with Olivia in the afternoons, what about an hour and a half after the short practices we have before home games?" I tap my keyboard. "If you start with Livvy next week, I could do Tuesday or Friday morning. Thursday we're in New York." I glance over at Hannah, confused when I find her gaping at me. I touch my cheek, worried I have pizza sauce all over my face. "What's wrong?"

"Nothing." She smiles and shakes her head. "This is the most I've ever heard you talk outside the bedroom, and I'm processing it."

"Don't get used to it," I grumble, trying not to blush. *The bedroom.* Where all I did was run my fucking mouth and told her how perfect she is. "This is an anomaly."

"We're going to have a blast." Hannah's smile morphs to a grin. "Tuesday is perfect. I really appreciate it, Brody. And if we could go back to what we were talking about earlier? That night in June?"

I pull at my collar. "What about it?"

"It's in the past. Yes, there was attraction. Yes, we had fun. But we're two adults who are going to be spending time together. Can we agree to be friends without any awkwardness?"

"Friends? You want to be friends?"

"Why not? It sounds more fun than skating in silence. Look." She pulls her phone from her pocket and holds up a text message thread. I recognize it as our conversation. "I officially removed you as an unknown number. You'll be henceforth saved in my phone as GC."

"What the hell does GC mean?"

"That's the best part. It can stand for so many things. Grant's Coach. Grumpy Coach. Good-looking Coach."

Hannah smirks. I get a brief glimpse at her lock screen when she clicks off her phone, noticing it's a photo of her and Grant after we won the Stanley Cup the first time. She's sitting on his shoulders with confetti stuck in her hair, and there's a pang in my chest. "Just kidding on the last one. Friends don't find their friends attractive."

"I think being around you is going to significantly raise my blood pressure."

"That's just old age," she quips, nodding once. "I'll be at the training facility Monday afternoon, ready to get started." Hannah swipes another slice of pizza from the box and pops to her feet. "Thank you for this opportunity. I'm so excited to work with Olivia, and I can't wait to see what she's going to accomplish. Text me if anything changes."

"Will do."

She walks to the door, pausing when she gets there. "Hey, Brody?"

"Hm?" I ask, doing my best not to gawk at her legs.

"Those flowers? They were beautiful. Thanks for sending them."

With a wave, she disappears. I stare after her, deciding this is going to be the longest season of my fucking life.

ELEVEN
BRODY

I PUT three plates on the kitchen island knowing Kali is bringing Olivia up and joining us for dinner. I messaged her after Hannah left my office, asking if she was free to talk about schedules. Communication is the most important part of our relationship, and we've done it damn well.

The older Liv gets, the more we both want to be present for those big life moments she's going to experience. Kali and I sit down together before every school year and plan out transportation. We divide holidays evenly and figure out how often we're going to shuttle Liv between our two houses.

We have a system. This *works*, and when something unexpected springs up—like hiring a new figure skating coach after the hockey season is underway—it's nice to have someone who is flexible and willing to work with me to keep Liv's life as uninterrupted as possible.

It's also nice to know I have an accomplice if I ever need to kick a future significant other's ass for not treating my daughter the right way down the road.

"We're here!" Liv calls out, bounding down the hall. She drops her backpack in the middle of the kitchen, racing toward me and the pile of food I have spread out. "Please tell me we're having tacos tonight."

"Nice to see you too, kid." I open the Styrofoam container housing the two dozen street tacos I ordered for us. "Of course we're having tacos."

"I'm glad to know you also leave a mess at your dad's house." Kali steps over the discarded backpack, nudging it out of the way with her shoe. "I thought it was just me."

"Don't go in her bathroom. It's scary as hell." I give Kali a quick hug and point to the food. "Grab a plate. There's something I need to talk to you all about."

"Oh, no." Olivia groans. "Did you get fired? Do we have to move to Canada? If you have the option to choose, could you pick California as your next place to coach? I really want to learn how to surf."

"Why would you go straight into thinking I got fired?" I take three tacos for myself and scoff. "Thanks for having confidence in your old man."

"The Stars are near the bottom of the standings to start the season." She hops onto the stool at the island and digs in. "People get fired for less."

"We've played twelve games."

"And you've only won six of them."

I look at Kali. "When did she turn into such a smart-ass?"

"She's *your* daughter." Kali laughs and takes the plate I offer her. "She's been this way since she could talk."

"What secret are you keeping, Dad?"

"First tell us about school," I say.

"It was fine. My math homework is kicking my ass, and I—"

"Language," Kali and I say in unison.

"Coming from the guy who got a $20,000 fine because he criticized the referees after his game last week? Is there going to be enough money to pay for my college tuition?"

A $20,000 fine is a drop in the bucket for me, and I know

how privileged I am to be able to say that. The deal I signed after my ELC was guaranteed. Money was funneled my way for years after my early retirement. Add in the contract extension with the Stars my agent secured two summers ago, and neither Olivia nor any of my great-great-great-great grandchildren will ever have to worry about money.

I give back when I can. I sponsor youth hockey camps in the city and set up a scholarship fund for local teenagers who want to play the sport in college. Doesn't feel right to keep it all to myself when there are people out there who need it more than I do.

"You're going to be fine." I wipe my mouth with a napkin. "I got some news today."

"News?" Kali frowns. "Is everything okay?"

"It will be. I found Livvy a skating coach."

My daughter gasps. "*What?* You did?"

"Yup."

"Who had space to bring me on? How much money did you have to pay them? Is this one of those arrangements where you owe someone a kidney down the road?"

"Jesus, Liv." I glance at Kali. "We need to take social media away from her."

"Agreed." She cuts a quick look at our daughter, pursing her lips, then refocuses on me. "That's great you found someone, Brody."

"Who is it?" Olivia practically bounces on her stool. "A former Olympian? Someone new in town? Are you sending me to a boarding school in another country?"

"Do you know Grant Everett? Second line left winger on the Stars?"

"Yeah." She giggles. "He's cute with his floppy hair."

"Absolutely not. You're not allowed to call any of the players on my team cute. Actually—scratch that. You're not allowed to call *anyone* cute. Ever."

"Why not?" Liv presses. "Half the girls in my grade have

boyfriends, Dad. It's going to happen for me at some point too."

"I'm ignoring everything you just said." I sigh, defeated, and look at Kali. "Grant has a sister. Her name is—"

"Hannah, duh," Liv interrupts, taking control of the conversation. "I know. I've told you about her, remember? She's so freaking talented. I've watched her World Championship program close to a hundred times. Her triple Lutz is the best I've ever seen! And, cooler than that, she's famous for her body composition."

"What does that mean?"

"She's taller than most skaters," Olivia gushes. "It gives me hope that one day I'll be as successful as her."

My fingers wrap around the counter. I am, unfortunately, very aware of how tall Hannah is. I know how it feels to have her long legs wrapped around my head, and inviting her back into my life was the worst decision I ever could've made.

"I see," I say.

"How the heck did you get *Hannah Everett* to agree to coach me? How does she even know who you are?"

"Her brother, remember?" I ignore how warm the room feels, distracting myself with the tacos so I don't have to give any more details. "She was available."

"She posted that she dropped out of Skate America, and I thought she was injured. I guess not. Oh, my god. *Dad*," Liv shrieks. "This is the best day of my life! When can she start? Where are we going to train? Do you think she'll let me hold her medals? I bet she's even prettier in real life."

She is, I think bitterly. *She's the prettiest woman in the world.*

But... why the hell did she drop out of a competition? Does it have to do with what she was talking about in my office—not being in love with the sport anymore? How skating is losing its magic?

Shit. I hope she's okay.

"You start next week at the Stars' training facility. Same

days as your previous schedule, and I have no clue about her medal."

"The girls at school are going to be *so* jealous." Olivia finishes her food in record time. "Permission to be excused so I can text my friends and give them the good news? Please, please, *please*?"

"Half an hour," I tell her. "Then homework."

"Deal." She squeals and jumps off the stool, stopping to give me a tight hug. "Thank you, Dad. This means so much to me."

I don't have a chance to hug her back. She's too busy sprinting down the hall, nose buried in her phone. Her bedroom door closes, and Kali laughs.

"Okay. Wow. You just snagged top spot for Dad of the Year," she tells me. "But you would've landed there without hiring her dream skating coach."

"Thanks, Kal." I dip my chin and point to the fridge. "Want some wine? Or a beer?"

"I shouldn't. Bryant and I have an appointment scheduled for tomorrow. Three years of trying to have a second kid, and nothing yet."

"Water it is then." I fill up two glasses and slide one her way. "I'll join you in solidarity."

"Thanks." She smiles and leans her elbows on the island. "So are you going to tell me why you were *blushing* a few minutes ago?"

"I have no clue what you're talking about. I got sunburned over the weekend."

"Sunburned? In November? Makes sense." She smirks, then takes a sip of her water. "You wanted to talk about schedules?"

"Yeah. Hannah is able to keep the same days for Olivia's training. I offered the Stars' facility because it's available, but I know it's farther from you than her usual rink."

"We'll figure it out. I haven't seen Liv that excited about something in months."

"If the travel gets to be too much on the days when you have her, I'll see if we can work out a few sessions at locations closer to your place."

"It's going to be fine, Brody. Really. We've made this work for years. A change in plans isn't going to be the end of the world. How the heck did you even pull this off?"

"I asked the guys if they had any recommendations." I shrug and put Olivia's empty plate in the sink. "Grant said his sister might be available to help, and she was. Sounds like she's taking a break from her career? I don't know. We didn't talk specifics."

"Let me know how much she charges and I'll pay half."

"Fuck no. Put that money toward redecorating the nursery you're going to use when your little one comes."

"If," Kali corrects.

"When," I answer.

"Brody Saunders is optimistic for once?" She grins. "There must be something in the air. The reason you were blushing earlier, perhaps? Is there a woman in the picture?"

"Don't push it. You know I don't date."

"Who said anything about dating? I'm sure half the city would throw themselves at your feet given the chance. A night of passion with the mysterious pro hockey coach? The line would stretch all the way to Meridian Hill Park."

"My hand works just fine."

"You're disgusting. Don't ever say that to me again." Kali makes a face. "Are you going to tell me why you're so adverse to having a personal relationship with someone? I know we had our whole accidental pregnancy thing—no complaints here, by the way—but you've never really given off playboy vibes. You're not secretly against monogamy, are you?"

"No." I lean against the counter and shrug again. "I'm

busy. Not sure when I have time to date in between being on the road and a parent."

"Your players make time."

"They're younger than me. And there's also the stupid reason."

"Oh?" Her eyes twinkle. "Do tell."

"I realize what I'm about to say sounds very narcissistic, but I don't mean it that way." I pause, crossing my arms. "When I met you, you didn't know who I was. When you found out, you didn't care. I was Brody Saunders, the hockey player. Nowadays, whenever I meet a woman, they tell me what a big fan they are. How much they love the team, then there's usually a sexual innuendo in there about *big sticks* or *nice pucks*." Kali stifles a laugh, and I rub the back of my neck. "I prefer keeping to myself. I always have. But if I'm going to be with someone, I want them to like Brody Saunders, the hockey coach. Not the hockey coach, Brody Saunders."

"Oh my *god*. You're a fucking romantic!"

"Shut up," I mumble. "I'm not. Like I said, I'm content with my life exactly as it is. I don't like change. I don't like disruptions to my routines, and dating is a big disruption. Leave me alone, dammit."

"Fine. I'll let you be, but only because I know you want to be *wooed*." She drags her finger through a spot of condensation, her mood turning serious. "Are you, um, okay with keeping Olivia until you head to New York? I'm not sure how I'm going to feel after my appointment. Last time I cried for twelve hours."

"Shit, Kal. Of course I'm okay with her being here a few extra days. You and Bryant will call me if you need anything?"

"You know, you're not making it easy for me to tell all my single girlfriends who ask what kind of father you are that you're a piece of trash." She slides off her stool and stands. "Why can't you be this nice to the general public?"

My lips twitch. "Because they don't deserve it. I like making people work for my respect. This kind of behavior is reserved for a very select group, and you happen to be part of it."

"Aren't I the luckiest girl in the world." Kali grins and gives me a quick hug. "Thanks for making this parenting thing a damn breeze, Saunders."

"Right back at you, Collins."

After Kali leaves, I clean up the kitchen and walk down the hall, pressing my ear to Olivia's door. She's talking to someone on the phone and I smile, moving to the other side of the condo where my room is. Closing the door behind me, I pull up my text thread with Hannah.

ME

Hey. I let Olivia know you're her new coach, and she's ecstatic. Apologies in advance for any fangirling she might do.

H.E.

Is that why two dozen teenagers just followed me on social media? I'm feeling really cool right now.

I fight off a smile and fire back a response.

ME

I'll have her at the rink on Monday afternoon.

H.E.

I can't wait!

ME

We'll talk pay then too.

H.E.

I'd do this for free.

ME

Not happening. Have a good night.

H.E.

You too, GC!

I toss my phone on my towel and stand under the hot water, stupidly optimistic for the second time tonight.

Friends.

I can be a friend.

Piece of fucking cake.

TWELVE
HANNAH

ME

I'm doing something new.

TIERNEY

Is it bangs??

ME

I'm coaching someone for the first time.

TIERNEY

Like. An actual human?

ME

Yup! Grant's coach has a daughter, and she needs someone for her lessons.

Through a weird twist of fate, I'm the one who is going to be working with her.

TIERNEY

Hannah, WHAT? Wait. I love this for you! You'd be a GREAT coach.

Are you excited?

FROM THE VERY FIRST day I started skating, I've been confident stepping onto the ice. Today, I'm nervous as hell. I could barely eat lunch. I spent all day prior to arriving at the Stars' practice facility making a list of things to discuss with Olivia.

I've racked my brain trying to remember what my coaches have taught me before we started working on program choreography. I don't want to assume Olivia knows or doesn't know certain terminology. I also don't want to push her so hard she winds up like me, stuck in limbo about whether or not I see a future for myself in this sport.

Being a good athlete doesn't mean you'll make a good coach, but I've taught a few Learn to Skate camps in the past. I've helped the younger skaters at the rink when they've struggled with some of their moves, and I'm going to rely on that directional instinct to help me get through our first couple of lessons.

No one will have any idea I'm flying by the seat of my fucking pants.

I fix my ribbon and walk down a long tunnel toward the players' bench. I pull out my skates and take off the soakers protecting the blades, reminding myself to breathe. Brody and I agreed on a four o'clock start, and a quick check of the time tells me I have fifteen minutes to shake out my jitters.

The ice is smooth, and the first lap has my shoulders relaxing away from my ears. My legs are lighter, and *this* is what I've been missing: complete peace. The ability to skate just to *skate*, not to perform for judges giving me scores. The second lap has me smiling. I go through some of my favorite moves on the third lap, landing a double Axel more perfectly than I have in months.

"If I tried to jump like that, I'd be taken away in an ambulance," someone yells.

I grin on instinct, finishing my turn to find Grant joining me on the ice in athletic shorts and a DC Stars Hockey hoodie. I move toward him, noticing freshly dried blood under his eye and a nick on his skin.

"What happened to your face?" I ask, stopping abruptly and spraying ice on his shins. He groans and tries to shove my shoulder, but in his slides, I'm much faster. "You weren't good-looking before, but now you look like a troll. I preferred the inch worm mustache."

"Glad I have such a loving sister who boosts my confidence."

"Like it needs boosting. I know you saw that social media page dedicated to making thirst trap edits of you."

"What can I say? I'm the people's princess." His grin is smug. "As for my face, I took a stick to the cheek during morning skate. I'm fine, and the battle wounds make me cooler."

"It would be even cooler if you were missing some teeth."

"Might happen in our next game. We're playing the team we beat for the Cup two years ago. It's shocking they're not fans of us."

"Are you all scheduled for an afternoon practice today? Please don't tell me my lesson is about to be taken over by twenty hockey players."

"Nah. Just wanted to stop by and say hi before your first official day as a coach. How're you feeling? Not stressed, I hope. You're going to knock this out of the park, Han."

It's impossible not to smile at his encouragement.

Grant's always been that kind of guy, the big brother who came to every competition and wore a shirt with my face plastered on it. Our skates were the oldest ones on the ice. We had to fundraise for games and competitions that required travel. When the summer came where only one of us could go to camp due to finances, he declined a developmental academy's invite to a prestigious event for select hockey players so I could spend two weeks in Boston training with a former Olympian.

He deserves every bit of success he's earned, from the contracts and sponsorships with Bauer and BodyArmor to two Stanley Cups. He doesn't even mind that he's not a starter, preferring to join the second line off the bench to give the team a spark when they need it. A lot of my friends have sibling relationships that are stilted and sad, but that's not ours, and I'm so glad.

"I'm a little stressed, but that's because I'm trying something new. And I really want it to go well," I tell him.

"It's going to go well. Your triple dipper quadruple—"

"That's an appetizer at Chili's."

"Whatever it's called. It's one of the best in the world because *you're* one of the best in the world."

"Even now?" I ask.

"Even now." Grant snaps. "What's that mantra you used to say? In the mirror, before a big event."

"'Inhale confidence, exhale fear?'"

"Yup. That. Here. I'll do it with you. Deep breath." He sucks in a long puff of air, and I mimic him. "That's the confidence. And now we're going to let go of the fear."

I blow out the breath, feeling lighter after. "Okay. That might've worked."

"Because you're a genius." He grins. "I should get going. We have a lifting session scheduled at the arena, then a team dinner. You still need to come to one of those, by the way."

"I don't have anything in common with the people there."

"The girls that are part of the team come. Lexi, Emmy, Madeline, and Piper. You know most of them."

"I'll think about it." I smile. "Thanks for stopping by, G."

"Confidence, remember? You're going to kill it," he adds, jogging over the ice toward the tunnel. He almost slips, righting himself at the last minute. "Whoops. Pretend like you didn't see that."

I laugh and do one last lap, repeating the mantra until voices echo over the ice. There's a deeper one, followed by a high-pitched laugh. I stop and fix my skirt, hoping I look professional enough. Brody comes into view, and beside him, there's a girl who is the spitting image of him.

They're a perfect pair, from her dark hair to the way she moves. Not nearly as broad, but her nose matches his, and so do her eyes. The only difference I can find after a quick once-over is her smile. Hers is big and bold, full of life from someone who hasn't been burned by the world yet while his is more subdued, like you're lucky to catch a glimpse of it.

"Hi." I wave and head their way. "I hope it's okay I'm here early. I wanted to get a quick warm up in."

"The ice is yours to use." Brody pins me with a look I can't decipher, his eyes briefly flicking to my legs before moving back to my face. "Hannah, this is my daughter, Olivia."

"Hey." I smile at her. "It's so nice to meet you."

"I'm going to get this out of the way now before I fall and embarrass myself, but I'm, um, a big fan." Olivia's cheeks flush. "I promise I'm not going to stalk you or anything."

"Liv." Brody shakes his head. "Why would you even mention that?"

"It's okay. I'm flattered. It's so nice to meet you, Olivia." I bounce my gaze over to her dad. "Are you going to hang out?"

"No. Liv won't let me watch her practice, so I'll be back in an hour and a half to pick her up." He fixes the bill of his backward hat and clears his throat. "I'm also, ah, not available tomorrow like I mentioned. Can we do next Monday instead?"

"Of course," I tell him. "I don't have a lot going on at the moment, so I'm flexible."

"Wait." Olivia glances between us. "You two hang out?"

"No," Brody says. "But we are friends."

"He's helping me with something. I might try my hand at hockey next," I joke.

"Please don't. Their jerseys smell horrifying." She wrinkles her nose. "Like, truly awful."

"You're so right. I think I'll stick to figure skating." I grin and hike my thumb over my shoulder. "Do you want to get started, Olivia?"

"Yes, please." She beams and gives her dad a quick one-armed hug, hurrying to the bench to change into her skates. "See ya, Dad!"

"The second she's on the ice, she forgets all about me," he says.

"It's good to know your place. We'll see you later," I say. "And, again, thanks for this opportunity, Brody. I can't wait to work with Olivia."

With a nod, he disappears down the tunnel. Olivia is already on her feet, leaning over the boards and waiting for my instructions, and I guess that makes me in charge.

"I'm so excited." She puts on her gloves, and I grab mine too. "I've been looking forward to this all day."

"Same." I smile. "I hear your previous coach is pregnant?"

"Yeah. I've been training with Susannah Sharp. She competed for Germany in the Olympics."

"We've been skating against each other for years. She's fantastic."

"You're much better." Olivia slaps a hand over her mouth. "Pretend I didn't say that. I swear I'm not unprofessional."

"Say what? I didn't hear anything." I grin and invite her onto the ice. We head for the Stars logo, and I check to see how she stands when we're not moving. Her balance is superb, and her posture makes me jealous. "Your dad mentioned the Potomac Memorial is your big upcoming event. What else do you have on the calendar?"

"Any competition I can enter, honestly. I want to be the best in the world. I know everyone says that, but I'm willing to put in the work."

"I have a feeling we're going to get along well, Olivia."

"You can call me Liv."

"Liv. I like that. You're on the taller side for a figure skater, like me. Have you noticed any issues with aerodynamics?"

"Yeah, I got the height from my dad. But I haven't noticed any issues when I start skating." She shrugs. "I have had a coach tell me I need to figure out a diet plan so I could lose a couple pounds, but I just got my period last year and—"

"Fuck that." It's my turn to cover my mouth. "Sorry. Pardon my language."

"Please." Liv laughs. "You should hear the things my dad says."

"I've had coaches tell me the same thing. And, like, I get it. Science, physics, all of that. It's hard not to let it get to you, but I've started using it as motivation. Nothing beats standing on a podium while someone who tried to control your eating habits watches you succeed. Have cookies and pasta three times a week. Food is fuel, and you're never going to catch me mentioning anything about your size, okay?"

"Is it too early to say that you might be my favorite coach of all time?"

"Way too early, because I'm going to put you through drills that will hurt like hell."

"I can't wait." She offers me a nervous look. "Am I allowed to ask why you're not competing right now? There are tons of rumors on the internet."

I hesitate before answering. Since my announcement about pulling out of Skate America and all the events on my calendar for the foreseeable future, my social media has been flooded with comments and DMs from fans as well as some of the women I've competed against checking in to make sure I'm okay.

"I've been skating since I was four years old. Over twenty years later, and fatigue is setting in. I'm burned out. I'm unhappy, but that's where your dad comes in. He's agreed to take me back to the basics of skating in hopes I'll fall in love with the sport again. When I'm here with you, we'll focus on the technical aspect of skating. When I'm with him, it will be like I'm a beginner all over again," I say, tilting my head. "Speaking of that—and we're about to get deep here—I don't ever want you to reach the point where you're unhappy during our time together. If you're having an off day or just don't feel like skating, I want you to tell me, okay? Making this your career is a great dream to have, but what good is it if you have to sacrifice your happiness to get there? Communication is key, and a lot of my coaches haven't put my mental health first. I'm not going to do that with you."

"I promise." Liv nods. "Dad talks to me all the time about not putting all my eggs in one basket, and I want to set myself up for success. I know taking care of myself is the way to do that."

"Good. I've been through a lot with this sport. If you ever have questions or need advice on something, I'm happy to help in any way I can."

"I appreciate that. I love my dad, but he's not a teenage girl. He's never been a teenage girl, and sometimes his solutions to problems are… not great."

"Same with my brother. They mean well, but they just don't understand certain things. And that's okay!" I laugh. "Ready to get to work?"

"No pressure or anything." She chuckles, shaking out her hands. "If I faceplant, I promise it's just nerves, not because I'm uncoordinated."

"There's no judgment if you fall. We all do it at some point."

We go through a warmup and do a few laps of easy skating. After, I pull off to the side, letting Liv take center stage. She shows me her waltz and salchow, followed by a flip jump. Her Lutz is clean, and so is her Axel, but she struggles with her double toe loop.

"I don't know why that one is so difficult for me." Liv sighs. "I can't grasp the concept."

"It's my least favorite move because of the weight transfer. We need to make sure our arms and shoulders are in line with our hips. We also don't want to curtsey. Here." I motion to the middle of the ice. "Let's do it slowly."

Liv runs an exercise I give her, focusing on her single toe loop first. After, we transition to another drill where she pays attention to her takeoff pivot. The last exercise is practicing rotations, and I talk her through landing in a controlled manner. We stop and adjust. I point out her body position, and after half an hour, she tries the double toe loop again.

"Holy cow." She laughs when she successfully lands the move, looking at me with wide eyes. "That felt so natural."

"Right? Your alignment was much stronger that time." I grin and give her a high-five. "I'm someone who likes tricks and flashy moves, but when the flashy moves don't seem to be working, I wind it back and go through the process step by step. That was beautiful, Liv."

"Coach Susannah is so nice, but she never explained things like you did. She would just tell me to do something again. I never knew what part of the move I was getting wrong."

"Every coach has a different feedback method. Mine promoted self-correction. She wouldn't get involved unless something was glaringly wrong. A lot of figure skating is trial and error, and you just nailed that, Liv. Great job."

We spend the next hour going through more drills, and by

the time we start to wrap up our lesson, Liv's confidence has only grown. I'm giddy at the thought of having made a positive impact on our first day together.

She pulls over to the bench and grabs her water bottle, taking a long sip while I do a triple Axel and wince at my landing.

"I'm sorry I'm late," Brody says, and I catch him standing in the tunnel. "I was on the phone and lost track of time."

"No problem." I skate over to him and pull out my light blue ribbon. He watches me wrap it around my wrist like a bracelet, his throat bobbing with a slow swallow. "Talking to anyone important?"

"Riley's agent and our PR department. He's going to start practicing with our AHL affiliate team next week, so we were trying to come up with a plan for announcing his two-way contract."

"No way. That's amazing! Grant told me how hard he's been working. It's going to be so special when he officially gets back on the ice."

"Yeah." He lifts his chin in Olivia's direction. "How did it go?"

"Great. Liv is so fun, and she's really talented, Brody. A lot of younger skaters have an ego. They don't like to be told what they're doing wrong, but Liv asks for that feedback and accepts it humbly."

"She's loved skating for as long as I can remember." Brody waves, his mouth twitching with a smile as he motions for his daughter to grab her gear. "I did some research."

"On?"

"Figure skating coaches and their salaries. I know what I was paying her old coach, but Liv is getting personalized, one-on-one lessons now. You're going to be with her four times a week, and I thought eight grand a month seemed fair? But tell me if I'm wrong."

I do quick math in my head and gape at him. "You want to pay me five hundred dollars a session?"

"Is that not enough? Damn the internet for lying to me. We can make it—"

"*Brody*. That's obscene. Especially for someone who has no experience coaching. I don't pay my coaches close to that."

"Is it obscene?" He folds his arms and peers over my shoulder again. "My daughter is smiling. She's not hurt, and from the way she's practically sprinting over here, I'd say she had a good time." There's pressure behind my ribs. It expands, taking up too much space when his eyes shift back to me. "There's no number you could come up with that would ever be too high a cost to make Liv this happy every day."

"Okay, well." My skin feels clammy. I'm flustered. In my head, I knew he was a good dad, but seeing it firsthand is beyond obnoxious in the best kind of way. "We can discuss it next time."

"Discussion is over. I'll get a contract drawn up, and we'll switch to biweekly payments going forward. Consider this a deposit." Brody pulls out his wallet and counts five hundred-dollar bills. His fingers wrap around my wrist, careful as he lifts my arm and unfolds my hand. He sets the money in my open palm, his thumb grazing my fingers when he pulls away. "Pleasure doing business with you, Hannah."

He drapes an arm around Liv's shoulders, nodding while she shares her rambled debrief about our session. Brody gives me a final, sweeping look and I watch them go, cash still in my hand and a warmth low in my belly.

Pleasure indeed.

THIRTEEN

BRODY

THE ARENA where the Minneapolis Loons play is cold as hell. I can't warm up my hands, and I rub my palms together as I join the coaching staff in the locker room.

"November sucks, doesn't it?" Mikal adjusts his suit jacket and grabs my whiteboard for me. "Everything is wet and dreary. The sun sets too early. Not a lot of redeeming qualities. Especially in Minnesota."

"Could be February." I gesture Riley's way, giving him the okay to gather up the guys for our pregame talk. He's still a part of this team even if he's not wearing the jersey, and he's slipped into the role of "extra assistant coach" well. "I'm making a lineup change before we submit tonight's roster, by the way."

"You are?" Mikal frowns. "Who's getting the boot?"

"I'm replacing Mulligan on the first line with Everett. Figured we could mix things up. Everett's passing has improved. His defense is some of the best on the team, and I need to reward the guy for working so hard."

"I support that decision," Parker Barnes, my other assistant coach, chimes in. "His effort has been great lately.

First one to morning skate. Last one to leave. No harm in trying something new."

"Listen up," I say, breaking away to address the locker room. Everyone quiets down and looks my way. "We had a rough night last night with that loss at home, but the slate is clean this evening. The Loons are last in the league in points, so expect weak defense and fewer shots on goal. We want to focus on our efficiency. Making the extra pass to someone who has the open shot instead of trying to be the hero. Starting lineup is Sullivan, Richardson, Hayes, Miller, Fitzpatrick, and Everett."

Grant drops his stick and stares at me, mouth open. Ethan wraps him in a hug and shakes him, grinning wildly. I look over at Maverick and he nods, silent in his agreement with my decision.

"Ten minutes until showtime, boys. Do what you need to do to set yourselves up for success," I say. Everyone turns their attention to their stalls and the last minute superstitions they like to go through, but Grant pops to his feet. He hurries my way, clutching his gloves tight to his chest. "What's up, Everett?"

"Coach. Are you, ah, sure about this? Mulligan has more experience, and I—"

"Experience doesn't win games. Heart does, and you have a lot of heart."

"Okay. Okay. Yeah." He dips his chin, mumbling something to himself. "Thank you, um, for this opportunity. I promise I won't let you down."

"I know you won't," I say, and when he moves back to his stall and accepts another hug from Ethan and Maverick, I almost smile.

"Think you just made his year," Mikal says. "Look how excited he is."

"Let's hope he delivers." I fix my tie and turn for the small office my bag is in. "I need to grab my marker. I'll see you out there in a few."

I rifle through my backpack, finding my favorite dry erase marker. I slide it behind my ear, frowning when my phone rings. It's buried under my stack of game notes on the Loons, and when I pull it out, I see that Kali is calling.

"Hey," I say, answering quickly. "Everything okay? I only have a second before puck drop."

"Brody Saunders," she says. "When were you going to tell me that Hannah Everett is *gorgeous*?"

"Fucking hell, Kal. I thought this was an emergency."

"I was picking up our daughter this afternoon and saw this stunning woman with golden hair spinning in the middle of the ice, and I realized it was Livvy's coach."

"How are you just realizing this? They have been working together for two weeks."

Two weeks of seeing Liv and Hannah together on the ice. Two weeks of hearing them laugh and wondering what's so funny. Two weeks of listening to Liv talk nonstop in the car about the new ways Hannah is challenging her, and two weeks of silky ribbons I want to tug out of Hannah's hair and keep for myself.

"And I hadn't met her before this afternoon. Now I understand why you were blushing when you mentioned her to Liv the first time." I know Kali is smirking even though I can't see her. "Because she's hot."

I unfasten the top button of my shirt, glad I'm hidden away. The last thing I need is an audience for this conversation or something to be taken out of context.

"I didn't hire her for her looks," I say, keeping my voice low. "I hired her because she's good at what she does."

"And she's also nice to look at."

"I'm hanging up. I have a game to coach."

"All I'm saying is Hannah seems fun. You could use some fun in your life."

"Appreciate the insight. Can I help you with anything else?"

"No." Kali laughs. It feels like she knows I'm hiding something, but I keep my mouth shut. "Have a good game, Brody."

"Coach." Mikal pops his head into the office when I hang up. "Waiting on you."

"Sorry," I grumble, tossing my phone back in my bag. I shove any thoughts of Hannah out of my mind. Hockey is my priority. "I'm ready."

WITH ONE MINUTE left on the clock in the third period, the game is tied.

The Loons came out with unanticipated aggression after having the last two days off while we're gassed after a short turnaround from last night's defeat. Liam's playing well in net, only giving up one goal, but we're coming down to the wire.

I take a timeout, using my whiteboard to plan out a play.

"We're dealing the puck to Miller." I draw an arrow from his dot toward the goal, signaling forward movement. "They're going to try to crowd you in the corner. If you get boxed in, chuck it over to Richardson and see if we can sneak another five-hole goal past them. We got lucky in the second with that first one, but they're anticipating Miller to do something flashy. We might be able to go two-for-two. We're not going with an empty net, so Fitzpatrick and Hayes, I want you past center ice. If we can get a rebound off a miss, anyone can take it."

"Hands in, boys," Maverick says, and all their gloved hands stack on top of each other. "Perseverance on three. One, two, three."

"Perseverance," they chant, and I knock their helmets with my knuckles.

We win the face-off, and Ethan passes the puck to

Hudson. Hayes sends it over to Maverick on the far side of the ice. He kicks it to Fitzpatrick who brings it back to Miller, and we're down to thirty seconds. I glance at the jumbotron then back to the play unfolding in front of me, groaning when Maverick takes a shot that bounces off the goal post.

"Shit," I mumble, lifting on my toes so I can see over the heads of the guys on the bench. They're all standing now, hitting the boards with their sticks as Ethan attempts a shot that's an inch too far to the left. "Someone needs to fucking do something."

"Coach." Riley elbows me, and I see it. "Look."

Grant is just outside the right face-off circle, calling for the puck. Ethan passes it his way, and I watch Grant pull his stick back and fire off the prettiest wrist shot I've ever seen. A player from the Loons dives in front of the puck, but he's too late. It's already soaring to the net. Flying past two defenders and slotting into the goal, right past the goalie's blocker as time expires.

The officials blow their whistles and the guys on the bench tumble over the boards, swarming the five on the ice and tackling Grant until they all fall into a dogpile. I pump my fist and Parker gives Mikal a high-five before reaching for me, patting my back in a celebratory hug.

"Fuck yeah, B," he yells. "Damn good call making that lineup change."

"Fucking ballsy of Everett to step up to the plate with that shot." I lift a hand in a wave toward the Loons coach. "That was big time."

"Hope it doesn't go to his head." Mikal laughs, giving Liam a fist bump as he skates past us to join the celebrations.

"Doubt it will. He's humble as hell. Let's try to get everyone out of here in one piece."

The guys drench Grant in sports drink when we get back to the locker room. Maverick hands him the game-winning puck and ruffles his hair, telling him he's proud of him before he gets pulled to do an interview. I sit in for a press conference where I'm hounded with questions about the lineup change.

By the time the mayhem dies down, I'm still buzzing with adrenaline. This is my favorite part about coaching and also what I miss the most about playing: the high a win brings. The camaraderie and excitement, and I take a breath before addressing the room.

"Good work out there, boys. Special accolades go to Sullivan for his forty-seven saves, and to Everett for the goal that gave us the W." I pause so everyone can clap. Grant grins from his stall, bare-chested and unlacing his skates. "We have three days off, a West Coast road trip, then we're back home for Thanksgiving to close out the month. Let's keep this momentum going forward. We need to be thinking about the games in June right now, and tonight's performance was an all-around team effort. You should be proud of yourselves. Bus for the airport leaves soon. No morning skate tomorrow, but we're back in action on Thursday. Grab a shower, pack it up, move it out."

There's another round of applause from the group, and head for the office. I sling my bag over my shoulder and check to make sure I have my laptop and charger. My phone chimes and I groan, knowing it's probably Kali giving me more shit. But when I pick it up, there's a text from Hannah, and my heart races.

I've been avoiding our coaching session. The first week we were supposed to work together, I had a scheduling conflict and needed to cancel. Last week I panicked when I wondered what the hell we were going to talk about for an hour. I lied and said a meeting came up, and it's been eating at me since.

Hannah is holding up her end of the agreement. She's with my daughter four days a week, doing exactly what I asked, while I'm over here with a stick up my ass because I'm fucking *afraid*.

I have no idea how to coach a figure skater who has

competed at the highest level. I have no idea how to be around her for an extended period of time without Liv as a buffer.

All of this falls outside of my carefully constructed routine. It's an interruption, and I don't like interruptions.

But I hate disappointing people more.

I slide my thumb across the screen, reading her message.

H.E.

Is this the most excited you've ever been about anything in your life?

Attachment: 1 video

It's a recording from her television taken after Grant's goal. She's zoomed in on me, Parker, and Mikal during our celebrations. You can see my obvious enthusiasm and I snort, firing off a quick response.

ME

One time I opened a jar of pickles on the first try. That probably takes the cake.

H.E.

I'm actually LOL. You know how some people say LOL but they aren't? I am.

ME

LOL?

H.E.

God, Brody. Don't you have a teenager? Laughing out loud.

ME

I knew what it meant. Just wanted to prove the point that it would've taken you less time to type that out first.

H.E.

You're a pain in the ass.

ME

I've heard that before.

H.E.

Grant just called. He's ecstatic. You have to admit you were a little pumped after that shot.

ME

Can't you hear my excitement through the phone?

H.E.

Oh, yeah. Calm down, killer.

I hold back a laugh.

ME

It was the best goal of the season. He earned it.

H.E.

Proud sister over here.

Anyway. I'm sure you're busy with your coaching responsibilities. I won't bother you... just couldn't resist sharing that clip. Have a good night!

ME

Not a bother. While I have you, I want to apologize for having to reschedule our first skating lesson so many times. Can you do tomorrow morning?

H.E.

I can, but won't you be tired? You're landing late tonight. I don't mind waiting until next week.

ME

I'm a big boy. I'll manage.

It takes a minute for her to respond, and I curse myself for making a stupid joke.

What the fuck was that?

That wasn't very *friendly* of me, and I hope I didn't make her uncomfortable. When she answers, shifting gears, I blow out a sigh of relief.

H.E.

Is 9 too early?

ME

9 works.

H.E.

Do you like coffee?

ME

I do like coffee.

H.E.

Let me guess. Black?

ME

Not even close. I go for iced brown sugar oat milk shaken espressos, but a regular coffee with cream and sugar is fine.

H.E.

Sugar oat WHAT?

Holy shit. That came out of left field, but I love surprises. I'm going to bring you the biggest size with as much espresso as the cup can fit. Since you're a big boy and all.

My cheeks flush at her response. Parker knocks on the

door to the office, and I nearly drop my phone.

"Ready, B? Boys are loaded up," he says.

"Yeah. Yes. Airport," I say.

He lifts an eyebrow. "Are you having a stroke? Do I need to get a doctor?"

"I'm fine." I shove my laptop and charger in my bag. "Let's get out of here."

My phone burns a hole in my pocket when I climb onto the team bus and take my seat. It stays there while I ignore the guys trying to get me to join some social media dance trend and board the plane. Right before takeoff, I read her message again. I can blame my response on the energy from tonight. Something fleeting I won't let myself indulge in tomorrow.

ME

Can't wait.

FOURTEEN
HANNAH

TIERNEY

Miss you, Han.

How's everything going?

ME

Today is day one in my attempt to find the magic in skating again.

TIERNEY

!!!!!

So excited for you.

The rink is less fun without you there, but I'm proud of you for taking care of yourself.

ME

Catch up after Thanksgiving?

TIERNEY

Please! Sending you a big hug and lots of love today.

ME

Thanks, T. I need it.

WITH TWO COFFEES in my hands, I take a seat on the players' bench, utterly exhausted. I tossed and turned all night, wondering how this session is going to go. It's an unconventional approach to burnout, but I'm so desperate to get to the root of my problems, I'm willing to try anything.

That includes enlisting the help of the hockey coach I hooked up with to make it happen.

Brody texted me early this morning to change our meeting location from the practice facility to the arena where the Stars play their home games, and I glance up at the championship banners proudly hanging from the rafters. Two of them were won under his helm, and if anyone knows anything about skating, it's the guy who brought a franchise back from the brink of death.

"Good morning." Brody walks my way in a hoodie, loose athletic shorts, and a backward hat. He's holding his skates in one hand, and there's a whistle looped around his neck that rests against the center of his chest. "You're here early."

Still hot as hell, I muse to myself, and I take a sip of my drink—burning my tongue in the process—to get the thought out of my head.

"Morning. Blame the nerves for my promptness." I hold up his coffee. "I come bearing caffeine."

"Thank you. We were delayed out of Minnesota because of weather, and I didn't make it home until almost three." He yawns and accepts the drink, taking a sip. "Tastes great."

"I can't tell you how much pressure I felt to get your order right."

"There doesn't need to be any pressure. It's not like I

would've thrown it at you if it was wrong." He huffs, fighting back a smile. "Probably would've screamed though."

"I asked the very nice barista if she could add an extra shot of espresso, and she was happy to oblige."

"Crisis averted." Brody looks at the ice, then at me. "How do you want this session to run?"

"I'm not sure, to be honest. I'm open to ideas."

"You're very clearly not a hockey player."

"That's a bold assumption," I tease. "Grant used to hit pucks at me so he could practice his slap shots."

"I hope you were wearing the right gear."

"Just a helmet, but I turned out okay."

"I'd say so." He moves to the bench, sitting next to me. "Why don't you tell me what you want to get out of our time together?" he asks after another sip of his drink.

I trace the crease of my cup. "Talk about an inter-rogation."

"Sorry. I don't mean to pry. Just might make things easier if I know your end goal."

"Permission to be totally honest with you?"

"Probably would be best if we implemented that going forward."

"And you won't judge me?"

"Never." Brody shifts his body, knee pressing into mine. "We're friends, right?"

"Yeah." I nod. "Friends."

"Friends tell each other shit. What's on your mind, Everett?"

"Okay, Saunders. Buckle up. For the entirety of my child-hood and most of my adult life, skating has been my source of joy. I'm fucking *good* at it. I've won championships. I've been people's favorite athlete. I've represented our country at the highest stages. Even when I was no longer winning, I was still glad to be out there. But recently, something has changed. The magic isn't there. I'm struggling mentally and physically.

Everything exhausts me." I sip my coffee, giving myself a second to think. "I know how privileged it is to have access to the resources and coaches I do. That privilege also brings high expectations. Expectations I'm no longer meeting because I'm not having fun. And trust me—I know how *stupid* that sounds. Do paramedics have fun at their job when they're resuscitating someone after a heart attack? Do oncologists have fun telling families their loved ones have cancer? Of course not." His knee is still there. Steady, calm. The reassuring presence I didn't know I needed to keep talking. "So why can't I get over myself, go out there, and perform like everyone wants me to for a few more years before I officially retire?"

"There's your problem. You're worrying what other people think. I haven't given a fuck in years, and life is great."

I burst out laughing. "And if I want to give a fuck?"

"You try to find the joy. In the little things. In the big moments. Under all that stress and pressure and strain from the outside world, you need to shut it down and do what makes you happy."

"Skating, at its most basic level, has *always* made me happy. No cameras, no judges to dock half a point because of my knee placement. It's me, it's the ice, and life is *good*." I blink up at Brody. "That's why you're here. To reteach me swizzles and snowplow stops. If this doesn't work, I either go back to competing and fight through the miserableness, or I give up."

"You don't strike me as someone who would ever give up."

"I'm not. Which is why I'm hoping this works."

"I've always performed well under pressure." He sets his drink down. "Can I ask a personal question?"

"Sure," I say.

"I apologize if this is overstepping, but have you considered therapy?" Brody asks. "I started seeing someone after my injury, and getting those feelings out… just having someone listen… it helped alleviate a lot of the weight I was carrying."

"I found a therapist a couple of weeks ago, actually. I'm

going in to see her twice a week to start, and I'm unpacking the things I've been holding onto for a while." I pause. "It's hard to strip yourself down like that. To show your flaws to someone else."

"It's really fucking hard. I didn't buy into at first, but finding an outlet to grieve what you lost is important." With another sip of his drink, he switches gears. "Funny that you mentioned swizzles and snowplow stops. Those are both in the USA Hockey Learn to Skate plan."

"Guess our sports aren't that different from each other." I unzip my bag, pulling out a scrunchie. I throw my hair up in a messy ponytail, adding a pink ribbon to it. "I know you're busy, but I don't need more than a few months with you to try this out."

"March." Brody rubs his jaw. "Four months, twice a week."

"Do you have time for that?"

"I'll make time. This is important to you, and I know what it's like to have something you love taken away from you prematurely. I wouldn't wish that feeling of being lost on anyone."

"Sounds like you have some firsthand experience. What happened?"

"You don't know my story?" Brody's eyebrows furrow. "It's hardly a secret."

"Do you think I spend my free time looking you up?"

"I hope not. You'd be bored to death."

I laugh. "In the spirit of honesty, I have read plenty of articles about you, but I've always preferred hearing things straight from the source."

"What do you know? The source is right here." He taps his right knee. A long, white scar stretches across his leg. I didn't notice it when we hooked up, too distracted by other parts of his body, but I see it now. "I came into the league at nineteen years old. Played four great seasons, but one game, an opponent's blade sliced through my gear and reached my skin. Cut a tendon, and I had to have surgery. It was a freak accident. My team wanted me back in the lineup as quickly as possible, but when I returned, my body wasn't healed. After three months of pain, poor playing, and a lot of frustration, I recognized I'd never be the same athlete again. So, I retired. It was the smartest thing I could've done, but I still did it unwillingly. It hurts like hell to lose a part of yourself, and I'm not going to let that happen to you." He kicks off his sneakers and slips on his skates, tying them tight. "Which means we have work to do."

Oh.

Hearing his story—and his eagerness to make sure history doesn't repeat itself with me—breathes fresh life into my motivation. It makes me lace up my own skates. Makes my blood hum with anticipation and excitement, and when was the last time I've been this ready to work on something as simple as my edge control?

Never, a voice whispers.

"Is that why you're wearing a whistle?" I ask, trying to keep the air between us light without giving away how much his agreement to help means to me. "Because you're about to go into coach mode?"

"Yup. Get your ass on the ice, Everett," Brody says, and I grin.

"Try to keep up," I say back, and the flicker of amusement in his eyes makes me think working with him is going to be a lot of fucking fun.

"Let's start with a couple easy laps." He moves clockwise around the ice. His legs are even longer with skates on, and I match his pace. "No specific focus. No thinking. Just skating."

"This is my favorite. Hey." I nudge him with my elbow. "I'm sorry about your injury."

"It was years ago."

"Still. I'm sorry things didn't turn out how you thought they would."

"They didn't," he agrees. "But I think they turned out better. If I kept playing, I wouldn't have Liv. I wouldn't be coaching a good group of guys."

"I'm going to tell them you said that."

"Don't you dare." He stops us after three laps and gestures to center ice. "You really want to get basic with this?"

"Yup. Pretend like this is my first time putting on skates."

"You're more elegant than the players I'm used to working them, but we can start with edge work."

"Sounds kinky." I smirk when his neck flushes red. "Bring it on, Saunders."

Brody takes me through a set of stationary drills. There are C-cuts. Outside and inside edge balancing. Dynamic exercises he tells me he runs with the guys, power pulls and crossovers that are new to me.

They're elementary components I haven't practiced in years. The moves come naturally to me as an adult, but away from a choreographed program or the jumps I rely on, I'm forced to think about each part of my body.

I have to remind myself to engage my core and the position of my shoulders. I keep dropping my chin, overthinking what comes next, until Brody blows his whistle and makes me jump.

"Eyes up." He lifts my chin with his finger, humming when my posture straightens. "That's better. We're going to do a gliding drill around the face-off circle next."

"Gliding is my favorite." I crouch low, pretending like I'm holding a stick. "How do you think I'd do as a hockey player?"

"Well, you're standing incorrectly, so pretty terribly."

"I am?" I look down. "How should I be standing?"

"Not like that." Brody positions himself in front of me. His skate knocks against mine. He hesitates, and when I look up, I find his hands frozen in the air. "Can I touch you?"

"Why? See something you like, Coach?" I tease.

"You're such a goddamn smart-ass," he mumbles. "See if I help you again."

"I'm kidding. Yes, Brody, you can touch me," I say, and, *oh*, I wish I had kept my mouth shut, because whatever humor is left dies out. Because his palms are on my shoulders, touching me, *controlling* me, and I remember how big and warm and powerful he is. I feel small in his hold, but at the same time, I know I'm safe. "Am I doing it right?"

"No. Spread your feet." His voice is raspier than it was before. I hear the whisper of off-limits in each syllable, but it's followed up with the touch of smoke. The hint of *I don't give a fuck*. "More," he adds, but my lack of movement has Brody bending from his hips. Has his hand traveling from my shoulder to my knee, guiding my legs apart so there's room between my skates. "That's better."

Did I honestly think I could get through this without feeling any sort of attraction to him? Did my stupid suggestion of friends really eliminate the chemistry we had when we tumbled into bed together? And, who could blame me? The man is devastatingly handsome, even more so with a thicker beard and tired eyes, and I have to remind myself to breathe.

The air around us is charged. We're standing so close I can see another scar above his eyebrow. I can hear his sharp inhale and smell the hint of his cologne and toothpaste. There's no reason for him to be in my orbit like this. It extends well beyond the scope of basic drills, but he doesn't pull away. I also don't ask him to. We stare at each other, and when his throat bobs, I'm hit with the memory of how utterly perfect he looks when his head is between my legs.

"Now what?" I ask. It's barely above a whisper, but it's all I can manage.

"Now I'd kick your ass and win the face-off because you're distracted," he murmurs.

"And you're not? Please. Ten bucks says I'm a faster skater than you."

"You probably are, but we're not here to skate fast. We're here to go slow, remember?" Brody's eyes bounce away from my mouth, gaze meeting mine. Caught red-handed, but he doesn't seem to have a care in the goddamn world. "Do you know how to go slow, Hannah?"

My breath hitches at the sound of my name from his lips. It's the first time he's used it since *that night*, but I do my best to play it cool. I do my best to appear unaffected, and it's a battle I might be losing. "I'm more of an instant gratification kind of girl."

"If that's the case, maybe you should show me, since you know how to do this drill correctly."

His tone is so commanding that I get why the guys listen to him. I feel it everywhere on my body, and it's *so fucking good.* "What drill?" I tip my head to the side, staring back at him. "You haven't told me what to do, Brody."

"Glide." His hand is still on my knee. "On one foot in a circle around me."

"And what is this focusing on?"

"Control." I swear a muscle in his jaw tightens as he says it. "Learning how to use your body to stay on that single edge."

"How fascinating." I back away from him. Push off with my left foot and balance on my right, circling him like he asked. "How's this?"

"Perfect," he says, and the praise makes me warm all over. "Now do it here where the puck would drop. Smaller space, less room to work with."

I don't know where he came up with this drill, but I like it. It's implementing the fundamentals more so than anything else we've done this morning, and I bite my tongue, paying attention to the limited surface area I have.

"Four more," Brody tells me. My balance wobbles, but I correct myself. "Good, Hannah. You're making this look easy."

I don't know the last time someone complimented my skating, and it kicks the competitive athlete in me into high gear. I make the last two rotations the best ones, not a toe out of line, and when I bring my right skate down, my leg muscles are screaming.

"Holy shit." I wipe my forehead and put my hands on my hips. "I haven't concentrated that hard since I attempted a quadruple Axel."

"How do you feel?"

"More aware of my body. Cognizant of every move and how it impacts the big picture."

"Exactly what I was going for. It wasn't too elementary?"

"Not at all." I beam. "What else do you have for me, Coach?"

He runs me through a few more drills, and I notice the shift in my mindset. I'm looking at the ice in a different way. There's nothing fancy, nothing advanced, but I appreciate this version I'm working on. When Brody pulls out his phone and curses under his breath, I'm disappointed.

"I need to get going. The guys have a weight training session." He takes the whistle off and tucks it in his pocket. "Then we have film review."

"Hang on. Wait. We haven't talked about how I'll pay you for these sessions. You strike me as an old school guy. Do you prefer check? Venmo?"

"Not necessary. I'm at the arena anyway. I like watching good skating."

"That's not really fair."

"Life isn't fair." Brody looks at me. "You're going to be all right, Hannah."

"You think so?"

"Yeah. I can tell you aren't going to go down without a fight. Friday the battle continues. You in?"

"Yeah." My heart squeezes in my chest. I can't stop my smile from bursting free. "I'm so in."

FIFTEEN

HANNAH

"I'M LATE. I'm late, and I'm sorry!" Liv comes tumbling into the practice rink with her backpack on her shoulder and a duffle bag in her hand. "My dad had a meeting that ran long so I had to take the Metro. Going to school across town is a pain the ass."

"Take a second to catch your breath." I laugh and help her unload her stuff. "I just got here a few minutes ago. Traffic sucked."

"The Metro wasn't much better. The red line was delayed by ten minutes. I can't wait until I learn to drive." She groans and sits down. "I hate when people don't show up to things on time. I'll make it up to you."

"Hey. Enough apologizing. It's fine, Liv." I smile to let her know I'm not mad. "Do you need to change? Your dad said there's a women's locker room in the building."

"I'm good. I did that before I left school." She unzips her coat, revealing black leggings and a white sweater. "Man. What a freaking day."

"If you ever need a ride from school, and it's okay with your parents, I don't mind picking you up if they're busy."

"They'll probably take you up on that. With the hockey

season in full swing, sometimes I wonder when the heck my dad is sleeping. And my mom lives outside the city, so making her way in to pick me up or drop me off can take forever."

"Have you ever had a nanny or babysitter?" I ask, and Liv shakes her head.

"Nope. Mom is all for it, but having someone unfamiliar in the condo makes Dad uncomfortable. He's very private." She follows it up with a laugh when she stretches out her leg, slipping on her left skate. "And, I get it. He's, like, kind of important. But he's not the freaking president. Not everyone wants his autograph."

"I fully support you keeping him humble." I grab my gloves and put them on. "When you're ready, I thought we could try something different today."

"Different how?"

"I know you've been anxious to get to your double Axel, so I figured we'll start working up to it." When Liv's mouth opens in surprise, I hold up a hand. "*Slowly.* You're not doing a 2A today, but we're going to lay the foundation that will make it beautiful when we do get there."

"Please, please, please, *please!*" She squeals and races to put on her other skate. "I've been waiting for this moment since I started skating!"

"We'll spend today perfecting your single Axel, then I'll give you some drills to practice off-ice so we can start gearing up for your double. Sound fair?"

"*So* fair. The day I land a 2A will be the best day of my life!"

I spend the first thirty minutes watching Liv perform her single Axel multiple times. I stop and correct her form when necessary, giving her pointers to remember throughout the sequence: *big movements. Deep knee bend. Speed, speed, speed.* Satisfied with how the move looks, we rewind it back to an easier sequence, implementing a standstill waltz jump and single loop combo.

"Initiate the rotation," I call out. "And hold your outside edge." She responds well to the feedback, the next cycle smoother than the last. "Yup. Just like that, Liv."

"That one felt really good." She stops to yank off her gloves, and I nod in agreement. "Breaking it down into two moves helped my brain understand what it needed to do."

"I'm so glad. That's the point of the exercise. The double is hard. You'll be in the air for almost half a second, so you need the height to clear the ice."

"How old were you when you landed yours the first time?"

"Ten, maybe? All it took was one time, and I was hooked. I wanted to spend more time in the air." I smile. "But we all learn at different paces. Getting comfortable with a move later in your career doesn't mean you're a bad skater. It's better to spend more time on getting the fundamentals right instead of rushing to do a move incorrectly."

"Dad always tells me to stay in my lane, but it's hard to see girls younger than me doing more advanced moves." Liv sighs. "I want that to be me."

"When did you start skating?"

"I was skating by the time I was two. There are photos of me and Dad on the ice together. He's holding me up under my arms. I barely come up to his shin. Doesn't help that he's a giant." She giggles. "I started taking lessons and getting serious about learning when I was nine? Maybe?"

"Well, there you go. I bet those younger girls have been competing since they were eight on novice teams. You can't compare yourself to them. Take it from me, Liv. Enjoy these moments of learning. The excitement you feel when you land a move for the first time? Gosh. That's special. There's nothing like it, and when it becomes part of your routine, it won't mean as much to you. Soak it up now."

"Wow." Liv offers me a smile. "That's a good way to look at it. Like, I won't know it's my last time practicing a move before I nail it until it's over."

"Don't tell your dad I said this, but he's right. The longer you stay in your lane, the more fun this is." I remember how eager I was at her age. My determination to be the best junior skater in the world and the thousands of hours I put in just to end up here: dejected. Lost. Not in any lane at all. "And I want this to be fun for you for a very long time."

Liv must hear the bite of pain under my wish for her, because she gives me a soft smile. An easy hug, and I'm not sure the thrill of winning any of my medals beats my reaction to seeing her land her single Axel so perfectly, my mouth drops open.

"*Liv!*" I jump up and down, giving her a high-five after another successful execution of the move. She shrieks with delight. "*Yes*, kiddo. Spectacular!"

"It's never felt so easy before. Hang on. I need to do it again so I know it's not a fluke."

I know it's not a fluke, but I nod. I quiet down and watch her nail it ten more times, so fucking proud I could *burst*.

When we wrap up for the afternoon, she's beaming. I am too, my adrenaline pumping like I'm at the World Championships.

"What a transformation. See what happens when you think about each step of the process?" I say, pushing my sleeve up my arm so she can see my goosebumps. "I got chills watching that."

"Why do I want to cry?" Liv fans her face and laughs. "I just love skating so much, and it makes me happy when I do something that I'm proud of."

"You deserve to be proud. You're working so hard, and after the holidays, we can start talking about your choreography for the Potomac Memorial. And, if you're up for it, we can take a look at some smaller local competitions you might want to enter."

"I didn't need motivation to work hard, but you just gave me some. Speaking of competitions, who do you think is going to win Skate America? I *love* Tierney Barnes. She's so majestic."

"Tierney is my best friend!" I smile when Liv screeches. "I'll see if she can stop by one of these days to say hi."

"I would *die*."

"I hope you're not planning on dying anytime soon," Brody says, and Liv and I turn our heads in his direction. He's in gray sweatpants today, the material loose on his hips and paired with a plain long-sleeved white shirt with the word STARS across his chest. Another backward hat, the ends of his hair sticking out by his ears. "I'd miss you."

"Hey, Dad. I'm just talking about figure skating royalty who Hannah *knows*. Like, in real life. Oh! My single Axel got so much better today. Do you want to see?" Liv asks.

"Of course I do." He shuffles to the players' bench and hops on the boards, legs dangling when he sits down. He blinks, looking our way, and I move so Liv can be the star. "The Olympics are on the horizon."

"I have a long way to go before that." She laughs and shakes out her arms and legs, getting loose. "Give me a second. I want to get this right."

"She's going to get it right," I say to Brody, leaning against the boards next to him. "Your daughter is very talented."

"Don't know where she gets it from. Her mother isn't coordinated, and the only skills I have on the ice are hitting a puck and ramming guys into the glass with my shoulders."

"Weird. That's what we spent this afternoon doing."

He smirks. "Sorry she was late today. That's on me. I had a meeting with a player that ran over. Liv is always my top priority, but it felt wrong to cut him off when he was talking to me about something personal."

"No worries. We had a great lesson and—"

"Okay, I'm ready." Liv inhales a deep breath and takes off, skating into the jump with speed. From the forward outside edge of her foot, she bends her left knee, lifting her right knee up. A rotation and a half later, she lands backward on her right foot, arms raised in the air. "Badabing, motherfucker!"

"*Olivia Elliot Saunders*," Brody hisses. "What have we talked about with the language?"

"I'm so proud of you, Liv," I say, shutting Brody out. "Way to implement what we worked on today. That was exactly how it should look."

"All thanks to you." She smiles from ear to ear and skates toward us, brushing her dark hair out of her eyes. "This was a great day."

"Agreed." I grin. "Are you guys heading out?"

"Yup. Someone has an English test to study for, and it isn't me. Shakespeare was never my friend." Brody climbs over the boards, picking up Liv's backpack from the bench. "Time to clear out, Mini-Me."

"Before we go, can we do something fun?" There's a conspiring look in Liv's eyes, and she gives me an innocent smile. "I think you two should race."

"No." He frowns. "Not a good idea."

"Is it because Hannah would obviously beat you?" She blows out a dramatic exhale. "I thought so too."

"For the record, I didn't pay her to say that," I say.

"Come on, Dad. I have straight A's. I'm the ninth grade student body president. I haven't missed a day of school all year, *and* I had the best figure skating lesson of my life. I never ask for anything."

"You asked me for a pony."

"For Christmas when I was four," she challenges, and I know how this argument is going to go. I know he's going to give in. I'm more certain of it when she sticks out her bottom lip and adds, "Please?"

Brody pinches the bridge of his nose and glances at me. "Are you okay with this? You don't have to be."

"I'm not going to risk being the uncool one. I'm okay with

it, but you don't have skates. If I'm going to win, I want to win fair and square."

"There are some in my office. I have multiple pairs."

"How convenient that you're prepared." I smile. "Could be fun. Could also be embarrassing, but I'm down to find out if you are."

"This is your one guilt trip of the year," Brody says to Liv, and she bobs her head in a nod. "You don't get another one. I'll be back."

"I'm so glad I'm using it on something good." She takes his spot on the bench, resting her elbows on the boards. "His turns are slow," she tells me when he disappears. "If you're with him at the halfway point, you'll probably win."

"I love insider knowledge. Thanks for the heads-up." I bump her knuckles with mine and move to the ice, stretching my hips. "I'm not very fast, but I am competitive."

"My dad might have you beat there. He's competitive with *everything*."

Brody is quick to return, mumbling under his breath about peer pressure and being ganged up on. He ties his laces and spins his hat so it's facing forward, and I decide he's one of those men who looks good no matter which way he wears a cap.

How unfair to all of us.

"What are the rules?" he asks, skating over to me. "A lap? Crease to crease?"

"Crease to crease." Liv winks at me, and he scowls. "Winner gets... the tiny origami star I made in Spanish class this morning!"

"You're going down," I whisper to Brody, and he grunts in response. "Do you think your legs are going to give out?"

"Be careful what you say, Tiny Everett. I'd hate to see you trip and fall."

"Tiny?" I laugh. "Please. Have you seen me?"

"I consider anyone I can lift with one arm tiny. That applies to you."

"I guess you can do that, huh?" I say, proud when his cheeks turn a deep shade of pink.

Making him blush might be one of my new favorite things.

There's no more trash talking, because Liv whistles, signaling the start of our race. We both take off, and I'm genuinely shocked by how fast Brody is. I was expecting to have the advantage due to his injury, but he's like a bullet. Gliding across the ice while looking like he's not even moving, and my legs burn as I approach the halfway mark, struggling to keep up.

It helps that Liv was right about Brody's rotation. It's clunky. He's heavy on his feet and his turn takes longer than it should. It's just enough time to allow me to catch him, and as we come into the final straightaway, I have a slight lead, ahead by a nose.

"Go, Hannah, go!" Liv cheers, and it's the motivation I need.

There's no trophy or grand prize. In the grand scheme of life, this event has no impact on anything else I'm ever going to do, but I'm suddenly *desperate* to win. Maybe it's to prove to myself that even though I'm going back to square one, I'm still one of the best skaters in the world. Maybe it's because I haven't won anything in so long. Whatever the reason, it's fuel to the fire, and with ten yards to go, the victory is within reach.

But Brody has other plans. I blink and he's there, right by my side, matching my pace. He's crouched low, keeping his center of gravity tight while swinging his arms, and I make the stupid mistake of looking over at him. When I do, I catch him smiling. Little eye wrinkles. An open mouth, like he's about to let out a low laugh.

He's *beautiful*.

It distracts me, and I lose my footing. The toe of my skate nicks the ice, and I tumble both forward and sideways, right into him.

"*Shit*," I cry out, hoping I hit the ice ass-first and not with my wrists.

The fall is inevitable. I brace myself, but I'm not met with the hard, cold surface I expect. Instead, it's warm. Soft in the middle, with an arm around my waist. I open one eye and find myself against Brody's chest, his back bearing much of the brunt force.

"Ow. Fuck. Dammit." He groans, head dropping back. He lost his hat somewhere, and there are pieces of ice in his hair. "That didn't go according to plan."

"What the hell even happened? How did you get under me?"

"You were falling. My reflexes are still quick. No one gets hurt on my ice." He winces. "I haven't been hit like that in years. You could have a future in hockey, Tiny Everett."

"Thank you." My arm is across his collarbone. My hand holds the waistband of his sweatpants. Our legs and skates are tangled together, and I don't know how to get out of this position. "You didn't have to sacrifice yourself. I've fallen thousands of times."

"No one gets hurt." Brody repeats the words as he lifts his head, sitting up slightly. His eyes sweep over my face. "You're okay?"

"I'm okay. Are *you* okay?"

"Yeah. My ass took most of the fall, and my daughter is in serious trouble."

"If you're going to be mad at anyone, be mad at me. It was my fault. I lost my footing, and I didn't mean to take you down with me."

"It's pretty clear I would've won if you hadn't interfered."

"Oh, *please*." I swat at his shoulder, and it earns me a chuckle. "I was kicking your bruised ass."

"Bruised is right." He moves, and when he does, I feel his hand on the small of my back. It moves higher, up the line of my spine, and I blow out a breath. "You sure you're not hurt?"

"I promise I'm fine. You didn't hit your head, did you?"

"Nope. I'm—"

"Are you two okay?" Liv skates up to us, a guilty gleam in her smile. "That wasn't part of the plan."

"We're fine," Brody grumbles.

He's the one to initiate the untangling of our limbs. His leg unwraps from around my calf. His hands fall away next, and I'm instantly cold without his touch. When I sneak a peek at him, his jaw is tight. His eyes are narrowed, and it's very obvious he's uncomfortable with the position we're in.

White-hot mortification grips me. I scramble out of his hold, rolling to the side. I swear he breathes a sigh of relief when I'm no longer manhandling him, and the flicker of awareness about how much he didn't enjoy a single minute of that is like getting doused with a bucket of cold water.

"It was stupid to suggest a game where you could've gotten hurt." Liv wrings her hands together with a sigh when Brody and I stand. "I'm so sorry, Hannah."

"It's okay, Liv. You couldn't have known we were going to fall." I smile. "That was fun. I needed an adrenaline boost, and beating your dad in a race was the perfect solution."

"Watch it, Tiny Everett. Beating is a very generous word." Brody points to the bench. "Let's go, Livvy."

"Hey." I put my hand on his arm. "You're not mad at her, are you?"

"I could never be mad at her." He sighs. "I'm mad I was so blatantly put in my place."

"You know what they say. Anything that boys can do, girls can do better."

"You're right. You'll let me know if something starts to hurt later? An ankle or elbow?"

"Do you think I'm going to sue the team because I got

injured on their property?" I laugh. "I promise I won't, and I'll sign a waiver before my next lesson with Liv."

"Fuck a waiver." The firmness in his tone makes me shiver. "I just want to make sure you're okay."

"Oh." I play with the ends of my ponytail. "Right. Okay. Yeah."

"Thank you." He gives me a nod and dusts off his sleeve. "Have a good night, Hannah."

"You too," I say, and when he checks over his shoulder, eyes locking with mine one more time, I think maybe he wasn't uncomfortable at all.

SIXTEEN

BRODY

Puck Kings (+ their savior, BS)

MILLER

Thanksgiving dinner starts at 4. You're allowed over any time after 2.

Hudson is on dessert duty. Mitchy is bringing salads. Sully has the cheese board covered.

EVERETT

I'm bringing the mashed potatoes! I've been peeling all morning.

MILLER

Great. Richardson, you have the stuffing?

RICHARDSON

I wish I was doing the stuffing, if you know what I mean ;)

MITCHELL

Ethan. Not on Thanksgiving.

ME

Why did I get added to a group chat? Hearing about Richardson's off-ice extracurricular activities is not how I wanted to start my day.

Remove me, or morning skate will be hell tomorrow.

MILLER

Come on, Coach. It's a holiday where we talk about what we're thankful for! And we're all thankful for you.

RICHARDSON

I'm also thankful for sundresses. I can't believe we have to wait until May before we see those again.

HAYES

You're coming to dinner, right Coach?

MILLER

I stuck my hand up a turkey's ass to get this food ready. He better be coming.

EVERETT

Who? Coach or the turkey?

RICHARDSON

I just gagged.

Liam Sullivan has left the chat
Ethan Richardson has added Liam Sullivan to the chat

RICHARDSON

Nice try, Goalie Daddy.

EVERETT

Is everyone bringing their better halves? I told Hannah to come, and I don't want her to feel like she has to stand in a corner with no one to talk to.

RICHARDSON

I'll keep her company, G-Money.

MITCHELL

Lexi will be there.

MILLER

Emmy girl too, obviously. But she's confined to the couch.

EVERETT

K, good!

RICHARDSON

You don't have anything to say about me keeping your sister company, G?

EVERETT

Nope. She'd never go for someone as conceited as you, so I'm not worried.

RICHARDSON

Challenge accepted.

ME

Every single one of you are on my shit list.

LIV

Happy Thanksgiving, Dad!

ME

Happy Thanksgiving, kiddo. Are you having fun at your mom's?

LIV

We're making pumpkin pie!

ME

Sounds fun. Bring a slice back with you tomorrow.

LIV

Will do! Love you!

ME

Love you too, Livvy.

KALI

I hope you're not spending the holiday alone.

ME

I was invited to Maverick Miller's house for dinner.

KALI

You should go!

ME

I might. Just don't want it to be weird.

KALI

It wouldn't be! They'll be happy to see you!

ME

We'll see.

KALI

What's Hannah doing today?

ME

How would I know?

KALI

Maybe you asked her when you picked Liv up from her lesson earlier this week.

It would be a shame if she had to spend the day alone.

ME

We're friends, but I don't know the details of her holiday plans.

KALI

Friends, huh?

ME

I'm not saying anything else. Happy Thanksgiving, Kal.

KALI

Happy Thanksgiving, Brody. Hope you have a chance to see your friend!

———

H.E.

Happy Thanksgiving, GC!

ME

Happy Thanksgiving, IQ.

H.E.

IQ?

ME

Ice Queen.

H.E.

Oh, I like that.

ME

Figured you might.

H.E.

Is your ass doing okay after that fall last week?

ME

I've had much worse. Does Monday still work for our lesson?

H.E.

Sounds great. Have a good day, Brody! Hope you have a lot of things you're thankful for.

ME

You too.

I STAND outside Maverick and Emmy's house with a bouquet of camellias wrapped in brown paper. I adjust the twine holding them together and wonder if I should knock or just walk in.

There are loud noises on the other side of the door. Laughter too, and now I'm worried I'm overstepping. Invading a safe space they've created without me, because they aren't professional athletes today. There aren't team rules they need to follow or workouts they have to complete. They're regular guys spending time with their friends, and I don't want to ruin that.

"Are you contemplating the meaning of life?" someone asks, and after hearing that voice moan my name, I'd recognize it anywhere.

Hannah.

I turn my head. She's sauntering toward me with a wide smile, blonde hair pulled out of her face and tossed over one of her shoulders. My grip on the flowers tightens as my eyes rake down her body, hoping my gawking isn't too obvious.

A short, pleated skirt that hits the tops of her thighs. The white sweater she paired it with that makes her skin look soft and smooth. Brown boots coming up to her knees and a long coat keeping her warm.

My tongue is heavy in my mouth. My palms are sweaty. It feels like my first day existing on this fucking planet, like the sight of her is a punch to my gut, and I have to remind myself to breathe.

The closer she gets, the more details I notice. Bright red lipstick, just like the night I kissed her the first time. Diamond earrings. A necklace clasped around her throat, and a possessive, unhinged part of my brain is smug with satisfaction in knowing my hand looked better around her neck than the simple silver chain.

She's still so goddamn beautiful, and I'm still so fucking attracted to her.

"Always," I draw out, shoving my hand in my pocket. It's safer than letting my fingers roam free. "Hello, Tiny Everett."

Casual, easy. *Friendly*, just like we decided.

"Hi there, Coach." She stops at my side, the scent of her perfume swirling around me. Vanilla, with the touch of strawberries. The same smell I licked off her when she was spread out on her bed. "Those flowers are beautiful. I didn't know you were a florist in your free time."

"I'm not. Some guy in Florida recommended them."

"So fragrant." Hannah leans forward, bringing her nose close to the petals. Her hair grazes my forearm and I freeze, not daring to move. "I wish I had a big backyard where I could grow flowers and vegetables. Since I don't, I collect keychains instead."

"Keychains?" I exhale when she takes a step back. "What do you mean?"

"It's a silly tradition I started when I traveled for competitions. I wanted to bring something home from each city I stayed in, and I've made it my mission to track down the funkiest, weirdest ones. Like, I have this one from Lake Placid that says *square dancers do it with seven other people*. Makes for a good conversation starter."

I bark out a laugh. "You have my attention."

"It's fun, right? If you ever find a bizarre keychain on your travels around the country, please send me a photo. They make me indescribably happy." Her elbow lands in my ribs with a gentle nudge. "Are you planning on going inside?"

"Debating on it. Might stay out here the rest of the afternoon."

"Wow. And here I thought Brody Saunders wasn't afraid of anything."

"I'm not afraid. Just…" I lift a shoulder in a shrug. "Sometimes I don't know how to act around them. My coaching style changed after Riley's accident. I never used to text my players. I didn't spend Thanksgiving with them. There was a clear separation. But now—"

"Now you know life is short, so you want to make an effort. You realize there's no harm in hanging out with them, but you're not used to *not* acting like their coach." Hannah cocks her hip to the side. "Did I get that right?"

"Yeah, and it's freaking me out." I mess with the twine wrapped around the flower stems. "I don't like people knowing all my secrets."

"Your secret is safe with me. Step one is going inside and knowing they'll be happy to see you. Step two is eating so much food, you have to unbutton your pants. Step three is walking it off so you can have another slice of pie when you get home." She rests her palm on my shoulder. "Here. I'll go first."

Hannah opens the door and steps inside. I follow her, lingering in the foyer while she takes off her coat and hangs it on the wall with a collection of other clothing. Warmth surrounds me. So does the smell of food and something sweet, and I relax when the door shuts behind me.

"Step one is complete," I mumble.

"You're doing great, BB," she tells me.

Looking down at her is a mistake. Her palm is flat on the wall. She's lifting her leg, unzipping her boot. I see those strong thighs. White socks that give me heart palpitations, and I wonder, fleetingly, if she'll ever be out of my system, even though I know the answer.

"What does BB mean?" There's chalk in my throat. I cough twice to try and clear it. "That's new."

"Broody Brody. I just thought of it." She pinches my cheek, the spot where my smile would be if I wasn't so mesmerized by the sight of her knees. "Have fun!"

"Who's here?" Ethan comes bounding around the corner, stopping in his tracks when he sees me hovering in the doorway like an unwanted guest. "*No fucking way*. Boys," he practically screams. "Get your asses in here!"

"I swear to god, someone better be dead, Easy E." Maverick appears with an apron tied around his neck, scowling Ethan's way. "Why are you—*Coach?*"

"Wait. Coach is here?" Grant stands on his toes, shoving past the other two. "He came," he whispers. "It's a miracle."

"Happy Thanksgiving." I hold out the flowers. "These are for your wife."

"She's going to love them. Thanks, man." Maverick beams and gestures for me to take off my shoes. "Come on in."

I follow them to the kitchen where I accept a water from Maverick. A quick lap around the house has me finding the rest of the guys and the significant others they brought. They all greet me with a hug. A hand on my shoulder and an excited whoop. By the time I reach a very pregnant Emmy sitting on the couch, I've finally relaxed.

"Emerson Hartwell." I shake my head when she tries to stand up. "Don't you dare. Not on my account."

"Brody Saunders." She grins. "I've lost a little bit of my speed."

"For good reason. How are you feeling?"

"I'm ready for this baby to get here. If Miller asks whether I need my pillow fluffed one more time, I'm going to induce labor myself."

I chuckle. "He's come a long way, hasn't he?"

"Yeah." Emmy's smile softens. She plays with the wedding ring on her finger and puts her hand on her stomach. "He has."

"Can I get you anything? A drink? Another pillow that needs to be fluffed?" I catch a glimpse of Hannah standing across the living room socializing with Piper, Liam's wife and the Stars' color commentator. I avert my eyes back to the redhead on the couch. "Something else?"

"I'm fine, thanks." She cranes her neck, finding the source of my lapse in attention, but doesn't call me out. "Maverick spent all morning wondering if you were going to stop by. He owes me fifty bucks."

"Betting on me? Not sure how I feel about that."

"More like believing in you."

"Thanks, Hartwell. You sure you don't need anything?"

"I promise I'm good. Thanks for coming, Coach."

Liam acknowledges me with a grunt I return with a nod. Ethan forces me to take a photo with him for social media. He uploads it, and within three minutes, it already has thousands of likes. Hudson brings me by to say hello to Madeline, his girlfriend. Lucy, her daughter, looks at the friendship bracelets on my wrist, and when I give her one to keep, she signs **thank you** with a giggle.

"She loves bracelets," Hudson tells me. "Doubt we're ever going to get her to take it off."

"So does my daughter. She makes me a new one every game. I keep most of them in my office, but I always wear a few so she knows I appreciate them."

"Dinner is ready," Maverick announces, and Lexi gives my arm a pat as she slips past with a stack of plates. "Ladies and kids first, then the heathens can be let loose. Easy E. What the hell are you doing? Get to the back of the line."

"God dammit," Ethan mutters, pouting. "I'm hungry."

"You're going to be fine. G-Money. Can't you put your notebook away for two seconds? I swear you're attached to that thing."

"Sorry, Cap." Grant grins and tucks a small black leather notebook in his back pocket along with his phone. "Important things require my attention."

"Coach." Riley slides up next to me. "Guess what?"

"What's up, Mitchell?" I ask.

"Marcus called," he says, mentioning his agent. "The Comets' coaching staff is proud of my progression at practice. They're eyeing a game in December for me to make my AHL debut."

"Holy shit." I grab him by the shirt and pull him into a hug. "I'm so fucking proud of you."

"Me too." He laughs and takes off his glasses, wiping his eyes. "Don't say anything to the guys. It's not a sure thing yet, and I don't want them to know until I'm positive it's going to happen."

"My lips are sealed. I promise."

"Thanks." He waves at Lexi, color invading his cheeks. "Glad you're here today."

"Me too," I say, meaning it.

Everything around me is chaotic and loud. I let the guys

grab food first, hanging back and waiting my turn. After I fill my plate, I scan the long table in the center of the living room, looking for a place to sit.

There aren't many empty spots, but I see an open chair next to Hannah. Her body is turned, deep in conversation with Ryan Fitzpatrick's wife, and I make my way over to her.

"Need anything, Coach?" Maverick asks, and I shake my head.

"No. Everything looks delicious."

"It was a group effort."

He grins, focusing his attention on Emmy. I remember the days I'd find him stumbling into the hotel lobby at away games with two girls under his arms, but now he's looking at his wife like there's no one else in the room.

I guess when someone's the center of your universe, everyone else ceases to exist.

"Grant cried when he saw you," Hannah says when I squeeze myself into the chair next to her. My knees barely fit under the table, and I accidentally bump her leg. "Like, actual tears."

"I don't know why. I'm not worthy."

"He's always been a sensitive guy. Where's Liv today?"

"With her mom and stepdad." I scoop a bite of mashed potatoes onto my fork. "I'm picking her up in the morning."

"I'm sorry you don't get to spend the day with her."

"Kali and I alternate holidays every year. I'll have Liv for Christmas. She already has the movie marathon planned out."

"That's cute." Her thigh hasn't moved away from mine. Heat radiates off her, and I adjust my position in the seat. "You and your ex are close. It's nice to see a healthy co-parenting relationship."

"No reason for us not to get along. I'm glad we realized early on we didn't work as partners. Better than dragging it out for Livvy's sake and resenting each other."

"A man who communicates. I like that." Hannah scoots back in her chair and crosses her legs. Her skirt inches up her thighs with the movement, and I jab a green bean like it personally offended me. "Anything you're thankful for this year?"

"A healthy team. A job I enjoy." I dare myself to look her way. When I do, I find a smirk on her lips. Fingers playing with the hem of her skirt. Maybe someone spiked my drink, because I swear she drags her thumb across her skin, right where I'm staring. "New friends."

"We work well as friends, don't we?" Her voice is low, husky. Amusement behind the question. "Training together has been fun."

"So much fun. Your edge work has gotten better. Your control too."

"I have a good teacher. Best coach in the league." Hannah reaches for her wine, taking a long sip. "I want to make you proud."

"Your drill performance isn't indicative of my level of pride in you," I say, not wanting her to think my support is contingent on how well she skates. My hand inadvertently falls to her leg, covering the curve of her knee. I don't realize I'm doing it until her sharp inhale makes me pull back, grabbing my fork. "You know that, right?"

"Right. But I like seeing you smile." Her eyes meet mine. "You don't do it enough."

"I could do it more." I wish I had grabbed a beer when it was offered to me. I could use one to get through this conversation. "If you wanted."

"I want a lot of things, Brody. But that would be a good start."

Flirting.

She's *flirting* with me.

There's the same hitch in her breath as that night in June. The undercut of teasing, and every part of me wonders why the hell I've tried to stay away from her when this is way more fun.

Fun.

Something I still need more of.

"I'll see if I can make that happen." There's a drop of wine on her lips. I want to lick it off, but I cut a piece of my turkey instead. "Just for you."

"I'm a lucky—"

"Two of my favorite people." Grant interrupts us, wedging his way between our chairs and kneeling on the rug. He drapes an arm over Hannah's shoulders, grinning at me. "Are you having a good time, Coach?"

"Can't complain." My eyes flick to the blush crawling up Hannah's neck. From the wine? Or from me? "Your sister makes excellent company."

"She does, doesn't she? Easy E hasn't hit on you, has he, Han?" Grant asks.

"Please." Hannah laughs. "Even if he did, I'm not interested."

"Good. Tell me if that changes. Locker room code says no player is allowed to touch another player's sister."

She wrinkles her nose. "Can't you all just keep your dicks in your pants?"

"*I* can, but I can't say the same for everyone else." He flips off Ethan from across the room. "I need to make my rounds, but I wanted to say hi."

"Bring me a slice of pumpkin pie," Hannah calls out when he pops to his feet and meanders to the kitchen. "Is there really a code?" she asks me.

"Mhm. First person to the showers turns them on for everyone else. Don't mess with the stuff someone keeps in their stall. You don't touch another team's goalie, and if someone touches yours, you have permission to kick their ass. Similarly, you don't touch a teammate's sister, mom, wife, or girlfriend. If you do, expect hell to break loose."

"Wonder if that applies to coaches too," Hannah says with the flip of her hair over her shoulder.

"Brat," I mumble.

"But that never happened, so it's purely hypothetical."

"Hey." I touch her wrist when she sets down her wine glass. "I know I said some things that night, but I don't regret it happening. You're not a mistake, Hannah."

"I know I'm not. I'm a goddamn prize," she tells me with the confidence that made me follow her back to her apartment in the first place. "I'm going to see if they need any help cleaning up."

"You never mentioned what you were thankful for," I say, watching her stand and smooth out her skirt.

"New friends. Hockey coaches." Hannah looks at my hands, a coy smile taking over her mouth. "And all the fun we're going to have the next few months."

Trouble, I think, when she leans in front of me to take my plate.

I'm in so much fucking trouble.

SEVENTEEN

BRODY

THE MALL three weeks before Christmas is hell on earth, I decide.

A woman with her arms full of shopping bags hits me in the shin, and I scowl at her as she walks away.

"Do you think I should get Hannah a Christmas gift?" Olivia stands on her toes, looking at the jewelry counter in a department store. I pull the brim of my hat low when a saleswoman eyes me like she recognizes me from somewhere. I regret agreeing to accompany my daughter on her shopping trip. "Or would that be weird?"

"I don't think a gift is necessary," I answer, folding my arms over my chest. "What about a card? I'll throw some money in there."

"That's not very personal." Liv rolls her eyes. "It's the holiday season, Dad. You have to show people you care about them. That you listen to them, and that doesn't include shoving a wad of cash their way."

"Why not? Everyone loves money."

"You're insufferable."

"Glad to know that early SAT prep course I signed you up for is working."

152

"I'm asking because it's been two months, and my technique is only getting better. Hannah is a big part of that, and I want her to know I appreciate all the work she's putting in with me." Liv sighs. "She's so talented. I hope she's able to come back to skating soon."

"What about a friendship bracelet? You have a million at home. I bet she'd love to wear something you created."

"Ugh. She's cool, Dad, and has like, so many Instagram followers. She wouldn't like a friendship bracelet."

"I like mine." I hold up my wrist so she can see the five I'm currently wearing. Different colors, different beads. Some bright pink and others light blue and red, matching the team colors. "Am I not cool?"

"No. You're old, and not many things bring you joy."

"You wound me, kid." I laugh and ruffle her hair, ignoring her when she tries to swat my hand away. "Tell me how you really feel."

"Mom says I get my bluntness from you." Liv grins. "You can only blame yourself."

"I'll say."

"Are *you* getting Hannah a gift?"

"Why would I get her a gift?" I lead her away from the diamond bracelets she's scoping out knowing I already bought her the one she wanted. "That also isn't necessary."

"I don't know. You're friends, aren't you?" Her smile is anything but innocent. "Friends get each other gifts."

"Yes, we are friends, but it's not a gift-giving level of friendship." I rub the back of my neck, bracing myself for an ambush. "We skate together. We spend Thanksgiving together. We don't exchange presents."

At least… I don't think we do.

Have I seen her eight times in the last month?

Yeah, but does that mean I'm obligated to get her a gift?

Shit. Is *she* getting *me* a gift?

I can't be the asshole who doesn't get her a present.

What the fuck do you get for the girl you slept with once and can't get out of your head?

Socks?

"You spent *Thanksgiving together?*" Liv gasps, yanking me out of my gift spiral, and what a terrible fucking idea that was. "*Dad!*"

"No. *No.* That's not—she was at the team dinner. I was at the team dinner. We spent Thanksgiving with my players." I almost knock over a display of perfume bottles as we wind our way through the store. "Not... not *alone.*"

"Interesting. Do you ever think you'll date someone?" Liv asks, switching gears. I'm fucking flustered. "Some of the girls at school have single dads, and they're on dating apps. You could be out meeting people."

"Why the sudden interest in my personal life?"

"Call it curiosity."

"I'm not out meeting people because I don't want to meet people. I have everything I need: you. The guys on the team. Hockey every day of my life. What else could make me happy?"

"Someone who makes you laugh? You're uptight, Dad."

"Gee." I huff. We pass a Dairy Queen and an Auntie Anne's. A kid wearing a Stars jersey and waiting in line to meet Santa tugs on his mom's dress to get her attention when he spots me. I give him the flash of a smile, and he waves. "You're piling on the compliments today, Livvy."

"You know I don't mean it like that." She sighs in that exasperated way teenagers do. I'm the biggest pain in her ass. Why don't I understand what she's trying to say? "Are you ever lonely when I'm at Mom's?"

"No." A long beat before I decide she deserves more of an answer. "I prefer to keep to myself. I always have."

"That's sad."

"I don't think of it that way."

"Well, if you ever *do* decide to date, I'd be okay with it."

Liv smiles. "I like Bryant. I'm sure I'd like whoever you started seeing. *Especially* if they're a pretty figure skater who could keep coaching me."

"Olivia Elliot. Knock it off."

"This is when I wish I had a twin sister so we could plan some 'Parent Trap' level scheming." She sighs, lighting up when she spots a photo booth. "Can we take pictures?"

I've never denied her anything, so I cram into the tiny stall with a curtain that shows off my entire lower body. Liv holds up a peace sign and I stick out my tongue. I give the camera my best menacing face and she puts her hands under her chin, batting her eyelashes. Two copies of the four snapshots print out, and I fold one up and stow it safely in my wallet.

"I'll split a milkshake with you before I take you to your mother's," I say, my attention catching on a store with lava lamps in the window. I squint at the racks of clothes and art prints hanging on the wall, veering left so we can step inside. "We're making a detour first."

"What do you want in here?" Liv rifles through a stack of shirts. "Whoa. Look at these cool graphic tees! What does *I survived Y2K* mean?"

"Jesus. I feel ancient." I scan the shop, smiling at the keychains on a back wall. "Bingo."

With Liv distracted, I touch the metal trinkets Hannah told me she likes to collect. They're not from halfway across the world or a memento commemorating one of her competitions, but they do make me chuckle. And, well, it's better than showing up somewhere empty-handed.

I grab two off a hook—one that's a jar of pickles with BIG DILL ENERGY written on it and another in the shape of a lemon with the words *when life gets tough, squeeze me*—and take them to the register. The bored-looking guy behind the counter asks if I want a bag and I politely decline, slipping the tiny knickknacks in my pocket.

"Do they have any of these clothes in a museum somewhere?" Liv asks when I track her down. "Is this how our founding fathers dressed?"

"You've reached your age joke limit for the day. Let's get you to your mom's so you can make fun of her instead. I'm going to drown my old man sorrows with my assistant coaches tonight," I say.

I walk slow so she can keep up with me, her stride shorter compared to mine. Our stop for milkshakes takes double the amount of time it should after a group of teenage boys in CCM beanies and Georgetown Hockey sweatshirts notice me. They ask for a photo and show me a video of their practices, asking for a couple of tips to improve their stick handling.

"Maybe you'll coach one of them one day," Liv tells me, handing over the cookies and cream milkshake.

"Maybe," I say, the keychains pressing into my thigh on our walk to the car.

"NO HOCKEY TALK," Mikal says when he sets a pitcher of beer on our table. "This is our one night a month where we're not obligated to talk about the sport we coach."

"Great. I can stare at the wall instead." I pour a cup for each of us, nudging the drinks to him and Parker. "That's my favorite pastime."

"I could talk about my kid," Parker suggests, tapping his phone and showing off his son on the lock screen. "But Mikal is scared of babies and Brody hasn't held an infant in years."

"For fuck's sake. I'm not *scared* of babies. They're just… judgy." Mikal shudders and brings his cup to his mouth. "When they stare at you, it's like they're staring into your soul."

"It's called being a good judge of character." I flip a coaster in the air, catching it between my thumb and pointer finger. "Babies and dogs. If they don't trust you, I don't trust you."

"Did you see that guy from the San Diego Iguanas got cast on a reality dating show?" Parker asks, holding up his hands when Mikal shoots him a look. "I said guy, not ECHL player. It could've been anyone."

"A reality dating show is my idea of hell." My phone buzzes on the table with a text message, and I discard the coaster. "You'd have to drag me on camera."

"I'd pay money to see that," Mikal says.

They start talking about the other reality shows they watch, but I'm distracted by Hannah's initials on my screen. I swipe my thumb across the notification, waiting for her text message to load.

> **H.E.**
>
> *Attachment: 1 link*
>
> Buzzfeed ranked the hottest coaches in professional sports. Guess where you finished?

> **ME**
>
> At the bottom, I hope.

> **H.E.**
>
> Do you have any self-confidence? You were first!
>
> Pretend I'm tossing streamers and confetti in the air.
>
> Anything to say about this accomplishment, Brody?

I'm trying my damnedest to hold back a smile. It's a losing battle.

ME

Is there nothing better to report on?

And who did I beat?

H.E.

The football coach for the DC Titans. Shawn Holmes? Do you know him?

ME

Yup. Good guy.

H.E.

There's a coach for the Sacramento hockey team. He's cute. What's his deal?

Irritation prickles at the top of my spine. I don't like that she's calling that dickbag *cute*, and my fingers fly across the keyboard to give her an answer.

ME

He's been divorced twice. Cheated on both wives.

H.E.

Darn. I knew he was too pretty to be true.

ME

They always are.

Three dots appear and disappear on her end of the text thread. I wait, wondering if she's going to say anything else. Just when I'm about to turn my phone face down, a new message pops up.

H.E.

What are you up to tonight?

ME

Out with my assistant coaches at a bar.

H.E.

Such a social butterfly. I'm so proud of you!

ME

What are you doing?

H.E.

I'm also at a bar. I got stood up? I think?

She told me she'd meet me at seven. It's now almost eight, and she's nowhere in sight. I'm still sitting at this high top alone, but the server was nice enough to bring over mozzarella sticks.

Nothing fried food can't fix!

I blink, something like anger bubbling in my stomach.

I don't like to picture her sitting alone, checking the door every time it opens and being disappointed when it's not who she thought it was. I shouldn't be asking this next question—there's nothing I can do to fix the problem—but I do it anyway, because for as hard as I try, this woman has me wrapped around her finger.

ME

Where are you?

H.E.

A sports bar called Intermission. It's near the arena, actually.

My head jerks up. I look around the crowded room—the same room she's in, and… there. At a table tucked away in the corner, under one of Maverick Miller's jerseys, is Hannah.

The universe has a sense of fucking humor.

I lock my phone, finishing off my beer.

"I'll be back in a minute," I say, and Mikal blinks at me.

"Everything okay?" he asks.

"Just need to help a friend with something." I hop off my stool and smile. "I'll be quick."

"He has friends?" Parker asks.

It's a valid question, because, no. I don't have a ton of friends, but Hannah has somehow become one of them.

And I don't like how sad she looks.

I dodge a group of drunk finance bros and round the bar. I run a hand through my hair then push the sleeves of my sweater up my arms, warm and loose from that first drink. Hannah exchanges her phone for a mozzarella stick, enjoying a long pull of the cheese.

"Is this seat taken?" I ask, and she nearly falls out of her chair. "Easy, Tiny Everett. It's just me."

"Brody?" she sputters. "What are you doing here?"

"Told you I was out at a bar."

"And it's the same bar where I am?"

"What a coincidence." I sit across from her and swipe a mozzarella stick from the basket. "Hi."

"Hi."

"Your date stood you up?"

"I wouldn't call it a date. We've talked on a dating app a few times, and we were meeting up to see what our connection was like in person." Hannah dusts off her hands and shrugs. "I guess I wasn't her type."

"That sucks. I'm sorry."

"My biggest fear is finding out she walked in, saw what I looked like, and left."

"If she did walk in, she wouldn't have left. She would've come over and stolen one of your mozzarella sticks. Struck up a conversation. Found a way to keep you talking." I dunk the appetizer in the cup of marinara sauce. "You're the best-looking person in this bar."

"You're just saying that." A throaty laugh. A lift of her highball glass and the sip of what smells like whiskey neat. "And buttering me up so I'll let you eat my food."

"Hannah." I lean over the table, tapping her elbow. She freezes. "Do I look like the kind of man who would butter someone up?"

Her lips part. Her eyes move from my hair to my chin. Lower, to my throat and down to my chest. She takes her time, and when she finds whatever she's searching for, her mouth quirks up with a smile.

"No," she says slowly. "You look like the kind of man who says exactly what he's thinking and gets whatever he wants."

"Not always." I pull my hand away, knuckles rapping on the table to give them something to do. "It's her loss."

"You know what? Yeah, it is her loss." Hannah snorts. "The first red flag was her name."

"Uh oh. What's wrong with her name?"

"People with J names tend to bring on higher disappointment than the other twenty-five letters. I've never met a Justin I liked."

"You know what?" I nod in agreement. "I haven't either."

"Cheers to that. Wow. I can't believe you're here. I like seeing you—" Hannah waves her hand in my direction with a smile. "Like this."

"Like what?" I fix my collar then touch the hair at the back of my neck, wishing I had worn a hat. It feels like I'm on display right now, waiting to hear what she has to say. "This is how I always am."

"Like without the whistle or the skates…" She trails off with a hum. "Makes you look more human."

"A shame, since I do love the robot allegations."

"Stop." Hannah laughs and swats at my arm. "It's a good look. Are you sure it's really you?"

"Brody Saunders, reporting for duty. If you think this is impressive, you should see the photos Liv and I took today," I say. "I fit into a photo booth."

"You *have* to show me."

"Hang on." I dig my wallet out of my back pocket, pulling

out the thin strip of photographs. I hand it her way, watching her hold the corners with her thumbs so she doesn't make any fingerprint smudges. "She asked. I couldn't resist."

"These are adorable. Can I please take a photo of this photo and save it as your contact information in my phone?" Hannah taps the one of me sticking out my tongue. "I promise I won't use it as blackmail."

"Go ahead. But only because I know how intimidating I look in the next one."

She laughs and snaps a couple pictures, her smile never dimming as she assesses the grainy photos one more time. "You love Liv so much, don't you?"

"More than words. She's my greatest joy."

"She's lucky to have a dad like you. Who invests in the things she likes. Who's involved, even when he's busy as hell." She puts a hand on my forearm, right on my bare skin. "It's wonderful to see."

"That's the bare minimum." I don't look at where she's touching me. "Do you want to come sit at my table? Socializing isn't my favorite thing in the world, but Parker and Mikal are good people. I can't promise your mood will improve, but you'd get free drinks out of it."

"Thanks for the offer, but my best friend invited me over. I'm going to curl up on her couch and wallow in how undesirable I am."

I'm still trying to understand why someone stood her up. "I bet there are ten people in this bar right now who would fight to the death to talk to you."

"I've always wanted someone to duel for my affection. Thanks for cheering me up, Brody. Seeing you has been the highlight of my night."

My chest warms with pride. I'm tipsy without having anything else to drink.

The Hannah Everett effect.

Everything is always brighter when she's around.

"Glad I could help," I say. "You want me to call you an Uber?"

"I've got it covered. Thanks for the offer." Another smile, and she climbs off her chair. She gathers her purse, but she doesn't leave. Not yet. "That code Grant was talking about on Thanksgiving."

I straighten my spine. "What about it?"

"You never told me if there's anything in there about a coach touching their player's sister." Her sweater shows off her sharp collarbone, the spot on her throat I'd like to kiss. "Or does it only apply to teammates?"

I knock over the salt shaker. I'm pretty sure my ears are ringing. "I, ah, haven't read anything about that. No."

"Good to know," she says.

If she's going to play this game, I am too.

"By the way, Hannah." I hop out of my seat. I walk toward her, our chests close. "You should go to sleep tonight knowing you're anything but undesirable."

She tips her chin up. Her lipstick is smudged on her bottom lip from drinking, and I want to wipe the rest of it away with my thumb. "Really?"

"Really." A shaky hand tucking away a piece of blonde hair behind her ear. Another brief touch. "Her loss, remember?"

"Yeah." She puts a palm on my sweater, fiddling with a loose thread. Nails grazing my chest. "Her loss."

Hannah steps away. With a last look at me, she heads for the door, hips swaying as she walks out into the December night. I'm practically floating on the way back to my table, like ten minutes with her really were the highlight of my day.

It's probably true.

"There he is." Parker clasps my shoulder. "We were getting worried about you."

"Told you I was talking to a friend." I pour myself another beer, sipping it like it's water. "It was good to see them."

"Must've been some friend," Mikal says with a smirk. "Brody is smiling."

I touch the corner of my mouth, a grin sitting there.

Guess I am.

EIGHTEEN
HANNAH

GRANT

Do you think I'd be a good dad?

ME

Something you need to tell me, G?

GRANT

No. God no! Nothing like that!

Mav and Emmy's baby will be here soon, and I'm contemplating.

ME

Yes, I think you'd be a great dad.

But I also think you'd be an exhausted dad, because you always put everyone else first. I know you. You'd never make time for yourself.

GRANT

Good point. I also love my sleep.

I'll table it for a few years.

ME

When you do decide it's time for kids, they're going to be so lucky to have you as their parent.

GRANT

Shucks, Han. That was sweet.

ME

Have you shaved your face yet? Your mustache is still horrifying.

GRANT

I knew the moment was too good to be true.

"THAT EDGE WORK WAS SHIT, EVERETT." Brody barely looks up from his clipboard as he says it, and I scowl his way. "You can do better."

"You're not paying attention. How can you be sure it wasn't perfect?"

"I see everything."

"That's obnoxious," I mumble under my breath.

"I heard that, Ice Queen."

"I'm going to grab some water," I tell him, heading for my bag.

Back at the bench, I hop on the boards and tug on my pink skirt, looking out at the ice. A deep breath helps. So does trying to recenter my thinking, but before I can get too deep in my thoughts, Brody is standing in front of me.

His presence is impossible to ignore. Backward hat, trimmed beard. Black joggers and a plain white shirt, he puts his hands on his hips and tips his head to the side.

"Hannah. Are you going to tell me what's going on?" he asks.

"It's stupid."

"I'll be the judge of that." After a long pause, he adds, "I'm not sure anything you're thinking or feeling could ever be stupid. What happened to being honest with each other?"

What happened is I'm a fucking liar, because ever since Thanksgiving and the night we ran into each other at that goddamn bar, I can't get him out of my head. I can't get over the feel of his hand on my knee, the weight of his gaze on my thighs, the flash of heat behind his eyes.

I might not know everything about Brody Saunders, but I know he's not a man who plays games. He's meticulous, intentional about everything he does, and those touches?

They weren't accidental.

He *meant* them, and I don't know what to do with that information.

Friends my ass.

"There's a big figure skating competition in Japan this weekend," I blurt, the words tumbling out of me without warning. "If I hadn't dropped out of the event I was supposed to skate in back in November, I might be there too. I'm grappling with this version of life where I'm not going to be one of the best skaters in the world this year. I haven't been the best skater in the world in *many* years, and that feeling of… of resentment? Of inadequacy? It's only being made worse by the fact that I can't do a basic edge control drill correctly."

Brody doesn't say anything. There's no rebuttal, no attempt to make me feel better.

He just *stares*, and the pressure is immense. Relentless no matter how hard I try to glance away, and the look he's pinning me with makes me squirm.

"Change of plans." His voice is a rough rasp. A caress against the inside of my thigh. "We're cutting out of here early."

"Early? It's not even noon. Where are we going?"

"Somewhere else. You hungry?"

"No." My stomach picks that moment to rumble. "Fine. I might be hungry."

"Are you a fan of burgers?"

"I don't trust anyone who isn't." My lungs deflate, wary. "I know what you're doing. You're deflecting so I don't think about the problem at hand. You're redirecting my thoughts. That kind of psychology won't work on me, Coach."

"I'm not doing anything besides offering you food, because that's a requirement for survival." He hitches his thumb over his shoulder. "Let's go."

"Okay, Daddy, calm down," I say, proud of myself when his hand flexes at his side. "Don't you have a game tonight?"

"I do, but I don't need to get to the arena until four. Plenty of time to eat a burger." Brody leads the way to the tunnel and I follow him with my bag and gloves and questioning how I wound up climbing into his Cadillac Escalade and relaxing into the heated seats he turns on. "Warm enough?"

"Yeah. Thanks." I hold my hands up to the air vents, sighing as the cold from the rink slips away. "Who are you playing tonight?"

"The worst team in the league. Which means we'll either win by one goal or lose by eight." He checks his mirrors, putting the car in reverse and pulling into traffic. "Have you been to a game yet this season?"

"Nope. That's my goal after the holidays. It's been a weird couple of months of trying to find a new routine that doesn't include regimented training and spending five hours practicing at my old rink. I finally feel like I'm balancing everything well, and that's going to open up more time to do fun things in my free time like go to hockey games and see my best friend."

"What about Riley's AHL debut?" Brody uses his blinker, then drapes his forearm over the steering wheel. "That's coming up. He doesn't think we'll be able to make it because of our travel schedule, but the guys are planning on surprising him. I'm pulling all the strings I can to make it happen."

"Stop." I put a hand over my heart. "To be honest, I had all these opinions about professional athletes before Grant was drafted. And I'm sure there are shitheads out there, but it's refreshing to see guys who aren't toxic pieces of trash. Who care about each other and aren't afraid to say they love each other. I was at my brother's house the other night, and he and Ethan had an argument over who needed to sign off their video game first. It's hysterical."

"That's changed over the years. When I played, guys weren't so open about their feelings. Maybe it's the social media effect." Brody shrugs, turning down a side street. "Digital affection is easier than other kinds of affection."

"You don't strike me as an affectionate guy." I burst out laughing. "Wait. You probably do some awkward bro hug, don't you?"

"I hug plenty of people the normal way," he grumbles. "I'm not an ogre."

"You sure?" I reach over and poke his cheek, squealing when his fingers fold around my wrist and pin my hand to the center console. "I see some green on your face."

"Watch your tone, Hannah," he warns, not releasing me from his grip. "What are you doing for the holidays?"

"Grant and I are going to Florida for two days. My best friend, Tierney, has a brother who plays in the NBA. He was traded to the DC Bullets, but he spent the first part of his career on the Orlando Blazers, who the Bullets are playing on Christmas. We have tickets to the game."

"That sounds fun." We pull into a gravel parking lot, finding a spot in the corner. "No snow in Florida."

"Thank god. This winter wonderland gets really old, really fast." I peer at the diner sign. "Are we here?"

"No. I thought we'd sit outside a different diner first," he deadpans.

"Please don't ever become a standup comedian."

I wiggle my hand free, but not before his fingers drag along the inside of my wrist. It's like he's sneaking the tiniest taste, stealing the smallest sip of something he shouldn't have. So quick it might not have happened at all, but his face gives him away. Pink cheeks. The dip of his chin.

The cold December air is welcomed when I leave the car, but I shiver when the wind ripples through my thin skating outfit.

"Here." Brody crowds my space, handing me a gray sweatshirt. "Put this on."

I look at the offering, realizing it's the same one he gave me that night in June. The same one he took off me in a frantic, desperate state, and I rub my thumb along the drawstring.

It's still soft. Still smells like him, and I wonder if it's his favorite hoodie. If it's one he sleeps in every night, because the sleeve has a hole in it. The hem is fraying, little threads coming loose, and I nudge it back his way.

Wearing it would be an admission. An acceptance that I remember exactly what happened the last time I put this on my body and the recognition that I want to do it again.

"I'm fine," I say. "We'll be inside soon."

"Hannah. Put on the sweatshirt."

Snow flurries start to fall from gray clouds, and the blast of heat when I open the door of the diner is magnificent. Ignoring Brody is the easiest option, so I spot the hostess. I slide up to her stand and give her a smile.

"Hi! Could we have a table for two, please?" I ask.

She flips through a stack of menus, and Brody is still there. The entryway is so small, my back is almost flush against his chest. His shoe bumps mine. My elbow knocks against his. I need more space, but he doesn't give it to me.

"You're in a skirt and tights." He bends his neck so he can whisper in my ear. "And shivering. Take the damn hoodie. Please."

"Fine." I accept the sweatshirt from him, and I swear he relaxes the second I yank it over my head. "But only because you know I like it when men beg."

"Have I told you today that you're a brat?" he murmurs, a hand on my lower back as we follow the hostess to a booth in the back.

"No. Say it again," I purr.

I'm pushing his buttons, but he doesn't bite. Not when he spins his hat forward to cover his face and lifts his menu, studying the options.

"How old were you when you started skating?" Brody asks, changing the direction of our conversation.

"Four." Our knees bump under the table. More accidental touching. More moments where he doesn't pull away. "Grant was playing hockey, and I was jealous he got to spend his summer in the air-conditioned rink while I was on the playground sweating in the Florida sun."

"Have you always been good?" He sets his menu down and folds his hands over the list of specials. "I, uh, watched some of your World Championship routines. I think I know the answer."

"Brody Saunders." I shove the ketchup bottle out of the way and lean forward. "Look at you being interested in me."

"Research. For Liv," he mumbles.

"Of course. For Liv." I grin. "I don't love that question. It negates the hard work I put in that no one sees. Like being gifted at something doesn't require hours of perfecting the craft."

"Ah. That's a good point. Let me rephrase. Does skating come naturally to you? In hockey, I can tell the guys who are naturally talented on the ice pretty easily."

"Which are you?" I ask.

"A natural. I was on a mini mite team when I was four. Played through middle school. Earned a spot in the United States Hockey League when I was sixteen. Won the World

Junior Ice Hockey Championships that first year. Boston College offered me a full ride, and I took it knowing I'd only be there one season. Left the NCAA for the NHL, and here we are."

"My god. You're like a prodigy." I laugh. "I didn't pay attention to all those stats when I looked you up."

There's a lull in our conversation when we order our meals, both going with a burger and fries. I try to stretch out my legs, but Brody takes up too much room. My knee bumps his again. He accidentally steps on my foot, and I give into the fact that we're not getting through this meal without *more goddamn touching.*

"It's funny you call me a prodigy when you have multiple important medals." Brody sips his water. On the table, his phone lights up. He checks the notification then turns it face down. "What about the Olympics?"

"I hear they happen every four years," I answer.

"I meant *you* in the Olympics. Have you ever been?"

"I have. I fell in my performance and didn't medal. That was the beginning of my demise, I think. Where it all started to go downhill."

"Would you go back?"

"If I felt like I could medal and give my program a fair and honest attempt? Yes."

"Going through waves is normal." Brody's thigh lines up with mine. "When I came back from my injury, I hated hockey because I wasn't as good at it as I used to be. Now that I'm coaching, I'm deeply in love with it again. When you give everything to a sport, it's hard when it doesn't give that love back to you. If it's not working, it doesn't mean it's the end. It's just time for a different path."

"I'm learning that." I hesitate before sharing this next part. "Working with Liv is showing me other ways I could have skating in my life, but it's really hard to separate myself from something I've been attached to for so long."

"I need you to do me a favor, Hannah," Brody says, and I swallow.

"What's that?"

"You said you were going to be honest, and I want you to be honest. When we're working together on the ice, I want you to talk to me. No shutting down. No pretending like you're okay when you're pissed—and you're allowed to be pissed. I can't fix things if I don't know what's going on. Okay?"

Brody tries to act like he's not interested in things. He gives off the impression of being unapproachable. Easily bothered by those around him, but deep down, under the gruff and all the ways he grumbles, there's a different man.

A helper with a big heart, and I've never found him more attractive than I do right now.

"Okay. I can… yeah. That's fair." I play with the ends of my hair, needing a distraction. "I'll remember that going forward."

"Good." A faint smile. His shoe tapping mine. "We're friends. We'd still be friends even if you never skated in another competition. But if you do, I'll be there to cheer you on. And take credit for your edge control."

A laugh whooshes out of me, but at the same time, there's a fist clamping around my heart. It gets tighter when he pays for our meal and drops me off at my apartment, letting me keep his hoodie.

Brody isn't broody at all.

He's fucking magnificent.

NINETEEN
BRODY

THE NOISE that pulls me from my dream is loud and incessant.

The bane of my fucking existence.

I open an eye. Moonlight sneaks through the curtains, and I know it's way too early to drag my ass out of bed.

But the noise won't stop.

Phone.

It's my phone.

Groaning, I sit up. I reach for the bedside table, knocking a stack of books to the floor. I answer without looking at the caller ID, grunting when I'm finally figure out how to slide my thumb across the screen in my state of deliriousness.

"Hello?" I rub my eyes, the room coming into focus. "Who is this?"

"Coach."

Maverick's voice. Brittle, scared, and I'm thrown back to the night of Riley's accident. I sit up straight, instantly awake. I fumble for the lamp so I can see, bracing myself and begging the universe not to be a cruel motherfucker to me twice in two years.

"Maverick. Are you okay?" I ask, twisting the sheets tight in my grip.

"Am I okay? Am I *okay*?" A sharp laugh. The slam of a door and heavy footsteps. "*No*, I'm not okay! I don't know what the fuck to do! I thought I had two more weeks. *Two more weeks*. Fourteen days! But nope. Not anymore. Why does no one teach you how to—"

"Maverick," I almost shout, cutting in. "You need to tell me what the hell is going on so I can figure out how to help."

"Emmy is in labor," he whispers. "And I'm going to have a heart attack."

"Fucking Christtttttt." I deflate, dropping my head against the wall. My heart is racing, and I shove aside the fear that's lodged in my throat. "Your wife is about to push a human out of her, and you're wondering what *you're* supposed to do? Get off the phone with me and get your ass in there with her."

"Yes. Yeah. *That*. I should do that, but I'm so fucking scared, Coach." There's a long pause. A crack in his voice. "How can I be a father when I didn't have one growing up? I'm fucking clueless on how I should act and what I should say. How do I punish my baby girl if she does something wrong? What if she hates me? What if she wants to grow up and play fucking *baseball*? And what about Emmy? I'm doing everything I can to be the best husband, and now I'm a father too? She's going to resent me. I'm not good enough and—"

"Take a breath, Mav," I tell him, and he blows out a long exhale. I don't want to laugh and have him think I'm making fun of him, but this is déjà vu. The exact thought process I went through before Olivia arrived. "Good. What hospital are you in?"

"MedStar. The same one where Riley lost his leg." A softer exhale. Gratitude in his next words. "I'm so glad whoever is up there looking down at this shitshow we call life decided to be fucking kind to us."

"How dilated is Emmy?"

"I don't know. Her water broke at the house. I drove her here. Then I came out to the hall because I'm *panicking*, man."

"Listen to me, Mav. That terrified feeling? I hate to break it to you, but it's never going to go away. You're going to spend the rest of your life wondering if what you're doing is good enough for your little girl, then one day, you'll blink and she's going to be a teenager. Getting ready to learn how to drive and going to school dances. I spend every second of every day scared *shitless*. I'm afraid I'm one step away from royally fucking up the single greatest accomplishment of my life. You have to figure it out as you go. There's no handbook. No set of rules to follow." I kick off the sheets and stand. "But guess what? You now have the greatest job in the world. You're going to be a girl dad, and there's no championship, no amount of money, *nothing* that will ever beat that."

"Oh my god." Maverick lets out a choked sob. "I'm going to be a girl dad. I'm such a lucky bastard."

"Yeah, buddy. You are. Hang up with me. Go be with Emmy. She's tough as hell, but she needs you. I'll let the guys know what's going on."

"You will?"

"You all are so codependent." I chuckle. "They'd hate me if I left them in the dark."

"We're pathetic, aren't we? I want them here. I want you here too."

"Then that's where we'll be. Mav?"

"Yeah?"

The hope in his voice clinches my heart and squeezes tight. It makes this next part easy to say.

"You're going to be the best dad in the world," I tell him. Slow, so each word registers. So there's not a doubt in his mind. "And when you're ever questioning that—which you will, trust me—you come find me, okay? I'll remind you."

He sniffs. "Thanks, Coach."

"We'll see you soon."

I find a shirt in my dresser and throw it on. Making a house call to the hospital in the middle of the night wasn't on the list of duties I was given when I took on this head coaching role, but that's something else I've learned along the way. When your guys need you, you show up for them.

Grabbing a pair of socks and my shoes, I switch my pajama bottoms for a pair of joggers. I pull on a sweatshirt while I type out a text to the team.

ME

Emmy is in labor.

I'm not surprised when responses start flying in.

SULLIVAN

Cool.

EVERETT

OH MY GOD. Are you seirious?! Where is she?11? Is Mavrick shtting hmself? Why am I crying????? It's not ev3n my kid!!!!!!!!!!!!!

Sully!!! I need some mre fkng enthsusm from you!

SULLIVAN

Learn to spell, then we'll talk.

EVERETT

I'm so excited I can't type right!!!!!!

RICHARDSON

DADDY MAVVY!!!!!!

HAYES

Is Maverick having a panic attack?

ME

He's having an appropriate response to the situation. They're at MedStar Georgetown.

MITCHELL

Maverick is the only person I'd go back to that hospital for.

ME

He'd understand if you didn't want to.

MITCHELL

No way. He was there for me. I'm going to be there for him.

ME

I'm sure they have a private room, but phones get turned off when we get there. No posting to social media. No photos. Same team rules apply. Got it?

RICHARDSON

Come on, Coach. We're always on our best behavior ;)

ME

Don't test me, Richardson.

THE MOOD in the hospital waiting room is different from the night we were here after Riley's accident. It's light, eager. Tears, yeah, but happy ones this time. Everyone is smiling and laughing. Emmy's best friends—Lexi, Piper, Madeline, and Maven, the team's sports photographer—keep asking for tissues. Maverick's buddies from outside the team, Reid and Dallas—a kicker for the DC Titans—are bouncing up and down. Grant joins the group of women and asks for a tissue too, blowing his nose and showing off the flowers he brought.

"Aren't they pretty?" He holds up the vase of lilies and sunflowers. "They symbolize joy, new beginnings, and love. What did everyone else bring?"

"Myself." Ethan grins from the chair he's sitting in. "When Emmy gets bored of Mavvy, I'll be waiting in the wings. We'll be the redheaded power couple."

"Maverick will literally kill you before that happens." Hudson adjusts his position on the couch, keeping a sleeping Lucy tucked tight to his chest. "Sully. What are you holding?"

"Nothing," Liam grumbles, but I catch sight of a small, patterned piece of fabric. "Mind your own fucking business."

"Is that a shirt?" Riley asks.

"It's a onesie," Piper says proudly, resting her cheek on Liam's arm. "He learned how to crochet, and he's been working on an outfit for the baby for *weeks*."

"Oh my god," Grant whispers. "That's the cutest fucking thing I've ever heard."

"It's not great." Liam scowls. "I messed up one of the sleeves. And the colors don't match."

"That's so sweet of you, Liam." Lexi beams. "Mav and Emmy are going to love it."

"On a scale of one to ten, how hard is childbirth?" Ethan asks. "Do you think it hurts as bad as getting hit in the balls with a puck?"

"It's worse," Madeline answers from her seat next to Hudson. "You wouldn't be able to handle it."

"Come on, Mads." He smirks. "I've lost teeth. I've taken a stick to the head. I'd be just fine."

"If you stand up, we could test the theory," she says sweetly, and Hudson buries his laugh in her hair. "I bet you'd cry within two minutes."

"Sit your ass down, Richardson," I warn, and he pouts.

"Come on, Coach. I want to—"

The doors to the lobby burst open, and Maverick comes staggering out. He's in a blue smock with booties covering his shoes, and he puts his hand on the wall. Takes a deep breath, and bursts into tears.

"I'm a dad," he wails, and the waiting room explodes with noise.

There are hugs and high-fives. Ethan pops a bottle of champagne I didn't know he brought, and Maverick refuses a glass. I shake his hand and he pulls me in close, clasping my back.

"How's Emmy?" I ask.

"She's a fucking champ. I almost passed out in there, but she powered through. I swear to god she's the most beautiful woman I've ever seen. I love her more right now than I did an hour ago." He laughs and wipes his nose with his sleeve. "And everyone knows how much I loved her then."

"And the baby?"

"Ten fingers, ten toes. Perfect red hair, just like her mom, and the cutest nose. She blinked up at me when I held her for the first time, and I cried more than Emmy." He looks at me. "I already know eighteen years with her isn't going to be enough."

"A hundred years wouldn't be enough," I say.

"Emmy's getting cleaned up. Baby girl is getting her measurements done. It might be a while before you guys can come back, so don't feel like you all have to wait around," Maverick says to our group. "I appreciate you being here."

Liam narrows his eyes in Maverick's direction. "I'm here in the middle of the night. I'm not leaving until I see that baby," he says. "And Emmy. I like her more than I like you."

Maverick laughs. "Don't blame you. I'll text when we're ready." He looks at everyone. Takes us all in. "I learned a long time ago that family isn't something you're born into. It's the people you find along the way, and I'm really glad I found you all."

THREE HOURS LATER, just as the sun is coming up, we get the okay to head to Emmy's room. Grant is crying. Ethan is falling asleep on Liam's shoulder, but the goalie doesn't shove him away. On the fourth floor, down a long hall, Maverick waves. He gestures for us all to come inside a large room, everyone rearranging where they're standing until we fill the space to the brim.

"Hi, guys," Emmy says, holding a baby wrapped in a blanket like she's the most precious, delicate being in the world. Maverick sits next to his wife on the hospital bed, an arm around her shoulders. "Thanks for sticking around."

"Is that our newest member?" Grant whispers. "She's so tiny."

"Meet Murphy Miller Hartwell." Maverick kisses Murphy's head. "It means sea warrior, and if she's anything like her mom, she's going to live up to the name and then some."

"We wanted to stick with the gender-neutral theme," Emmy explains. "That way, when a hockey coach signs her to his team in twenty-eight years, the arrogant captain will think he's meeting a guy."

"But instead, it'll be a kick-ass woman who's going to sweep him off his feet." Maverick brushes his nose against Emmy's. His attention turns to me, eyes wet with tears. "This is all because of you, Coach."

"I don't think I can take any credit for your spawn, Miller," I say, walking over to them. "This was all you two."

"Yes, you can." Emmy smiles at me then tucks her chin to her chest. "Do you want to hold her?"

"I haven't held a baby in years. Grant's right. She's too tiny. I don't—" My argument snuffs out when Emmy puts Murphy in my arms. "God dammit." I stare at the ceiling. "I don't like getting emotional in front of people, Hartwell."

"The only reason this is possible"—Emmy gestures between her and Maverick—"Is because you took a chance on me. You didn't sign me because it would check a box or be a good headline in the media. You didn't treat me any different because I'm a woman. You saw a player with a dream, and because of that, I got so much more than I could have ever imagined."

"I don't have many years left in the league," Maverick adds, looking only at me. "Three, maybe? Two tops if it means Em can come back and have another season before she retires, because I want her to have a chance to win the Cup. I know we have a player-coach relationship, and I want to be respectful of that boundary for the time that I have left on your team." He turns to the rest of the group. "All of you are going to be aunts and uncles, obviously. Huddy Boy, I hope you're okay with being godfather number one and sharing the honors with Reid and Dallas."

"Jesus, Mav. Of course I am," Hudson says with a laugh. "I'd be honored."

"Good. And I hope after I retire, you'll consider being godfather number two, Coach," he says, and I freeze. "Signing Emmy to the team..." He trails off and bites his fist. A tear rolls down his cheek. "You gave me everything I've ever wanted in life. A partner. A family. A home. I'm not worthy of any of it, but I'm going to spend every second of every day doing my best to prove that I am."

"We'll talk," I rasp, hating how my voice cracks. "But only if I get first dibs on Murphy's playing rights after she's done a year in college."

Maverick knows what my answer is, and I'm glad I don't have to say it outright. If I did, I'd be a fucking mess, because how the hell did this group of kids who pissed me off to no end grow into a group of good, hardworking men starting their own families they want me to be part of?

"Fuck you, Saunders," Liam says, breaking the heaviness in the room. "All I got them was a onesie."

That makes everyone laugh. Murphy gets passed around,

already so loved by so many people. Maverick and Emmy can't stop looking at each other, and I have to take a deep breath.

I've had a lot of highs as a hockey player. I've won championships. Broken league records. Been the best player in the world, but I think at the end of my career, when I walk away from the sport for good, this moment right here is going to be the one I'm proudest of.

TWENTY

HANNAH

"HOW WAS JAPAN?" I ask Tierney, pressing my phone to my ear. "Your program was incredible, T. You deserved a higher score."

"Thanks, Han." She pauses to close a door, letting out a deep sigh. "I did the best I could, and other people's best was better than mine. It happens."

"Humble even in defeat. I'm so proud of you."

"How are things going with you? That video you posted to social media yesterday of your Axel was literally stunning."

"Stop. My foot placement was all messed up." I tap speakerphone so I can put in an earring. "Coaching is going well. I have no clue if what I'm doing is having an impact or not, but Olivia—that's the girl I'm working with—is improving. That has to mean something. *Oh.* She's a big fan of yours, so if you ever feel like stopping by the Stars' practice rink during one of our lessons, it would probably earn me a lot of cool points."

"We'll make it happen. World Championships aren't until March, so I'm giving myself a week after the holidays to fucking relax before I amp up my training for Boston. I'll come by then." Tierney decides to FaceTime me, and I smile when her face fills my screen. "Speaking of Boston. Any thought about showing up to the World Championships?"

"Honestly? No. This break has been good for me, and I don't want to rush myself. There is a small competition in Virginia happening in March I've been looking at. It's the weekend before Worlds. If January and February go well, I might give it a shot." I grab my lipstick and put a light shade of red on my lips. "But if it doesn't happen, I'm perfectly content with what I'm doing right now."

The two scheduled sessions that Brody and I talked about have turned into seeing each other three or four times a week. He'll text me in the morning and let me know he has an hour between practice and a meeting, an open invitation to head to the rink if I'm free.

Some days we'll run drills, but lately, most of our time is just spent skating. Side by side, with easy conversation. He tells me about the gifts he got Liv for Christmas. I talk about my idea to create a social media page dedicated to teaching beginner moves to people new to figure skating. We alternate who brings coffee, and by the time I leave the arena, I'm always in a better mood.

"Tell me the date. I want to be there to support you." She tilts her head, assessing me. "You look good, Han. *Happy*. Is there someone new in your life?"

"God, no. I got stood up recently, and that was a humbling experience." I groan. "I am happy. At least, I think I am. Things are good. I'm letting myself enjoy small moments, like when Liv tries a Biellmann spin for the first time and makes it look beautiful. Seeing others enjoy the sport I love makes everything more fun, and I'm taking it day by day."

"It would be so easy to fall off the face of the earth, but you're still showing up. I'm so proud of you." Tierney assesses my outfit. "Where the hell are you going dressed so cute?"

"Oh." I smile and touch the white turtleneck and leather pants I slipped into thirty minutes ago. "Riley Mitchell is playing in his first game since his accident tonight. Grant is picking me up so we can head to the AHL arena."

"*Fun.* Tell Grant I say hi. You two are still good to come to the Blazers and Bullets game in Orlando, right?"

"Wouldn't miss it." A text message from Grant pops up, and I grab my clear purse. "I have to run. Grant is outside. I'll see you next week! We'll pick you up on the way to the airport."

"Can't wait! Have a blast tonight!"

Tierney blows me a kiss and we hang up. I hustle through my apartment, grabbing my winter coat and a beanie in case the arena is cold. With a check of my reflection in the mirror, I lock up and hurry downstairs.

"Hi," I say, breathless when I climb into Grant's Range Rover parked near the curb. "Sorry, I was talking to Tierney."

"No worries. Traffic was light, and I had a minute to drink my coffee." He yawns and rubs his eyes. "I'm so tired."

"When did you get home?" I buckle my seatbelt and tilt the air vents my way. "Early this morning?"

"I wish. We literally landed two hours ago. Our redeye in from California was delayed for a mechanical issue we found out about after we boarded the plane. We sat in the hangar for-fucking-ever." Grant checks his mirrors and heads for the arena. "I thought Coach was going to lose it. I don't know who he called or what kind of strings he pulled, but the part that wasn't going to arrive in Orange County until this afternoon magically showed up early this morning. A miracle worker, I'll tell ya."

"Want me to drive? We don't need you falling asleep at the wheel."

"Nah. My adrenaline outweighs the fatigue." He turns the radio down. "I brought you one of Riley's jerseys in case you want to wear it. We all have one on, and we're sitting right on the glass. When he comes out from the locker room, he'll see us. He has no clue we'll be there."

"This is going to mean so much to him." I twist, reaching for the backseat so I can grab the folded jersey next to a pair of Nikes. "Please tell me this is clean."

"Uh. It's not *not* clean." Grant gives me a sheepish grin. "It's been through one cycle in the washing machine, but there might still be a smell. I didn't have time for anything more than that, and these things hold a stench for weeks."

"Lovely. Hope I don't meet my future life partner tonight. They'll think I smell like dirty socks." I wrinkle my nose and set the jersey in my lap. "What's new with you, G? You're busier than usual this season. I haven't seen you in two weeks."

"Nothing. Everything is exactly the same," he says. "Boring, boring, boring."

"Grant Calloway Everett. You are the world's worst liar. What the *hell* are you hiding?"

"Okay, watch it with the government name, Hannah Tabitha Everett. I'm not hiding anything!" A lock of his hair falls in his face, and he brushes it away. "Mind your business."

"A girl." Understanding dawns. "You're seeing someone. *Who*?"

"I can't talk about it."

"Is it serious? Is she married? Is that why you're so secretive?"

"No one is married, and, ah, I'd like for it to be serious." His smile falls. "But I'm not sure it ever could be. Too many factors. Too much scrutiny. Maybe one day."

"Do I know her?" I ask.

"No. Well, maybe? Probably not. Anyway." He drums his fingers on the steering wheel, coming to a stop at a red light. Grant unlocks his phone and tosses it to me. "Look at the photo Mitchy sent us earlier in his jersey. Isn't it cute?"

"This is precious." I zoom in on the shot of Riley with his glasses on, hockey stick in hand and eyes closed. His smile is wide, and the messages under it are from the guys telling him how good he looks. "I'm so glad you guys get to be there for him tonight."

"Me too." The light changes, and Grant moves with traffic. "He's my Secret Santa this year, so I asked the equipment manager for the Comets to steal his jersey after the game. I'm going to have it framed and put a plaque at the bottom with the date and final score on it. He'll always have something to remind him of tonight."

"You're so thoughtful, G. What a big night. He's going to love it."

"Might get overshadowed by the other thing happening. Scroll down," he says, and I read through the rest of the group chat until I see a photo of a piece of paper, the words Riley's Life List written at the top. "He's proposing to Lexi. Okay. Well it's not an actual proposal, but he's going to ask her to spend the rest of her life with him."

"*Shut up*. That is so exciting! Wait. Does she have any idea this is happening? They haven't been together that long, have they?"

"A year and then some? Maybe? Not too long, but when you know, you know. Right?"

"Don't ask me." I laugh. "I don't know anything about relationships."

I haven't dated someone in a couple of years. There was a girlfriend back when I was nineteen that lasted for eight months. The other figure skater I went out with when I was twenty-one who told me he loved me then slept with someone else. A few casual hook ups, but nothing serious. Nothing earth-shattering, and I wonder what it would be like to find someone like that. Someone you want to be around all of the time, who lights up when you walk into a room. Who you can't live without, but I'm not sure it even exists.

"Neither do I." Grant laughs and pulls into the VIP parking lot adjacent to the arena. We climb out of the car, making our way to the large glass doors. "There's an entrance over here for us. Security didn't want us getting mobbed by fans before we get inside."

"I forget how popular you all are. Women must throw themselves at you."

"Yeah, but most of us don't want that kind of attention. Maverick is a dad—you get to meet Murphy tonight, by the way. Liam will deck someone in the face if they look at Piper the wrong way. Riley's been obsessed with Lexi for years."

"That leaves you and Ethan," I point out.

"Easy E might be a lost cause. Don't let him stand next to you tonight, by the way. He keeps joking that he's going to get you to fall in love with him, and I do *not* want him as my brother-in-law."

"Is it true his dick is—"

"Please stop." Grant groans. "My ears are going to bleed. Pierced? Yes, it's true. Yes, I've seen it. Too many times."

We scan our tickets and go through a metal detector. When we make our way onto the concourse, we're bombarded by fans asking for autographs and photos. By the time we make it to our seats, there are only a few minutes before the Comets are supposed to take the ice.

"Hannah!" Lexi gives me a hug and I smile. "It's so good to see you again!"

"I'm so happy to be here. How are you feeling? Grant told me how much you've been working with Riley to get him ready for tonight," I say.

"I'm terrified." She laughs and plays with her necklace. "I don't want him to get hurt, but I know he's going to be pissed if anyone takes it easy on him. I just want him to have a good time out there."

I wave to Piper, Madeline, and Emmy, who puts a pair of headphones over Murphy's ears. I find a seat near the aisle, draping my coat over the back of my chair, when a shadow falls over me. I tip my head back and find Brody staring down at me.

"Ice Queen." His eyes flicker with amusement. "Good to see you."

"Hi, BB." I don't bother holding back my smile. "How are you?"

"Running on fumes. Delirious. Happy to be here." He points to the empty seat next to me, ignoring the woman three rows over who is screaming his name. "Is that seat open?"

"All yours if you want it."

"That would be nice," he murmurs.

"Come on down, Coach."

Brody sits down. The chair can't be comfortable for him, but he doesn't complain. He drapes an arm over the back of my seat, fingers brushing against the ends of my ponytail.

"You always wear a ribbon in your hair." A gentle touch to the light blue bow I tied to match the Comets' team colors and a low hum. "I don't know how I feel about them."

I turn my body his direction, leaning close so I can hear him. "Are they too girlie for the guy who used to get in fights on the ice?"

"No." His hand falls away. He stares out at the ice with a set jaw. A secret he's not revealing. "They're fucking distracting."

"How so?" I ask.

"When you wear them, I want to—"

A roar from the crowd interrupts him, cheering as the players skate out of the tunnel. Riley is the last one on the ice and moving more carefully than his teammates. He scans the arena with a grin, taking in the signs and banners welcoming him back. He laughs, accepting a puck from a teammate and lining up to take a practice shot on goal, but then he spots us. He does a double take, dropping his stick. Covering his mouth with his gloved hand, and then, chaos unfolds.

"Look at everyone here for him," I yell over the noise, clapping with the rest of the crowd.

"I'll be back," Brody says, squeezing my shoulder once and stepping into the aisle. "Gotta say hi to our boy."

Someone from the team's staff escorts the Stars players to the bench so Riley can have a moment with them. I hang back, watching them with a full heart and tears in my eyes. There are photos and high-fives. Riley holding Murphy then reaching for Lexi, kissing her like the world is going to end tomorrow. They're so deeply in love it almost hurts.

The lights turn back on. Everyone settles down. The fans take their seats, the refs huddle close, and it's almost time for the puck drop. The guys from the Stars climb over people to make it back to our row, and Brody is smiling when he appears at my side again.

"I'm going to tell you a secret," he says.

"I can't wait to hear." I pat his chair and he sits, leaning forward with his elbows on his knees. "Make it something good, please."

"Well. Since you're begging," he muses, glancing my way. "That's how it works, right?"

Hell.

Surrounded by the team, and this is the most brazen he's ever been. My lips part. I blink, following the path of his hand as he grazes my ponytail again.

"I don't know," I answer, not bothering to keep my voice down. With the noise from the crowd, there's no way anyone is able to overhear us. "You're usually the one begging."

The curl of a smirk on his mouth. The bold, carefree way he steals my ribbon and wraps it around his fingers. It's sensory overload, a side I haven't seen from Brody before.

And I *like* it.

"I guess I am. There are far worse things in life than being on my knees." A soft chuckle. His guard coming down. "I act like being around my players is a detriment to my health, but I really love it. They're stupid as hell, and it's fun to see."

"You softie. I *knew* you didn't hate it as much as you said you did." I look down the row of seats, at the family they created. "You did all of this, Brody. This camaraderie. This love. It doesn't happen everywhere, but when it does, it's magic."

"Magic," he repeats, twisting my ribbon in a knot on his wrist. "Can I tell you another secret?"

"You're so free with your admissions tonight. Have you been drinking?" I tease, but the shake of his head makes me want to stop joking.

"No. I'm in full control of my thoughts." Brody pauses and shifts closer to me, cupping my ear. "I know I fucked up after our night together, but having you here? Seeing you part of the team? I like that too. A lot. It might be my favorite thing."

"Mine too." My heart races. I can't talk above a whisper. "I've felt so lost lately, but thanks to you, I'm finding my way."

"We make a good pair, don't we?" he asks, pulling away so he can tuck my ribbon in his pocket. "Who would've thought?"

I try my best to focus on the game. I cheer when the Comets score. I jump to my feet after Riley makes a beautiful pass to an open teammate. It's fun and it's lively and the best night I've had in a long time, but I can't tell if that's because of the energy around me or Brody's arm staying over the back of my chair and the glances he keeps tossing my way.

TWENTY-ONE

BRODY

THE HOTEL WHERE THE STARS' holiday gala is taking place is festive as hell. There's garland around the windows. Ornaments hang from chandeliers and fake snow falls from the ceiling. On one side of the ballroom, someone set up a photo op with Santa and a handcrafted sleigh, and I blink down at the shrimp appetizer a waiter offers me on a tiny cocktail napkin.

"No, thank you," I grumble, taking a slider instead.

"Dude. This is a fundraiser for charity. Can you attempt to be in the holiday spirit?" Parker asks. "Less Grinch, more jolly."

"Ho. Ho. Ho. Is that better?" I nod my appreciation to the bartender who brings over a double whiskey neat. I slide him a hundred-dollar bill as a tip and down half of it. "I spent thirty minutes being forced to network with a group of men who told me I made them lose a thousand dollars after I pulled Liam from the net the other night. As if my coaching decisions are a contributing factor to their gambling addiction."

"Sports betting is ruining the game, and it's a shame to see." He shakes his head at the next tray of appetizers that come by. "Grilled octopus? Really?"

"Hell. I would've been happy with a hot dog." I take another sip of my drink and lean against the bar. "How much longer do you think I have to hang around before I can make an escape?"

"Given you're the one delivering the speech to thank all the donors for their generous contributions this season? At least another hour."

"We could've done this at an Applebee's." I finish my drink and set down the empty glass. "At least the guys are behaving."

"Probably because you told them we have a weight lifting session at six tomorrow morning. Watching them puke while doing bench presses sounds delightful," Parker says, and I snort in agreement.

A flash of color from across the room catches my eye and pulls me away from our conversation. I crane my neck, trying to find the source of it, and when I do, my heart skips a fucking beat.

Goddamn this woman and her inability to get out of my fucking head.

Hannah walks into the ballroom with Grant by her side. Her hair is down tonight and hangs halfway down her back. Her light blue dress matches her eyes, the thin straps showing off her shoulders and too much bare skin. There's a slit up the side, but the most devastating part is the way the material dips low to her chest. How it hugs the curves of her breasts, showing off the cleavage that makes my brain go foggy.

People turn her way. At least three guys start walking toward her. My fingers curl around the edge of the bar to restrain myself from walking over there, giving her my jacket, and not letting anyone else look at her.

She breaks away from her brother who's greeting Maverick and Hudson, scanning the room. Her gaze bounces from person to person, and when her attention lands on me, she lights up brighter than the twenty-foot Christmas tree in the lobby.

Her smile stretches into something big, something beautiful, and the twinkle in her eye when she lifts her hand in a wave tells me she knows exactly how good she looks tonight.

"*Fuck*," I whisper, scrambling when she starts to make her way over to me. "Do I have anything on my face? Is my tie straight?"

"What?" Parker blinks. Stares at me and frowns. "You look great, B. Are you nervous for your speech or something?"

"Or something. I'm going to do a lap," I say, stepping away from him and finding a cocktail table off to the side.

The champagne is flowing. A string quartet starts up a holiday tune, and I'm fighting for my fucking life. Hannah weaves her way across the room, a drink in her hand by the time she makes it over to me.

"Well." She looks me up and down, an appreciative hum working its way up her throat. "A bowtie *and* cufflinks? You sure do clean up well, Brody."

"Hey." I reach for her like I'm going to hug her but stop when I'm halfway there. I throw out my hand instead, offering her a handshake. "Good to see you, Hannah."

"Wow. Going with the formalities tonight?" Hannah laughs and takes my hand with hers, squeezing my palm. She's soft and warm, and a bracelet slides down her wrist with the movement. "Good to see you too, Mr. Saunders."

"I didn't know you'd be here tonight. These things are pretty boring."

"Boring? I see free food and alcohol. And I know there's a chance to bid on some of the players later." She sets her drink down, an elbow propped on the table. "Is the coach up for auction too?"

"Hannah." I pull on my collar, lowering my voice in warning. "You can't say that to me. Not here."

"Oh." Her face falls. She shuffles back, lifting her dress so she doesn't trip on the hem with her silver shoes that make her impossibly tall. "You're right. That was totally inappropriate. I'm sorry. I'm going to find some of the girls and a grab bite to eat. It's good to see you, Brody."

Hannah turns, gliding past a group of kids who stop me for an autograph. I do my best to plaster on a smile and sign all the rookie trading cards they brought, excusing myself after I get to the end of their stack. A reporter tries to snag me for an interview, and I politely ask to circle back in half an hour to answer any questions they have.

"Hey." I finally reach Hannah and spot a door off to the side of the room. I put my hand on her elbow, gently guiding her into a hallway that's quiet and deserted. "I'm sorry for how that came out."

"No, I get it. I shouldn't be saying things like that to you when we're around people who could hear." Hannah leans against the wall behind her, arms crossed over her chest. "I don't want to make you uncomfortable, and I'm sorry."

"You know you could never make me uncomfortable." I step toward her, resting a palm flat on the wall near her head. Her inhale is subtle, but I hear the hitch in her breathing. "You didn't then. You don't now. When you say stuff like that to me, all flirty and cute and fun, you make me want to be reckless. You make me start wanting things I know I can't have."

"What kind of things?" she asks, tipping her chin up. Our eyes meet and hold. "What other secrets do you have, Brody?"

"I want you." I bend, whispering in her ear. "I want you so fucking bad, it's getting so hard to stay away."

"I thought you didn't play games." Hannah's mouth twists into a frown. Disappointment in her eyes. Hopes dashed. "Why are you saying that after you already rejected me?"

"Rejected you?" I move even closer, until the tips of my shoes touch hers. Until I can smell the wine she was just sipping on her breath. Until I can see the collection of freckles on her right shoulder. "I've spent every day since that June night going out of my goddamn mind with missing you. With wondering what you were up to or how much you hated me for not coming back to apologize. I couldn't, Hannah, because I knew the second I did, you'd suck me in. I'd be a lost cause. And being on the ice with you? Seeing you at dinner and bars and when you're in a fancy dress that should be criminal it looks so stunning on you? I get weaker every day. So close to giving in. So sick of trying to fight it." My mouth drops to her neck. I press a kiss to her throat, indulging in irresponsibility. Just for a second. "I fall asleep dreaming about you, and I wake up mad as hell that I let you get away."

"You don't mean that." She loops an arm around my neck. Grabs a fistful of my shirt with her other hand. "It was one night. Just sex. That's what we said."

I sneak out from her hold. I keep my eyes on her while I take off my jacket and drape it over my forearm. Rolling up my right sleeve, I point to the tattoo I got last year on a night when I was drunk and stupid and missing the hell out of her. When I thought I'd never see her again.

It's been easy to pretend it's something for Olivia. A design I had made to celebrate her accomplishments, but I know who it's really for. Blonde hair. Long legs. A laugh I can't stop hearing.

"What do you think this is?" I ask.

Hannah holds my arm. "A tattoo?"

"Look closer."

Her thumb traces the outline of a pair of skates with a ribbon threaded through them. It's the same color, the same pattern as the one she was wearing the night we were together, and her gasp is a dagger to my chest.

"Brody." She blinks up at me with long lashes and brings her mouth to my arm. She kisses the small piece of artwork, and my body is electrified with long-lost pleasure. "Is that my ribbon?"

"Nothing I've ever done has been without a purpose." My voice is hoarse. My heart is thumping so loudly, I'm surprised she can't hear it. How pathetic would it make me if I asked her to kiss the tattoo again? "I torture myself by spending time with you. I know nothing can come out of it, but I can't stay away. Not anymore."

Hannah grabs my shirt. She tugs me toward her, not stopping until our bodies are flush together. Her mouth is inches away from mine, and I haven't breathed in what feels like years.

Fuck.

How often have I thought about her mouth and the things I would do it if given the chance? How badly have I wanted to kiss her during one of our sessions, just so I could taste her again? How long have I felt like I've been searching for the sun, only for it to be right in front of me the whole time?

"Kiss me," she says, a challenge behind it.

"No."

"Brody." Hannah puts her fingers under my chin, turning my face until her palm rests on my cheek. "Kiss me."

"I can't." I try to swallow, but my throat is on fire. "I won't be able to stop if I do."

"Stopping is the last thing I want you to do."

A million different ways our conversation could have gone, and this right here—with her stroking my jaw, with her asking for the thing I've wanted to do for *months* but didn't think I could—is the biggest fucking surprise.

"Are you sure?" I rest my forehead against hers. It's the last bit of my sanity telling me to slow down. To make sure we're on the same page, because once this door opens, there's no going back. Not for a second time. "My self-control is dwindling by the fucking second, but I can walk away."

"You did that once." Her fingers trail down my chest, palm splaying out across my stomach. Her thumb brushes along the waistband of my slacks, teasing. "And look how it turned out."

"Horribly," I croak. "You need to be the one to do it, Hannah. So I know—"

"What was it you said?" she murmurs, her exhale tickling my skin. "Fuck it, right?"

Her lips are soft and sweet on mine, but there's a roughness to the way she kisses. Her hands work up to my hair, threading through the stands and giving a sharp tug that almost makes my knees buckle. I cup the back of her head so she doesn't hurt herself, a soft moan tumbling from her when I rock my hips, wanting her to feel what she does to me.

"More." She untucks my shirt from my pants. I let my jacket fall to the ground and bump her ear with my nose. "*Please*, Brody."

"I love it when you beg." I lick a hot swipe up the line of her throat, laughing when she squirms. "It's nice to be in control around you for once in my fucking life."

"Do you want me to get on my knees?" She touches my belt, and I hold back a groan. "Because I will."

"Not here. Not where someone can see." I kiss her collarbone, glad when she pulls on my hair again. "And not because I'm embarrassed of you, but because I'm selfish, sweetheart. What's mine is mine, and I don't want anyone else to see what they can't have."

"Your place or mine?" Hannah ghosts her fingers down the front of my pants. Her knuckles tease my cock through the fabric, and I have to hold back a groan. "Preferably soon, please."

"Mine. Liv is with her mom for the weekend." I have to shift away from her and scrub a hand over my face to make this decision. "But I have to give a speech before I leave."

"You have to go out there and talk to people again?" Her eyes travel to the hard dick I'm supporting, and I can't help but burst out laughing when she gives me a proud grin. "I wish you all the best."

"Think I need a second before I go out there." I tuck in my shirt and roll my sleeve back down. Shucking on my jacket, I hold out my arms. "How do I look?"

"Unbelievably hot and like you can't wait to be thoroughly fucked. Except…" She licks her thumb and touches the corner of my mouth. "There. No lipstick that will give you away."

"Hey." I cup her cheeks. "Just give me a little time. I'm not leaving you. Not again."

"I know." Hannah smiles, and all feels right in the world. "I'm not big on second chances, but I have a feeling you're not going to let me down."

With a kiss to each of her knuckles, I move away and find my way back into the gala. No one notices my absence, and I charm the fuck out of everyone I'm introduced to over the next hour. I pose for photos. I sign more autographs. I give advice to a season ticket holder's daughter who wants to play hockey at a higher level, but is afraid of the kickback from the boys on her small club team who say she's not good enough.

"They're jealous," I tell her, "Which means you're doing something right."

When it's time for my speech, I get a standing ovation as I stress the importance of camaraderie and working together toward a common goal. Hannah stands in the back, her eyes never leaving me as I shake the hands of our owner and CEO. My assistant coaches rib me for speaking so eloquently when they're used to only seeing me scowl, and when I make it to the bar for one more drink, a relieved sigh loosens out of me.

"Nice job out there," Maverick says, leaning against the bar next to me. "You light a fire under the boys' asses."

"Where's your better half tonight?" I ask, sipping on my last whiskey.

"Emmy didn't feel like coming." He plays with his cufflinks and shrugs. "I get it. All the questions lately are when is she going to be back on the ice? How is she planning to lose the baby weight? How does she feel about her husband traveling across the country to hit a puck while she's at home with a newborn?" Maverick glances my way. "That shit hurts."

"Being an athlete is really fucking hard. Being a female athlete? You and I can't comprehend the scrutiny they're under." I sneak a look at Hannah, watching her talk to Piper and Lexi. "As long as you're there for her when she needs you, that's all that matters."

"I'm trying to be." His jaw tightens. "The guys want to double check what time practice is in the morning."

Thinking about dragging myself to the arena a few hours from now while Hannah is still in my bed sounds unappealing. I swirl my drink around and drum my fingers against the glass, contemplating.

I never missed a practice during my playing career. High school, college, and the NHL all saw perfect attendance from me. It stretched into my coaching days, with the exception of one game last season when Liv had appendicitis and I rushed home to be with her.

When I'm scheduled to be somewhere, I show up.

But how fun would it be not to for once?

"You know what?" I finish the whiskey and slide the empty glass across the bar. "Let's scrub practice tomorrow. Take the day off."

"Uh." Maverick looks down at his hand and pinches his skin, wincing when a red mark appears. "I'm not dreaming. You actually just said that to me?"

"I did."

"You never cancel practice. Ever."

"There's a first time for everything." Hannah makes eye contact with me. She mimes tapping the invisible watch on her wrist, and I don't bother holding back my smile. "Might as well make it tomorrow. Weather looks nice too. You guys can go get brunch."

"*Brunch?*" He pulls out his phone. His fingers fly across the screen, and I roll my eyes when my own phone buzzes in my pocket. I pull it out to see what he has to say. "Holy shit."

Puck Kings (+ their savior, BS)

MILLER

911. Emergency. Coach is canceling practice tomorrow morning.

Said we could go to fucking BRUNCH?

Around the room, the guys' heads pop up. They look at their phones, then at me, then down again. Ethan stands and gestures to the server passing with champagne, grabbing the bottle and chugging it.

HAYES

Uh. Did someone spike his drink?

EVERETT

There's no way this is happening. Coach canceling practice the day my favorite spot is doing bottomless mimosas AND pancake stacks? I believe in MIRACLES.

RICHARDSON

We're partying hard tonight boys!!!!!!!!!!!!! No sleep until Brooklyn! Strip club. Bar. Night club. Casino. We're doing it all!!!!!!!!

SULLIVAN

I'm not going to a strip club. Nothing I want to see there.

MITCHELL

Same

RICHARDSON

Okay you boring ass married men. The REST
of us will go, and we'll send pictures of all the
women you're missing out on.

"Tell me I didn't make a mistake, Miller." I pinch the bridge of my nose. "He can't possibly do all of that in one night, can he?"

"Oh, Coach. Best not to question what Ethan can or cannot do." Maverick laughs. "It's better for everyone."

EVERETT

Wait a second. If his drink isn't spiked, and
this is really happening… Coach has to have a
very, VERY good reason for not wanting to
show up bright and early tomorrow.

Is it a woman????

"Let Everett know I expect him on the ice an hour before film review on Monday," I say to Maverick, tucking my phone away. "And make Richardson join too for talking about women like that."

"Happy to pass along the message, but he makes a valid point. *Is* there someone involved with this decision of yours?"

"Miller. This is an inappropriate conversation for us to be having."

"Oh, fuck off, dude. We've spent years working together, and you're barely older than me. When I retire, we'll go to the bar, grab a beer, and shoot the shit. We'll probably even be friends." He clasps my shoulder. "I'm sure you have a shit ton of pressure on you. I'm sure it's hard balancing work and a kid. Hell. I'm struggling to keep my head above water and Murph can't even walk yet. You're allowed to be happy, just like the rest of us."

"Noted. Thanks for the pep talk, Miller." Hannah tips her

head to the door, and I pat Maverick's chest. "Now leave me the hell alone."

TWENTY-TWO
BRODY

> There's a coffee shop two blocks up the road. I'll meet you there and we can split a car to my place.

> Give me fifteen minutes.

H.E.

> If I send you a picture of what's underneath my dress, will it get you to move faster?

ME

> Ten minuets, and I don't need bribing.

IT'S THRILLING to be sneaking out of here with Hannah. The adrenaline coursing through me is new, unfamiliar, and so different from what I used to experience when I was on the ice. She exits through a set of doors away from the lobby and I veer to the right, doing one last lap to make it obvious as hell I'm still here while she's not.

My plan is foiled when Grant appears in front of me. He's missing his tie, and the champagne glass in his hand is almost empty. He looks wary when his gaze locks on mine, and I stop in my tracks.

"Everett," I say, checking my watch. "What's up?"

"Hey, Coach." He runs a hand through his hair and shifts on his feet. "Can I, um, talk to you for a second?"

"That depends. Are you going to try to get out of the extra skating I gave you?"

"What? No. I'll give you two extra hours if you want. It's more… personal?"

It comes out like a question, and I tip my head back, blowing out a breath while I look at the ceiling. It would be so fucking easy to brush him off and dash out of here, but that doesn't fall under the values I try to implement with the team.

I want Hannah more than I've ever wanted anything else in my life, and I hope to every higher power out there she understands why I'm late.

"Come here." I motion to a quiet alcove in the breezeway that leads to the lobby. "What's going on?"

"I'm afraid I'm going to get in trouble with the league," he whispers. "And I want to know if you can forward me a copy of our CBA."

"Our CBA," I repeat. "What did you do, Everett?"

"*Nothing*. I just want to make sure my, ah, extracurricular activities aren't going to get me suspended." His ears are bright red. He downs the rest of his drink and holds the champagne flute with a tight grip. "It's nothing illegal."

"Okay. Are you betting on games?"

"I don't know how any of that stuff works."

"Are you physically assaulting someone when you're off the ice? Roughing up the person you're sleeping with and threatening them if they talk?"

"*What?*" The color drains from his face. His mouth falls open, aghast. "I've never... I would never put my hands on a woman. *Ever.*"

"Are you threatening fans on social media?" I ask, trying to run through things players have been reprimanded for in the past. Article 18-A from the CBA that outlines commissioner discipline for off-ice conduct is fuzzy. Even fuzzier after drinking and kissing Hannah, and I can't remember the procedure. "You're looking at a fine, suspension, or an expulsion if—"

"I haven't done anything like that, and I never will. It relates more to, ah, personal relationships? And who I'm allowed to be in one with?"

"Grant. You know our team policy is inclusive to *all* relationships, right? And you don't have to disclose anything you're not comfortable with. Private things are allowed to stay private, even if you're a public figure." I drag my knuckles over my chest, thinking about Hannah waiting for me. "If it makes you feel better, I'll forward you the CBA in the morning."

"Thanks, Coach." Grant's shoulders sag with relief. "That would be amazing."

"Thanks for trusting me. You need anything else, let one of the older guys know. Hudson and Maverick are good people."

"I know they are. See ya on Monday." With a salute, he turns, practically skipping away.

Knowing I'm behind schedule, I hightail it down the steps of the hotel. I ignore the ache in my knee, jogging the two blocks it takes for me to get to the coffee shop I suggested. Hannah is standing on the corner, arms wrapped around herself to stay warm, and I rip my jacket off.

"I'm sorry." I drape it over her shoulders and rub my hands up and down her arms. "I was talking to your brother."

"Grant?" She lifts an eyebrow. "Did he—"

"No. Had some questions about team related stuff, but we're good." I dig out my phone, ordering us an Uber. "Are you cold? There's a bar a few doors up we can sit it while we wait."

"I'm better now." Her nose brushes against the lapel of my jacket, giving it a deep inhale. "Tell me your place is going to be nice and cozy when we get there."

"I already adjusted the temperature on my phone. You'll be toasty. And if you're not, I also have a towel warmer. We can throw a couple blankets in there and make a heated tent."

"Now you're talking." Hannah smiles up at me. "How much have you had to drink?"

"Enough to be a slightly buzzed. Not enough to start stumbling." I pull my jacket tighter around her. "What about you?"

"Perfectly sober. I don't want to forget anything about tonight."

"I don't either." My phone chimes, telling me our car is arriving. "I canceled practice in the morning."

"*What?*" She laughs, her hands resting on my chest. "Why?"

"Don't think four or five hours with you is going to be enough." I wrap my arms around her waist, burying my face in her hair. "I want you so fucking bad, Hannah."

"I want you too, Brody." Her lips, featherlight against my throat. "Tonight. Tomorrow morning. As many times as you'll have me."

A car honks, and I wave down our Uber driver. We settle in the back seat, Hannah sitting in the middle so I can keep my arms around her. She rests her cheek on my shoulder, thumb stroking over my knuckles, and I blow out a breath to keep my heart rate steady.

"What are you thinking about?" she murmurs, a hand on my leg. Her fingers dance up my thigh, all the way to my hip, then stop at my belt. "Anything good?"

"If I told you, I'd lose my perfect Uber rating." I turn my head, my lips finding her ear. "I'm thinking about how easy it would be to hike your dress up. I could put my jacket over your lap and slip two fingers inside you. The driver wouldn't know I was fucking you, but I would."

"God." Hannah drops her head against the seats behind us. "I forgot how talkative you are in bed."

"I'm happy to remind you." I pull down on her bottom lip with my thumb. "And stop calling me god, sweetheart. You know my name. You screamed it last time, didn't you?"

"Careful, Brody." A palm, right over my cock. Thank fuck it's dark as hell outside so the driver can't see what she's doing. "Keep talking like that, and I'll make you get on your knees."

"Like I wouldn't do it willingly." I brush her hair away from her neck, kissing her throat. I'm not normally this handsy, not normally so flustered I get hard in the back seat of a rideshare, but Hannah is addicting. I've gone too long without getting my fill, and I don't know if I want to savor her or devour her. "Are you wet, Hannah?"

"You'll have to wait to find out." Her smirk is coy. She knows exactly what she's doing to me. "Are we there yet?"

We are, thank fuck. We pull up to my building and I leave Hannah in the warm car, rounding the vehicle so I can open her door. Fishing out some bills from my wallet, I toss the money to the driver and thank them for the safe drive, trying not to look too desperate when I tug on her arm.

"Before we get started," I say, practically smashing the button for the elevator in the lobby, "we need to have a quick conversation."

Hannah presses into my side, her hand on my back. "About what?"

"Testing. Partners. I haven't, ah, been with anyone since we slept together."

"Wait." She files into the elevator, pulling me behind her. "You haven't?"

"No. Didn't seem fair to lead another woman on when I was picturing you the whole time," I mumble. "Even after I ran away from you. Even when I knew I didn't have a chance. I was still thinking about you."

"*Oh.*" Hannah touches my cheek. "I haven't slept with anyone either. I kissed a couple people, but nothing else. Not like what we had."

"Does it make me a terrible person to say I'm glad that woman stood you up?" I move my jacket away from her arms, bending to kiss her shoulder. "Because now I get to have you."

"I won't dock a point," she says. We reach my floor, and I'm proud of myself for not kicking open the door to my condo. "But only if you make me come."

"What else do you want, baby? The moon? I'll bring it out of the fucking sky for you."

Her grin is bold. She holds my neck, pulling my mouth to hers as we step inside. She kisses me carefully, a change of pace from how frantic I feel. She swipes her tongue against mine, moving with me as I lock the door behind us.

"My god," she whispers, turning to look around the foyer that leads to a large living room. "I'm going to need a tour later. This place is massive. Do you require a vial of blood for me to enter? Proof of my income?"

"Such a brat." I take her purse and my jacket, leaving them on the floor. Sweeping her off her feet, I carry her down the hall, flipping on a couple lights as we go. "And a pain in my ass."

"You like it." Hannah makes quick work of my tie, tossing it behind us. "Wow. A headboard? Curtains? An *armoire*? You have a grown up room, Brody Saunders."

"I'm a big boy, remember?" I set her on the mattress, kicking off my shoes and socks. My shirt comes next, the buttons pissing me off. That gets discarded too, and she reaches for me to join her on the bed. "Hi."

"Hi." She smiles, sitting up on her knees. "Will you tell me about your other tattoos?"

"The rose on the back of my hand is the flower from Olivia's birth month. Got it when she was born." I falter when Hannah kisses my chest, fingers fanning out over my stomach muscles. "Hockey sticks. That one is easy. Olivia's initials." I tap the small O in the middle of a heart above my wrist. "Many, many more. I could tell you all the stories, if you want."

"No. Let me see the flower again."

"This one?" My left hand slides up her neck, wrapping around her throat. "Look at you wearing my jewelry."

"I've always liked necklaces." Her eyes flutter closed. She sighs, the strap of her dress slipping down her arm. "The tighter the better."

My cock hardens at her admission. My skin burns hot, and I need her so badly everything fucking *aches*.

"Come here." I stand, helping her to her feet. When she

has her balance, I drop to the floor, running a hand up her leg. Over her knee, up her thigh, under her dress. I stop when I reach her underwear, twisting the lace. "I'm not going to be gentle with you, Hannah."

"Good." Her fingers thread through my hair. A tug. The scrape of her nails against my scalp. *Heaven.* "I don't want you to be."

"I'm going to mark you." I lift her calf, setting her foot on my shoulder. Her strappy shoes are difficult to take off, but I get there eventually, letting the heel hit the hardwood while I suck on the skin above her knee. "I might leave a few bruises behind." I move to the other foot, repeating the process. "I like to be in control."

"What if I like to be in control too?" She looks down at me, eyes heavy-lidded. "Who's going to win?"

You, I think pathetically.

Because I'm a helpless fucking wreck.

"We can take turns," I say. "Each share the victory."

"Would you crawl for me, Brody?" Hannah backs up, taking a seat on the edge of the bed. She spreads her legs, knees opening wide, and I whimper when she bunches her dress at her hips. I see light pink lace. A damp spot already. She pulls her underwear to the side, eyes on me. "What would you do to taste me again?"

"Anything." I lick my lips. My hands tremble as I unbuckle my belt and unzip my pants, the slacks falling to my ankles. "Anything you want."

Leaning back on an elbow, she grins. This smile is pure power. She knows she has the upper hand, and she's proud of it.

"Prove it."

TWENTY-THREE
HANNAH

I'VE ALWAYS THOUGHT a man looked infinitely better when he was on his knees, and Brody is proving my theory correct. Eyes locked on mine. Cock thick and hard in his briefs. His palms—those big palms—are flat on the rug, and he's crawling to me on all fours.

It's the hottest thing I've ever seen, and I'd never admit I'm holding back a moan while the muscles in his arm flex with every inch he moves. A lock of hair falls in his face but he ignores it, and I decide I want him like this a thousand fucking times.

His shoulders fill the space between my legs, his big and broad body bathed in shades of gold and yellow in the dimly lit room. Brody lifts his chin, bottom lip caught between his teeth while his hand flexes on the rug.

"Can I?" he rasps, attention moving from my face to my underwear. "Please?"

"You've been so patient, Brody."

I sit up and reach behind me, pulling down the zipper on my gown. I make a show of it, slipping the straps off my shoulders and letting the dress pool around my stomach. I lift my hips, leaving me in my new lingerie set—a light pink strapless top that pushes my breasts together and matching bottoms that show off my ass—and smile.

"You're a goddess." Up on his knees, Brody puts both hands on the inside of my thighs. "I'm not worthy. Not after what I did last time."

"Hey." I bend so I can kiss him. He tastes like alcohol and something sweet. The hint of forbidden. A trace of *I don't give a shit*. "The past is in the past. We talked about it, and now we're moving on. You want me, don't you?"

"I might die if I can't have you." He runs his knuckles along the front of my underwear before giving them a firm yank, ripping the delicate material. When I start to protest, he puts his mouth on my hip, sucking a small pink mark on my skin. "I'll buy you a new pair. A hundred pairs. I'll do whatever you ask, but only because I know how wet it gets you." He pushes a single finger inside me, and my back arches. A moan escapes me when he turns his wrist, getting deeper. "Yeah," he whispers, licking my belly. "Just like that."

The anticipation of waiting for this for the last two hours —the last two *years*—takes hold of me. I want him more now than I did that first night, and I didn't think that was possible.

"That feels so good," I tell him, letting him know how much I like what he's doing. My nails dig into his shoulder, trying to grasp hold. "The perfect spot."

"Mark me up, Hannah." A kiss to my stomach, but lower than before. He's so close to where I need him the most. Taunting me with a second finger and a warm breath at the apex of my thighs. "Give me a badge of honor to wear when I go back to practice on Monday."

It's satisfying to think about him walking around with a reminder of our night together in a place no one can see. It makes me urge his head down my body and place my feet on his shoulders. It's why I spread my legs wider. It's why I reach out, curl my fingers under his chin and say, "You look hungry. You should eat, Brody."

His dark eyes flash with desire, liquid heat I feel on every inch of my body. Bliss greets me, refuses to let go when he licks my pussy. Gaze on me. Focused beyond belief, his tongue presses against my clit, a satisfied noise rattling out of him when I moan his name.

"I've thought about this almost every night." Brody bites my thigh, soothing over the sting with a trail of kisses. "The sounds you make." A third finger, and color sparks behind my eyes. My gasp is lodged somewhere in my throat, unable to make any noise because he's finding a rhythm. Alternating the press of his tongue with the slick glide of his fingers, I know the reason I haven't wanted to hook up with anyone else is because nothing, *no one*, would ever be better than him. "The taste of your cum on my tongue. How tight you are, but how perfectly we fit together."

My pleasure is building. My body is yielding to him, greedy for every single thing he gives me. Another kiss. A sharper bite. A lick that tells me he's holding back, drawing this out for as long as he can, and I don't know if I hate him or love him.

My legs press against his head. I sigh, touching him wherever I can reach. Brody pulls his fingers out of me and puts both hands under my thighs, yanking me all the way to the edge of the bed. My ass hangs over the mattress. I'm close to falling, but he doesn't let me. He's still there. Still devouring me, and when he circles my clit with his tongue, I almost jolt off the bed.

"Stop moving," he growls, lifting an arm over my stomach to hold me still with a heavy weight. The awareness of being trapped is heady, and his low chuckle makes me smile. "You're so fucking needy."

"For you. I want you inside me, Brody. I want you to fuck me."

"Not until you come." A long, slow lick that has me questioning how much longer I can hold on. He doesn't give in to my plea. "You know I make it so good for you, Hannah."

So fucking good.

He starts again, each press of his fingers bringing me closer to the precipice of ecstasy. He's like a god on his knees, a willing worshipper of my body and my undoing. Wet fingers —four now—and hurried kisses. My body is his canvas and he doesn't stop, not until I finally, *finally* feel that satisfaction within reach.

It only makes Brody work harder. He grunts, a bead of sweat rolling from his forehead to his cheek. He whispers silly things, telling me how beautiful I am, how I was made for him, how much he missed having me like this, and when he drags his fingers from my clit, across my entrance, and all the way to my ass, I lose it.

I explode, completely undone. He doesn't offer me a break, stealing a second orgasm from me before I can recover from the first. His forehead rests against my thigh, shoulders heaving as he holds up his hand. Languid movements. Deep breaths, he traces my lips with his wet fingers.

"Open up and suck," he says, and my mouth parts. I taste myself on his finger, licking from tip to knuckle. His groan could shake the walls, and his free hand rests on my knee as I suck his finger clean. "*Fuck.* Look at you."

"I'm on cloud nine." My vision is hazy. Everything around me looks dreamlike, fuzzy outlines of colors and shapes. "You deserve a gold star, Coach."

Brody kisses my shin. "The highest honor."

"Will you fuck me now? You already know how needy I am."

"Not yet." His thumb digs into my calf, coaxing out another moan from me. "I need a minute."

"A minute?" I bring my feet away from his shoulders, my muscles objecting. I wince when I sit upright, everything heavy and sated. "Are you okay?"

"Finished in my fucking briefs," he says, and my eyes snap to the front of his gray underwear. I see the wet circle on the cotton, the obvious effect I've had on him, and he covers my mouth with his hand. "No jokes. No calling me old. I'm fully capable of fucking you, and I'm going to."

"Brody Saunders. The guy who likes to eat women out." I smile against his palm. "I can't tell you how hot that is."

"Is it?" He grimaces when he stands, stretching out his legs. "That's the first time it's ever happened to me."

"Yeah. It makes me feel…" A quiet laugh. "Wanted, I guess."

"Oh, Hannah." He cups my cheek, thumb tracing the curve of my jaw. "I want you in so many ways."

"Tell me about them." I reach behind my back, unclasping my bra so my breasts spill free. "Where? When? How often?"

"If I tell you the answers are everywhere, every second, and every day, will it go to your head?" Brody motions for me to scoot back on the bed and I do, relaxing against the sheets while my hair scatters across his pillows. He holds himself above me, my nipple caught between his thumb and pointer finger with a rough pinch. "Probably."

"Sounds like we're going to have to do this again, then. Would more than one time hooking up be okay with you?" I ask.

"You made me come, and you didn't even touch me." His laugh is self-deprecating. Fucking cute as hell. "You know I'd be more than okay with seeing you again."

"Okay." I wet my lips. Guess we're talking about this now. "We're two adults who like to spend time together. Who are good in bed together. Calling it friends with benefits—even though we *are* friends who *are* indulging in benefits—feels too—"

"Casual?" Brody finishes for me, and I nod. "But labeling it as a relationship seems—"

"Too serious, too soon?" I say, and it's his turn to nod.

"I haven't dated anyone in a very long time. With Liv and coaching, my attention is all over the place. But I acknowledge that I like you, Hannah. That I want to keep spending time with you, even if we don't have a way to define it yet."

"Are we exclusive?" I ask. I'm afraid I'm moving the conversation along too quickly, but then I remember what Brody has said to me in the past: he doesn't bullshit anyone. He's going to tell you exactly what's on his mind, and if he didn't want to figure this out right now, he'd shut it down. "Or also sleeping with other people?"

"I'd like for us to be exclusive. I'm thirty-nine, Hannah. I'm too old for hookup culture." He kisses me, and I let myself daydream about what this would be like every night. I'd wait up for him to get home from a road trip. Maybe I'd surprise him in his hotel room. "But I know that isn't only up to me to decide."

"Exclusive it is. I've never been a fan of sharing my favorite things." I touch his tattoo, the one he got for me, and my heart surges in my chest. "And you're becoming one of my favorite things, Brody."

"People tell me I need to have more fun. What do you think?" Brody pins my arms above my head, and I gasp. He rocks his hips, the head of his cock pressing against my entrance through his briefs. "I asked you a question, Hannah," he whispers in my ear, and *oh*. That possessive, raw scratch of his voice electrifies me. "You should answer it."

"Fun is good. We'll have plenty of fun," I blurt, squirming beneath him. "Do you want me to sign on a dotted line or something?"

"No." His laugh is a caress. "Just spread your legs, sweetheart, so I can feel your tight cunt."

TWENTY-FOUR
HANNAH

THE WEIGHT of the mattress shifts when Brody moves away from me. I turn my head, watching him take off his briefs and toss them in the corner. He rubs his thighs and walks to his dresser, glorious ass on display.

"Do you still work out?" I ask, watching his lean muscles stretch and shift. "Your body is beautiful."

"Minus the scars all over my knee."

"Those are beautiful too."

"I do work out." He looks at me over his shoulder, a box of condoms in his hand. "I skate with the team at practice. I'll also run drills with them and hit the weight room. Some of the guys from my draft class are still in the league. They're slower than they were when we were teenagers, obviously, but I'm not letting a dude sitting on the fourth line for a shitty team be in better shape than me."

"Liv told me you were competitive. That checks out." I laugh. "You lift me pretty easily, and I'm not light."

"Hush, Hannah. I squat double your body weight before I start my workout." Brody brings the box to the bedside table, taking out a packet. "Want to sit on my face so I can prove it to you?"

"I do." I run my nails down the front of his chest when he climbs back on the mattress. I look at him, every angle, every dip of his body something beyond my wildest dreams. "But I want you to open that wrapper and take care of me more."

"One more minute." Brody grips his cock, hand wrapped around his shaft and giving himself a long stroke. "I'm almost ready."

"Want me to talk about my childhood to pass the time?"

"No." He smiles. Messy hair, lipstick stains on his neck. For as meticulous a man as he is, right now he looks thoroughly wrecked. "Just let me look at you."

I do let him look at me, but not without trying to rile him up while he does it. My palms trail down my neck, across my chest. I push my breasts together and his moan is strangled, fracturing right at the edges. His pupils go wide when I dip my hands lower between my legs, making easy circles on my clit.

"Do you like what you see, Brody?" I whisper.

The heat in the room swells around us. The tension grows when he rips the condom wrapper open with his teeth. He rolls it down his length and lifts my leg, pinning it to his hip.

"Very much." The bob of his head. Anguish in his eyes because he doesn't know where to look. "You are so beautiful, Hannah."

My body is an inferno, set ablaze by the soft drift of his fingers to my cheek. He holds my neck gently, a silent question behind the slight pressure against my windpipe. I nod and he rocks forward, the tip of his cock pushing inside me.

Pain comes first, the flash of uncomfortableness nudging its way from the stretch. Brody chokes out a groan but doesn't move, waiting for me to get used to the sensation. I grip his bicep, trying to remember to breathe.

"Big," I manage to get out. "I forgot how big you are."

"You're going to feel me everywhere." He rocks forward another inch, the pain giving way to delight. "Is this okay?"

"Yes." My laugh splinters with the quick move of his hips, his cock halfway buried inside me. "I'm in heaven."

"Tight. Wet. Perfect pussy." His thumb moves down my neck, pressing at the base of my throat. "Deep breath, baby."

Baby.

It's far too soft a word for how he's treating me right now, burying himself all the way to the hilt as we moan in unison. Brody's hands fall to my legs, bringing my knees to my chest. He holds me in place, fucking me with quick snaps of his hips. The whole bed shakes. The headboard hits the wall, and I grab his wrists, trying to stabilize myself.

"*Fuck,*" I slur. I feel drunk. Absolutely delirious. "I want more."

"More?" His laugh is wild. "More might kill me. But I told you I'd give you anything you want." With a move that happens so fast I'm still trying to process the logistics, he switches our positions. Brody lies with his back on the bed and holds me above his shaft, handing over control. "Take what you need, Hannah. Use me. Fucking *wreck* me."

I lean forward, my hands near the pillows. I lower myself, just enough to only take the head of his cock before pulling off of him. "Ask nicely," I say, and he growls.

"Please." Brody grips my hips so tight he's going to leave bruises in the shape of his fingerprints behind. "Please fuck me."

"Such a good boy." I smile and sink back on him, rolling my hips as I do. "Such a good big boy."

The room blurs. Time stands still but also speeds up. It's impossible to figure out where I stop and where Brody begins. Our hands roam. We kiss each other mercilessly, like we're seeing who can get the other to the finish line first. When Brody slips out of me, condom wet from my arousal, he shifts me onto my side. When I ask to change our position again, he puts me on my hands and knees, ass in the air while he fucks me from behind.

It's messy and loud, but soon his movements turn ragged. So does his breathing, and he wraps a fistful of my hair around his wrist and tugs.

"Going to come," he mumbles, the words disjointed. "Did you—"

"No. But I want you to finish. We can take care of me later."

If it's a blow to his ego, Brody doesn't show it. He grunts, snapping his hips one more time. His cock throbs inside me, filling the condom, and I gasp when he touches my clit again. When he makes quick circles, drawing an orgasm out of me, and I fall apart. It's unexpected, but I ride the high of the euphoria, savoring the way his cock hits the spot I can rarely reach with any of my toys.

Labored breathing fills the quiet in the room, and Brody pulls out of me. He takes off the condom, ties it up, and disposes of it in the trash. I close my eyes, sighing as he brings me to his side and runs his fingers through my hair.

"Hi," I whisper. I touch his long eyelashes, smiling at the way he relaxes into me. "Are you alive?"

"I haven't come like that since my twenties," he pants. "And twice in one night? Jesus, help me."

"He'll help you repent for your sins, that's for sure. We defiled your bed." I giggle when he kisses my neck, the scruff of his beard rough against my skin. "I think spending time with me is going to be great for your cardiovascular health."

"Great. I'll become invincible." His arms wrap around my waist. "Stay the night?"

"If you think I'm dragging my ass out of this warm, comfy bed and into the cold, you've lost your mind. Besides. I still need to give you your Christmas present."

"Christmas present? You didn't need to get me anything."

"Don't get your hopes up. It's small. Like, really small. And I have something for Liv too. They're in my purse in the foyer."

"I'll grab it for you." Brody untangles our limbs. "Do you want some water? Something to eat?"

"Water would be great." I tuck the sheets under my arms, leaning against the headboard. "And maybe a snack later."

"Be back in a second," he says, and when he disappears down the hall, I glance around his room.

Everything is clean, organized. A phone charger plugged into the wall and a laptop on a long desk. The rich mahogany of the armoire and light blue paint on the walls. There's a photo of him and Liv when they're both younger, and I touch the glass frame and their smiling faces.

"I'm surprised you're not snooping." Brody reappears, leaning against the door frame. He's naked, one ankle crossed over the other, and he lifts my purse in the air. He's holding a glass of water in his other hand. "I come bearing gifts."

"I'll snoop in the morning when you give me the full tour. And, again, what is in the bag is small. Silly, really, but I saw them and thought of you two."

"I have something for you too." He hands over my bag and walks to his desk, opening one of the small drawers. "I didn't have a chance to wrap it."

"For *me*? I'm so excited." I fold my legs under my butt and rifle through my purse, finding the two gift bags I put together before I left my apartment. "Here you go."

"You first." Brody motions for me to open my hand. "Hold out your palm, please."

"Please don't tell me it's an animal. I will scream if a spider touches me."

"No animals. And don't put that idea in Liv's head. She's begging me for a cat, and I know if we go down to the shelter, we're going to come home with a kitten." He sits next to me and puts a small object in my hold. "There you go."

"Wait." I blink, looking down at the two metal keychains in my hand. My thumb runs along the grooved edges of the design. "These are for me?"

"You mentioned you like to collect them. I saw a store at the mall and thought I'd get you a couple. I know they're not from France or Beijing or wherever else you might've competed, but I thought maybe you could start a new collection with keychains you find when you're just... living your life. Having a good day. Skating doesn't have to be involved."

"Brody." I don't know if I want to smile or cry. They're perfectly hysterical, unique in a special way because I understand the joke. "They're perfect."

"Do you like them?"

"I love them." I clutch them tight to my chest, a laugh bubbling out of me. "They're going on my wall."

"You have a whole wall dedicated to keychains? Please tell me I can see it one of these days," Brody says.

"Only if you don't make fun of me," I warn.

"I'd never make fun of something that makes you happy."

The moment feels too heavy, too important for something so small, so I shove the gift bags his way. I watch him pluck the festive paper from the bag, nervous when he pulls out the gift.

"It's a whistle," I say. "I thought you could use it at practice or during one of our sessions. Yours looked old and rusty, but now I'm realizing coaches probably have emotional attachment to their whistles, so—"

Brody cuts me off with a kiss. "I have been needing a new whistle for a very long time. Thank you, Hannah."

"You're welcome." I smile when he rests his forehead against mine. "I'll let you give Liv her present. It's new laces for her skates. Pink, because she told me that's her favorite color."

"She's going to be ecstatic. Thanks for thinking of her too." He moves the gifts out of the way, and I set the keychains down, not wanting to scratch them. "How do you feel about pancakes?"

"In general? I'm a fan."

"And for breakfast in the morning?"

I have to hide my smile in his bicep. "Sounds perfect."

Brody drags me to the shower and cleans me up. After, he wraps me in a big, fluffy towel before giving me one of his old Boston College shirts with his name on the back. I curl up in his arms, and right before I drift off to sleep, I feel him press a kiss to my cheek.

TWENTY-FIVE
BRODY

H.E.

Merry Christmas, Brody!!

ME

Merry Christmas, Hannah.

H.E.

How is the movie marathon with Liv going?

ME

Great. We're watching Die Hard.

H.E.

Please tell me you're joking.

ME

One will never know.

She loved the laces, by the way. There were tears. And screams. And photos.

H.E.

Aw! Give her a hug for me! I'm glad they made her happy!

ME

How's Florida?

H.E.

Warm. I might never come back to DC. I'm heading to the basketball game now. I'll text you later?

ME

Sounds good. Have a good day, Hannah.

H.E.

You too, Brody.

H.E.

I miss the sun not setting at 4 in the afternoon.

These gray skies are so sad.

ME

How was your flight back?

H.E.

Besides listening to my brother snore for two hours? It was great.

The flight attendant gave me four bags of pretzels, and this must be what it feels like to be God's favorite.

ME

I could never get into the pretzel craze. Now popcorn? I can eat a bucket in minutes.

H.E.

Oooh, what about popcorn with M&Ms mixed in? That's a delicious combo.

ME

I've never tried that. Might need to give it a whirl and see for myself.

H.E.

I'm picturing you whirling and I'm giggling.

ME

Glad I made you smile.

See you bright and early on the ice.

We're doing swizzles all morning.

H.E.

I can't wait!

H.E.

Happy New Year's Eve! What exciting plans do you have today?

ME

Do you really think I have exciting plans?

H.E.

Okay, true. You're probably going to spend your night staring at the wall. Right?

ME

I hate that I'm so predictable.

What are you up to?

H.E.

Nothing at all. Grant is going out with some of the guys. My best friend is out of town. It'll probably be an uneventful night on the couch.

ME

Feel like taking an adventure?

H.E.

Do I get to take my clothes off and sit on your face?

ME

Eventually, yes. But not at first.

We'll pick you up at three.

H.E.

We? Who is we?

ME

You might want to bring a helmet.

"DAD. It's very distracting when you hold the 'oh shit' handle before I shift out of park," Liv says from the driver's seat of my Cadillac. "Can you chill, please? For like, thirty minutes."

"She's right," Hannah pipes up from the back seat. "We need a calm environment. You look like you want to rip that handle off, and that gives the tone of nervous energy right off the bat."

"I don't appreciate being ganged up on," I grumble, slowly relaxing my grip. I look down at my seat belt, checking to make sure it's tight, and take a deep breath. "This is serious shit, everyone."

"We're in an open parking lot with no other cars. What do you think is going to happen?" Hannah asks, and when her eyes meet mine in the mirror, it's easy to tell she's trying not to laugh. It makes my lips twitch. "A meteor is going to crash into earth and we're all going to die?"

"Yes," I answer. "Do you not see the threats all around us?"

"Hang on." She makes a show of leaning over the center console and looking out the dashboard. "Oh, *no*. Liv! Look out! There's a crushed water bottle sixty yards away!"

"There's also hot dog wrapper up ahead." Liv giggles and turns on the radio, starting to blast a pop song before I reach for the dials and lower the volume. "Could be dangerous."

"You can't even get your permit yet. Why are we rushing to get you behind the wheel?" I put a hand over my chest, positive I'm having heart palpitations. "And why is it so hot in here?"

"I think your father is panicking, Liv." Hannah reaches for the dials on the dashboard. She switches from heat to air conditioning, and I heave a sigh of relief at the cool blast of air. "Brody? May I speak to you outside?"

"Sure. Yeah. Outside." I open my door and unbuckle my seat belt, almost rolling to the asphalt. My knees shake when I stand, and I lean against the car when I shut the door behind me. "What's up?"

"Are you okay?" Hannah asks. "You seem jumpy."

"Maybe that's because my only daughter wants to learn how to drive. That means tomorrow, she's going off to college." I press the heels of my palms into my eyes. "And then getting married and having her own kids."

"I see what's going on here."

"What's going on here is time is moving too fast. She just learned to walk, and now she's driving? Where did the last—"

"Brody." Hannah puts her fingers around my wrist, guiding my hands away from my face. "Take a breath."

"I was fine this morning." A deep inhale, a long exhale. "When she asked if I would teach her to drive, I thought this would be easy. But now we're here, and I'm—"

"A very good father," she says gently, letting go of my wrists. Somewhere, behind my panic and anxiety, I appreciate her discretion with PDA around Liv. That's a conversation I'm *really* not sure how to have. "Liv is so lucky she has someone who cares about her and her safety so much. I'm not a parent. I'm not going to pretend to understand anything parent-related or tell you how to act, because that's your domain, but as a former fourteen-year-old girl, I'm here to tell you that you can't stop time."

"You'd think with all my money I'd be able to find a way," I tell her, and she smiles.

"It would be nice, wouldn't it? I think I'm going to call an Uber and head home. This feels like an important moment for you all, and I don't want to overstep." Hannah pats my chest. "Text me later? We could—"

"Will you stay? I could use some moral support. Clearly, I'm not doing that great." I huff out a laugh and shove my hands in my pockets. "And it's nice to have someone call me out when I'm acting irrationally."

"I never said anything about being irrational! Just that—"

"I know. I'm giving you a hard time." It's cold as hell out here, but I smile. "I mean that in the sense of you're not oblig-ated to handle the absurdity that comes with being a parent, but I'm glad you're letting me know when I'm overreacting."

"Feels like I'm invested now." Hannah bites her lip. "I'll stay with you. But only because I can't wait to see how much you panic when she gets up to ten miles an hour."

"Brat," I tell her. "If you're not doing anything tonight, Liv is going to Kali's. I'll probably be asleep by ten, but if you want to come by and enjoy some early festivities before the ball drops, my door is open."

"Yeah?" She steps closer. "What kind of festivities?"

"Pineapple pizza. Whiskey. Three fingers," I murmur, and her cheeks turn bright red. "Maybe four."

"Can't think of a better way to ring in the new year than with good dick and good food." Hannah opens the back door, dropping into the leather seat. "Count me in, Brody."

I don't let myself look too excited when I sit next to Liv again. "Okay, kid. Go from park to drive, and make sure you keep your foot on the brake when you shift gears."

"What was it like when you learned to drive?" Liv raises her seat up and checks the mirrors before following my instructions. "Did you have to use a horse and buggy?"

"Ouch." I groan and shake my head. "My own daughter is attacking me."

"I'm sure you had those crank windows, right?" Hannah asks, adding fuel to the fire. "You'd have to manually roll the windows down, Liv. And if it started to rain, you'd have to roll them right back up."

"I was born in this century. Let's go to that light post at the other end of the parking lot, Livvy. If you could keep your speed under five miles an hour, that would be great."

"Floor it, Liv," Hannah says, and my daughter giggles.

"This is good practice. I have someone trying to peer pressure me and someone who is being a back seat driver from the front seat." Her hands stay at ten and two on the wheel, and we lurch toward our checkpoint. "Wait. If I want to stop do I just—"

"Jesus fucking Christ." I fly forward when she slams on the brakes, my seat belt locking in place. "Congratulations, kid. You found the brakes."

"I should probably buckle up. We've got a speed demon out here." Hannah bursts out laughing when Liv smashes the accelerator and I fly back against the seat. "I wish I had this on camera."

"Gentle, Liv. And go slow, please. Wait. Why are you turning? The light is up ahead, not to the left."

"Just getting a feel for the wheel," Liv says, but it's anything but innocent. "I bet this car can go fast, can't it? What kind of car does your brother have, Hannah?"

"A Range Rover. I drive a Hyundai, but that's because anything more advanced confuses the hell out of me. Like, this thing has heated *and* cooling seats? You're fancy as hell, Saunders."

"I want my ass to be warm in the winter and cool in the summer." I glance at Liv, who looks as carefree as can be. "Two hands on the wheel, please."

"This is so easy. Uh oh, Dad. Look out. There's a soda can up ahead. How should I avoid it?"

"Smart-ass. Everyone in this car is a smart-ass." I fold my arms over my chest, miming that I'm keeping my mouth closed. "You're on your own, kid."

And, of fucking course, the less I talk, the better Liv does. She uses her blinker and completes a full circle turn. She puts the car in reverse, neutral, then back to drive, taking her time to accelerate through the gear shifts. I start to breathe easier, folding my hands in my lap instead of trying to secretly reach for the door handle in case I need to make an escape.

"This was *so* worth skipping one of our skating lessons, Hannah." Liv rolls to a stop and puts the car in park, clapping loudly. "What do you think, Dad? Did I pass?"

"Not hitting that pigeon earned you extra points," I say. "For day one, you did well."

"A miracle, because I've been listening to you yell about shitty drivers for *years*." Liv smiles and drums her fingers on the center console. "Can I drive home?"

"And break the law under my nose? No. You can sit in the back seat so Hannah can stretch her legs in the front."

"Oh, don't worry about me. It's like a movie theater back here." Hannah puts her hands on the armrests, leaning between us. "Are you excited to spend New Year's Eve with your mom, Liv?"

"Yeah! We're doing a spa night with manis and pedis and watching romcoms. I'm going to do my nails pink to match my new skating laces." Liv unbuckles her seat belt and retracts the seat from the steering wheel. "Are you going to any parties, Hannah?"

"No parties for me. It's funny. When I was your age, I couldn't *wait* to grow up so I could do all this fun stuff like stay up past the ball drop and drink champagne in a sparkly dress. Now that I'm older, I'm happy with being on the couch and making a list of all the things I want to work on in the new year." Hannah smiles, and I listen to every word. "Do you want to know what my top two focuses are?"

"*Yes.*" Liv spins to look at her, eyes wide. "I bet they're good."

"I want to prioritize my patience. Your dad has been so kind to spend time with me on the ice, and every day we're out there together, I see myself making improvements. But I also know there is joy in going slow, and I'm having so much fun doing drills I would've written off six months ago."

"That's a really good one. What's your other focus?" Liv asks, and I see the spark of wonder in her eye. I can tell how much she looks up to Hannah, how much she values her opinion, and it says so much about her character that she's here, with us, when she could be anywhere else.

"I want to say yes more. To things that scare me—like the competition I officially entered in March." Pride practically bursts from her with the admission, and Liv squeals. "To things I wouldn't normally try—like coaching you, Liv. Think of all the fun I would have missed out on if I didn't give this a shot." Hannah gives her a high-five, and the strangest sensation settles over me as I watch her interact with my daughter. Peace, almost, and knowing Liv is in the best fucking hands. "I can't wait to see where that takes me."

"I'm going to focus on not comparing myself to other people," Liv announces. "A girl who is younger than me already nailed her double Axel? That's fine. Mine will happen when it's meant to happen. My friend at school has a boyfriend and I don't? No big deal. Boys my age are *gross.*"

"That's my girl," Hannah says. "Brody? What are you going to focus on in the new year?"

I stall before I answer. I could go the coaching route: focusing on getting my guys to play better. More attention to detail when it comes to what's happening on the ice. But these two are sharing important things with me. It doesn't seem fair to take the easy road.

"My daughter lovingly tells me I need to lighten up," I say, and Liv rolls her eyes. "I think I'd like to focus on having more fun." My gaze meets Hannah's in the mirror. She's watching me, listening to me, and it makes me feel like a million bucks. "With people who know how to have a good time."

"That's a good focus," Hannah answers. "Any idea how you're going to do that?"

My smile is easy, slow. "I have a few ideas."

LATER THAT NIGHT, after I drop Liv off at Kali's, there's a knock on my door. I open it to find Hannah in a sparkly silver dress, holding a bottle of champagne.

"After our conversation with Liv earlier this afternoon, I felt like mixing it up this year and going for the best of both worlds: a sparkly dress while I'm sitting on the couch because the thought of being at a crowded bar sounds absolutely horrible." She grins. "Want to join me?"

"I'm a terrible father." I yank her inside and close the door, pressing my lips to hers. She tastes like sugar, and she laughs against my mouth when I take off her jacket. "I was excited for Liv to spend the night at her mom's so I could see you."

"I'm excited to see you too, but I had fun with you and Liv today." Hannah puts a hand on my shoulder so she can take off her shoes. "She's a good kid."

"The best." We walk down the hall to the living room where I have the electric fireplace going. "Want to open the champagne?"

"Honestly? It was kind of for show. I'll take a glass if you're having one though."

"It's the year of saying yes, right?" I lead us to the kitchen and open the cabinet, pulling down two cups. "This is the fanciest thing I have."

"It'll get the job done." Hannah hands over the bottle. "I've actually never opened one of these before, so I'm going to defer to you."

"I've opened plenty in the locker room after a championship win." I walk her through the steps, popping the cork and pouring the alcohol into our glasses. "Cheers, Hannah."

"Cheers." She smiles and bumps her cup against mine, taking a sip. "So. What time are you aiming to be in bed by? Ten, right?"

"I could be persuaded to stay up later." I loop an arm around her waist, pulling her to me. Did you have something in mind that would pass the time?"

"Scrabble?" Hannah teases, and I laugh. "Gosh. I like that sound."

"What?"

"You. Laughing." Her fingers press into my cheek with a sigh. "It's funny. Grant tells me about the guy at practice who rarely smiles and barks out orders, but I almost don't believe he exists. You're not that guy around me."

"Can't explain it. There are expectations that come with coaching, yeah, but when I'm with you…" I shrug, sipping my champagne. "I don't feel any of that. I feel…" How is it that she makes finishing a sentence almost impossible? "Different, I guess."

Hannah hops on the kitchen counter and swings her legs back and forth. "Is it a good different?"

"Yeah. It is."

"Good." Her whole face lights up when she says it, and her happiness hits me square in the chest. She's so fucking pretty, and out of every option she could've picked tonight, she chose me. How lucky am I? "I'm glad."

"You officially signed up for that competition in March?" I ask, trying to get rid of the pressure sitting on my chest. It's persistent, heavy the longer I look at her. "How are you feeling?"

"Terrified, but also grateful. Working with you has meant so much to me, and I'm ready to see how our training has paid off." Her foot nudges my thigh. "I'm really proud of myself, and I'm not sure that would be possible without you."

"Hannah." I set my drink down and nudge my way between her legs, putting my hands on her knees. "You would've gotten here without me. I've only given you the drills. You're the one executing them. You're the one showing up. And while I hope this is the cure for your burnout because you're so fucking beautiful on the ice, I also know I'm going to be so proud of you no matter how your story ends."

She puts a hand on my shoulder, hope in her eyes. "Really?"

"Yeah." I step closer, cupping her cheek. "This year is going to be your year, Ice Queen, and I can't wait to watch you shine."

TWENTY-SIX

HANNAH

I SETTLE on my couch with a glass of wine and my phone when a message from Brody pops up on my screen. My grin is undeniable at the sight of his name, and I don't waste any time seeing what he has to say.

GC

Hi, Ice Queen.

ME

Hi, BB. How was the flight to Dallas?

GC

Long. The boys are always amped up this time of year because we're in the back half of the season. Games have more significance. The standings for the playoffs are starting to take shape. We're playing well, and it makes for a very loud travel day.

Tell me about your day.

ME

I went to the gym this morning then did some solo skating. Liv and I had a great lesson mapping out her choreography for the Potomac Memorial. I was going to grab dinner with Tierney, but I'm so tired. I'm taking it easy tonight.

GC

Best friend Tierney, right?

ME

That's her!

What are you up to? Heading to a strip club? Finding some barbecue? Exploring all the fun Dallas has to offer?

GC

None of the above. I'm heading to my hotel room.

ME

It's 8 p.m.

GC

Yup, it is. The team dinner was chaos, as usual. Sitting in the peace and quiet is going to be the highlight of my day.

ME

If you want to FaceTime when you get there, I'll be around.

My phone rings five seconds later and I laugh, drawing my legs to my chest to answer the video call.

"Hi," I say, resting my chin on my knees. "You look tired."

"I can't wait to shower and pass out." He yawns and sits in a chair, a big window behind him. "But I wanted to see you first."

"Here I am. What did you all do for dinner?"

"We had Italian delivered to the hotel. There was a fight over garlic bread, and Ethan spilled marinara sauce all over the carpet in the meeting room." Brody sighs, rubbing his forehead. "Pretty tame night, actually."

"I'd fight someone for garlic bread too." I shift on the cushions and set my wine down. "Don't let me keep you too long."

"I lied when I said sitting in peace and quiet was the highlight of my day. This is." Brody leans back, stifling another yawn. "Can I see your keychain collection?"

"Damn, Saunders. Buy me dinner first." I smile and pop to my feet, walking down the hall. "It's in the guest room, so we're taking a field trip."

"I don't know what I would collect if I did collect things. Coasters from bars? Magnets?" He shrugs. "Guess the possibilities are endless."

"Stamps. Antique plates." I turn on a light and switch the camera so he can see the wall in front of me. Dozens and dozens of keychains sit on small pegs, various shapes and colors and sizes. "Ta-da!"

"Look at all of them. Get closer so I can see what they say. What's that one on the left?"

"It's from Las Vegas." I zoom in, laughing at the one he picked. "It says 'don't hate me because I'm a little cooler.' And it's written on a tiny cooler. Get it?"

"Oh, I get it. Fascinating," Brody murmurs, genuinely interested. "Are those the ones I got you?"

"Yup. Front and center." I tap the recent additions and smile before flipping the camera back so he sees me. "They fit in well with the rest of the group."

"Looks great. Thanks for showing me." His eyes flick from my face to my shirt. "Hang on. That shirt looks familiar."

"This one?" I hold up my phone to show off the shirt I

stole from him, *BC HOCKEY* written across the front. "You didn't think I was going to give it back to you, did you?"

"It looks better on you anyway."

"And it's comfortable." I pad back to the living room, dropping on the couch. "The back is the best part, in my opinion."

Brody's gaze flares. "My last name." He leans forward, elbows on his knees and a hand rubbing his jaw. "Can I see?"

"Of course you can." I give him a coy smile and lean my phone against a stack of books. Standing, I move my hair away from my neck and turn so he can see his name stretched across my shoulders. His old number, nineteen, sits right in the center of my spine, and I swear a growl leaves his end of the line. "What do you think?"

"Lift it up." His voice drops low, a commanding lilt behind the ask. The shirt is so big on me it hangs down to my knees, and deciding not to wear pants was the smartest decision of the day. I glance over my shoulder, watching him as I pull the hem of the soft material up the curve of my ass. Brody brings his fist to his mouth, biting his knuckles while his eyes never leave the screen. "*Fuck*, Hannah."

"See something you like?"

"Saunders looks good on you."

"It does, doesn't it?" I bite my bottom lip and let go of the shirt, covering my backside. Brody groans and scrubs a hand over his face. "Would you like it better if it was off? Or should I leave it on?"

"*Hannah.*" A plea. A prayer. Exquisite music to my ears.

"I asked you a question, Brody." I grab the shirt again, bringing it halfway up my stomach. I keep going, pulling it over my head, and I look at him again. A whimper leaves him when he sees my boy short underwear and nothing else. "You should answer," I say, tossing his words from the night of the gala back to him.

"You're going to kill me. Off. Off is definitely better. Turn around again. Let me see the rest of you."

"So demanding." I sink back on the couch and put my feet on the edge of the table with a smirk. "If I'm going to show you mine, it's only fair that you show me yours."

"Is that what you want? To watch me jerk off?"

"I want you to be next to me right now, but since that's not possible, I'll take the next best thing."

Brody stands and moves to the bed in his room. He leans his phone on something out of frame and kicks off his shoes. He drags his sweatpants down his thighs, showing off his cock straining in his briefs when he sits back down, shoving a hand in his underwear.

"Better?" he asks, and I smile.

"Perfect."

I relax into the cushions, my hands roaming over my chest.

This is my first time having phone sex. Knowing someone from his team could be on the other side of his wall listening is exhilarating. The secrecy is heightened by Brody getting rid of his briefs and dragging his thumb over the head of his cock. Pre-cum slicks his fingers, and he holds them up to the camera.

"This could be yours," he says. "It *is* yours."

"Not tonight it isn't." I angle my phone so he can see my whole body. "But I wish it was."

"I swear this isn't what I had in mind when I called you." He strokes his length up and down, blowing out a breath. "I wanted to hear about your day. I wanted to see your cute face. I like you for reasons outside of sex, Hannah. I swear."

I know he does.

He sends me texts throughout the day. Pops in at the end of Liv's lesson and lingers with me at my car when we finish one of our skating sessions in the morning. His affection when we're in a public place is always subtle—the hook of his pinky in mine when he passes by. The graze of his palm. A thumb bushing against the small of my back. It's just enough to know he's there, to know he's thinking about me, and I have *such* a crush on him.

When we're alone, it's amplified. Rough kisses. Teeth scraping along my hip and a burn on the inside of my thighs from his beard. Tangled limbs while we fall asleep wrapped around each other on the nights he doesn't have Liv or a game, and I find myself wondering how the hell something can be so good, so soon.

"I can grab a blanket," I suggest. "If that would—"

"Two fingers in your cunt. And let me watch while you fuck yourself," he says, and I've never been so turned on.

The position is awkward after I take my underwear off. I have to bend my leg in a way that gives me a cramp. I overthink briefly, wondering how the lighting looks and if my hair is a mess, but Brody doesn't care. He stares at me, watching my every move.

"Okay, Daddy," I whisper, delighted when his palm slips on his cock. When he fists the sheets with his other hand. "It feels so good. But not as good as it would be if you were here."

"Are you tight? How wet are you? Can you scoot to the edge of the couch, baby, so I can really see you?"

I adjust my position and bring the camera closer. It's intimate, the most exposed I've ever been, but I feel so powerful.

"So wet. I've been thinking about you all night, Brody." I pull out my fingers and show them off to the camera. He pumps his shaft harder, a determined spark in his eye as he follows the path of my hand. "I can't believe I have to go a week without seeing you in person."

"I'm about to buy you a plane ticket and fly you to Dallas tonight so I can wake up with you in my bed. So I can fuck you and bring you breakfast and clean you up before I make a mess of you again." Sweat rolls down his chest. There's restraint in his movements. A softness to his exhale. "I wish I could be louder, but I don't know who is in the room next to me."

"Just watch." I rub my thumbs over my nipples, pushing my breasts together. His fist moves faster. His gaze is as dark as night, and understanding dawns. "You like when I do that."

"I want to fuck you there." Brody pulls his hand away, spitting in the center of his palm. "I always thought I was an ass guy, but I'm a big fan of your tits."

"Next time." I sigh, parting my thighs wider. I touch my clit, sliding two fingers back inside me. My toes curl, pleasure building at the base of my spine. "I should've grabbed my toy."

"You have toys? What do you like to use?"

"I have different ones I use when I'm with a woman and when I'm by myself. When I'm alone, I have a favorite vibrator. Different speeds, different settings. It always makes me come."

"And when you're with a man?"

"They've never been a fan. Called them a hindrance." My back arches. "It's not my fault men don't know how to get the job done."

"Can I tell you something?" Brody's hair is messy. His eyes are turning glassy, lust behind each blink. "I've never been with a woman so open about her sexuality. And it's hot. Not because I'm picturing you with another woman or anything like that, but because you know exactly what you want, and you get it."

"Do you see what you do to me, Brody?" My fingers fall away from between my legs. I use my thumbs to spread myself open, really giving him a show. "This is all for you."

"I see." A shadow of anguish passes over his face. Jealousy that he's not here. The ache of wanting to touch me. "I see, and it's fucking *torturing* me."

Three fingers back inside me, and I imagine it's Brody who is fucking me when I press on my clit. I imagine he's holding himself above me, breath warm on my skin and kissing me until I can't think straight. That's how it always seems to go with him, and my mouth curls into a smile.

"Can you do something for me, Hannah?" he asks. "Please?

"As long as I get an orgasm out of it, I'll do anything."

"I'd never deny you that. You're so beautiful when you come." Brody's throat bobs. "Can you wear my shirt again? Backward, so you're wearing my name when you come? Countless women have shown up to games in my jerseys, but there's never been anyone I want to see in it."

I sit up, throwing the shirt back on and rolling it to my stomach so his name stays visible. "How's that?"

"Perfect," he mumbles. "Fucking perfect. I'm not going to last much longer."

"I'm not either." The shirt smells like him. I picture him wearing it late at night, in bed when he's missing me. "Race you there?"

We fall into silence after that, watching each other. Brody curses when I put my fingers in my mouth, wetting them. I hold back a moan when he strips off his shirt, leaving him naked with his body on display.

Each push of my fingers brings me closer to the edge. Shyness threatens to overtake me when Brody asks if can take a screenshot of our call, but it disappears when he tells me I'm the most beautiful woman in the world.

"I think I'm going to come," I whisper, and a muscle in his neck jumps.

"Thank fuck. I've been running hockey drills in my head so I don't finish before you," he says, the pace of his hand increasing on his shaft.

"You waited for me? That's sweet."

"Sweet. Right. That's exactly what I am while I think about putting you on all fours and finishing on your ass."

There's something about the raw scratch of his voice, the

explicit dream of something I want too that sends me over the edge. It's a freefall, the pleasure spreading to every inch of my body as I chase it, holding on to it for as long as I can.

When I finally return to earth with heavy breathing and heavy limbs, I open an eye to find Brody flat on his back on his bed. His arm is draped over his face. There's cum covering his hand, and his grip slowly slackens as he blows out a long exhale.

"How is it possible that you killed me through the phone?" He props himself up on an elbow, wincing. "You're not even here and I'm suffering."

"Doesn't look like suffering." I smile and draw my fingers out of myself. My legs close. I turn onto my side, stretching out on the couch. "That was *good*."

"I'm going to be asleep in ten minutes. It would be less than five if I didn't have to shower." Brody blinks, rubbing his eyes with his clean hand. "If this is the kind of fun everyone else is having, I can see why they're in such good moods all the time."

"You know what they say. Orgasms make the world go round."

"Think you might be on to something, Hannah." He stretches his arm above his head. "Let me shower, and I'll call you back in a few?"

"You're tired. You should get some sleep," I say. "I don't want to be the reason why you're cranky tomorrow."

"Highly doubt that's possible." With a long yawn, Brody swings his legs over the side of the bed. "Five minutes."

"Make it ten so I can rinse off too."

We hang up, both cleaning up before he calls me back like he said he would. I climb into bed and so does he. When he pulls out a pair of glasses, I almost drop my phone on my face.

"What the *fuck*, Brody? You wear glasses? You can't have all four things," I say.

"What are the four things?" he asks, pushing them up his nose.

"Glasses. Backward hats. Gray sweatpants. Tattoos. It's not fair."

"I don't wear glasses. I use them at night when my eyes are tired and I'm doing the crossword puzzle. The print is too small."

"Oh my god." I pull a pillow over my face and scream into it. "You're not serious."

"When have you ever seen me joke about something, Hannah?"

"Can I tell you something stupid?"

"Nothing you could ever say would be stupid."

"I like you. I think you're so fun. And, yeah, the mutual orgasms are great, but this?" I gesture between us, that same happiness from earlier when I first saw his text message making itself known. "This is even better."

"You know I don't like talking to people." A long pause. A slow blink behind his thick-framed glasses, and Brody adds, "But I like talking to you."

We stay up another hour on our video call. His eyes get heavy, and so do mine. When he starts to fall asleep, glasses slipping down his nose and phone falling out of his grip, I force him to hang up, knowing I could've talked to him until the sun came up and never gotten bored.

TWENTY-SEVEN

BRODY

"AGAIN," I yell to the guys. With their hands on their thighs, they hang their heads. Someone drops a stick. Another person groans. When no one moves, I blow the whistle Hannah got me for Christmas. "Now."

"Who pissed in Coach's cereal this morning?" Maverick groans. "He woke up on the wrong side of the bed."

"I can hear you, Miller, and I'm adding three extra laps because of your commentary."

"I should've taken paternity leave. Changing twenty diapers a day is more enjoyable than the hell you're putting us through," my captain grumbles.

Grant gags. Ethan wails, hanging half his body over the boards by the bench. Even Hudson, the guy who usually works the hardest without any complaints, is panting, and I grin.

I'm not pissed off at all.

I'm fucking *giddy*, and I can't remember the last time I felt this good.

I got the best sleep of my life last night after Hannah came over. I made her pasta, and we talked while we ate dinner. She showed me pictures from her first figure skating competition and I brought out the photo album of all my mini mite playing days. We put on a television show, muting it halfway through so she could ask me about Liv and what it was like in those early days of being a parent. When we got in bed, she opened a book while I read over game notes, keeping my hand on her thigh until we fell asleep.

There was no sex, no orgasms, but that's how it is sometimes, and I'm not going to complain. It makes it feel like this relationship is something that exists outside the bedroom too, and when I made her pancakes this morning, dodging the spatula of batter she tried to lodge at my face, I laughed for ten minutes straight.

Easy.

Everything with her is fucking *easy*. I don't have much experience to go off of—my dating history is minimal at best —but Hannah is different. I feel good around her, and that fun people tell me I need?

I'm having a lot of it.

"Again," I repeat, nodding when the players pull themselves together. "What did you think about that shift, Mitchell?"

"Huh?" Riley blinks. "What? Sorry. My head is in ten different places right now."

"If you could refrain from thinking about your girlfriend for the rest of morning skate, it would be appreciated," I say.

"Fiancée," he corrects with a sharp tone. "And there's no need to bring her into our conversation. I'm thinking about my AHL game tomorrow."

"Think you'll be with the second line?" I ask.

"I hope so. Practices are going well. I'm not afraid of hurting myself anymore, which was holding me back in the beginning."

"You looked good from what I saw when I sat in the other day. Head down, keep working, yeah?"

"Yeah." Riley nods. "What did you ask me a second ago?"

"What you thought about that shift the boys just ran. Grant is still playing really well, and I want to continue to reward that."

"I'm going to be honest with you, Coach. I don't know when Grant grew up, but he has a good head on his shoulders. He's making more of an effort on and off the ice. That positive reinforcement is going to go a long way." Riley pauses, leaning back at his hips to adjust his prosthetic leg. "You have to know he looks up to you, right? You're his role model."

I bristle with the compliment, but I know it's true. I see how Grant looks to me for approval. It might be his age—he's one of the youngest on the team. It might be because he's more locked in this season, more attentive when he's at practice. Whatever he's doing, it's working. He's playing the best hockey of his career, and I don't want to be the one to mess up his groove.

"Thanks for the feedback, Mitchell. We'll keep the lineup as is." I blow my whistle after the guys finish another run-through of their drill. "Good effort today. Three laps, then you can head for the showers. I want you to focus on building speed for the first lap. Second lap is an all-out effort. Third lap is a cooldown. And when you're finished, Richardson, I need to see you in my office."

"Oooh," Grant teases, elbowing Ethan's pads. "What did you do, Easy E?"

"Last person to the locker room is on laundry duty," I add, and everyone starts moving.

Thirty minutes later, there's a knock on my office door. I put my phone on silent and shove it in a drawer.

"Come in," I call out, and Ethan steps inside. "Take a seat, Richardson."

He looks around, shoulders up by his ears while he slides into the seat near the door. "Am I in trouble, Coach?"

"Do you think you should be in trouble?"

"No. But if this is about the video I posted where I was

dancing in front of my motorcycle, I didn't show my face. *Technically* I didn't break any team rules, and I—"

I hold up my hand to stop him. "I don't need to know what you do in your off time unless it starts to impact your performance on the ice." I pause, narrowing my eyes. God damn my curiosity. "You post dancing videos?"

"You bet I do." He digs into the pocket of his athletic shorts, pulling out two phones. He taps the screen of one and hands it over with a sheepish grin. I hit play on the video that has one million likes and ten million views, confused. A guy dances to some rap song I've never heard before in full motorcycle gear, helmet and all. "That's me."

"Huh. This isn't the worst thing I've ever seen."

"Shit, Coach." He grins and relaxes in the chair, fingers linked behind his head. "You're going to make me blush."

"Hang on." I tap the profile. "You have *five million followers?*"

"Yup. More than I have on my athlete page. What can I say? The ladies love a masked man." Ethan smirks. "I'm a chameleon. I can be whoever they want me to be."

"They don't know it's you? What about your voice? Do you talk?"

"Voiceovers, Coach. Unless you know my freckles—which would be really fucking creepy—there's no way you'd put two and two together." He frowns when I give him back his phone. "This isn't about that?"

"No. Ethan, I got a call yesterday letting me know you're leading the league in penalty minutes. Again. You got into multiple fights with the St. Louis Tigers' assistant captain the other night. Again."

"Shit," he whispers. "The league really tracks how much time I spend in the sin bin?"

"Yup. They're looking for patterns. Repeat offenders, repeat victims. Most of your penalty minutes aren't for majors, but they're worried about how this could progress if we don't talk about it." I sigh. "Look. I think it's bullshit. The league encourages fighting, but they punish you after if they deem it too severe. I just need to bring it to your attention."

"The Tigers' assistant captain." Ethan fidgets with a loose thread on his shirt. "He and I, uh, aren't the best of friends."

"I'm all for being rough, but this is obviously personal."

"Does the team get access to our high school and college transcripts during the draft combine?"

"No." I frown. "Why the hell would I care about what grade you got in calculus? All I want to know is how fast you can get down the ice to protect Sullivan in goal."

"I wasn't a very good student." He rubs the back of his neck. "I've struggled with learning disabilities pretty much my entire life."

"Ah." I look at him, wanting him to know he has my full attention. "Sullivan has dyslexia."

"I know. We've talked about it a few times. It's hard when everyone around you finds things easy and you struggle to read a sentence." A shrug, a sigh. "I wish dyslexia is where my disabilities stopped. I also have dyscalculia. ADHD. The hint of dysgraphia. Needless to say, I was bullied a lot as a kid. Someone who couldn't turn their thoughts into words? Flipping things and having trouble with math? People had a field day with me."

What the *fuck*?

I remember all the times at practice I've seen Ethan counting things out on his fingers. How often he asks how many reps we've done and how many we have left. I assumed it was because he was being lazy, because he wanted to know when we were finished for the day, but boy was I wrong.

There are all the times he's asked to take the charity items he needs to autograph home with him so he can finish them later. His barely legible handwriting every month when I ask the guys to write a reflection on how their season is going and his request to type it up.

My stomach drops to my feet.

"Ethan. I know I'm tough on you all on the ice, but my door is always open. Why didn't you tell me? It wouldn't have impacted your position on this team. We could've made accommodations or—"

"No," he snaps. "Hockey is the one part of my life where I don't have to use my brain. It's the only thing that comes naturally to me, and mentioning all the places where I struggled would mean I'd be treated differently. I've spent so much of my life being treated different, and I hate it. I do my best to hide it from the guys. From you. No one knows."

Hell.

I know the pressure of being on a championship team at such a young age. I know the scrutiny you're under from the media, from the fans. To carry all of that *and* this isn't easy fucking work, and my respect for him multiplies.

"Can you tell me how your learning disabilities correlate to your behavior on the ice and all those penalties? You already have as many minutes as some guys had all last season. I'm not mad. I just want to understand so we can come up with a plan going forward."

"Brady Williams, the Tigers' assistant captain, played at BU when I was at BC. We also went to rival high schools in Canada, so the fucker has been in my life for way too long. He knows I struggle when I'm off the ice, and he likes to start shit with me. Saying things under his breath. Calling me names. I'm sick of it. Punching him in the face is exactly what that dickbag deserves. He's lucky I haven't run into him off the ice. I'd fucking destroy him."

"I get why you're frustrated, Ethan, but you have to know he's doing it because it'll get a rise out of you."

"Trust me, Coach. I've tried ignoring him, but he's a piece of shit." Ethan leans back and folds his arms over his chest. "It's not just me he targets. It's anyone he deems weaker than him. When Emmy was on the team, he said things about her.

Thank fucking god Maverick never heard, or Brady would be six feet under. I know I joke around about women, but my mom raised me right. I respect them, but he doesn't. When he mentions his ex-wife, I want to strangle him on her behalf."

"Okay. Look. We don't play the Tigers again until the first week in April. I need you to try to keep your temper under wraps until then."

"Come on, Coach. Half of the fighting is to get the fans involved. You know they love it when we go at each other."

"I'm asking you to knock it off, Ethan, and behave yourself."

"Okay. Yeah." Ethan nods. "I'm sorry. I don't mean anything by it. I love this sport, and all that stuff makes it more fun."

I pinch the bridge of my nose. I've always hated bullies. "As for Brady Williams, I'll talk to the league. I won't mention names, only that I've heard there might be some inappropriate behavior happening behind the scenes that doesn't align with our values. And if that doesn't work, I played with Williams's coach at BC. I'll give him a heads-up."

"That means a lot." Ethan smiles, visibly relaxing. "I don't want to be a problem child. It just… happens. I'm protective of things that are important to me, and being treated right is very important to me."

"You have a good head on your shoulders, kid. I'm proud of you."

"Thank my mom. She's the one who got me started in rec hockey when I was first diagnosed. Saved my life. Gave me something to focus on rather than all the things I wasn't good at."

"Don't forget your dancing videos." I give him a nod. "Keep them PG, and we won't have a problem."

"What about PG-13?"

"Fine. But if I catch wind of you recording something without clothes on, your ass is in for a world of hurt."

"Yes sir." He grins and pops to his feet. "Anything else you need from me?"

"Yeah. I'm here, okay? I'm not going to make you feel different, but if there's something I can help with, let me. The team has resources. Ways to make things easier. You have to tell me though. I'm not a goddamn mind reader."

"Thanks, Coach. I appreciate you." My phone buzzes twice in my desk drawer, and he smirks. "Something else requiring your attention?"

"Scammers, probably. Go get some rest, Richardson. And no minutes in the box in tomorrow's game. Got it?"

"Got it. See you tomorrow morning."

When he leaves, I grab a sticky note and jot down a list of things I'm going to look into that might ease some of the stress he's carrying. I make a note to talk to our community outreach staff to see if we can find an autographing method that might be more accommodating for him. I add the coaching staff to the list, wanting to fill them in on what's going on so we don't set Ethan up for failure.

Forty-five minutes later, I have a plan of action I'm going to implement. I finally let myself look at my text messages, smiling at the ones from Hannah that have come through.

H.E.

I'm not someone who can sit around all day, so I left your place.

But I'll see you tomorrow morning for some skating!

ME

Sorry for not responding. Coaching stuff. The boys have practice tomorrow, so can we do 12?

H.E.

Don't apologize. I know you're busy. 12 Is great!

ME

See you then, IQ.

H.E.

Can't wait, BB.

"Sorry, Coach, I forgot my—holy *shit*." Ethan stands in the doorway to my office with his mouth open. "Are you *smiling*?" He glances around. "Is the world ending? Is this a simulation? What the *hell*?"

"I'm not smiling." I scowl and scrub a hand over my face. "Mind your business."

"You are *grinning*. And that's not a 'I just watched a funny video' grin. That's a *smitten* grin. Oh, shit. The boys are going to love this."

"Don't you dare."

"Sorry, C." Ethan shrugs and holds up his phone. "I've already told the masses. We have bets on your love life."

"You all need new hobbies."

"I get it, Coach. Love is scary."

"I'm not—don't use that word."

"Someone is defensive." He winks. "For what it's worth, happiness looks good on you."

"I don't know what you're talking about. I look exactly the same."

"Sure you do." Ethan swipes his other phone off my desk and waves. "Don't forget to invite us to the wedding!"

When he leaves again, I pull up my phone camera. I study myself and frown.

Same beard. Same circles under my eyes from not getting enough sleep. Same nose I've broken half a dozen times.

I don't really look different, do I?

Another message from Hannah comes through. This time, it's a photo of her in the grocery store holding up a pineapple, *your least favorite fruit!!!* written under it, and I catch a glimpse of my reflection in my laptop screen.

Smiling.

I'm fucking *smiling* just at the sight of her, and I guess that tracks.

I like her.

I like her in a completely normal, completely acceptable *I don't want to just fuck you, I also want to feed you three meals a day* kind of way.

I like her in a *how the fuck do we make this work long-term even though there are fourteen years between us* kind of way.

That's a problem for Later Brody, because Current Brody takes a selfie sticking out his tongue. Types *the bane of my existence* and tries not to get fucking butterflies when Hannah hearts the message in response.

"YOU ARE *GLOWING*, HAN." Tierney knocks her glass against mine in a cheers. "Who are you sleeping with and why haven't you told me about them?"

"What?" I fan my face, pulling my hair up in a high ponytail. The bar we're in is warm with bodies cramped together at tall tables, and I scoot closer so I can hear her. "Why do you think I'm sleeping with someone?"

"Because it's not the economy that has you smiling like that. Spill, woman."

"Okay, okay." I down half my white wine and set my drink aside. "I am seeing someone. It's new. I don't know how to define it yet, and I'm also not sure I should be sharing it with the world."

"That sounds scandalous." She arches an eyebrow. "Is it someone famous? A politician? *Please* tell me it's the president's daughter. She is so hot."

"Daphne Montgomery? I'm so far out of her league, but it's a nice daydream. This glow you think I have? It's thanks to a man, which, I know. Shocking, right? But we've been spending time together, and I'm having a lot of fun."

"A *man* making people smile? My god. The world might be ending. Who is he?"

"I guess technically he's famous? The girl I'm coaching, Olivia, it's her dad. Who also happens to be Grant's coach."

Tierney chokes on her wine. "You're sleeping with *Brody Saunders*? You're not serious, Han."

"Oh, I'm eight inches and a dirty mouth serious."

"Holy shit. How did this even start?"

"Almost two years ago at a club." I laugh and trace the rim of my glass with my finger. "The night the Stars won the Stanley Cup, he came back to my place, and we hooked up. That was also the night of Riley Mitchell's accident, and Brody had to leave early to be with the team."

"Makes sense. Gosh, I was so sad for Riley."

"Me too, but he's doing better. I didn't talk to Brody again until he reached out and asked if I would be interested in coaching his daughter. And while I've been doing that, he's been helping me on my edge work. Running drills with me and just…" I shrug. "Skating? Having a good time? One thing led to another, and we hooked up again before Christmas. We've been hooking up since."

"Does Grant know?" she asks, and I'm quick to shake my head.

"No way. I'm not sure how that would go. Would he be mad at me? Mad at Brody? Is it breaking some team rule I don't know about?"

"How can it be breaking a team rule if you're not a member of the team?"

"I don't know. I haven't considered the logistics of Grant finding out, and honestly, I don't want to. It feels like Brody and I are in a bubble right now, T, and I'm afraid if word gets out that we're sleeping together, hell will break loose." I sigh. "I keep my personal life private because I don't need the media digging into my previous relationships just because I'm Grant's sister. Brody has a daughter, and that's not fair to drag her into something public just because people want some gossip."

"Does his daughter know about you two?" Tierney crosses her legs and sips her wine. "Would she be okay with it?"

"I think she would be. When Brody comes to pick her up from our lessons, she's always making comments to him about how pretty my hair is or how cute my figure skating outfit is." I laugh. "She's definitely trying to play matchmaker."

"Hannah and the hockey coach. *Wow*." She grins. "How's the sex?"

"God help me. It's the best I've ever had. I told him the first night we were together that I don't come from penetration, and no man has ever made me finish during foreplay either. Then along comes Brody, with his magic fingers and magic tongue, and suddenly there are no issues. It's like he's written by a fucking woman."

"Can I ask the question I'm not sure I should ask, but I feel like I need to because you're my best friend and I love you."

"Anything." I reach for Tierney's hand. "And I'll answer."

"How old is he? If he has a kid, he has to be—"

"He's thirty-nine. I don't even notice the age difference, if we're being honest, and it doesn't feel… dirty? I know that's a creepy word to use. If I was four years younger, I might feel differently, but I've always thought I had an old soul. And Brody is… *fun*. He has this persona he slips into when he's in coach mode and on the ice, but away from all of that, he's…" I shrug again, the words to perfectly describe him hard to find. "Lovely."

"Hannah. This is so cute. I'm happy for you. Are you two dating? Seeing other people?" She tips her head to the side. "Falling madly in love?"

"Way too soon for that word." I laugh. "We're exclusive, and he told me he didn't sleep with anyone in the eighteen months apart because he didn't think it would be fair to lead another woman on when he was still thinking about me."

"What the fuck?" Tierney groans. "Okay. So he *is* written by a woman. I'm not jealous at all."

"I'm excited to see where it goes, and you know that's not my usual approach to dating." Reaching for my glass, I take another sip of wine. "I even have a contact photo for him."

"Let me see."

She makes grabby hands and I grin, tapping over to his name in my phone. The picture of him and Liv is there, and my heart swells at the sight of the them. Matching faces, matching expressions, they're the perfect pair.

Liv has been busy with a science fair project and Brody was on a four-game road trip, and it's been over a week since I've seen them. I *miss* them, I realize, the admission hitting me straight in the chest. I hope they're having a good night. I hope they're laughing at whatever funny story Liv is sharing, and as if I've manifested them to reach out to me, a message from Brody appears on my screen.

"He's hot," Tierney concludes. "And he's messaging you this late? He's down bad."

"Stop." I smile, biting my lip as I tap over to his text. "We always text late at night."

"What did he say?"

GC

I've been requested to ask you something, and please do not feel compelled to answer yes.

ME

I have no clue where this is going, but I need to know.

GC

Liv doesn't have school tomorrow, and we're about to head out to do some cosmic bowling. The pins glow in the dark or something? I don't know.

She wanted me to ask if you wanted to join us, but given it's Thursday and almost ten o'clock at night, I'm certain you have something better going on.

"He and his daughter are going bowling, and she invited me to come." I tap the sides of my phone and look at Tierney. "What do I say?"

"Do you want to see him? To see her?"

"Yeah. I do." I nod. "But I don't want to ditch you. We just got here and—"

"Sweetie, that man is an adult who knows how to communicate. Wait." Tierney sits up. "What about his ex? Is she still in the picture?"

"Amicably separated, with the healthiest co-parenting relationship I've ever seen," I tell her, and she's pushing my chair away from the table.

"You need to go right this second, because people—men—like this don't exist on every street corner. And you should enjoy it."

"I should, shouldn't I?" I grin, answering him as fast as my thumbs can type.

ME

I'm in. And I'm an excellent bowler.

GC

So am I. Care to wager a bet?

ME

You're on, Saunders. Which alley are you going to?

GC

Attachment: 1 link

Want us to pick you up?

ME

I'm out with Tierney, so I'll grab a rideshare.
Are you on your way now?

GC

ETA 20 minutes.

ME

See you soon!

"Okay. I'm going to go." I click off my phone and grab my purse, making sure to leave enough cash to cover the tip. "Because why the hell not?"

"I love this for you, Han. Text me if you need anything?" Tierney says, and I grin.

"I will."

TECHNO MUSIC PLAYS from the speakers over the lanes. Brody fixes the Velcro on his shoes and stands, jumping up and down.

"Is that a new technique I don't know about?" I ask, lacing my own shoes.

"He has weird superstitions about things," Liv tells me. "The shoes have to feel right, or he'll blame his bad score on them being a half size too big or too small."

"And I thought hockey was the only sport he cared deeply about."

"Nope, and it's best to let him just… do whatever the heck that is," she says.

"How did the science fair go?" I ask, and she lights up.

"So well. I got second place! I recreated a volcanic eruption, and my teacher loved it. Kind of makes me want to think about doing some higher level science classes. Maybe I'll study it in college."

"She gets that from Kali," Brody says, lifting a ball and testing its weight. "Not me. I don't know shit about chemical relationships."

"I didn't go to college, but science would have been a fun thing to study." I grab my own ball, slipping my fingers in the holes. "It's all around us. In the air we breathe. In the light we see. In weather. I follow this meteorologist down in Florida who seems so fun."

"You didn't go to college?" Liv turns to her dad. "See, Dad. I don't *have* to have an education."

"I only skipped college so I could skate. In hindsight, I wish I had gone to school. Just in case," I say, and when Liv goes to grab a soda, I offer Brody an apologetic look. "I'm sorry. I hope I'm not bringing up a sore subject."

"You're not. I've been trying to tell Liv there's a world outside of skating, but she's focused on the sport right now. To her, that means no college. Trying to make an Olympic team, even if the chances are slim."

"I'm the leading example of why you should always keep your options open." I laugh. "People I went to high school with have their lives figured out, but I'm still unsure about what the future looks like for me. And it's terrifying."

"Hey." Brody glances over his shoulder, finding Liv still in line and staring at her phone. He touches my hip and frowns. "Are you okay?"

"I'm good. I'm *so* good, and that's the issue. The more time I spend away from skating at a such high level, the more I realize all the things I've missed out on. Like, take tonight. Eight months ago, if you had asked me to go bowling this late, I would've said no because I had an early training session in the morning. But here I am, ready to kick your ass," I say. "And I'm *happy* about that."

"Balance. Priorities. It's all important. Finding the happy medium. You're doing great, Hannah." A finger in my belt loop, giving me a gentle tug. "And I'm glad you're here with us, even if I can't hear a fucking thing over this music. Do you think if I complain, they'll turn it down?"

"Probably, but only because you're intimidating as hell." I stand on my toes, flipping his hat backward so you can see his face. "There. Now you're more approachable."

"I don't want to be approachable." He scowls, but he's smiling too. Stepping away when Liv comes back with a Coke and a bag of popcorn. "You're up first, Livvy."

I like that photo of Brody and Liv on my phone, but seeing them together like this is even better. She steps on the foul line when it's his turn to bowl. He sneaks up behind her and rolls a ball between her legs, laughing when it ends up in the gutter. Liv stops and talks with me, asking if she can braid my hair then tying a ribbon to the end of it.

"Distracting," Brody whispers in my ear when Liv takes a break to use the bathroom. He plays with the end of my ponytail, giving it a hard tug. "I want to tie you up with those ribbons so you can't fucking move."

"If I remember correctly, you have two of them at your place." I put my hand on his shirt. "Maybe you should put them to good use."

"Next time." He's slower to move away, his eyes roaming down my jeans. "Everything about you is maddening in the best possible way, Hannah."

"What did I miss?" Liv asks, sitting next to me. "Did someone recognize Dad?"

"We were just talking about how much your dad loves this song." I point to the music video on the television with flashing lights. "I'm going to ask if they can play it again."

"Yeah, right. Dad only likes to listen to classical music, and only before a game. Otherwise, he prefers silence."

"Wow." I give Brody a look. "Is that true?"

"It's good for concentration. The one time I didn't listen to classical music before a game, I got injured. It's part of my routine now." He hands a ball to Liv and gestures at the lane. "You're up, kid. Let's see if you can beat your score of ninety-eight from the last game."

"It's not my fault you were sabotaging me!" Liv pops to her feet, huffing under her breath.

"Speaking of the last game, you lost, Saunders," I say. "How does that make you feel?"

"Did I? Didn't even realize." His eyes lock on mine. "Kind of feels like I won."

TWENTY-NINE

HANNAH

GC

Liv is at her mom's tonight. Do you want to
come over?

I miss you.

ME

I'll be there in an hour.

GC

Can't wait to see you.

"HI," I say, breathless from the cold when Brody opens his door.

"Hi." He smiles and leans against the frame, looking me up and down. "I like your skirt."

"It's new." I touch the pleated material and step close to him. "And it has pockets."

"A genius invention, really." Brody gestures me inside the

267

warm condo. He helps me take off my winter coat and kisses the top of my head. "Want something to drink?"

"Are you going to have anything?"

"I need a whole handle of whiskey. I just finished a league-mandated anti-sports betting computer module, and I think my brain is going to explode."

"Sounds irresponsible. I'm in," I say, giggling when he swats at my ass. "Have you had dinner yet?"

"Nope. I'll order us something later." He threads his fingers through mine and leads me down the hall to the living room. "Tell me about your day."

"I spent this morning finalizing the choreography for the program I'm going to perform at my upcoming competition. It didn't go as well as I'd hoped, but what can you do?" I sit on the couch, folding my feet under me. "I'm nervous. *Really* nervous, if we're being honest, and I'm afraid I'm making a mistake."

"Hey." Brody pulls me into his lap, keeping me tight to his chest. "What are you nervous about?"

"Will you judge me if I say everything?" I laugh and bury my face in his shirt. "When we first started working together, I dreaded going on the ice. I wanted nothing to do with it. Now I'm… scared, I guess? Because I've felt so optimistic the last few months. Because I'm excited to skate again. I'm worried I'm one poor landing away from never skating again. And I'd rather be burnt out than walk away from the sport completely."

"I'm going to tell you something, and it's not because I'm sleeping with you. It's not because I have any stake in your success, but because it's the truth, and you need to hear it. I'm sure you've met a lot of people in your life who are starstruck by your accomplishments. They see your medals. They see the money you've earned. They see your social media following. But under all of that, you're still Hannah Everett." Brody kisses my jaw. "And Hannah Everett, the figure skater, Hannah

Everett, the coach, and Hannah Everet, the regular human who is surprisingly good at bowling are all the same to me. You're kind. You're funny. You're sarcastic as hell, and no matter if you wind up on your ass or winning first place at this competition, I'm still going to cheer for you."

"That… is a very nice thing for you to say." I clear my throat to fight back tears, trying to wipe under my eyes without Brody noticing. "I hope you know I feel the same way about you. I know you have, like, five Stanley Cups or something like that, but I don't see all those championships. I see a devoted dad. A loyal coach. A guy who works hard for the people in his life, and it's special. Makes me want to be a better person too."

"You already are the best person." His hand rests on my thigh. "Do you know how I know that?"

"How?" I ask, changing my position in his lap so I'm facing him, straddling his thighs.

"Because all the days I get to see you? Those are my favorite days." He cups my cheeks with both palms. "I don't have to spend two hours going over drills you could do in your sleep. I don't have to get to Liv's lessons early, but I do. Because it means more time with you."

It feels like a confession without saying the words. A recognition of how this relationship between us has grown, has blossomed into something real, something *wonderful*, and I like this man so fucking much.

"Brody?" I whisper, brushing my nose against his.

"Yeah, sweetheart?" he answers, thumb stroking along my jaw.

"Will you come to my competition and watch me?" I ask.

For all the years I've spent spinning in the air with moves I've spent hours perfecting, none of them have ever made me feel as high as he does in this very moment.

His laugh is soft, surprised. He kisses my forehead, the corner of my mouth. "I'll be in the front row, baby."

"You will?"

"If you want me there, that's where I'll be."

"You know, I'm starting to get a little freaked out," I say, and Brody frowns.

"By what?"

"You. How have you been single for so long?" I rest my hand on the back of his neck, playing with the long strands of his hair. "What skeletons aren't you showing me?"

"No skeletons. You know not many people interest me." His mouth is on my neck. His words are hot on my skin. "But you do. You've always interested me."

"For a while now, right?" My skirt fans out around us, and he grips the hem. "Tell me about the first time you really noticed me."

"Friends and Family night. Three years ago. You were in the middle of the ice doing some pretty spin, and I couldn't look away. I didn't *want* to look away, and it frustrated me to no end. I see plenty of women. Half of Liv's teachers try to get my attention, but none of them have ever been able to have it. But you? You, Hannah Everett," Brody grabs my chin, kissing me. "You have *always* had my attention."

"I'm here now." I reach for my shirt, pulling it over my head to reveal a new lingerie set. "Why don't you show me how much you've been paying attention to me?"

"Before we do that, I want to try something new with you," he says, kissing down my chest. He sucks on my nipple over the fabric of my bra, and I wiggle my hips. "Something I mentioned the other night."

"Does it have to do with my ass?" I hold his shoulder, eyes fluttering closed when he moves to my other breast. "I'd be interested in hearing more."

"No, but we can table that for another day." Brody lifts me off his lap, setting me on the couch. He stands, rubbing his hand over the front of his jeans. "Stay here. I'll be back in a minute."

"Okay." I frown, not sure where this is going. I brush my hair out of my eyes while I wait for him to return, my frown deepening when I see his hand behind his back. "Should I be nervous?"

"You told me to put these to good use." He holds up two of my long ribbons and stares at me. "What do you say?"

"*Oh.*" I blow out a breath, my heart thundering in my chest. "You want to tie me up."

"Just your wrists." He joins me on the couch again, running the ribbon along the back of my hand. "And only if you're comfortable with it."

"I've never done this before. But I'd like to try." I touch the ends of the ribbon and nod. "Do you like to tie people up?"

"How honest do you want me to be with answering that question?"

"Honest." My voice is a rasp. My hands are shaking. Anticipation swirls low in my belly, and I touch his chest. "I want to know."

"I haven't slept with many women, but I do like to tie people up. It comes from my desire to be in control. With you, I don't mind handing that control over. Deep down though, there's something inside me that likes to be in charge." He kisses my collarbone, tongue swiping up my throat. "I like when people do what I say. I like when they listen to me. It's why I enjoy coaching so much: I see it play out in real time when someone does what I ask. In the bedroom, it's not necessarily a dominant and submissive thing. It's the enjoyment of a partner handing over their trust to me. I get off without any of this stuff just fine, but it's sexy as hell to watch, and I think I'd like to watch you."

"I'm not very submissive," I whisper. "I don't want to follow orders in the bedroom."

"You don't have a submissive bone in your body, sweetheart, and there's nothing wrong with that."

"I could try." I reach for Brody's shirt, tugging it over his head. I run my nails down the front of his bare chest then back up, moving to his shoulders. "I want to try. With you."

"Are you sure? I already think sex with you is out of this world."

"I'm positive." I hold out my wrists, handing over control. "Tie me up, Brody."

THIRTY

BRODY

"DO YOU STILL TRUST ME?" I murmur in Hannah's ear. I crowd her space, spinning her so she's facing the arm of the couch and I'm behind her. I kiss the top of her spine. Below her ear. "Do you, Hannah?"

"With everything I have," she says, watching with wonder as I reach around her.

I knot the ribbons together to make a longer strand that will fit her hands. I loop it carefully around her wrists, tying them together. I check the security of her hands, knowing she can release herself at any time with a quick pull.

"Give it a gentle tug and tell me how that feels," I tell her. She lets out a soft gasp when the ribbons strain against her skin. "Too tight? Uncomfortable at all?"

"No. *No.* It feels… right?"

"Good." I run my hand up her leg, finding the zipper of her skirt. "You'll tell me if that changes?"

"All this talking." Hannah drops her head, resting it in the crook of my shoulder. She arches her back, and the things I want to do to her tits would get me in a world of fucking trouble. "When you could be doing things that are far more fun. Make yourself useful, Brody."

"Yeah?" I grab her cheek. "How can I be useful, princess? Tell me, and I'll do it."

"You could start by lifting up my skirt," she breathes out, smiling when I bring my palm under the hem of the soft material. I find fancy underwear there, and I hiss when I drag my knuckles across the front of it. Already wet. Legs spread open for me. "And fucking me."

Her demand snaps me to attention, and I get rid of her skirt as quick as I can. My brain nearly short-circuits at the red thong she's wearing, and I pull away from her so I can trace the underside of her breast.

"You wear this under your clothes?" I ask, using my teeth to bring one of the straps of her bra down her shoulders. I do the same on the other side until her tits are free. "You just… walk around looking like this?"

"Is that a problem?" Hannah's eyes flutter closed when I pluck her nipples. "I've always liked wearing cute outfits. I've always liked to feel pretty, and I like knowing if someone asked me to get naked, I'd look damn good doing it."

"It's only a problem because I'm not going to be able to look at you the same way again." I unclasp the hook in the back, letting the bra portion of the set fall to her bound wrists. "I'm going to be wondering what you have on under your outfits. What color you're wearing that day. Christ, Hannah." I gather her hair, brushing it to the side so I can kiss her neck. "This is really bad news for me. My productivity is going out the fucking window."

"Permission granted to strip me down every time you see me." She wiggles on the couch, her hips pressing into the front of my jeans. I hold her there so she can feel my hard cock. So she can know how much she turns me on. "You should take the rest of it off."

"I'm going to leave the stockings on." There's a lump in my throat when I try to swallow. When I snap the top of the thigh-highs against her skin, then rub over the sting with my thumb. I have a new fetish I didn't even know existed. "If that's okay."

"It's more than okay." Hannah leans forward, lifting off the couch. I work the red bottoms down, giving her cheek a smack when I'm greeted by bare, creamy skin. She rocks her hips, a groan caught in her chest, and I smile. "That wasn't too hard, by the way."

"Good to know." I kiss her hip and pull away, rising to my feet. She follows my movements, watching me stand. "Stay there."

"See something you like, Saunders?"

"So many things I like," I croak. "Look at you practically naked and bound for me." I pull the zipper down on my jeans, letting the denim pool at the floor. I step out of my pants, getting rid of my briefs next. "Keep your hands on the arm of the couch."

"What are you doing?" she asks.

"Something I've wanted to do for fucking *weeks*." I step toward her, spitting in my hand. I grip my cock, giving it few rough strokes. "Fucking your tits."

"Another first." Her smile is sexy. "We're crossing so many things off the list tonight."

"The height should work." I put hand in her hair. "Get me wet first, Hannah."

"Okay, Daddy," she says, and I hate myself when my cock gets even harder.

Hannah holds out her tongue and I rest the head on it, letting her lick and suck me. She starts at the tip, taking me down her throat, deeper with every thrust of my hips. When she reaches the root of my shaft, I groan, knowing I can't let her do this for too long.

"That's enough," I say, twisting my fingers in her hair. "Take me out." She does, saliva sticking to her lips when I pull away. I drag it down her cheek with my thumb, smiling when she moans. "Did you like that, sweetheart?"

"You're the one with all the pre-cum when I called you Daddy. I think you liked it more than me." She smirks. "Come on, Brody. Show me what else you can give me."

Not a single fucking submissive bone, and I'm glad for it.

I bring her to the edge of the couch and push her knees open. I reach my hand between her legs, dragging my fingers through her entrance.

"Says the girl who is fucking *soaked*." I rub her arousal up my length and step closer. "Bring your hands in front of you. I want you to push your tits together with your upper arms. *Perfect*, Hannah. There you go." I wedge my cock between her breasts, groaning at the sensation. "*Fuck*."

"Be rough with me," Hannah whispers.

I *am* rough with her. I fist my cock, jerking my hips as I slide up and down her chest. I close my eyes, imagining it's her pussy I'm fucking, and groan when she makes her cleavage even tighter. I stop every few thrusts and let her suck my length again, delighted when she gags.

My grunts fill the living room. I should've moved us to my bed where we'd be more comfortable, but there's no stopping now. Not when Hannah rolls her hips, grinding against the couch and trying to get herself off. Not when she bends her neck, her tongue finding my balls before I start to fuck her again.

It's the crudest thing I've ever done, but Hannah meets me every step of the way. When I think I'm hurting her by yanking on her hair, her eyes twinkle. When I'm about to ask if she needs to take a second to breathe, she shakes her head. I'm hanging on by a thread, not sure if I want to finish all over her chest or with her riding me, and I make a split second decision when pleasure builds in my stomach.

"Stand up," I pant, fumbling with my jeans. I find the condom I shoved in there on my way back from grabbing the ribbons and rip it open. Rolling it down my length, I stretch out on the couch, reaching for her. "Come ride me, sweetheart."

"I love being on top." Hannah leans into me for balance, her wrists still bound in front of her. "I like to watch you fall apart."

"I've been falling apart for the last eight minutes." I rest my hands on her waist, guiding her onto my length. There's no foreplay, no chance to stretch her out, and she groans at the first press of my cock inside her. "*Jesus Christ*. You're so fucking tight."

"Give me a second." Hannah relaxes, sinking down another inch. "Okay. Okay. That feels good."

"I need more than a second," I say, but this isn't about me. This is about her, and she works my cock up and down. Faster, as she finds a rhythm, and she's in complete control. "Use me, Hannah."

Those must be the magic words, because her pace quickens. She lets out a sharp breath, burying me deep inside her. I open my mouth to try and groan, but no sound comes out. It's disjointed thoughts. Bodies fused together, and I press my thumb on her clit, determined to get her to come.

"*Brody.*"

"How do your wrists feel, sweetheart?" I rub a slow circle, savoring the way she squirms on top of me. "Do you like being at my mercy?"

"So much." Her head falls back, hair brushing against my knees. "You're the only one I would want to do this with."

I hold her in place, lifting my hips and thrusting into her. I take over, watching her tits bounce. I give her ass a smack, and when she tightens around me, I know I'm going to come.

"I can't last much longer, sweetheart. Are you—"

"I'm going to come too. Touch my clit. *Please*," she says, and because hearing her beg is my favorite thing in the world, I do what she says.

Hannah moans my name, and that's all it takes for me to

tip over the edge. She follows me, riding the high while I hold her in place, not stopping until I fill the condom with my release.

"I've got you," I whisper, ripping the ribbons in half with a single yank to free her wrists. Her bra falls away. I kiss the pink marks on her skin, soothing over them with my thumb. "Are you okay?"

"I think you might have killed me," she mumbles, the words slurring at the edges. "Wholly and completely."

"Hang on." I lift her by her hips, groaning at the loss of contact. I set her next to me on the couch, tying off the used condom and dropping it on the table. I'll clean it up later. Turning on my side, I bring her flush against me, stroking her shoulders while her breathing returns to normal. "Is that better?"

"Yeah. That felt different from the other times, and I don't know why." Hannah nuzzles into my embrace, my arms snaking around her waist. "Maybe because I couldn't touch you how I wanted? It all felt… heightened."

"Take away one sense, the others work harder." I bring her hand to my mouth, kissing her knuckles. "Thank you for letting me try that with you."

"I'm not sure I'll ever be able to look at my ribbons the same way again." Her laugh is barely a puff of air. She melts into me, the adrenaline waning. "All I'm going to see is you."

"Is that such a terrible thing?"

"No." She traces the rose on the back of my hand. "You told me the days you get to see me are your favorite days. The ribbons. Skating. The way my outside edge work has only improved… all of those have become my favorite things because you're there too. The joy in the little moments. Like you said."

It feels heavy to say after the sex we just had. Like we're taking the next step down a road I'm not sure where it leads, but I want to find out. With her.

I press a kiss to the back of her head, the smell of her shampoo tickling my nose. Tomorrow I'm going out to buy a bottle for her to keep here. I'll buy a thousand bottles if it means she's still around.

"Do you want to spend the night?" I ask. "I'll even try pineapple on my pizza."

"*No.*" Hannah turns in my arms, facing me. Her lipstick is smudged. Her hair is a messy, a piece matted to her cheek with sweat. Beautiful. *She's so fucking beautiful.* "Who are you, and what have you done with Brody Saunders?"

"Compromise, sweetheart. You let me tie your wrists together. I can eat pineapple on my pizza for one night."

"Wow." She props up on an elbow, looking down at me. "From the sound of it, I'd say you like me."

"And if I do?" I ask, touching her chin.

"I'd say I like you too," she murmurs, bringing her mouth to mine. "What a lucky, lucky girl am I."

THIRTY-ONE
BRODY

H.E.

I'm sorry about the loss tonight. I'm sure you want some space, but my door is always open if you feel like stopping by. No pressure. Xoxo

ME

You have nothing to be sorry for. You weren't out there giving up goals.

H.E.

No, but I know how much you care about your guys. Losing 8-1 can't be fun.

ME

No. It fucking sucks.

I'll stop by, but it's going to be a while. My captain has been playing like shit this week, and I need to have a conversation with him.

Contrary to popular belief, I don't like being an asshole, but I think I'm going to have to be.

H.E.

You're just doing your job. Take your time. I
can't wait to see you and give you a big hug.

READING Hannah's message as I walk down the tunnel after an embarrassing defeat is the only thing keeping me calm. Piper doesn't try to wrangle me for an interview. Our social media intern doesn't bother asking if I want to speak to the group of reporters waiting in the media room. Everyone knows better than to put me in front of a microphone after getting our asses handed to us.

"Miller," I bark out, and my captain stops to look at me. Behind him, Liam throws his goalie stick to the ground. "Shower. My office."

"Yeah." Maverick nods, his eye purple from where he got decked in the face in the second period. His shoulders curl forward, and he has to lean on his stick to stay upright. "Okay."

I brush past the rest of the guys heading for the locker room and kick open the door to my office. I drop in my chair and open my email, waiting for our film team to send me the condensed footage from tonight's game so I can start seeing how fucking *awful* we played.

The knock forty-five minutes later barely grabs my attention, but Maverick's voice does.

"Coach." Maverick steps inside and shuts the door. "You wanted to see me?"

"Sit down." I point to the chairs, not waiting for him to get comfortable. "You and I have never bullshited each other, Miller, and we're not going to start now. I'm going to ask you a question, and I want you to answer it honestly."

He slides into the chair and fixes his hoodie, folding his hands in his lap. "Okay."

"What is going on with you this week? You're late to practice. You're playing like shit. Every time I look at you, you're seconds away from falling asleep while standing up. If you can't figure this out, I'm going to have to bench you. It's not something I want to do, but you can't honestly tell me you're playing at the top of your game right now."

Maverick blinks. His bottom lip quivers, and he takes a deep breath. "It's Emmy," he whispers. "Things aren't good with us right now. She's… I think… I've been doing a lot of research on postpartum depression? I'm afraid of what's going on with her, but she won't fucking *talk* to me even though I'm trying to help." He pulls at his hair. A sob works out of him, and I freeze. "She's not sleeping. She's not working out because she just had a fucking baby and she needs to let her body recover, but people flood her social media asking when she's going to be back. When I try to help with Murphy, Emmy doesn't let me because she thinks Murphy likes me more than she likes her. I don't know what to fucking do. I'm scared, Coach. For her. For Murphy. For *me*, because I'm a selfish fucking asshole. Emmy is everything to me. If something happened to her, I wouldn't forgive myself and—"

I grab the landline phone sitting on my desk and punch the code for the locker room, feeling like the world's biggest asshole. It rings three times before Lexi picks up.

"Hey, Coach," she answers. "What's up?"

"Send me Hayes, Sullivan, Everett, Mitchell, and Richardson. Now," I say, hanging up.

I stand. Maverick is staring at his hands. His shoulders shake. Tears run down his face and I sit beside him, putting a hand on his arm. He jerks his chin up, staring at me, and I give his bicep a squeeze.

"Olivia's mom went through the same thing," I say.

"She did?"

"Yeah. It was the worst year of my life. I didn't know how to help her. I didn't know what to say. Of course I don't fucking know what it's like to give birth. That's not something I'll ever experience, so I was clueless on what to do."

"What *did* you do?" he asks.

"I used my resources. I paid for her therapy appointments. I watched Liv when she went to support groups. I listened to her when she told me what she needed, even if it hurt my feelings. I made sure she was eating and sleeping, and I didn't argue when she said she needed a night off, no matter how fucking tired I was."

"I can't do a lot of that. We're in the middle of the season and—"

"I'm making you a non-roster player," I say. "Family comes first on this team. Always. Your spot will be here when you're ready to come back. And if you never feel like coming back, we can have that conversation down the road."

"I don't even know what a non-roster player is," he whispers.

"It was added to the CBA a couple years back and requires league approval. It means you're not playing due to a reason other than injury, illness, or disability. We can replace you with an AHL player, and it won't count against our roster limit."

"Does that mean I get to be home with Emmy?"

"Yes. No practicing. No traveling. No games. I don't want to see you at any of the Stars' facilities for at least a month, Miller." The door to my office opens again, and five more players file inside. There's barely any room for all of them, but I pop to my feet anyway. "Good. You all are here."

"What's going on?" Hudson looks at Maverick, then at me. "That loss wasn't all on Mav."

"I gave up eight fucking goals." Liam scowls at the floor. "That was the worst game of my career."

"Forget the game," I say, and the room goes silent. "Miller is going to be taking some time away from the team effective immediately. Hayes, you'll assume captain duties during his absence. Everett, you're wearing the A on your jersey now."

"Shit," Grant whispers. "Are you okay, Mavvy?"

"No." Maverick looks at his teammates. We've been working together for years—through losing seasons. Through roster changes and new lines. Through the worst years this organization has ever seen, and I've never seen him so distraught. "I'm not okay. I think Emmy is going through post-partum depression and—"

"How can we help?" Riley interrupts, wrapping his arms around Maverick from behind. "What can we do?"

"Why didn't you tell us, Mav?" Hudson asks. "Why do you have to be such a stubborn motherfucker who doesn't like to ask for help?"

"Doesn't the league offer paternity leave?" Liam asks. "Fitzpatrick was out for two weeks when his kid was born."

"They do, but Emmy told me to keep playing. She said it wasn't that many days, that she was handling everything just fine, but it's a lot of fucking days. And she *is* handling things fine, but she shouldn't have to do it on her own." Maverick sighs. "I love hockey, but at what cost?"

"Here's the plan." I scratch my jaw, an idea coming to mind as I survey the room. "There are five of you. If Miller and Hartwell agree to it, you're each going to pick up three days when we're in town. You'll go to their place and help with cooking and cleaning for a couple of hours. Laundry? Watching Murphy while her parents eat a meal? Cleaning the bathrooms? Changing sheets? All on the list. Rotating sched-ule, so you're not missing too much practice, but you're still available if they need you."

"Hang on. You want *me* to watch a *baby*?" Ethan asks.

"I don't know about that, Coach. Ethan burned the hot dogs he made for dinner the other night." Grant laughs. "A baby is a lot of responsibility."

"I'm not asking you to be a father, Richardson. I'm asking

you to help Emmy warm up a bottle and Maverick fold a sheet so they have some extra hands," I say.

"Fitted sheets are a bitch," Liam grumbles.

"Right. Of course. I understand. I can help." Ethan lifts his chin. "I *want* to help."

"If Ethan needs to tap out, I'm sure Goalie Daddy would be happy to jump in," Grant adds. "He likes kids."

"No, I don't." Liam scowls. "II don't know what you're talking about."

"Oh really?" Grant rolls his eyes. "Is that why you're an asshole to everyone *but* kids? I see the jerseys you sign and the pucks you give out during warmups."

"They offer to trade me candy," Liam says. "I love Starbursts."

"Wow." Riley smiles. "He does have a heart."

"I'm serious, Miller. A month off. We'll evaluate things in March," I tell him, and he nods.

"Thanks, Coach." His smile is weak, but the life is returning to his eyes. "I love Emmy and Murphy more than anything."

"Maverick the family man Miller." Ethan grins. "Who would've thought?"

* * *

IT'S another hour and a half before I can leave the arena, and when I do, the moon is high in the sky. The temperature is biting and cold, the late February wind brutal on my face. I ask my Uber driver to drop me two blocks from Hannah's apartment so I can walk the rest of the way, taking a deep breath for the first time all night.

The call to the commissioner's office about getting Maverick taken care of has been made. I've scoured our AHL team's roster and a couple other players in the ECHL I've had my eye on. There's a girl out in Chicago with a playing style similar to the offense we like to run I'm hoping to talk to, but I'm trying to not get too excited. Maverick told me he'd call me later, and we're figuring this shit out.

By the time I get to the hallway that leads to Hannah's apartment, I'm exhausted, but she's there, opening the door in one of the DC Stars T-shirts I left at her place and giving me a smile that's as bright as can be.

"Coach," she says, her voice sultry and sweet.

"Everett." My eyes rake down her legs. There's a charm bracelet clasped around her ankle. Bright pink painted toes, and she has a tiny braid in her hair. "It's good to see you."

"You too." She holds the door open for me. I step inside, kicking off my shoes in the foyer. "Are you hungry?"

"No. Just drained." I rub my forehead, a headache forming there from the stress. From wanting to make sure my guys are taken care of and everyone is safe. "Can we go to your room so I can stretch my legs? My knee is killing me."

"Of course." Hannah stands on her toes to kiss my cheek, then offers me her hand. I follow her down the hall, rubbing my thumb over her knuckles and savoring in the warmth of her palm. She climbs on the bed, propping herself up on an elbow, and pats the spot next to her. "If you want to take off some clothes, I wouldn't mind."

I chuckle and get rid of my suit and tie, draping everything over her desk chair so they don't wrinkle. I settle next to her on the mattress, an arm behind my head and a hand on her thigh.

"Hi," I say.

"Hi." She doesn't try to hide her smile, and neither do I. "Did you yell at the guys after that loss?"

"No. Didn't feel right." My hand moves to her hair, and I play with the braid framing her face. "There are days when being a good coach takes the back seat to being a decent human."

"For what it's worth, I think you're both." Hannah scoots closer. "Anything I can do to help?"

"I don't want to share too many details and disrespect my players' privacy, but I had a conversation with some of the guys about helping with Murphy, Maverick and Emmy's baby, and around their house." I sigh. "Lots of moving parts."

"I'd never want you to share something a player told you in a trusted environment." She puts a hand flat on my chest. "Do you want more kids?"

"I don't know. Liv is perfect, but can I really get that lucky twice in a row?" I laugh. "I guess my answer is a tentative maybe, but with the caveat of knowing I'm perfectly happy with how things are now."

"Imagine teaching another kid how to drive in fifteen or twenty years. We'll probably all have spaceships by then."

"What about you?" I ask, playing with her sleeve. "Do you want kids?"

"No." There's a long pause. "I'm not sure I even want to get married. Apparently, that's controversial? So many marriages end in divorce—and I'm not saying people who are in non-legally binding relationships don't break up—but I guess I can't comprehend being tied to someone for the rest of my life." A soft chuckle now. "Guess that makes me cynical."

"Not cynical at all. Kali and I never got married, even after having Liv. What works for one person might not work for everyone else. Who gives a fuck what people do with their lives? Marriage, no marriage. Kids, no kids. Everyone needs to mind their own fucking business and let people just *live*."

"Wow." Hannah draws circles on my skin, and I shiver under her touch. "You're hot when you get fired up about things."

"If you think that was fired up, you should've seen me on the bench during tonight's game. I broke a clipboard."

"I saw. That was also hot." When I frown and steal a glance at her, I find her blushing. "I, um, might've subscribed to ESPN+ so I could watch all the Stars games. This isn't just about you, by the way. It's so I can see my brother play too."

"Of course." I smile. "I could've given you a ticket so you could watch it in person."

"Grant always leaves me tickets. I like watching from my couch better." Hannah straddles me, a leg over both of my thighs. I put my hands on her hips, inching her shirt up to her waist. "That way, no one can see me drool over you."

"You flatter me," I murmur, reaching up to cup her cheek. She turns her chin, kissing my palm. "While I have you here, I need to talk to you about two things."

"Uh oh. Are you mad that I offered to help Liv with her bowling skills so next time we play, we'll both kick your ass?"

"No." My smile grows. Knowing she and my daughter get along makes me happy as hell. "Do you want the bad news or the good news first?"

"Bad first. Always."

"I'm not going to be able to make it to your competition next month." I swallow, dreading this conversation. "The league changed our puck drop in Boston from one p.m. to four p.m. that day. Something about an arena conflict with an NBA game?" I stroke my thumb along her skin, disappointed. "I'm so sorry, Hannah. I know how much this means to you, and I hate that I can't be there to support you."

"That's okay." Her smile falters. She plays with the ends of her hair, not looking at me. "It's no big deal. I know you have other priorities, and a local figure skating competition can't be high on the list. It's not like you're my boy—"

"I'm almost forty." When her eyebrows wrinkle, I keep going. "I like you. Very much. I like sleeping with you. I like spending time with you. I like that you're there to keep me from having a panic attack when Liv almost hits a pedestrian."

"She was two football fields away," Hannah argues. "Personally, after three driving sessions, I think she's getting *much* better."

"Debatable."

"Why are you telling me how old you are?"

"Because I want you to know this?" I gesture between us. "It's not just physical for me. You're important to me, and I…" I swallow, nervous. It's been years since I asked this question, and my heart rate kicks up a notch. "I want to know if you'll have dinner with me."

"Oh." Hannah rolls her lips together. The spark is back in her eyes. A dimple shows up on her left cheek, and the more time I spend with her, the more I want to do this every day. "I'd love that, Brody." She hesitates, running her fingers through my hair. "But I think we need to have a conversation about how this could impact people around us."

"What do you mean?"

"If my brother found out. Or Liv. Or the league. Would you get in trouble for dating me?"

"Not with the league, though." I clear my throat. "Liv would be okay with it. She'd probably be fucking ecstatic. As for Grant…"

"I don't know how he'd react, to be honest. I told you he doesn't know about my bisexuality because my personal life shouldn't be brought into conversations with his professional life. This… it mixes the two." Hannah climbs off me, curling up under my arm with her cheek on my chest. "He's very protective of the people he loves. Maybe we… I don't know. Keep enjoying this privately, and cross that bridge when we get there?"

"Not a bad idea." I run my finger down the line of her arm then back up. I think about the offseason only a few short months away. Things will calm down by then. There's not as much media coverage or reporters digging into team dynamics to see if there's a rift that might cause a feud heading into the playoffs. "The guys do think I'm seeing someone though."

"Really?"

"Yup. Ethan caught me smiling at a text you sent me a couple weeks back. And that night we left the gala together, they asked if I canceled practice because of a woman."

"Wow. Who knew you smiling would be such a hot topic?" Hannah drums her fingers on my chest. "You smile plenty around me."

Because you make me happy.

Because no one else has ever made me feel this way.

Because I miss you when you're not around.

"Must mean you're special. What do you think about dinner?" I ask, and she kisses my jaw.

"It's a date," she says, and I feel on top of the fucking world.

THIRTY-TWO

BRODY

Puck Kings and Daddy Things (+ our savior, BS)

EVERETT

Figured it was time to change the chat name.

Attachment: 1 image

Look at me and Murphy chilling! I got us matching sunglasses!

RICHARDSON

Wait. Fuck. That picture is cute as hell. Can I come help again? I bet she'll help me score all the women.

MILLER

You're not allowed to use my daughter as your wingwoman, Ethan.

HAYES

How's everything going, Mavvy? How is Emmy?

MILLER

She's at the spa right now with Piper, Lexi, and Madeline. Started therapy earlier this week, and I went with her. We slept for four hours when G-Money came over earlier to help with Murph and the house.

I know it's not something that's going to change overnight. I know I'm going to have to work my ass off to make sure I'm doing enough so she never feels like she's handling everything by herself. But Emmy smiled this afternoon, and I swear to god it was the most beautiful thing I've ever seen.

MITCHELL

Why does that make me want to cry?

Happy for you two, man. And after these two weeks, I'm more than happy to still help out.

EVERETT

Same!

SULLIVAN

Your replacement is shit, Miller. Coach could've done some better scouting.

MILLER

Miss you too, Sully.

Miss all of you.

ME

Watch yourself, Sullivan.

RICHARDSON

Shit! I forgot Coach was in here!

What it do, Brody boo?

ME

> You can't be serious, Richardson.

> You just earned an extra forty-five minutes in the weight room.

RICHARDSON

> Joke is on you. I love sled pushes.

Liam Sullivan has left the chat
Ethan Richardson has added Liam Sullivan to the chat

RICHARDSON

> Just accept it, Sully. There's no escaping us.

SULLIVAN

> Fuck my life.

THE WEEK we had off during the league's international competition was a welcomed relief. Hannah and I skated every day. She showed me some of the routine she's working on for her competition, and when she fell after trying to land a move I can't pronounce, I gave her a hug and told her I was proud of her before she could start to doubt herself.

The two weeks after the break at the start of March are some of the toughest of the season. We have ten games over fifteen days. Six are at home, but the cross-country flights nearly knock me on my ass. Maverick is still away from the team, the guys who have been helping him and Emmy are dragging too, and I made a last-minute decision to cancel tomorrow's morning skate so everyone can take a fucking breath.

I lean against the doorframe of Hannah's apartment, my

head on my forearm while I contemplate taking a power nap before I take her out.

"Falling asleep on me, Saunders?" Hannah asks, opening the door in a jean skirt and sweater. "Our date hasn't even started."

"Sorry." I yawn and stand up straight. "I'm exhausted."

"We can reschedule if you want to—"

"No." I grab her by the belt loop and bring her to me, kissing her forehead. "Hi, Ice Queen."

"Hi, baby." Hannah stares at me horrified, a hand over her mouth. "Oh my god. No. *Nope.* Pretend I didn't say that. I meant BB. Not baby."

"Hannah Everett. Dropping the pet names on me." My hands slide into her back pockets, giving her ass a squeeze. "I'm *scandalized.*"

"Sorry. Was that weird? It felt weird." Pink cheeks. Hurried tone. Her nerves make me smile. "Are you ready? We should go."

"Why are you freaking out? I don't think that was weird, sweetheart," I say to make a point. It's my turn for flushed cheeks. "I liked it."

"Wait a second. Are you secretly a big softie? A romantic?" She stands on her toes and touches my cheek. "I knew there was so much more to you than all the grunts and groans."

"Layers." I kiss her ear, her jaw. "I'm full of surprises."

"Like where you're taking me tonight?"

"My mental capacity for planning things is pretty low right now," I admit. "There's a lot going on with our schedule, making sure my players are taking care of themselves, and Liv recovering from the stomach bug. Is it okay if we keep it lowkey tonight?"

"Lowkey sounds perfect." Hannah pats my chest and grabs her purse, lacing our fingers together. "Sounds like you have a lot on your plate."

"That's coaching a professional sport." I watch her lock up and we file into the elevator. "I'd say the summers are quieter, but that's when all the roster changes happen."

"Is coaching something you see yourself doing the rest of your life?"

"I'd like it to be. Coaching at the Olympics is the short-term goal, but long-term? Yeah. I'd like to put in twenty more years. I enjoy it. I'm decent at it. I don't see myself as a commentator or analyst, and you'd have to pay all the money in the fucking world to be on television."

"You don't want to make small talk with people in front of dozens of cameras? I'm *shocked*." She hops in the passenger seat of my SUV, and I turn on the heat to make sure she's warm. "Do you want to stay in DC?"

"Pending getting fired? Yeah. I moved Liv around so much when she was younger because I only spent a season or two with a team before I got a better offer and headed to the next city. That meant Kali moved too. We've been here for years now, and uprooting them at this point feels cruel. They have friends and routines, and I like the Stars' management. I like the culture and the team we've put together. I like the fans. I'm happy here." I pull out of the parking garage and head for the bar I scouted out for tonight. "Speaking of Liv and being happy in DC, I see she gave you a friendship bracelet."

"She did!" Hannah holds her wrist, proud of the pink and white beads. "It's my good luck charm for my competition in eleven days."

"Her bracelets are magic." I show off my matching one. "I haven't taken mine off from the Stanley Cup two years ago."

"That makes me so happy." She relaxes in the seat and turns her body my way. "Can I ask you a personal question?"

"Sure."

"Do you do a lot of dating?"

"Nope." I drum my fingers on the steering wheel. "Privacy

has a big thing to do with it. I'm protective of Liv. Of people having access to my players. And, like you saw tonight, I'm exhausted. I'm pulled eighteen different directions, and with the limited free time I do have, I don't want to spend it making small talk with someone I'm not interested in." I glance over at her. She's smiling at me as we pass streetlights, and it makes me smile too. "There are some exceptions, of course."

"Of course." She taps my hand resting on the center console. "And aren't they lucky?"

We talk the rest of the way to the bar and order a round of drinks. After a story from Hannah that involves a first date with a woman and a wedding ring, I'm laughing so hard she has to hit my back so I don't choke.

"You kicked my ass in bowling, but how do you think you'll fare with air hockey?" I take her hand and lead her through the crowded room. "That's your side there."

"Am I allowed to flash you? I think it's the only way I'm going to win. You're very good at hockey."

"Come on, sweetheart. Air hockey and hockey aren't the same thing." I set the puck in front of my striker and wait for Hannah to grab hers. She crouches low, moving side to side, and *my fucking god*. She's the cutest person I've ever seen. "Ready?"

"Come on, Daddy." Her grin is sharp. "Give me your best shot."

It's a goddamn miracle I'm able to bring my wrist back and hit the puck as hard as I can, and when I do, it sails past her hand and goes into the goal. "Oh, Hannah. You need to at least try to stop it."

"Bullshit! You can't be out here acting like you're quali-fying for the Olympic team. Bring it down three notches, Saunders, or you'll be playing by yourself."

"I play by myself a lot," I answer with a grin. She huffs under the breath, and I motion for the puck. "Funny how it's

Daddy when you want to get your way, but not when you lose."

"Funny how you pretend like you don't like it when I call you Daddy, but your forearm is flexing," she tosses back. "And you just looked at my tits."

I grind my teeth to stop myself from bending her over the table because, no, I don't hate it when she calls me that, and I wish I could fucking explain why. "I don't know what you're talking about," I say. "Let me try again."

This time, I go comically slow. I exaggerate pulling my arm back. I hit the puck gently, watching it inch across the table. When it gets close to her, Hannah knocks it as hard as she can. It lifts off the table, into the air, and spins before knocking me in the forehead.

"Oh my god." She gapes at me. "Are you okay?"

"Dirty, dirty play, Everett." I shake my head, but there's no way I can fight off my smile. "It's time for payback."

"If you hurt me, I'm going to kick your ass next time we're on the ice."

"Last time we raced, you blatantly interfered with my victory." I line the puck up with her goal. "And I hope you know I would never hurt you."

"I do know that." Her face softens. "I call for a redo."

The next play has Hannah flailing, trying to stop my goal, but she looks so ridiculous, I fucking *giggle*. I put my hands on the table, keeling over, and when her striker goes flying off the table, I completely lose it.

I've always strived to be the hardest worker in any room. I've sacrificed so much to get to where I am today. I missed out on birthdays and parties and big life moments. There's been no dating, no excitement, no *fun*.

Boundaries in place. Clear expectations of everyone in my life, including myself. But as I lift my chin and look at Hannah leaning over the hockey table, her blue eyes sparkling with glee, it hits me that every good moment I've had over the last five months, every moment that's pushed me out of my comfort zone and forced me to live a little, has included her.

The winning is great. Watching good hockey is a blast. But for the first time in my life, I want a partner to share all of that with.

And I want it to be her.

"Hey," Hannah snaps, and my gaze shifts to her. She's grinning, and looking at her makes my breath loosen from my lungs. "You're in la-la-land over there. What's going on in that head of yours? Plotting other ways to make me look ridiculous?"

I'm considering getting on one knee and asking if you'll hang out with me for the rest of my life so I can laugh like this forever. I want to bend you over this table and show you how much you mean to me. I think I might be falling in love with you, and it scares the hell out of me because the last thing I ever want to do is hold you back or not be good enough for you. I don't know what I'm doing, but I want to try with you.

"Nothing." I set down the puck and walk around the table, pulling her in a tight hug. She relaxes against me, cheek on my chest. Hand over my heart, and everything is right in the world. "Just daydreaming."

Peace.

That's the way to describe what it's like to have her in my arms.

The outside noises, the responsibilities, the list of things I need to accomplish tomorrow—everything else on my plate disappears. It narrows down to a single thing, the only woman who has ever had so much of my attention.

Her.

"Brody?" she says, my name muffled in my sweater.

"Yeah, sweetheart?"

"Don't ever make me play air hockey again."

"Okay." I bury my face in her hair, feeling drunk. Fucking intoxicated and goddamn giddy when she's in my orbit. If everyone was like her, I'd always walk around with the biggest smile on my face. "I promise I won't."

"Can we grab a bite to eat? I'll pay, since you wiped the floor with me."

"Abso-fucking-lutley not. I might kick your ass, but I'm going to take care of you too."

With a hand on the back of her neck, we find a table near a large wooden beam. A jukebox sits in the corner and plays some sappy love ballad from the eighties I remember my mom listening to when I was young. Hannah orders a burger and I go for the chicken sandwich, not putting up a fight when she steals a tater tot from my tray.

"Do you have a bucket list?" I ask, grabbing an extra stack of napkins from a server passing by. "The guys were talking about them at practice the other day."

"Oh, good question. As far as athletic achievements go, medaling at the Olympics is at the top, but that feels out of reach these days." Hannah pauses to add ketchup to her burger and take off a piece of lettuce. "Non-athletic things would be a trip around the world. Tierney and I have talked about visiting Paris and London and Tokyo, but we haven't made it happen yet. Maybe pick up a new hobby and be good at it? Make an impact on someone's life. Riding in a racecar would be freaking cool. I'd also like to love someone deeply. Like, that romcom movie level kind of love, you know?"

"Can't eat, can't sleep, reach for the stars World Series kind of love?"

"Did you just quote a Mary Kate and Ashley Olsen movie to me? Are you *cultured*?"

"Thank my daughter. We spent one summer watching their entire filmography, and if held at gunpoint, I could recite a quote from each one," I tell her, and she drops her head back with a laugh.

"I'm impressed," she says.

"So. A movie kind of love, huh?" I ask.

"Yeah. I don't know. It sounds cheesy, but it feels like a rite of passage. I don't think a relationship is indicative of a life well lived, but those warm, fuzzy feelings? The butterflies? Smiling so hard your cheeks hurt? A grand gesture with a boombox outside my window?" She shrugs, reaching for another tater tot. "Sounds like it could be fun until you get your heart broken, then everything sucks."

"The circle of life, apparently."

"What would be on your bucket list?"

"I have no clue. I've never thought about it, which is sad, since I'm almost forty." I wipe my hands and fold my napkin in half. "My entire life, ever since I was four years old, has been perfectly laid out. I was on a travel hockey team by the time I was ten. Colleges were knocking on my door when I was fifteen. NHL scouts came to every one of my games at BC. Then Liv was born, and everything else took a back seat to being a father—which I'm grateful for. But I haven't had any time to decide what the hell *I* want."

"Do you want to travel? Skate at some famous rink?" Hannah asks.

"I think I'd just like to…" I huff out a laugh. "Breathe? Uninterrupted? For just a minute? Maybe somewhere beautiful with someone I enjoy."

"You *are* a romantic." Her foot nudges mine. "If you want someone to join you, I know a girl. She has a lot of free time, and for as much as people say the hockey coach is a grumpy asshole, she knows differently." She looks at me from across the table. "And she would be very excited to accompany you."

I don't care that we're in a public place. I don't care who might be able to see us. I stand, walking to her chair, and put both hands on her cheeks. I tip her head back until our eyes meet. Then, I kiss her. I kiss her because I fucking *can*, and that just jumped to the top of my list.

THIRTY-THREE

HANNAH

GRANT

Good luck tonight, Han!

All the guys say good luck too!

Wish I could be there to watch you.

ME

Thanks, G.

GRANT

Feeling okay?

ME

I think once I get out there, I'll be okay.

But right now, I'm so nervous.

GRANT

Inhale confidence, exhale fear, remember?

ME

I remember!

I hope you guys have a good game too!

GRANT

Who doesn't love Boston?!

Text me after so I can hear about how it went.

ME

I will, I will.

Thank you for checking in.

GRANT

Course. Love ya, sis.

Knock 'em dead!

"WE MADE it to your big day. How are you feeling?" Tierney asks in the small dressing room at the Washington Figure Skating Club's rink. She pulls my hair out of my face, securing it with a pink ribbon. "You look beautiful."

"Thanks, T." I fix my sleeve and take a deep breath. "I'm feeling everything right now, to be honest. Scared. Hesitant. I'm happy too, but I overheard two teenage girls ask what I was doing at a competition as small as this one, and their friend answered with, 'she sucks now.' That's jarring."

"Fuck 'em," Tierney says, setting down the brush. Her dark eyes find mine in the mirror, encouragement behind her gaze. "Might as well go out there and give them something to talk about."

"You're right." I smile. "At the end of the day, I don't need to listen to what anyone else says. I'm doing this for me."

"Anything else on your mind?" She rests her hand on my shoulder and squeezes once. "You seem distracted."

"I just…" I bite my bottom lip. "Promise not to judge me for what I'm about to say?"

"Never."

"Brody was supposed to be here tonight to watch me, but a conflict with his game means he's still in Boston. And... I miss him. I didn't realize how *much* I missed him until I checked my phone all afternoon, waiting for a text from him, only to not have one." I grab my lipstick and open the tube. "He's busy. I *know* he's busy. I just... I was hopeful, you know?"

"Oh, sweetie. It's okay to be disappointed." Tierney bends to give me a hug. "If he could text, I'm sure he would. That doesn't mean he doesn't support you."

"You're right. I'm the one going out there and performing. I'm the one who has spent hours rehearsing the choreography, but I don't think any of this would be possible without him. He made skating *fun* again, and I wish he could see how excited I am."

"I'll make sure to record it so you can send it to him." Tierney taps her phone to check the time. "You should get going. It's almost your turn."

"Shit. Let me grab my skates." I pop to my feet and fix my pink skirt. "I'll find you after."

"You're going to be incredible." She pulls me into another tight embrace, and I savor the energy she's sending my way. "You're Hannah fucking Everett. You belong out there. Okay?"

"Okay." I roll my shoulders back, more sure of myself. "Thanks, T."

When I slip into the hall, I force myself to take a deep breath.

Inhale confidence, exhale fear, I repeat, shaking out my arms and starting for my skates. Ahead of me, a door flies open and hits the wall. I jerk my neck up, trying to see what the commotion is, and halt in my tracks.

Someone is walking toward me in a black sweater and dark joggers. White sneakers, backward hat on his head. Long strides that bring him closer and closer. I blink, positive this must be a dream, and then he's there. Right in front of me, and the earth stops moving.

Brody.

"I thought I was late. I thought I missed it." He scrubs a hand over his face, but I can't answer. "But I made it."

"What—" I glance around. The music from a competitor's program echoes from the other side of the wall, and I blink. Stare up at him, mouth open. "You're here? Aren't you supposed to be in… New York? Philadelphia? Somewhere else? But you're… you're here?"

"Boston," he says. "And I was. The good thing about earning the kind of money I do is I can spend that money however I want. And tonight, that meant arranging for a private plane, leaving halfway through the third period when we were winning 6-0, and taking the short flight so I could see you." He takes my face in his hands, thumbs stroking over the curve of my cheek. "This is important to you, which means it's important to me."

"What about the team? Coaching? The game?"

"One of my assistants took over. He's hoping to interview for a head coaching position next season, and the experience would be good for him. I said I wasn't feeling well." Brody's mouth pulls up in a smile. He pretends to cough. "I'd hate to get anyone sick."

"You did that for me? Hockey… that's your life."

"Maybe it's time I rearrange a few things." He digs in his pocket and pulls out a bracelet. "A new one from Liv. She's out in the stands too—I swung by Kali's and picked her up on the way—and wants me to let you know she's proud of you. She says you're the best coach she's ever had." He pauses, resting his forehead against mine. "You're the best skater I've ever had, and I'm so proud of you too."

My eyes prick with tears. My nose stings. I'm dangerously close to splitting at the seams because Brody is *here*. He's here, and I've never been so happy.

I throw my arms around his neck. He laughs into my shoulder, palms on my waist and pulling me flush to his body.

"When you didn't text me, I thought you were busy. Or you forgot." I swallow the lump in my throat, emotion welling inside me. "It made me sad, and I don't know why it made me sad."

"I'd never forget today. I've had it in my phone calendar for weeks." He's careful as he strokes my hair, playing with the end of my ponytail with gentle brushes of his fingers. "I wanted to text you, but I also didn't want to get your hopes up if I couldn't pull this off. I'm so glad I did."

"Thank you," I whisper. "This means so much to me."

"I'll let you finish getting ready." Brody drops a kiss to the top of my head and pulls away. "You're going to kill it, sweetheart."

"I can't believe you're here." I wipe under my eyes, fanning my face so my tears don't ruin my makeup. "All the way from Boston."

With one more kiss to my cheek, we turn to go our separate ways. Before I can get too far, his pinky loops around mine. I look at him over my shoulder, and it hits me like a goddamn wrecking ball when I find his eyes sweeping down my outfit. When he smiles at me again, bright enough to light up a room.

Butterflies.

Warm and fuzzy.

Smiling so hard my cheeks hurt.

Going out of his way so he can be where I need him.

I'm falling for this man. I'm falling for him so hard, and I don't know what to do.

"There's nowhere else I'd rather be," Brody says, and it feels like the wind gets knocked out of my chest.

I STAND along the curve of the rink, watching the woman before me finish her program. It's beautiful. Incredibly smooth for someone who's not professionally trained, and when she hits her final mark, I join the crowd in applauding her.

The music cuts off and she gives the crowd a curtsy. She waves as she skates away, hopping over the small ledge to the rubber mats and stopping when she sees me.

"That was great," I say. "Your camel spin is beautiful."

"Holy shit. You're Hannah Everett. I thought there was a misprint with the entries when I saw your name." She looks me up and down. "You're my favorite skater. I have your World Championship program memorized."

I smile. "It's so nice to meet you."

"Okay. Wow. I'm going to be riding this high for a long time. Good luck out there. I'm sure you're going to do great," she says.

"Wish I could shake these nerves." The announcer calls my name, and I double-check my laces to make sure they're tight. "Thanks for the luck. I'm going to need it."

The world around me quiets when I step out. It always does, and I stand in the center, leaving everything behind me. I take solace in the crowd, finding Tierney in the front row grinning at me. Toward the top of the stands, with his hat pulled low, is Brody. He's sitting forward, elbows on his knees, hands covering his mouth, and my heart jumpstarts when he gives me a nod. Next to him is Liv, her fingers crossed and palms clasped in front of her.

All of my favorite people are here to watch me, and I'm the luckiest girl in the world.

The first chord of the song plays over the speaker, and my body moves on instinct, taking off like it has done thousands of times before. A shaky triple Axel. A more confident triple Lutz. The more I travel across the ice, the more I relax. The more I feel reconnected to the sport that used to own my heart.

It's a different program than what I've done before. Less flashy and less risky, I stick to elements I perfected by the time I was eighteen, but the crowd enjoys it. There's applause with my butterfly spin, one of the best I've ever done. There's a sigh of relief when I nail my jump combination, and two minutes and thirty seconds goes by far too quick.

By the time I finish, every part of my body aches. My muscles are sore, my brain is foggy from performing in front of a crowd for the first time in months, but when I lift my arm above my head and hold my final pose, I'm ecstatic.

The arena explodes in applause again and I wave, skating off the ice and wiping a bead of sweat from my forehead, a gentle reminder my conditioning needs work if I'm going to consider making a comeback. When my score comes in, the judges give me something I'm damn proud of.

"Hannah!" Tierney rushes to me. "Holy *fuck*. That was stunning."

"My 3A was shit, wasn't it?"

"You made up for it with your 3Lz. Forget that. What was it like being back out there?"

"Exhilarating. And humbling." I laugh. "Also… exciting? Like I kind of want to do it again?"

"I'm so happy for you, Han. I recorded the whole thing so you can send it to Brody," she says.

"I don't need to do that." I gesture to where Brody and Liv are lingering by the stairs. "He surprised me."

"*Fucking hell.* Of course he did, because he's a man, not a fuckboy." Tierney grins. "Go talk to them."

"I'll be right back," I promise.

"You better not be. That man deserves more than two minutes of your time." She pins me with a look. "He *surprised you*, Han."

"Yeah, I know. And my brain is mush because of it." I find my bag and switch my skates for my slides. "I really like him, T."

I maneuver through the crowd to where the two of them are standing. Liv squeals when she sees me, jumping up and down and giving me a hug.

"Hannah! That was so good!" she muses. "Your airtime is *wild*. You're just like, *floating*!"

"That will be you one day," I say, looking over at Brody. "Thank you so much for coming, you all. I can't tell you how much it means to me that you're here."

"I knew you were good. I knew you were popular." Brody's gaze shifts from my skirt to my ribbon. "But watching you skate at full strength and speed in person? That was the most beautiful fucking thing."

My cheeks flush with heat. "I messed up a few times. Some of my entries were shaky and—"

"You did the damn thing, Hannah. And your edge work?" He reaches out like he wants to touch me, then remembers who is around. "Perfect."

"I had a great teacher," I say.

"Is that Tierney Barnes?" Liv asks, craning her neck. "Oh my *god*. She's stunning in real life! *Dad*. Did you know she's the second Black woman to medal at the World Figure Skating Championships? She's *royalty*."

"And one of the sweetest people in the world. Go talk to her," I urge. "She'd love to meet you. If you have any extra friendship bracelets, she'll take one." I show Liv my wrist, the gift she made me carrying me through my program. "We can all match."

"You *and* Tierney wearing one of my bracelets? I would die. Okay." Liv takes a deep breathe. "I'm going to say hi."

Brody and I watch her walk up to my best friend, and he puts a hand on the small of my back.

"You've given my daughter so much," he tells me. "I don't think I could ever repay you."

"Says the guy who went out of his way to see me." I relax when his thumb strokes up my spine. "Knowing you were in the crowd reminded me it's okay if I mess up. At the end of the day, I have people who support me, and that's what is most important."

"Any anxiety?" Brody asks. "Feeling overwhelmed?"

"No. I'm always happy when I skate, but I'm not always happy when I perform. Right now, I'm happy. It's a start."

His hand moves up back, between my shoulders, stopping when he gets to my hair. "Another ribbon. Still the bane of my existence."

"Should I stop wearing them?" I ask.

"Please don't."

I laugh and undo the bow looped through my ponytail. I pull it free, then take his hand, tying it around his wrist. "There. Now you have one you haven't ripped."

"Wow." Brody brings it to his nose, giving it a deep inhale. "Smells like your shampoo and perfume. I'm never taking this off."

"Unless it's to tie my wrists together, right?"

"Right." He smiles and looks over his shoulder. He kisses his palm then rests it on the back of my neck, the briefest of touches to my skin. "What are you doing now?"

"Tierney and I are probably going to grab some food. Do you want to come?" I ask.

"I do, but you should go without me. This is your big night. She's been your cheerleader for years. Go enjoy it with her," Brody says.

Oh, no.

The butterflies are back, swarming in the center of my chest.

This man and his soft, considerate heart.

"Thank you," I whisper. "I'll text you later?"

"Looking forward to it." He steps back, and I miss him already. "I know I already said it, but I'm going to say it again, because it's worth hearing twice. I'm so proud of you, Hannah. Small, local competitions. The Olympics. Doesn't matter what the stage is. I do support you and whatever your dreams look like."

With the graze of his knuckles against my elbow he heads for Liv, leading her toward the exit. Brody looks at me one final time before they step outside, and I feel it. The cosmic shift when his eyes find mine.

He's part of my dreams now, and I don't think I could ever be any happier than this.

THIRTY-FOUR
BRODY

KALI

How was Hannah's competition?

ME

How do you know about that?

KALI

We have a fourteen-year-old daughter, Brody.
She's the biggest gossip.

Liv seemed like she had a good time.

ME

It was fun. Cool to see her skate like that.

KALI

Anything else?

ME

We might be spending time together.

And I might like her. A lot.

Haven't felt this way before, really.

KALI

I KNEW it.

Oh, Brody. I'm so happy for you.

Do you love her?

ME

I've never really been in love with anyone before. I love Liv. I love you. I love my guys. But that's different from how I feel about Hannah.

It's almost like she completes me.

KALI

You have been smiling a lot more lately.

And Liv adores her.

ME

I'm not sure what I'm supposed to do about it.

KALI

Just let it be. Enjoy it. Enjoy her.

You take care of a lot of people in your life. You deserve to be taken care of too.

ME

I appreciate you, Kal.

KALI

Are you seeing her tonight?

ME

Yeah. She's coming over. Think you could keep Liv until tomorrow night? I'll swing by and pick her up after the game.

KALI

Happy to :).

"WHAT DO you like to do for fun when I'm not around?" Hannah stretches out on my bed, a leg thrown over mine. "Or are you unfamiliar with what that word means?"

"I do know how to exist when I'm not with you." I poke her ribs, my fingers fanning out over her stomach. "Though it's much more fun when you're here. My heart health is the best it's ever been. Apparently, I'm laughing more?"

"I'm a miracle worker, what can I say?" She rests her hand in the center of my bare chest. Her nails scrape over my skin, and I like the pink lines she leaves behind. "Say it's a Friday night and Liv is with Kali. What would you do with your free time?"

"You're going to make fun of me." I groan and grab a pillow, covering my face. "And probably say something about my old age."

"Oh, I can't wait to hear." Hannah moves the pillow away, smiling down at me with her hair in a messy bun on her head. "Spill, Saunders."

"I'd be reviewing game notes or watching game footage. Maybe answering an email or text from our CEO asking about a potential trade. After that? I might read? Or watch a movie? I don't know. Back when I played, a lot of my team-mates were into partying and drinking and hooking up with random women in random cities until sunup, but I never liked any of that. Always kept to myself, I guess. Now that I'm older and Liv is spending more time with friends and less time at home, I'm realizing I need to get some more hobbies outside of crossword puzzles." I reach up, twisting a loose piece of her hair around my finger. "Should I learn to golf?"

"Golfers are hot. I'd like to see you in a pair of khakis."

She grins and crosses her legs. "I have an idea for something fun we can do."

"Should I be afraid to hear what it is?"

"Are there any cameras in the practice facility?"

"No. They kept the security features to a minimum. Wanted to protect the players and their privacy, so the only digital recording is when we open our practices to the public." I narrow my eyes and sit up, pulling her into my lap. "Why?"

"We could go down there." Hannah rolls her hips against my thigh. I wonder if she could get off just from grinding on me. No fingers, no tongue. "And play a game of strip skating."

"Strip skating?" Thinking clearly is proving to be difficult when she leans forward and presses a kiss to my neck, licking up my throat. "I've never heard of that game."

"It's like poker. Or HORSE. We take turns doing a move on the ice. The person who doesn't perform the move correctly has to ditch an article of clothing." She pauses so she can whisper this next part in my ear. "First person to be naked loses."

"Jesus." I close my eyes when she drops her hand and strokes my shaft over my briefs. "What happens when you're naked?"

"Whatever you want. The winner gets to decide. So, if you were victorious, you could tie my wrists together again. Bend me over your desk or fuck me in the locker room."

My cock jumps at the idea of having her in a place I spend hours of my day. I've been protective over the thought of someone from the team seeing her in a way I don't want them to, but this is different.

It would only be us. No chance of getting caught, no chance of being overheard. I could spread her out. Fuck her in the showers. Maybe I wouldn't bother with any of that, instead pressing her against the glass surrounding the ice and making her come on my cock while she screams my name.

"Whatever I want to do to you?" I repeat, grabbing her

chin so she looks at me. Big, blue eyes. The jut of her bottom lip I want to bite. "That sounds dangerous, sweetheart."

"Whatever you want. But if I win, I get the same reward." She trails a finger along my jaw. Down my chest and my stomach, stopping at my cock. "Have you ever crawled on the ice before, Brody?"

I growl and stand, lifting her off of me. I climb off the bed and toss a pair of pants at her, already reaching for my clothes. "Get dressed, Hannah. You're about to see how competitive I can be."

"You're hot when you go into athlete mode." She giggles and switches out my oversize shirt with her white one. "You're going down, Saunders."

I'm going to let her think she has the upper hand. I'm going to let her pretend she's in control, because being naked and letting her have her way with me doesn't sound like losing at all.

***

I KEEP the arena lights dim when we get to the practice facility. It's colder in the building without sweaty bodies in it, and I wish I had worn pants instead of athletic shorts and a hoodie.

"I need to grab my skates from my office," I say. "Glad you had yours at my place. We don't have anything that would fit you here."

She flashes me a smile and takes a seat on the players' bench. "I'll wait for you here."

"Be back in five," I say, jogging down the tunnel.

I snag my skates from where they're sitting in the spare chair and head back to the ice. Hannah is in the same spot, and I sit next to her, my thigh pressing against hers.

"This place is creepy when there aren't other people around." She glances at the rafters and across to the rows of seats. "Do you think it's haunted? Do you think the Grim Reaper has visited here to take someone's soul?"

"Unless she also visited the trees and overgrown grass that used to be here, I wouldn't expect any ghosts to surprise us."

"I think the Grim Reaper is a woman *too*!" Hannah nudges my arm with her elbow. "I knew you were a smart man."

"Women are far superior." I slip my left foot into my skate, tying it tight. "Tell me about the rules of this game. You know I can't do a triple quadruple backward Axel or whatever the hell it is you do."

"You're kind of close." She kisses my cheek, and my right foot misses the skate entirely. "The rules are simple: you can do hockey shots, and I'll do figure skating moves, with the exception of no jumps or flips."

"*Flips*? You can flip while you're on your skates?"

"There's a reason why it's hockey players who hang out with figure skaters in the offseason and not the other way around: because we're really fucking talented. Flipping on skates is difficult. Almost impossible. The ISU—that's the International Skating Union—banned somersaults in competitions decades ago. You were probably alive then."

"Brat." I reach down and squeeze her knee. "Are they still banned?"

"Not anymore. I could give you a whole history lesson, but we have more important things to focus on. No flips from me, which means you're not allowed to do any fancy goals."

"So, we each perform the move. If we're successful, and the other person isn't, they lose an article of clothing."

"Exactly," Hannah says.

"How many layers are we ditching?" I ask.

"Well, that depends." She pops to her feet. The spin she does on the ice is effortless, beautiful. I'm mesmerized every time I watch her. "How bad do you want me, Brody?"

I lace my other skate and move toward her, towering over

her. I wrap her hair around my wrist and give it a hard tug, humming when she blinks up at me.

"I want you more than I want any other thing in my life, Hannah," I murmur. "And when I win, I'm going to spread you out on the logo. I'm going to make you wait until you're begging for my cock. Then I'm going to fuck you in the same spot my players will be tomorrow, and they'll have no idea I made you come right there, just a few hours before."

She whines and squeezes her legs together, and I can see her nipples turning hard through the thin fabric of her shirt. "And if I win?" she asks, a hand resting on my hip. "Would you get on your knees for me, Brody?"

"I have before. I would again. But that's not going to happen," I say into her ear. "Get your ass on the blue line, angel, so we can start. I'll let you go first."

I grab two sticks and a puck and lean them against the boards. Hannah stretches her hamstrings and calves. With her eyes on me, she does a turn with her arms above her head, pirouetting in three full rotations before coming to a stop.

"I'm starting easy," she says.

"No making fun of me," I grumble.

"What happens at the practice rink stays at the practice rink." Hannah taps her heart. "I promise. But I believe in you, Brody."

It's stupid how her faith in me makes me want to puff out my chest. It's stupid how I check to see if she's watching before I stand up straight. It's stupid how I don't care about winning, but I do care about showing off.

I'm flustered as I try to mimic her position. I push off with my left skate, unsteady as I make the first rotation. I pick a spot on the ice and put all my focus on it, my arms swaying dangerously until Hannah lets out a whoop and claps.

"I messed up, didn't I?" I ask when I stop. "I didn't turn enough times."

"Yes, you did! That was so good!" She kisses my cheek,

and I'm flustered all over again. "How do you feel about pairs figure skating? We'd make a great team."

"I appreciate your faith in me, but I am not lifting you over my head in a way that could get you hurt. I'll leave that to the professionals." I tap her hip. "Do I get to keep my clothes on?"

"For now." She grabs one of the hockey sticks and crouches low. "What move are you going to make me do, Coach?"

"A quick lesson first." I stand behind her, crowding her space. I put my hands above and below hers on the shaft. "A wrist shot starts with your stick low, then coming up to shoulder height, keeping contact with the puck the whole time. A slap shot will start with your stick in the air, then come down to the puck where you'll accelerate with a brief separation from the puck." I walk her through each shot. "Backhand shot uses the back of the stick, and a snapshot is faster than a wrist shot without a full wind-up. Understand?"

"Yeah," she breathes out. "I understand, Coach."

I kiss the back of her head and pull away, deciding on a wrist shot without a lot of momentum. The puck sails easily into the net when I hit it, but it goes wide right on Hannah's turn. She decides on ditching her hair tie first, and after a brief argument, I agree that, *fine*, she can count that as an article of clothing, as long as I can count my friendship bracelets.

We go back and forth, finding a good rhythm of accomplishing every move, but I get sloppy with an in-and-out sequence she executes perfectly. I have to pull off my hoodie, and her shirt comes off when she misses an easy shot from the crease, the puck clanking off the post and away from the net.

I can't do a spin sit to save my life and almost pull a muscle in the process. She's hopelessly optimistic when she attempts a bar down goal, not able to get the puck in the air. Soon, I'm in just my briefs, the cool arena air welcome on my overheated skin. Hannah is left in a pair of underwear that shows off the curve of her ass, and her tits are distracting the fuck out of me.

"My eyes are up here, Brody," she says, and I wouldn't be surprised if my tongue was hanging out of my mouth.

"Don't need to see your eyes." I pluck her nipple, smiling when she drops her head back and moans. "This is just fine."

"If you miss this, I win. Are you ready for your punishment?"

I'm ready for this game to end. My self-control is hanging by a thread. All I want to do is throw her over my shoulder, take her somewhere warm, and eat her out.

"Don't get ahead of yourself." I move my hand down, dragging my knuckles over the front of her underwear. There's a damp spot in the center, and I'm seconds away from ripping them in half. Seconds away from proudly declaring myself a loser, just so she can use me however she sees fit. "You have to complete the move too."

"I could do it in my sleep."

Turning her back to me, she brushes her ass against the front of my briefs. She tries to pull away, but I loop an arm around her waist, keeping her there. Her head drops back against my chest, blonde hair going everywhere while I pull her underwear to the side and push a single finger inside her. Hannah hisses, spreading her legs open. My skates frame hers, and I watch her breathe out a slow exhale.

"What are you waiting for, angel?" I kiss her cheek, her neck. She rolls her hips on my finger, looking for more friction, but I don't give it to her. "Let me see your move, then you can have what you want."

"You're mean." She whimpers when I drop to my knees, grabbing her ass with both hands. I knead the soft skin of her cheeks and bite the curve of her backside. "And not fair."

"You have free will." I pull on her underwear, my middle finger running along the line of her crack. "You could've done your move at any time, but you haven't, have you? Because you like when I touch you. And you're going to like it even more when you lose."

With a rough smack to her ass, I stand back up, not caring that my cock is leaking pre-cum in my briefs. It wouldn't be the first time I finished in my pants around her, but Hannah slowly skates away. Her knees tremble and she fans her face, trying to regain her composure.

"Bunny hop jump," she tells me, but when she takes off and tries to bring her swinging knee in the air, she loses her balance. Her toe pick hits the ice, and she falls forward. She catches herself with her hands, but I still rush over to her. "God dammit."

"Are you okay? Are you hurt?"

"My ego is hurt. I've never *not* landed that move, and the one time I need to, I can't." Hannah groans and shivers, dusting ice off her knees. "But I don't think you'll be able to do it either."

"Oh yeah?" I crouch low, holding out a palm to help her up. When her fingers lace through mine, I give her a wicked grin. "Is this the part where I tell you I did a figure skating class with Liv when she was ten, and I fucking *nailed* the bunny hop jump?"

THIRTY-FIVE
BRODY

Puck Kings and Daddy Things (+ our savior, BS)

MILLER

Guess what, boys? I'm officially returning next week.

The last month and a half off has been incredible. Thanks for the extension, Coach.

EVERETT

HELL YEAH. MAVVY DADDY IS BACK, BABY!

RICHARDSON

Just in time, too. We play against St. Louis in a couple of weeks, and I need my captain there to keep my ass in line.

SULLIVAN

Why haven't I seen a photo of your daughter wearing the onesie I made for her, Miller?

I spent weeks crocheting that hat.

MILLER

Attachment: 1 image

Better, Sully?

SULLIVAN

Much. Thank god she looks like Emmy and not you.

HAYES

Glad to hear you're coming back, Mav. Happy to return your captain title to you whenever you're ready.

EVERETT

Wait. Are we all at home on a Friday night not doing anything fun? Lol. When did we get so boring?

MILLER

Married with a kid, G-Money. I'm fine never leaving the house again.

HAYES

Madeline made brownies tonight, and now we're on the couch watching some romcom based on a best-selling book? Motioning for it to be our next book club read.

MITCHELL

I'm with Lexi. She kicked my ass in the athletic trainer's room today. She's so hot when she's torturing me.

SULLIVAN

Piper.

EVERETT

I'm afraid to ask what Easy E is doing.

RICHARDSON

Nothing, actually. Might turn in early.

EVERETT

Whoaaaaaa. What in the world?

Maybe Coach is doing something fun!

RICHARDSON

Brody boo! Where are you?

EVERETT

Coachhhhh?

RICHARDSON

Must be pretty important if he doesn't even
tell us to shut up.

HANNAH GAPES AT ME, but she lets me pull her up.

"You're not serious," she says.

"Wish I had pictures of the blisters to prove it. Four classes. Four Sundays of my life twirling around. Four Sundays with other dads who had two left feet. Four Sundays of wondering how the hell I played professional hockey when I couldn't cut a lap in figure skates." I kiss her knuckles. "And four Sundays of learning the bunny hop."

"Why didn't you tell me? That's not fair at all!"

"Oh, please. Like you never joined Grant on the ice," I say, and her guilty smile tells me all I need to know.

"He might've taught me what a slap shot is," she says, letting out a yelp when I throw her over my shoulder. I move to the penalty box and deposit her on the cold metal bench, laughing when she huffs at me under her breath. "What are you doing to me?"

"Sit in the sin bin and think about what you did. After I

execute this bunny hop perfectly, I'm going to bind your wrists together with tape. I'm going to fuck you so hard, your ass is going to have bruises from my desk."

"That's not the threat you think it is." Hannah sits back, looking me up and down. "Go on, Coach. Show me what the big boy can do."

I should be embarrassed by how my body reacts to her. I should hate how hard I am, how badly I want her, but I don't give a fuck. How can I when she's grinning at me? When she's pushing her tits together in an effort to distract me, and I cover my eyes so I don't lose sight of the goal.

Now that I've put it into the universe, having her like that—completely at my mercy in the sacred spot of my office—is exactly what I want. Exactly what I *need*, and I stretch my neck. I bend my knees, testing my weight, and dare myself to look at her again.

"Are you watching?" I call out, and she stands. Leans over the boards and whistles. "I'll take that as a yes."

"Let's go, baby!" she yells, and I bite back a grin.

I don't know shit about figure skating judging and scoring, but I know I deserve a perfect ten for how goddamn good my bunny hop is. Even Hannah thinks so, because she cheers. Bursts out laughing and reaches for me, throwing herself into my arms when I skate up to her.

"Pretty sure I dislocated something doing that." I hold her, scooping up our clothes, the sticks, and the puck. I hustle down the hall, not caring about my blades touching the ground when I'm off the rubber mats. Fuck the damage. "Worth it."

"You're going with your office? I thought you were going to fuck me on the ice," Hannah says. "And the boys would have no idea."

"Thought about it, but I don't want you to get too cold." I blaze into my office and slam the door shut after us. I lock it and wedge a stick under the handle just in case. No interruptions, no unwanted visitors. "On the desk. With your skates on."

"This is kinky. And exactly what I pictured when you say *edge work* to me in our sessions." She smiles when I shove a stack of papers out of the way. The pen jar goes flying. I toss my keyboard on the couch shoved against the wall and move my mouse to a drawer. "I like this unhinged, frantic side of you."

"Feels like that's how I always am around you."

I set her on the wood, pulling her underwear down her legs, over her knees. I get the pair over her skates and shove them in the pocket of my hoodie, wanting to keep them for myself. When she's naked, I shove her thighs open and look down at her.

"See something you like?" she whispers.

"You're already so wet." I run my knuckles over her slit, groaning when I bring them to my mouth and lick them clean. "Hold yourself open and tell me what part about tonight turned you on the most, Hannah."

Her hands drop to her legs. She spreads her pussy open with her thumbs, and I blow out a shaky breath. I'm supposed to be in charge here, but seeing her pussy—pink, wet, fucking *ready* for me—I worry I should have let her win.

"Watching you skate." Her voice catches when I rub a circle over her clit with my thumb. "Your body. Your focus and concentration." A moan rattles out of her when I put a hand on her stomach and press two fingers inside her. "Everything about you turns me on, Brody."

"Going to tape your wrists together. Don't move," I tell her, fucking her deeper.

"Wouldn't dream of it, baby," she answers with a gasp.

My tongue is heavy in my mouth. My brain is still somewhere out on the ice or in the hall. I'm slow to catch up, and I don't want to stop touching her. I don't want to stop coaxing those soft noises out of her, but I want her in a way that's new.

In a way I've never had anyone else, and I fumble with a roll of athletic tape.

"I was going to use the hockey tape you would use to wrap a stick, but I don't want it to be too tight. This will get the job done." I lift her arm and kiss her hand. "Tell me if it hurts?"

"I will. It's just like the ribbons, right?"

I nod, ripping off a piece of tape with my teeth. I hold her hands together, wrapping the tape around her wrists three times. When they're bound, I give them a tug, satisfied with the snugness.

"How does that feel?" I ask.

"Perfect," she breathes out.

"Good." I move her ass across the desk, stopping when she's at the edge. "You're so beautiful," I tell her, dragging my finger through her entrance. I push back inside her and Hannah moans, dropping her head back. "Even when you lose, you're so pretty." The heel of her skate presses into my back, urging me forward, and I shake my head. "I call the shots here, sweetheart. You're going to have to be patient."

I start by licking her clit. Light, slow laps of my tongue, and for as much as I want to tell her to stay still, I like when she lifts her hips. I like when she takes her bound hands and puts them on my head, pulling my hair.

"Brody." She wiggles her ass. I reach up, my thumb grazing over her hard nipple. "I've been turned on for over an hour. I don't want to be teased. My wrists… being here with you. It's a lot. I need you."

"It's not about you want, remember?" I give her clit a slap, smirking when she arches her back. "If you had won, then you could tell me to hurry up and fuck you. But you got me on my knees. It's not a total loss, right?" My shoulders push her legs open. The feel of her skates on my bare skin is dangerous given that a blade to the knee is what ended my playing career, but I can't stop now. "Let me worship you my way."

"Okay."

Her agreement is soft, resigned. On the edge of blissfulness when I give her what she wants: three fingers in her cunt and my tongue back on her clit. I devour her like the world is going to end tomorrow, my cock hard as hell when she moans my name and gets my beard nice and wet.

"Like that, angel?" I ask.

"You could teach a pussy eating class, Brody."

"Wouldn't want to do it with anyone but you." The tips of my ears turn pink. My skin is on fire. "No one tastes as good as you."

She moans when I hold her open and bury my tongue inside her. She's the sweetest thing I've ever had, and I'd be perfectly content to die just like this: with her thighs squeezing around my neck. With her panting my name. With a drop of sweat rolling down her knee.

I grin and give her clit another light slap that makes her hips buck. Her whispered words turn explicit, sharp, and a needy demand falls from her mouth.

"Please," she begs, and I've never been one to deny her what she wants.

Her orgasm starts to build when I switch back to my fingers—four of them, to get her ready for my cock—and curl them inside her. Her breathing shifts to a raw, desperate whisper of my name, and I feel it too. The animalistic way I *need* her like I need oxygen, and when she rides my fingers, hips rolling, tits bouncing as she takes, and takes, and *takes*, I watch in pure fucking awe of how goddamn beautiful she is when she comes undone.

And, *fuck*, does she come undone. All over my hand. On my tongue in panting, strangled groans as she collapses onto her back. Her body convulses when I slow my fingers. When I pull out of her and watch her pussy beg for my cock, a second jolt of pleasure hitting her when I tap her clit until a tear rolls down her cheek.

"I can't—" Hannah writhes on the desk. I hold her, a

hand on her hip so she's not in danger of falling. "It's too much. *Brody*. Please."

That word again. It's enough to make me lose my senses. To turn me absolutely fucking stupid.

"Please what, princess?" I unlace her first skate, letting it fall to the floor. I make quick work of the other and pull off her socks, kicking everything out of the way so I don't step on them. "Please fuck you? Please fill you up with my cum? What do you want, Hannah?"

"Both of those things." She rests her bound hands on her chest. Her skin is a pretty shade of red. Her hair is everywhere, and she props her feet on the wood. "Anything. I'll take anything you give me."

I remove my own skates and my briefs. Her sated smile turns wicked, *hungry* when she sees my cock thick and hard between my legs. I grip her knee, lining myself with her entrance, then freeze.

"Shit," I say. "Fuck. We can't do this."

"What?" She tries to prop herself up on an elbow, but can't. "Why not?"

"I didn't bring a condom with me."

"You don't have any here?"

"Fucking someone on my desk at our practice rink was never something I considered." I scrub a hand over my face. "We'll have to table this until we get back to my place."

"We could not use one," Hannah suggests, and I stare down at her. Everything goes still and quiet. I'm not sure I'm breathing. "The first time we were together, we almost—"

"Are you still on birth control?" I manage to get out.

Irresponsible. Hasty. So fucking reckless.

"Yeah. I take it religiously." Her ankles circle my waist. She smiles, no disappointment about possibly cutting this short. "Or we can wait."

"I always told myself I would never fuck a woman without a condom unless it was serious between us. Unless I knew I could trust her with everything I have." I pause and lick my lips, wanting to make this next point very clear. "Unless I knew I could see a future with her."

"Let me grab my clothes and—"

"Bring your thighs to your chest, Hannah, and let me fuck you like you're mine. Because we both know you are."

Her lips part. Her gaze stays on me as she bobs her head, moving painstakingly slow, and I guide her to the position I want her in.

"Are you sure?" she asks.

I've never been *more* sure about anything. Ever. It feels like we've been building to this moment from the very first time I laid eyes on her. For the first time she looked my way, the first time I kissed her.

Mine.

"Yes. But only if you're okay with it."

"I'm okay with it," Hannah answers. "Go ahead, Brody. Show me I'm yours," she adds, and this has to be my time of death.

"I want your eyes on me when you feel me for the first time." My thumb traces over the curve of her knee. She relaxes under my touch, and I tease her with the head of my cock. "Deep breath for me, sweetheart. Let's see how well you take me without anything between us."

The first few inches of sinking inside her are agony. I fight off a roar. I resist the urge to fuck her as rough as I can, to claim her, and her stilted groan snaps me back to reality.

"*Fuck*," she cries out. "It was never like this the other times."

No, it wasn't. This is the closest I'll ever get to heaven. Divine exquisiteness in its perfect form.

"Hannah. I need—*shit*. I need to move. Can I move, baby?"

"Yes. *Yes*, Brody. I want every inch of you. I want to feel full. I want you everywhere."

She already is everywhere. In my blood. In my fucking head. Written in my DNA too, I think, but it's easy to give her that when it's what I want too. A palm on her throat, the other still grasping her hip, I rock forward. I grunt, burying my cock in her with incessant urgency clawing at my back.

"*Jesus*," I groan. "You're so goddamn tight around me."

"More like Satan," she pants. "Jesus would be *very* displeased." My laugh is a rumble and her giggle is pure ecstasy. I move the hand on her hip to her clit, touching her there too. "I want to kiss you. Can you kiss me, Brody?"

What else do you want, Hannah? The stars? The fucking sun? Give me a list, and I'll give you everything you ask for.

With my height and the angle of the desk, it's difficult to find a position that works, but we figure it out. When we do, I ease her onto her back until she's flat against the wood. I keep a hand behind her head, protecting her from my rough thrusts, and I kiss her. She kisses me back, teeth nipping at my bottom lip. Tongue swiping against mine, greedy for whatever she can get.

"You need to tell me where you want me to come," I say. The snap of my hips is quick, bruising, but she meets me each time. Sinking down my cock, then sliding back up. It's too much. "I don't want there to be any misunderstanding."

"Inside me. I want to walk out of here with your cum trailing down my leg. I want everyone to know who I belong to."

I'm never going to be able to look at this place the same way again. Every time I walk in my office, I'm going to think about her here. Spread out. Asking for my cum. Asking to make her mine. It makes my mind go numb. It renders me fucking speechless, and all I can do is nod. Lick my thumb and find her clit, relishing in her moan.

"You're going to have to ride home like that. Up the elevator, all the way to my floor, and hope no one sees. If they did, they'd know you were full of my cum." I suck on the skin below her ear. "The pretty figure skater, so fucking needy for my cock."

"I'm close, Brody. Keep—I like when you talk to me."

"Yeah?" Another thrust, even deeper. I must hit a spot she likes because Hannah gasps. Screws her eyes shut and starts to tighten around me. "Have I told you how much of an honor it is to be the oldest guy you've fucked? And to be the only one who can make you come like this? You joke about my age, but deep down, you know it's because you're scared. Scared that this is so good, you'll never find anyone better. Who knew that under those cute skirts and ribbons you like to wear was someone who just needed Daddy to take care of them."

I have no fucking clue what I'm saying. I have no fucking clue if she likes it, but I guess she does, because she's falling apart. Yelling my name like I'm her goddamn savior, and I can't last any longer. I groan, holding her in place while I spill inside her. It's a full-body experience, and by the time I calm down, there's sweat at my hairline. My heart is threatening to fall out of my chest, and I'm gasping for breath.

"Holy fucking shit." I rest my forehead against Hannah's knee, weightless. "Was that—I didn't mean to—"

"Perfect." Her eyelashes flutter open. There are tears in her eyes, but she's smiling. Touching my chin with her clasped wrists and rolling her hips, making me hiss. As if what we did wasn't enough. As if she hasn't splintered me into a million fucking pieces and ripped my heart out of my chest in the process. "It was perfect."

"Hang on." I pull out of her with a groan. I can see my cum inside her, and possessiveness rips through me when I drag my thumb through it, spreading it over her pussy. "You are the most beautiful woman I've ever seen, Hannah."

"You make me feel beautiful."

"If I wasn't around twenty nosy motherfuckers every day of my life, I'd take a picture of you like this. I'd have it as my phone background so I could stare at you every minute of every day. My favorite girl in my favorite place."

"You'd probably get bored."

"Of you? Never."

She smiles and lifts her hands. "Will you free me, please?"

I use scissors to cut the tape. I kiss the inside of her wrists, running my thumb over the residue left behind. "Stay the night at my place?"

Hannah scoots to the edge of the desk. She touches my cheek and hums, tipping her head to the side. "I'd like that."

It takes us a minute to get dressed. We're both moving slow, and Hannah stops me halfway through putting my shorts on to kiss me again. By the time we make it to my place, she's asleep in the front seat. I take her in my arms and carry her upstairs, knowing what I told her earlier was true.

I do see a future with her.

I see her everywhere I look, and if I'm going to fall in love with someone, I'm glad it can be her.

THIRTY-SIX
HANNAH

GC

Hi.

ME

Well, hi, BB. How are you?

GC

Liv has been talking my ear off about some TV show she's watching. There are brothers involved? And a cousin?

ME

Oh, my god. Ask if she's Team Jeremiah or Team Conrad!

GC

She says Team Conrad? Am I supposed to know what that means?

ME

You can quote Mary Kate and Ashley but you don't know about this love triangle?!

GC

I'll try and catch up.

What are you doing tonight?

ME

What if I told you I'm coming to the game?

GC

I'd say I'm very happy.

ME

And what happens if I show up in one of the guy's jerseys?

GC

They'll be skating laps tomorrow until their legs give out.

ME

Event if it was Grant's?

GC

Even his.

ME

Tempting.

GC

I have a jersey you can borrow.

ME

Who's to say I don't already have one? Maybe I sleep in it when you're out of town.

GC

I'm going to need a picture. Immediately.

Liv and Kali will be there tonight. I can get you a ticket next to them.

ME

Is it weird if I'm hanging out with your daughter's mother? To be honest, I think she's cooler than you.

GC

She is absolutely cooler than me.

I let Piper know you'll be there. She can meet you at the VIP entrance and show you around.

I won't be able to catch up with you until later.

ME

That's okay. I know you're coming home with me!

Now to pick a guy whose name I want to rep.

I'm thinking Ethan…

GC

Hannah.

ME

See you tonight, Coach!

THE STARS' arena is electric as I follow Piper past the locker room and media area. I can feel the energy from the fans pouring in, and with only a month left in the regular season, I imagine everyone will be excited tonight.

"Is it a sellout?" I ask.

"It always is." She pulls on the sleeve of her pink blazer and waves to someone wearing a Stars polo. "Where are you sitting?"

"With Brody's daughter, Olivia. We're down by the ice,

and she let me know in our lesson the other day she's *very* intense when it comes to games."

"Like father, like daughter." We make a right turn, heading down another hallway. "Are you hungry? Your ticket has access to the friends and family room where they have food set up. I swear, the fried mac and cheese is probably the best thing I've ever eaten."

"That sounds great. I didn't have a chance to eat before I left my place," I say.

"I'll take you there and point out how to get to the ice. I need to track someone down for an interview, but—"

"Hi." Lexi jogs up, her hair slicked back in a high pony-tail. She gives us each a quick hug before letting out a groan. "I think I need to start working for a women's team."

"Oh, no." Piper sighs. "Did you get flashed today?"

"Unfortunately." Lexi glances at me. "By your brother. Poor guy had his headphones in and dropped his towel in the athletic training room without realizing I was there. I've never heard someone scream so loudly."

"Poor Grant is right." I laugh. "He does have a high-pitched scream, doesn't he?"

"I'm surprised glass didn't break." Lexi grins. "Anyway. I'm off to give your husband a quick massage before the boys take the ice, P—and, yeah, I recognize that in any other circumstance, what I just said would be grounds for a fight."

"Nope, that's all you! You do a much better job than me, and I like that he doesn't want my massages. They hurt my hands." Piper checks her phone and waves at us. "I have to run. I'll come say hi at intermission."

"And I have to check Hudson's shoulder before they take the ice. He said he was stiff after warmups, and I'm going to keep this team healthy all the way to the playoffs if it's the last thing I do." Lexi eyes my jersey and smirks. "BC, huh?"

"Boston's a *great* city," I say, knowing she's going to see the name on the back when I walk away. "Who doesn't love a lobster roll?"

After Piper leads me to an empty room set up with trays of food, I load up a plate and take a seat at one of the tables. There's a television on the wall, and I turn up the volume when I spy Brody on the screen.

He's giving an interview, running through what the team is going to focus on tonight, but before I can get too invested, he's apologizing to the guy holding the microphone.

"I need to check in with the team before they take the ice," he says. "Thanks for the questions."

I snap a photo of the food and send it to Tierney. I fire off a quick message to Grant wishing him good luck tonight, and I turn when I hear the door to the room open. Brody is slipping inside, his suit tailored and pressed and fitting him like a goddamn glove.

"There you are," he says.

"Did you know there are three kinds of hot dogs over there?" I ask. "Seems excessive, no?"

"Blame Ethan. He's obsessed with the damn things." Brody smiles. Looks over his shoulder and walks my way. "Glad you got here okay."

"Piper gave me a tour. That Stanley Cup photo of you guys from a few seasons ago is precious. Liv looks so small sitting on your shoulders."

"Doesn't she? She hit a serious growth spurt the summer after those pictures were taken."

I pop to my feet and meet him halfway. "You look nice in your suit. How much do you hate wearing that tie?"

"Somedays I wish I coached in the NBA so I could show up in joggers and sneakers and not get fined." His gaze roams down my body, stopping when he gets to my jersey. He falters, touching the stitching on the shoulders. "Did you actually track down one of my jerseys from Boston College?"

"You have a lot of fans on the internet. Some guy named

StickLover69—yeah, the irony isn't lost on me either—had it for sale, and I figured I had to have it." I do a slow circle, stopping when my back is to him. "What do you think?"

"I think it's a real shame I have a job that needs my attention for the next four hours." A thrill races through me when his fingers graze the hem of my short skirt and the boots I paired the outfit with. Anyone could walk in and see us like this. "Every guy in the arena—and probably on both benches —is going to be looking at you."

I spin, facing him again. "Are you going to be looking at me, Brody?"

"I'm not going to be able to stop looking at you."

"That's all I care about."

"I wish I could stay," he says, "but I—"

"Am a very important coach getting paid a lot of money to lead his team to a victory." I smile. "I know. I get it."

"I'll come find you after. The media got two answers out of me. They don't need anything the rest of the game." Brody checks the door. Sure that we're all alone, he kisses the top of my head with the faintest brush of his lips. "Have fun tonight, sweetheart. I'm glad you're here."

THE STARS ARE PLAYING WELL, but Grant is on fire. He's the first one down the ice every possession, and from the way he's taking shots and diving to protect Liam's net, I swear there's someone in the crowd he's trying to impress.

He has two goals through the first two periods, and during the last intermission, I stand and stretch my legs.

"Did either of your parents skate?" Kali asks, standing with me. She waves to Liv who disappears down the tunnel to grab a bucket of popcorn, then looks my way. "You and Grant are both so talented."

"Nope. We're from Florida, so it's a mystery how we both

ended up playing sports on the ice." I smile. "He puts in so much work."

"I had no idea who Brody was when I met him for the first time. Come to find out he's the greatest skater in the last twenty years, and it's very apparent our daughter takes after him, not me." Kali shrugs. "I don't give two shits about sports."

"Funny, because Liv is really talented."

"She loves the sport, but that's all her. We don't pressure her. We never forced her to put on a pair of skates. Brody even signed her up for a gymnastics class so she wouldn't feel like she had to follow in his footsteps, but nothing stuck like skating did."

"That's important," I say. "My parents weren't pushy at all —these sports are *so* expensive, and I think they were actively hoping I'd pick up something that cost less money. But so many of the other adults in my life were forceful about my skating. When I finished fifth at an event when I was fourteen, my coach told me if I put in ten more hours of work a week, I'd finish fourth. So, I did. And I did finish fourth." I shift on my feet, the prickle of unease rising when I think of the people in the past who have failed me. "The cycle continued until I recently broke out of it. Now I'm skating when I want to skate and how I want to do it, which is something I wish more young skaters did."

"Liv talks really highly of you. About your skills, yeah, and how beautiful your program was at your recent competition, but also you as a coach." She pauses. "Your encouragement means a lot to her. You speak to her like she's an adult. You listen. We'd love if you kept working with her after her event in August."

"Gosh. I'd be so honored." Pride blooms in my chest. I pull on the hem of Brody's jersey to distract myself from that warm and bubbly feeling nestling behind my ribs. "This is going to sound silly, but working with her—and Brody—has really made me appreciate skating again. Liv encourages *me*, and it's my motivation."

"She's a good kid." Kali clears her throat. "Brody told me you and him are spending time together."

The pride shifts to the hint of anxiety. Does Kali think I'm too young for him? Does she not want Liv around me now that she knows we're sleeping together? "He did?"

"To be fair, I kind of pulled it out of him, but, yeah. He did." She nudges me with her elbow. "I've been around that man for many, many years. And I've never seen him so happy as he's been these last few months."

"Oh." Butterflies again. They never seem to go away when Brody's around. "Really?"

"Really. He's not very open about his feelings, but I learned a long time ago Brody's love language is acts of service. He says the right things, of course, but he also shows you he cares by the things he does for you. Being there when you need him. Remembering your favorite food or favorite movie. Hell." Kali snorts. "I promise I'm not in love with him."

"I didn't take it that way," I hurry to say. "You do know him better than anyone else."

"A blessing and a curse. He doesn't do casual. If you're in his life, it's because you're important to him. And I can tell that you are."

Liv bounds up the stairs, dropping in her seat with a snack and a water.

"What are you two talking about?" she asks, tucking her hair away from her face.

"You." Kali smiles. "And how wonderful you are."

"Okay, Mom." She rolls her eyes, but I see her soft smile. "Did Dad give you that jersey, Hannah? He usually hates when women wear his name and number."

"Does he?" I ask, spotting at least five Saunders jerseys in the surrounding area. "Why?"

"He doesn't like the attention it puts on him apparently? If that's the case, maybe don't be a professional athlete."

"So true, Liv. Don't tell him this, but I'm only wearing it so he feels included." Grant skates up to the glass and motions my way. "Be right back!"

"Are you having fun?" he practically yells when I get down to the ice.

"Am I done?" I yell back.

He rolls his eyes. "FUN," he yells again, and I grin.

"I heard you the first time. Dude. Nice game tonight. Who are you showing off for?"

"Just want the fans to see a good game." The buzzer sounds, and he lifts his glove. I bump his knuckles against the glass. "Wait. Whose jersey is that?"

"Ethan's. He's a BC boy, and it felt weird to wear something that belonged to the other guys when I'm friends with their significant others," I say, easily pulling the lie out of my ass.

"You couldn't think to wear *mine*? Geez, sis. Appreciate the support and having *Ethan* picked over me." He groans. "He's such a fuckboy."

"Relax, G. He's not old enough for me."

"Please spare me from the details of your personal life," he says. "Gotta go. Don't want Coach pissed at me!"

"Have a good third period!" I call out, waving as he skates back to the bench.

When he does, Brody's eyes bounce away from the small whiteboard he's holding. Twenty thousand fans are cheering, but with one lift of his chin, his attention is zeroed in on me.

He holds up his finger, gesturing for me to spin, and I blush. I turn, skipping to my seat and giving him the perfect view of my jersey and his name stretched across the back. He uncaps a marker with his teeth, scribbling something on the board, then holding it up.

I squint, trying to read what it says, but I can't make it out.

I take a photo and tell myself I'll zoom in on it later, not when I have a nosy teenager looking over my shoulder.

And, I'm glad my focus is on the game, because Grant comes out of intermission like a bullet. He scores his third goal and sends the arena into a frenzy. Hats go flying onto the ice and play stops. He does a lap, accepting high-fives and hugs from his teammates while he soaks up his first career hat trick. I scream so loudly, I almost lose my voice. I've never been prouder.

Later, after the pandemonium dies down and the Stars win by two, I pull my phone out of my purse. I zoom in on the picture I took of Brody's whiteboard, discovering the secret only for me.

Mine.

THIRTY-SEVEN
HANNAH

IT'S BEEN weeks since I stepped foot in the Skating Club of Washington's rink, and I stop to say hello to some familiar faces on my walk to Justine's office.

"How are you feeling?" Tierney asks, falling in step beside me. "Talking to Coach is scary, but important."

"I'm kind of shitting bricks. I'm a grown woman. Why am I dreading this so much?"

"Because it's a conversation about your future, and that's terrifying. Did you decide what you're going to say?"

"I'm going to talk about a hybrid schedule and mention that while I'm feeling rejuvenated, I'm not ready to fully commit to high intensity training. But I do want to be more present with the club again." I cringe. "I hope all of it makes sense."

"It does." She takes my hand when we reach the door tucked away at the back of the rink. "I'll be here when you're finished. We can either celebrate with a glass of wine to welcome you back or bitch about shitty business decisions over a glass of wine."

"Have I told you today how thankful I am for you? I appreciate you keeping me so level-headed, T."

"You're my girl, Han. I just want you to be happy."

Justine welcomes me into her office, and I perch in one of the uncomfortable chairs across from her desk. We exchange pleasantries and a few minutes of conversation before she stops me with a heavy look.

"Hannah," she says. "Are you going to tell me why you're really here? I'm sure it's not to let me know Lauren's flip jump has improved."

"You know I made the decision to step away from competing, but I performed a couple weeks ago at a small event and placed second. The break in the rigorous activity and schedule has been beneficial to my mental health and how I'm approaching the sport as a whole." I stop to cross my ankles and smile. "I wanted to propose the idea of a hybrid training program to you."

"I don't understand what that means," Justine says.

"There are less than two years until the Winter Olympics, and while I know I'm not ready to dive headfirst into ten-hour days, I thought easing into a part-time schedule would be a good balance. I'd train for three days a week with you, and the other four days I'll do my own training."

"Hannah." She sighs and clasps her hands together. "Do you know I have a waitlist of skaters who want to join our program that's four years long?"

"No." I swallow. "That's very impressive."

"All of them are willing to put in the full effort it takes to perform at the level we pride ourselves on. How fair would it be if I bypassed them for someone who only wants to be here a few hours a week when they're willing to give it their all?"

"I'm not asking for special treatment. I just—"

"You've been doing this sport a long time, and you know it's like a relationship. No relationship is great every second of every day, but you have to push through the rough patches, and not run when it gets tough. You ran," Justine says, and my blood turns to ice. "How can I be sure you can handle the caliber of training the Olympics are going to take? How do I know you aren't going to quit on me halfway through the year and make me scramble to find an alternate to compete at another Grand Prix event? You disappointed me, and you disappointed this club. Going forward, we're prioritizing skaters who are all in on their development. We can't have people representing us who want to skate on their terms, even if they have World Championship medals. It's not fair." There's a long stretch of silence. "Your performance at that competition was not the results this club boasts. Your 3A was abysmal, Hannah, and a complete disappointment."

Fair.

Abysmal.

As if I willingly decided to fall out of love with the most important thing in my life. As if I haven't gone through hell trying to find who the fuck I am when I'm not skating at the World Championships. As if I haven't been agonizing over whether people think I'm not credible anymore because I walked away from opportunities that were handed to me on a silver platter.

"Thank you for your honesty," I say, but every word tastes like lead. "I appreciate the feedback."

"You either want to be out there, or you don't, and I think it's best if we end our partnership so we can both move on," Justine says, landing the final blow.

"Of course. I'll just—" I gesture vaguely to the door and stand. I have to get out of here before I break down. I have to get out of here before she can see me cry. "Have a nice day, Coach."

I manage to hold it together until I'm back out at the rink and staring at the ice I've spent so many hours of my life on. I left my home, my friends to move here and try to create magic, but that's the part no one tells you about when you're wishing on a dream: it's all fleeting. Something that could be yanked away at any moment, and you're left with your greatest heartache.

"How did it go?" Tierney asks, and I plaster on a smile. I'm too embarrassed to tell her the truth.

"Great. We'll see what she says. Hey, I totally forgot I have a lesson with Liv this afternoon. Can we raincheck on that wine date?"

"You know I'll always make time for you." She searches my face with a frown. "Are you sure you're okay, Han?"

A complete disappointment.

"I'm fine. I'll text you later tonight." I wrap her in a quick hug, letting go far too soon when I can feel myself starting to break. "Have a good practice, T."

I make it to my car before the tears start to fall, but then they don't stop. The anger comes in waves, and I'm mad at Justine. I'm mad at myself and I'm mad at this sport too, for making me love it so fucking much.

I grab my phone, fingers shaking as I type out a blurry message to Brody.

ME

I know you're in Dallas getting ready for your game, but I just wanted to say hi. I'm not having a good day. I'm feeling very lonely, which is not a problem you can solve, but speaking it into existence helps, I guess.

Sorry for bothering you. You're busy, so you don't need to respond. I just… I miss you. That's all.

I toss my phone in my bag, watching it land next to the skates I optimistically brought with me today.

The irony.

It might be time to retire for good.

THE KUNG PAO chicken I order from my favorite Chinese restaurant helps my mood. So does the fried rice and the glass of wine I have with my meal. I change into a DC Stars shirt and lounge pants, dozing into a fitful nap on the couch as the moon comes out and rises high in the sky.

Brody doesn't answer my texts, but I don't expect him to. Checking the score of the game when I wake up at some point, I see they lost by one, and he has other things on his mind. More important things, like his career, and I'm hoping I wasn't a distraction to him.

I turn on my side, staring out the living room window. Some of the city lights twinkle below me, and my eyes flutter closed. I take a deep breath, ready to drift off to sleep again when a knock on my door has me bolting upright.

It's a Saturday night. It's probably someone getting back from the bar, tipsy and on the wrong floor. I wait, listening for retreating footsteps, but then there's another knock.

"Han?" a voice calls out, and I recognize it instantly.

Brody.

I kick off the blanket draped over my legs and sprint to the foyer. I fling the door open and Brody is there, suit jacket and tie draped over one arm. Sleeves rolled to his elbows, and I can't fight off the choked sob lodged in my throat.

"Hi, sweetheart," he says. "Can I come in?"

"Is this a dream?" I rub my eyes and take a step back, welcoming him inside. He carefully folds his clothes and puts them on the entry table, a laugh wobbling out of me when he kicks off his shoes too. "I was just asleep."

"Very real, if the cramp in my knee from sitting on an airplane is any indication." The warm press of his mouth on my forehead confirms he's telling the truth, and I do my best not to melt into him. "I'm so sorry I woke you up."

"It's okay." I head for the nest I've made for myself on the couch. Brody sits on the free cushion, and I stretch out my legs, resting them in his lap. "Must've been a quick flight from Dallas."

"The tailwind helped."

"Do you want to stay the night?" I yawn. "What time is practice tomorrow?"

"Ten a.m. In Cleveland."

"Cleveland?" I blink. "Your next game isn't at home?"

"No. We're on the road again. We'll be back on Wednesday."

"But you're here."

"I am here."

"Is everything okay with Liv?" I ask.

"Hope so. She's at a sleepover tonight, and I haven't gotten any 911 texts asking to pick her up."

"And Kali?"

"At home with Bryant. Asleep, probably, given that it's midnight."

"So why did you—" I sit up, caught off guard. "Did you fly back to DC? For me?" I ask.

"You said you were lonely, and I missed you too." Brody holds my leg, massaging out the soreness in my calf. Soft, gentle pressure all while he stares into my eyes. "You needed me, so I'm here. The lack of sleep is worth it, because this is exactly where I need to be. Where I want to be."

Acts of service.

You're important to him.

My conversation with Kali comes flooding back, and then my heart does something silly. It flip flops. Skips a damn beat and almost falls out of my chest, because this man flew *across the country* to see me.

All because I was lonely.

If this isn't the standard, I don't know what is, and no one else will ever be able to measure up.

There's another word floating in my head. It's not one Kali mentioned, but I've been hearing whispers of it for weeks: when Brody showed up to my competition. When he fucked me on his desk and told me he saw a future with me. Every time he smiles, and it feels like I'm seeing the sun for the first time in days.

Love.

"Talk to me, Hannah," Brody says, bringing me out of the fog. "What happened today that made you upset?"

"I had a conversation with my figure skating coach—former figure skating coach, I guess I should say—about training with them again. The competition was a confidence booster, and I thought I was ready to test the waters again." I play with the friendship bracelet on my wrist, keeping Liv's gift with me all this time. "It didn't go well. She told me that I gave up. She told me I disappointed her, and there are people waiting for my spot."

"She said that to you?" Brody's thumb digs deeper into my skin. "Fuck that. Why are you being punished for prioritizing your mental health?"

"The saddest part is, she's right. What privilege do I think I have over everyone else? A couple medals that I won years ago?" I shrug. "I need to make the decision about where my career is going. Do I want to put my body through months of training and exercise only to panic and withdraw weeks before a qualifying event? Or do I walk away now, proud of everything I've accomplished?"

"Only you can answer that, but it boils down to what makes you happy. If you woke up tomorrow and only had one day to live, how would you spend it?"

"I'm not sure I have the capacity to answer that question."

"I'm sure you do."

"I'd want to go skating for an hour or two," I tell him. "Not with choreography or drills or intense training. I'd just glide around the rink, happy as can be." My smile starts slow.

"I'd work with Liv, and you'd be there too. I'd go to sleep proud. I'd know it was a good day because I did the things I wanted to do, not what other people wanted me to do."

"I think you have your answer, sweetheart."

"Wow. Am I really going to retire at twenty-five?"

"If you do, skating will always be there." Brody adjusts our positions, both of us lying on our sides. "I read about a woman who stopped skating for sixteen years, came back, and now does pairs. She just won a world title at forty."

I giggle at the thought of him reading the article on his iPad, glasses slipping down his nose. "Thank you for making me feel better, but you know you could've told me this on the phone, right? So you didn't have to sacrifice your sleep schedule."

"I could've, but why would I let you sit at home alone when I could easily get to you?" His fingers comb through my hair, taking his time when he finds a knot. "I'll catch the seven a.m. flight out of DCA and be at the arena in time for morning skate. And, between you and me, your bed is much more comfortable than another stay at a Holiday Inn."

"True, but you don't get the free continental breakfast here." I spin in his arms, finding his eyes closed. Blissful, content. "No biscuits. No oatmeal."

"But it has you, and that's more than enough," he says.

"Brody?"

"Yeah?"

"You are, without a doubt, my favorite person in the world."

"Funny." He cracks open an eyes, gaze meeting mine. "I was thinking the same thing about you."

A fresh wave of tears starts to fall, and I don't know if it's the loss I'm grieving or the enormity of my feelings for him. Brody doesn't ask, holding me in his arms in an embrace that feels like coming home after a long day.

That word echoes in my ears again, even louder when he lifts me off the couch and carries me to my bed. When he takes off the rest of his clothes and joins me under the covers, murmuring how proud he is of me while we doze off to sleep.

Love.

BRODY

Puck Kings and Daddy Things (+ our savior, BS)

MILLER

Book club has been moved to Tuesday
evening at Grant's house.

Please confirm your attendance!

ME

Book club?

Why am I getting notifications about book
club?

MILLER

Whoops. Sorry, Coach. This chat is pinned in
my messages, and it's easier than finding our
other one.

EVERETT

I am VERY excited to be hosting everyone. I
have a full spread planned out, along with
themed treats that go along with the book.

RICHARDSON

That was my first time reading a bodyguard romance. I'm a fan.

SULLIVAN

Didn't like the narrator for the audiobook.

He sounded miserable.

RICHARDSON

… are you looking in a mirror, Sully?

EVERETT

I'll narrate the next one to you, Goalie Daddy.

RICHARDSON

Damn. We have a lot of daddies in here. Mavvy Daddy. Goalie Daddy. Coach Daddy.

ME

Don't you fucking dare.

EVERETT

Uh, duh, Easy E. That's the point of the chat name.

RICHARDSON

If you feel like joining us, Coach, the book is called Untouchable. We have a 7 p.m. start time.

ME

No, thank you.

And leave me alone.

This is supposed to be the time I'm free from you all.

RICHARDSON

Yet here you are. Texting us back.

EVERETT

He likes us. He really, really likes us!

Liam Sullivan has left the chat
You have left the chat
Ethan Richardson has added you to the chat
Ethan Richardson has added Liam Sullivan to the chat

ME

Hope you enjoy the extra drills we're running tomorrow, Richardson.

RICHARDSON

Worth it <3

ME

Hi. I wanted to run something by you.

H.E.

Anal?

ME

You can't text me that when I'm about to walk into a meeting, Hannah.

H.E.

You're the one who didn't give me any context!

ME

I want to tell Liv about us.

It doesn't seem fair to hide it when she sees you four times a week and lives with me part-time.

But I wanted to know how you felt about it first.

H.E.

We've been sleeping together for, what? Four months? And spent some time before that as friends.

I mean... I don't want to speak on your behalf, but that feels pretty serious to me.

ME

Feels pretty serious to me too.

H.E.

Liv is the most important person in your life. She deserves to not be kept in the dark about something that will impact her.

Like, if she can't stand me, you'll take her side (as you should!).

ME

You know you're her idol, right?

H.E.

I'm nervous!

ME

I'll talk to her this afternoon.

H.E.

Please report back.

ME

You're going to be anxious all day, aren't you?

H.E.

I don't think you understand how important a teenage girl's opinion is. They're brutally honest.

ME

Oh, I'm well aware. Two nights ago, Liv told me my hair is starting to turn gray at the temples.

H.E.

I could dig the silver fox look.

ME

Noted.

MARCH TURNS TO APRIL, and with it, the last two weeks of the regular season arrive. We've held on to a playoff spot, sitting pretty at second in the East and first in the Metropolitan division. Practices amp up. The guys are exhausted, and so am I, but I spend hours in my office studying lineups. I stay up late watching footage of our weaker games so I can address any persistent issues before the playoffs starts, and I don't know where the hell this year has gone.

No one is expecting us to make a deep run. With Maverick's intermittent playing time this season and our slow start in October and November, we've already been written off.

I've always liked being an underdog, and hearing analysts throw out words like *lucky* and *easy schedule* about our year only fuels the boys' fire with their training efforts.

I shut my laptop and press my palms into my eyes knowing Liv is on her way up. Kali is dropping her off after her skating lesson, and I should figure out what we're going to have for dinner.

"I'm home!" Liv calls out. There's a loud thump from the foyer and the slam of the front door. "Mom says hi!"

"I say hi back," I answer, rising and stretching my shoulders. "How was school? And skating?"

"I'm up to the first forty-five seconds of my choreography!

Hannah said she was proud of my double Axel, which makes me very happy because I've been working on that for *months*." She climbs on a barstool at the island and accepts the glass of chocolate milk I hand her way. "School sucks. Algebra blows, and I really don't see how anyone uses it in their daily life."

"Olivia Elliot." I sigh. "Can we watch the word choices, please? Your principal already called me once this semester to let me know your vocabulary was colorful."

"What's wrong with colorful? This world is too dreary."

"Nothing. I'd just prefer if people didn't think I walked around the house only using four-lettered words."

"You kind of do," she says, and I huff. "I will do better with not being *so* profane."

"Thank you." I fold my arms over my chest. "If you wanted to know, I don't use algebra at all in my daily life. Geometry and angles? Oh, yeah. But algebra? It's kind of bullshit."

Liv grins. "That's what I thought."

I chuckle. "What do you want to do for dinner?"

"Maybe some soup? And I can chop the onions?" she asks, batting her eyelashes. "Please?"

"Okay, Gordon Ramsey. We can make that happen. Can I talk to you about something first?" I ask. "It requires you putting your phone down for fifteen minutes."

"Okay." Liv's smile fades to a grin. "What's up?"

"I, uh, hang on. I'm trying to figure out how to word this without making it weird."

"You went with me to buy my first bra. You pick up tampons for me. Is any of that weird?"

"No. That's the bare minimum." I sigh, taking the seat next to her. "Okay, look. You were much younger when your mom and Bryant got together, so I'm not sure if you all talked about anything like this, but I wanted to get your opinion on dating. Specifically, me dating someone."

"Oh, my god. I knew it. I *knew* it! That's why I've been

spending more time at Mom's. That's why you're always smiling at your phone. That's why there's a candle in the living room." She hums. "And I know who it is. I've known this whole time!"

"You do?" I freeze. "How?"

"Come *on*, Dad. You show up before my lessons are finished when you used to wait in the car until I was done. You charted a freaking plane to DC so you wouldn't miss Hannah's competition." Liv holds up a hand and starts ticking off items on her fingers. "She came to a game and wore *your* jersey. You're *happy* happy."

I rub a hand over my chest, trying to stop my heart from racing. My fingers moves to the tattoo on my arm, the figure skates wrapped up with a pretty ribbon.

I am *happy* happy because Hannah makes me that way.

Must be pretty fucking obvious if Liv is noticing too.

"How does all of that make you feel?" I ask, trying to broach this topic as tactfully as possible. "I know I've never brought a woman around before, and—"

"I figured that's because you hadn't met the right one yet. Fireworks, right?" She giggles. "Do you think I'd be mad? Dad. I *love* Hannah. She's so freaking cool and nice and so pretty. Wait. Is it serious between you two? Is she moving in? *Areyougoingtopropose?*"

The last question comes out in a rush of words, and I pinch the bridge of my nose.

I know the interrogation is part of the process of telling a teenager I'm dating someone they like, but it also makes me sweat. It's forcing me to confront my feelings, and, *no*, I'm not proposing, because Hannah has made it clear that's not something she would be interested in, but it *is* serious, and I *am* trying to find the right word for it.

How do you describe the person you look for in every room?

How do you describe the person who is the best part of your day?

How do you describe the rush of adrenaline you get when she touches your hand?

How do you describe the peace you feel when she's in your arms?

How do you describe the way you'd do absolutely anything for her and ask for nothing in return?

I don't have a lot of practice with it, but every day I wake up with Hannah next to me, the definition narrows down to a single word.

Love.

I fucking *love* her, and I grin at the revelation.

"Yes," I say, holding up a hand when she opens her mouth to scream. "It is serious, but the rest of your questions don't apply. I'm not rushing this because I care about her very much. This is new territory for me, and I don't want to mess it up."

"Dad is in *love*," Liv squeals, spinning on her stool with her arms out at her sides. "I'm so glad you don't care that she's younger than you!"

"What do you mean?"

"She's cool and hip. You're old and go to bed at nine p.m. No offense," she adds, and I wave her off. "What if she meets someone while she's out? What if he flies her to Paris or wants to take her to all the cool F1 races?"

"Hannah doesn't like F1." I frown. "At least, I don't think she does."

"These are important things to know!"

My stomach twists. I imagine Hannah's bucket list and all the things she wants to do, and I hate that Liv called out our age difference so easily.

I don't care about her actual age. The shitty part about life is we're constantly getting older. Young today doesn't mean young forever.

I just don't want to be the reason why she doesn't do something she loves.

"I'll find out about F1," I say, and Liv claps.

"Good! I'm so excited for you, Dad. She should come over and have dinner with us sometime. Like, tomorrow. And the day after." Her excited yelp has me covering my ears. "I am *so* a matchmaker."

"Hey. I know you're happy about this, but can you do me a favor, Liv? Can you keep this to yourself? You know I'm a private person, and I don't want this getting out to the world before I'm ready to share her with everyone. I'm telling you because I love you, and I don't want any secrets between us," I say.

"I promise." Liv's face softens. "But you shouldn't wait too long to talk about her. If you love someone, you should want to show them off to the world. If not, someone else might," she says, and I wonder how the hell she got so goddamn smart for her age.

WITH LIV in her room and the kitchen cleaned up, I climb in bed and grab my phone from the nightstand. I debate texting Hannah again, but that seems too casual.

The last thing I want is for her to think this is casual.

I settle on the pillows with an arm behind my head, waiting for the FaceTime call to connect. It doesn't take long for Hannah to answer from her own bed where she's propped on her side.

"Hi," she says, blinking at me like I pulled her out of a dream.

"Hi." I smile at her messy hair in a bun on the top of her head and the crease on her cheek from her sheets. "I woke you up again."

"Why does that keep happening?" Hannah yawns and cradles her chin in her palm. "How did it go with Liv?"

"I hate to be the one to break this to you, Hannah," I say, and her eyes widen. She sits up, pulling the sheets to her chin. "But Liv was ecstatic, and she claims she *knew it all along*. Whatever that means."

"Really? She doesn't care that it's me you're seeing?"

"Her exact words consisted of how nice and cool and pretty you are." I smile at the camera. "All true, I'd say."

"That makes me so happy." Hannah blows out a sigh of relief. "I can't believe she knew."

"I've made it obvious for her, apparently. I used to wait in the car during her lessons, but now I wait inside so I can have a chance to talk to you." I chuckle. "Hearing it all back makes me sound pretty pathetic, and she's claiming to be a matchmaker."

"Without her, this wouldn't have ever happened." Hannah gestures between us. "Aren't you glad you have a daughter who loves figure skating?"

"Very. And I'm even more glad her previous coach got pregnant. Hey. Question for you," I say, switching gears. "Do you like F1?"

"That… is not the question I thought you would ask. I do not like F1," she says, and my shoulders loosen. "Why? Do *you* like F1?"

"Not particularly, no. Just going off of something Liv said. She mentioned how you're young and hip—"

"True," Hannah agrees.

"And I'm old and like to be in bed early," I finish.

"They do say opposites attract. Are you afraid I'm going to run off with an F1 driver, Brody?"

"No." I rub my jaw. "I just want to make sure I'm not holding you back from doing things you want to do."

"I don't have a ton of relationship experience, but from what I've heard, communication is pretty important." Hannah slinks down her pillows, nestling back under her covers. "And when two people care about each other, they communicate. Is that right, ole wise one?"

"It is. I communicate with all the important people in my life: Kali. The guys. Some more reluctantly than others, but I still do it. I guess I want us to be on the same page when it comes to talking about things that come up between us. You know you're important to me." I smile again. "But I also remember my lack of communication the first time we hooked up. I promise I'll be honest with you."

"Me too. Which is why you should know some driver just slid into my DMs," she teases. "Communication. What a piece of cake."

"Are you headed to bed?"

"Yeah. I wish you were here."

"Same." *I think I'm in love with you.* "Not sure how I feel about having you stay over when Liv is in the house, but maybe you want to come over for dinner with us sometime? If you want."

"Yeah, Brody." Hannah grins. She might not be next to me, but it feels like she is. In the smell of her perfume on my pillows. In her extra phone charger plugged in on her side of the bed. In the space in my heart she's carved out for herself, but I think she's been there all along. "I want."

THIRTY-NINE

BRODY

"DAMMIT." I look at my phone and check the time. "What's the holdup now?"

"Weather." Parker stretches out his legs in front of him. "The flight attendant said it could be another hour."

"An *hour*? Fucking hell."

"You in a rush to get home?" Mikal asks. "Everything okay with Liv?"

"Liv is fine. It's… never mind. I'm not in a rush. Just tired of sitting on the runway for forty-five minutes."

"Coach," one of the guys yells from behind me.

"What?" I bark out.

"Want to come play a game?" Ethan asks, and I narrow my eyes, turning to look at the group over my shoulder.

"What kind of game?"

"Poker. But before you get all pissy, we're not betting real money. Just locker room spots," Maverick says.

"I don't want to be closest to the bathroom anymore," Grant declares. "It's not fair."

"You're the youngest on the team. It's a rite of passage," Ethan says.

"You're literally seven months older than me. We share a birth year, doofus."

"Yeah, and that's enough to make me a year ahead of you in the league." Ethan grins. "Sorry, G-Money. You get the shitty locker."

"This is hazing," Grant whines. "Mavvy. Do something."

"It's not hazing, G-Money. It's just how it worked out." Maverick pats his shoulder. "Next year will be better."

"I see why Sully keeps asking for a trade." Grant huffs and glares at the group. "I don't feel like playing poker anymore."

My phone chimes, saving me from being pulled into their game. Hannah's initials pop up, and I turn the brightness down on my screen so no one can read over my shoulder.

> **H.E.**
>
> Can you hurry up and get home?
>
> *Attachment: 1 image*
>
> I miss you.

I have to dig my nails into my palms to keep from moaning. It's a photo of her spread out on her bed in a blue lingerie set, the sheets hiding her lower half while her bra pushes her tits together. The angle of the picture doesn't help my imagination either, showing off the arch in her back and one hand disappearing under the covers.

Dirty fucking girl.

> **ME**
>
> I need a warning before you send something like that.
>
> I'm on the team plane, delayed because of weather. Anyone could see what you're texting me.

> **H.E.**
>
> Maybe I should send one to Ethan too.

I whip around and glare at the poker game happening ten rows back. I shove my phone in my pocket and stand, storming to the rear of the plane and not stopping until I'm next to Ethan, holding out my hand.

"Give me your phone," I say, and he blinks up at me.

"Huh?" He frowns. "Why?"

"You don't need to know why. Your phone. Now."

"*Oooh.*"

"Easy E is busted!"

"I didn't do anything! I know what the team rules say about posting to social media before, during, and after games, and I haven't violated that." Ethan digs into his pockets and pulls out two iPhones. He reaches into his backpack and retrieves a third one, dropping them all in my hands. "But there ya go, Coach. Whatever is going on, I'm innocent."

"You have *three* goddamn phones?" I stare at the devices. "What the fuck for?"

"One is for all of you. One is for my agent and all the business shit I have coming in. Sponsorships, ya know? Gotta make the money I can since our league literally refuses to pay us as much as the fucking NBA. The last one, well." He smirks. "It's for my fans."

"Don't look at the photos, Coach," Riley offers. "It's probably a gallery of dick pics."

"*Pierced* dick pics," Ethan adds, and I swallow down vomit.

"I should ban you from social media," I say under my breath, and Ethan stares at me, horrified. "And I never want to hear anything about a pierced dick ever again."

"People would miss me too much. You can't do that," he argues.

"You'll get these back at the end of the flight."

I don't give the group another look, walking back to my row and laying all three of his phones on my tray table. I snap a quick picture, ignoring the seventy-five notifications that come in on his personal phone. My hands need to be disinfected.

"Everything okay?" Mikal asks, and I snort.

"Sometimes I'm glad I don't know what the fuck these guys do in their free time. I think I would be fucking appalled," I grumble, firing off another text to Hannah.

ME

Attachment: 1 image

The best part of being a head coach is all the power I have.

Anyone else's phone I should confiscate?

H.E.

Those are all Ethan's?!

I can't believe you took them.

ME

Unfortunately. I'm afraid of what I might find while they're in my care, and I'm having regrets.

Jokes or not, he doesn't deserve to see you like that.

H.E.

You might have been a little dramatic.

ME

I'm not the one pretending like I'm going to send a photo like that to someone else.

H.E.

Do you want to punish me, Brody?

Goddamn her. I jab the reading light above me to turn it off, afraid I might need to track down a blanket to put in my lap. A text message like that shouldn't turn me on at thirty-nine, but here I am: daydreaming about her over my knee while I make her ass nice and red.

ME

Do you think you should be punished?

Three dots appear, then disappear. I'm sitting on the edge of my seat, wondering where the hell this is going to go when another message comes through.

Too much? Past a boundary we haven't talked about yet?

H.E.

I think I'd like to be.

I have to blow out a breath to keep myself from begging the gods above to fix the weather so the pilots can take off.

Fucking unprofessional, Saunders, my brain screams. *You are around your players right now,* it adds, but my fingers are already flying across the keyboard.

ME

Get comfortable for the next few hours, sweetheart.

Take a bath. Have some wine.

I'll let you know when I'm in my car heading to your place, then we're playing by my rules.

H.E.

I lost the last game we played, and I'm determined to not let that happen this time. What are the rules?

ME

When I get to your apartment, I want you on the bed. Ass up. Face in the pillows. A vibrator between your legs. You're not allowed to come until I get there, and if you do, I'll take you over my knee and spank you.

H.E.

Sorry. I dropped my phone.

That's hot as hell, Brody.

ME

Too much?

H.E.

No. Not at all.

It was perfect.

I can't wait to see you.

ME

I can't wait to see you too, sweetheart.

WE LAND in DC three hours late. All the guys and my coaching staff are half asleep, but I'm buzzing with energy. Awake and knowing what's waiting for me once I get away from this godforsaken airport. It's a goddamn feat to not snap at anyone who talks to me, and when the boarding door is finally opened, I make my escape down the airstairs and practically sprint to the hangar where my car is waiting.

"See you in the morning, Coach!" Maverick calls out.

"Why is he running?" Grant asks.

"Maybe he has to shit," Ethan answers, and I slam the door of my SUV shut.

I call Hannah through the Bluetooth, and it rings six times before she finally answers.

"Hello?" she says, voice tinted with exhaustion.

"I woke you up," I say. "I'm sorry."

"No, no. I'm awake. Just resting my eyes." There's a beat where I think she's yawning. Where she's turning on her lamp and sitting up in her bed. "Are you on your way over?"

"Yeah, but we can raincheck. It's late."

"It's not too late." I can hear her smile through the phone, beautiful and bright. "I want to see you."

"I'll be there in twenty. Did you already eat dinner?"

"Six hours ago, like a normal human being. But stop on the way if you're hungry."

"I'm not grabbing shitty takeout when there's something better waiting for me," I tell her.

"You mean pineapple pizza?" The rustle of sheets. A quiet laugh. "I have an extra slice in the fridge."

"Don't make me sick, Everett."

"I'll leave the front door unlocked. You know where I'll be."

I break almost every traffic law on the way to her place. I have to tuck the head of my cock in the waistband of my jeans before I nod hello to the security guard on duty, not wanting to traumatize the nice man who buzzes me in and congratulates me on tonight's win.

Hannah's apartment is dark when I step inside and lock the door. I smell a candle down the hall, and I follow the scent to her bedroom, frantic as I toe off the sneakers I changed into on the plane.

The floor creaks under my feet and I nudge my way into her room, unable to fight off my groan at the sight of her on her bed, exactly how I asked.

She's leaning forward, one elbow on the sheets while her other hand holds a toy against her underwear. Spread legs, ass up, the navy-blue material showing off the curve of her backside.

"Look at you following directions." The rest of my clothes don't last another minute, and I don't give a shit about the wrinkles in my shirt when I throw them all haphazardly on the ground. I climb on the bed, the mattress shifting under my weight, and trace my thumb down the line of her spine. Hannah whimpers, rocking her hips. Her knees open wider, her chest resting on the mattress. "Get up on all fours."

"I have been teasing myself since you called." She swallows, and I brush a piece of hair out of her face. "Do you know how hard it is not to come when I'm thinking about you?"

"You're telling me." I kiss her shoulder and position myself in front of her so I can see her. I turn her cheek, lifting her chin so our eyes meet. "I almost jerked off in the car on the way here because I didn't think I could wait to touch you."

"Please don't make me wait too long. You've been gone a week, and I've missed you."

"Yeah?" I relax against the pillows, smirking at her. "Why don't you tell me about your day? And bump your toy up a notch while you do."

"*Brody*." She moans when I pull down the cup of her bra and pinch her nipple, but she listens, adjusting the speed of her toy. The soft sound of the vibrator fills the room, and, *god*. How have we not done this yet? Why haven't I sat back and watched her take what she needs? Seeing her fuck herself would send me into cardiac arrest. "That feels so good."

"It looks like *you've* been so good, Hannah. Here." I lift her, moving her so she's on top of me. Her knees bracket mine. Her palm sits by my head, and I pull her underwear to the side. "Touch the toy to your clit and pretend it's my fingers. Nice and slow to start, with those circles you like. *Yeah*, sweetheart. *Fuck*. You're so pretty."

"That's my favorite spot. I love when you touch me there." She sighs, body starting to go slack. I use my thighs to push her legs open wider, a hand on her waist to catch her if she falls. "Sometimes I think about surprising you in your office in a short skirt or one of my skating outfits. You'd put me back on your desk like the night at the practice facility and make me spread my legs."

"Do you?" I have to move my hand away from her hip to

stroke my cock. I'm so hard it fucking *hurts*, but I wouldn't fucking dare get myself off before I see her finish. "What else do I do?"

"You use my underwear to keep me quiet while the team is on the other side of the door. You tease me, then stop, making me wait. And when I make too much noise when I come, you bend me over your desk and use a hockey stick to slap my ass."

My brain goes fucking haywire. I swear I almost spill cum all over my hand, because it's the raunchiest thing she's ever said to me, and I don't know how to react.

I know that I like it. I know that I'm picturing her with her skirt hiked up to her waist and marks on her ass. I know that I'd love to stuff her mouth with her underwear to keep her quiet, and I kind of love knowing we could get caught.

"I'd have to use a new stick," I rasp, playing into this fantasy. "One that hasn't been on the ice. Sanitary. Cleanliness. You know." My eyes shift to her hand, watching her increase the pace of her toy. She pushes it inside herself, then pulls it out, and I see how wet it is. I see how much she's liking this, how I turn her on, and if her underwear wasn't so fucking pretty, I'd rip it in two. I'd flip us and put her on her back, fucking her with the toy and making her suck off her cum from the silicone. "Gotta take care of my girl."

Her eyelashes flutter. Her cheeks turn a rosy shade of pink and she bends her neck, kissing me. I meet her halfway, jerking my cock with rough strokes while I kiss her back.

"I am your girl, aren't I?" Hannah whispers, and I nod. "How lucky am I?"

"I'm the lucky one. Being here with you. Having you like this." I take my hand out of my briefs and lift my hips, letting her feel how hard I am just from the sight of her. *Pathetic, stupid man.* "Think we need to do this more often."

"I'm so close. It feels so good and—I want you to finish me off. With my toy. *Please.*"

My fingers wrap around her wrist, taking the toy out of her grasp. It's lightweight, easy to move, and I want to buy one for my place so she'll have one there too. "Like this?"

"A little higher. That's—*ah*." She moans as I drag the toy across her entrance and bring it to her clit. "Perfect."

Without being in control of the toy, Hannah can move more freely, and *hell* does she move. Circling her hips to the pulsing rhythm. Up and down, fucking herself with her hands on my chest. The slick glide of the vibrator filling her up rings in my ears. So does the creak of the bed when I tap it against her nipples and dance it across her stomach.

"So good, sweetheart. You've held out for so long. Do you want me to stop teasing you, Hannah?"

"Yes." A choked sound leaves her. Her shoulders shake, legs trembling. "Please."

"Beg a little more for me, baby. What does this tight pussy want?"

"To come on the toy and pretend it's your cock." Her moan cracks at the edges when I grab her by the waist and set her in my lap, the vibrator in the perfect spot to make her squirm. "That's...I'm going to—" I cut her off with a kiss, a hand on her nape as she falls apart. She drops her head back. Her body jolts, electrified, and she tries to push my hand away when I increase the speed on the toy. "I can't. *I can't*. It's too much, Brody, and I—"

"One more. *There you go*, baby. Look at you taking it. You're so perfect, Hannah. Make a mess so I can clean you up." She opens her mouth, but no noise comes out. I take my time, bringing her down from the high slowly. I decrease the intensity on the vibrator, still holding it to her clit. I grin when she rolls her hips with a whimper. "Greedy girl wants three, doesn't she?"

Sweat rolls down her chest, catching between her tits. The strap of her bra is twisted, and her hair is stuck to her face. I sneak one more small orgasm out of her, finally shutting off the toy when she collapses on my chest.

Hannah buries her face in my shoulder, her tears sticking to my bare skin. I stroke her hair, holding her there until she sniffs and pulls away, looking down at me.

"That was the most intense orgasm of my life," she says.

"Yeah?"

"I've only ever used toys with women because they know how to work them. They know the spots that are most sensitive and don't try to fuck me with them when all I want is some stimulation. But that?" Her laugh is low, sexy. Pleased. *I did that.* "That was fantastic."

My fingers trace along the curve of her jaw. "If you have any videos to help me get better with toys, send them my way."

"I don't think that's necessary. Not when you have this." She touches the front of my briefs, and I groan. "I need a second, Brody, but then I'm going to fuck you like I'm your girl."

FORTY

HANNAH

I'M THOROUGHLY WORN out and could sleep for hours, but Brody is sprawled across my bed with one knee up and his other leg out straight. He takes up so much space, barely fitting on the mattress, but he doesn't seem to care. Not when he reaches up and touches my cheek, smiling in that special, secret way that crinkles his eyes and scrunches his nose.

"What are you thinking about?" he murmurs. "It looks like the wheels are turning in that pretty head of yours."

"Nothing." I kiss his palm. "I'm just happy."

"So am I." He moves onto his side, fixing the straps of my bra. "I'm still trying to figure out how you do it."

"Do what?"

"Make everything you wear look so good. My T-shirts, my jerseys. Expensive lingerie. You're so beautiful, Hannah, and I don't think I could ever tell you that enough." He kisses my back, fingers dancing over my skin. His mouth moves to my shoulder, kissing there too. "Look at us," he says, gesturing to the mirror leaning against the wall. "We look good, don't we?"

"Yeah." I trace over the design of his tattoo, all of the rose petals covering the back of his hand. "We do."

"Take a picture," he says.

"Why? So I can post it on social media and announce to the world I'm sleeping with my brother's hockey coach?" I laugh. "I'm sure that would go over well."

"No." Brody snakes an arm around my waist. His fingers fan out over my ribs, his other hand pulling at my underwear. "So I can use it to get off when I'm not with you."

"*Oh*," I breathe out. Liquid heat inundates my blood, and I squeeze my thighs together at the thought of him in a hotel room. Curtains drawn, lights down low. His hand fisting his cock while he looks at the photo of me. "Is that something you want?"

"Yes." He snaps the waistband of my underwear against my skin, smoothing over the sting with his thumb. I want him to do it again, but so much harder. "I do."

I have photos of him on my phone, candid snapshots I've taken over the last few months. There's one of him on the ice with his backward hat and hands on his hips. Another of him in bed, glasses slipping down his nose and the crossword puzzle in his hand. One of just our hands, blurry on our walk back to his car after a night out at dinner.

I've seen him take photos of me too. He has the screenshot from our FaceTime call and one of me half-asleep, a pillow over my head. Me and Liv on the ice, posing with our backs against each other.

They aren't incriminating. Anyone could've taken them, but something this personal, something this *intimate* feels like a big step. An announcement to the world that we're sleeping together, but I don't think it's scary. Not at all.

I swipe my phone off the bedside table and hold it up, the screen covering my face. You can see Brody's profile, a lock of hair falling across his forehead, but you wouldn't be able to tell it was him unless you knew his tattoos like I do.

He could be any broad, big guy in bed with an unnamed blonde woman, but I know it's us. I know it's his thumb swiping the underside of my breast. I know it's him inching my underwear lower, showing off the dips in my hips, and by the time I finish taking the pictures and send them to him, my body is humming with anticipation. With aching *need*, because I don't think I'll ever get enough of this beautiful man.

I toss my phone on the floor with Brody's clothes and roll on top of him. He smiles up at me, and I touch his nose, his sharp cheekbones, unable to not smile back.

"You said something about fucking me." Brody puts both hands on my thighs. He moves his palms back up, thumbs pressing into my waist then hooking in my underwear, trying to tug the lace down. "How much longer do I have to wait before you put me out of my misery?"

"That desperate for me, huh?" I ask, lifting my ass so he can get rid of the underwear entirely. I grind over the front of his briefs, the tight and dark material doing nothing to conceal his erection from view. He's hard and hot through the cotton, and I sigh as the head of his cock brushes against my pussy lips. "What's the magic word, Coach?"

"Please, baby." He blows out a breath, restraint wavering. He's doing his best to stay still, trying not to raise his hips to meet the slow, controlled roll I'm torturing him with, but he falters. He unhooks my bra and cups both of my breasts, thumbs pinching my nipples hard enough to make me cry out. "I've been good."

The way he's rough yet gentle with me is one of my favorite things. He could be buried inside me in one quick thrust. He could cut off my air supply with a squeeze of his hand to my throat, but he doesn't. He treats me like I'm precious, like I'm *adored*, and there's reverence behind the sweep of his heavy gaze. His eyes bounce all over my body as he struggles for another breath, not sure where he wants to look first.

It's always like this: awe sparking behind his features like he's never had me this way even though I'm so familiar with his body, I could recognize it in my sleep.

The brush of his fingertips. The whisper of a plea falling from his lips. I want to give him everything he wants and more, and I can't believe what he wants is me.

"You've been so good." I move his briefs down his thighs, leaving them tangled at his feet. He helps me adjust my position until I'm hovering above him. The heat from his body is intoxicating, stronger than any shot of liquor, and I let out a startled gasp when he teases my clit with the head of his cock. "*Oh.*"

"Still okay without a condom?" he asks, propping up on an elbow so he can take my nipple in his mouth. He leaves bite marks on the sensitive skin, and my eyes roll to the back of my head. "Answer me, Hannah."

"Of course I'm okay without a condom. Are you?"

"Am I sure that I want to fuck you without any protection because I see a future with you?" The pause is heavy, telling. A hundred things I want to say as I wait for him to keep talking. "Yeah, I am."

A future.

Crying in the middle of sex is the least flattering thing I could do. He's spreading his pre-cum over my pussy. Licking his fingers and rubbing my clit, chin tipped back with a spark of wonder in his eye, but here I am: my heart clenched in a vise-like grip. It's spiraling, *tumbling*, and I have to tuck away the wave of excitement I feel when I look down at him, seeing a future with him too.

Watching Liv at figure skating competitions. Joking about his age and falling asleep with him every night. Joining him on the road and being there to welcome him home after a disappointing loss.

It doesn't come without hurdles and obstacles, without pushback we're sure to get from people who see our differences, but I don't care. I don't care, because I'll have him by my side, and I *love* him.

My bottom lip wobbles. Brody freezes, quick to sit up and gather me in his arms.

"Baby," he whispers. Tender, loving, down to the brittle of each syllable. "What's wrong?"

"Nothing. *Nothing.*" I give a watery laugh and kiss him with everything I have. "I promise I'm okay."

"Are you sure? We don't have to do this. You know I never expect—"

"I know. I want to, but I know it's going to be different this time."

"Different?" He takes my hand, letting me switch our positions. He's on top now, and I wrap a leg around his waist. "Different how?"

"I'll know it when I feel it," I whisper back. His mouth parts. He dips his chin, kissing my knee, my calf. My tongue runs over my shin. "And I think you'll feel it too."

"Yeah," he croaks. "I already do."

When Brody pushes into me, inch by inch, it's not rough. It's soft. The rock of his hips, the flex of his arms. His thumb on my bottom lip that I suck into my mouth, kissing him so I can stay tethered to the ground. I'm afraid if I let him get too far away, this feeling won't last.

And I want it to last.

I've never given all of myself to someone before, too afraid of the consequences of what might happen if I handed my heart over, but as I stare into Brody's eyes, I know it will be him.

Wholly, completely. With every fiber of my being.

"More." I put a hand on his ass, urging him deeper. So many meanings behind the word, and I don't know which one I want him to hear. "I want more, Brody."

"You have it. All of it," he says. He touches me everywhere—my cheek. A hand over my heart. Between my legs where I'm wet and aching for him. "I think you always have."

Brody fucks me like we have all the time in the world, and

maybe we do. We can stay in this bubble, this life we've built for ourselves, where we skate side by side and laugh for hours.

There's no rush, no hurry. He moves us into different positions, finding new angles, finally landing on one that has my back flush to his chest. I can feel his heart, every breath. Tied together.

I moan when his palms roam over me, touching, memorizing with his touch.

"These fucking thighs." Hard fingers press into my skin, gripping me tight. "They're my favorite part about you."

"Because they fit nicely around your head?" I gasp, the first burst of pleasure starting as his hand rests heavy on my throat. "You do like that position."

"No. Because you're so fucking strong and beautiful."

"Even without skating?" I ask, afraid of what his answer might be, afraid of who I am without it, and he buries his face in my neck.

"I've been watching you longer than I've been watching you skate. You could never touch the ice again and I'd still think you were the most magnetic, magnificent thing in this universe."

God.

I love him so much.

"Right there." I ride his cock and toss my head back, sinking into the ecstasy cresting over me. He plucks me apart, knowing exactly what I want. Exactly what I need. "You make me feel so alive, Brody."

"Open your eyes, Hannah. And see what you do to me. How thoroughly fucking wrecked I am by you."

I blink, squinting into the dim light of the room. I see us in the mirror, our bodies moving together in choreographed synchronization that makes color spark behind my vision.

Brody looks anguished. Pure lust in his eyes, desperation in the hungry, greedy way he nips at my neck and ear. He's a man tortured, and when he tilts his chin, attention moving to me, I know I'm his salvation.

"We look so good together," I whisper.

I reach down, finding his balls and cupping them in my hands. His groan is ragged, and he pulls out of me. Lies on the bed and slams me down on his shaft, my breath stuttering out as I take his length.

"Make me come," he practically begs. "Ruin me."

My surroundings blur. I work him up and down, each rotation of his hips helping him get deeper, *deeper* until his muscles constrict. Until he sputters out my name, falling over the edge in a fit of tangled limbs.

I don't stop until my own orgasm hits me, using him to chase the high. I join him, gasping as he holds me in place, filling me up with warm spurts of his release until he has nothing left. My body gives out, exhausted from the physical and emotional exertion, and Brody gathers me in his arms. Kisses me until I finally feel like I return to earth.

"I don't want this to go to your head, but sex with a man has never been this good before for me." My cheek rests on his shoulder, and I trace over the dark hair on his chest. "You make me forget my name."

"For me too. It's a whole new world when you're on top of me."

We're slow to pull apart, taking our time to climb in the shower and clean up. Brody washes my hair, scrubbing my scalp with featherlight fingers. After, he warms up the leftover pizza in my fridge and brings it to me in bed. He climbs in next to me, stealing a bite of the slice covered in pineapple, and hums.

"You know what?" he says, a drop of tomato sauce on the corner of his mouth. "I kind of like that."

"*See.* You've been missing out on so much because you're a stubborn man who doesn't want to try something new." I hold up the slice to him and he takes another bite. "Hopefully you've learned your lesson."

"Many, many lessons."

"Did you find anything good on Ethan's phone earlier?" I ask.

"God." He groans and puts his forehead on my arm. "Don't remind me. I'm afraid I need to teach a sex ed class so everyone knows what happens when you sleep with someone without protection. Can you imagine? All of the guys and their kids running around the arena? I can barely control *one* Richardson, let alone a mini version."

"Daddy Saunders talking about the importance of safe sex and wrapping up." I smirk. "That's hot."

"You're the only one allowed to call me that," he huffs. "The playoffs start next week. Will you come to the home games?"

"Of course I'll be there." I prop up on an elbow. "It's important to you, which means it's important to me."

"Hey." He moves his hand to my cheek. "Have I told you tonight that you're my favorite person in the world?"

"Am I? Out of eight billion humans, you're picking me?" I ask.

"Every single time," Brody murmurs. "And I think that means I win at life."

FORTY-ONE

BRODY

Puck Kings and Daddy Things (+ our savior, BS)

MILLER

Don't forget team dinner starts at six sharp.

Last one to arrive is on dishes duty.

EVERETT

I'm going to be outside your house at 5:30 so I can see my girl Murph.

MILLER

She really likes you, G.

EVERETT

Maybe I'm her real dad.

MILLER

I will murder you, Everett.

HAYES

Boys. Settle down.

ME

Do you have room for one more at dinner?

RICHARDSON

HOLD UP. COACH IS COMING TO DINNER?

EVERETT

This might be the best day of my life.

SULLIVAN

Are you sure you want to subject yourself to video games and fighting over who gets what on their plate? It's not worth it.

MITCHELL

Says the guy who brought pie last time and stayed for two hours.

SULLIVAN

Piper was socializing. That wasn't my choice.

MILLER

Of course there's room, Coach.

EVERETT

This really is going to be such a good night. Hannah is coming to dinner too, which means all my favorite people are in one place. WAYYYY UP, I feel blessed.

ME

Nobody else send me a message or I'll rescind my invitation.

RICHARDSON

Please. You'll be there, and you're excited about it, aren't you?

Coach?

Coachhhhhhhh?

K. Bye.

ME

I hear I'm seeing you at dinner tonight.

H.E.

Lexi and Piper invited me. Is it okay if I'm there?

ME

Of course it's okay that you're there.

H.E.

It's your team and I'm not a part of it, so I don't want to overstep.

ME

If it's my team, I get to make the rules, and the rules say you should be there.

H.E.

Bossy.

I'll be there.

Come to my place after?

ME

Only if you're okay with me staying up late to look at game notes.

The playoffs start tomorrow.

H.E.

Will you wear your glasses?

ME

I don't need them, but I'll wear them for you.

H.E.

Then, yes. I'm okay with you staying up to
look at game notes.

ME

See you later, sweetheart.

H.E.

It's going to be hard not touching you, but I
think I have some self-control.

ME

We'll see about that.

MAVERICK AND EMMY'S house is loud. After thirty minutes of video games, yelling over who gets food first, and a stack of napkins that Ethan throws at Grant, Emmy saunters over to me where I've been hiding out in the kitchen. She holds out Murphy, deposits her in my arms, then turns and leaves me for a glass of wine.

"Uh." I look down at the redheaded baby blinking at me. Her little arm reaches up, trying to grab my chin, and I cradle her head. "What am I supposed to do with this?"

"You have one of these." Maverick leans against the counter with a glass of water. "Shouldn't you be a pro?"

"Tell me, Miller. In the time Murphy has been on this earth, have you ever felt like a pro?"

"Fuck, no." He laughs. "I'm flying by the seat of my pants."

"That never goes away. You're going to be clueless for the rest of your life." I pause and stick my tongue out at Murphy.

She giggles, lighting up, and I forgot how goddamn precious babies are. "Fuck you for making a cute kid, Miller."

"That's all Em." He sighs, so in love it makes me sick. "I hope she inherits her skating skills too."

"Hartwell did have a way of putting you in your place on the ice."

"Yeah." Maverick glances out to the open living room, a dopey grin taking over his face when he finds his wife. "She did."

"How are you two doing?" I ask.

We've had conversations after practice and in our monthly meetings, but I've made it a point to check in every time I see him. The last thing I want is for him and Emmy to feel broken and defeated again, and I'll use all of my resources to help where I can.

"Better than ever. I can't tell you what taking that time off meant to me, and I appreciate you being so flexible. I think you saved my marriage. Saved Emmy, too, and for that, I owe you my life." He rubs his chest. "You're a good guy, Coach. I hope I'm half the man you are when I grow up."

"Shut up, Miller. You're not much younger than me."

"And feeling it every day." There's a long beat. He waits for a couple of the guys to grab a plate and file out of the kitchen before he adds, "I'm reaching the end, dude."

"You already decided?"

"I'm going to honor my contract. Two years, then I'm out." Maverick walks over and touches Murphy's cheek. I see the same gleam in his eyes I know I have when I look at Liv. It's been there from the moment I first held her, and it's never going to go away. "Hockey was my first love. I have no clue what my life is going to look like without it, and it's going to hurt like hell to walk away. But I have more important things calling my name. Don't want to spend all my time hitting a puck and miss out on the greatest gift I've ever been given."

"You don't need to do any growing up, Miller. You're a

man now, and I don't know If I've ever told you this, but I'm proud of you. When I first got to DC, you were a piece of work. I did damage control for you too many times to count. I thought you were lazy. I thought you were a guy who had god-given talent but cared about other things more than what he was blessed with." I pause. There's a lump in my throat, and I turn my head away from Murphy so I can cough to clear it away. "But you've changed. It's been an honor to have you on my team, and the day you retire, I'll have a seat at the bar saved for you."

"Jesus, man. You need to stop." Maverick wipes his eyes. "We've got the playoffs to get through. Two more seasons together."

"You say that, but look at her." Murphy wraps her tiny hand around my finger. I huff out a laugh. Maybe I'd like to have another one. "She's perfect. No Stanley Cup is ever going to beat this, Maverick. I would never hold it against you for wanting to go now. You deserve to rest with the people you love."

"We'll talk after the summer. And fuck you for making me emotional." Maverick glares at me. "Aren't you supposed to be an asshole?"

"If Grant keeps playing as well as he has been, he'll be a better player than you in five years," I deadpan. "How's that?"

"There's the guy I know." He waves to Hudson. "You want me to take Murph?"

"Nah. Go eat." I shift out of the way from everyone filing in to the kitchen to fill their plates. "We're fine."

I find a chair in the formal living room where it's quieter and take a seat, rocking Murphy in my arms. She blinks up at me with big, green eyes. I wait for her to scream, to demand to be handed back to someone she knows, but she never does, yawning instead.

"Well, shit," I mumble. "You're making it very difficult to want to be done with this life, kid."

"The theories are true," a soft voice says.

I look up to find Hannah staring at us with a smile.

"What theories?" I ask.

"A man holding a baby is right up there on the hot scale with backward hats and gray sweatpants."

My lips twitch. "Yeah?"

"Without a doubt." She walks over, perching on the arm of my chair. "Hi, Murphy. Gosh, you're stinking cute."

"Takes after her mother. Her father is a troll," I say, and Hannah giggles.

"Why are your eyes red?" she asks.

"Allergies," I mumble.

"Inside this gorgeous house? What are you allergic to? People?"

"You didn't know that about me?" I sigh. "And Maverick and I were having a heart-to-heart."

"Yeah?" Her fingers rest on my neck, playing with the ends of my hair. "Is everything okay?"

"It will be. We talked about his next steps. What the future looks like for him now that he has all of this." I glance down at Murphy closing her eyes. "It's hard to find other things important when you already have everything you need."

"That's a good sentiment. We have to enjoy the moment we're in, right?" Hannah laughs when Murphy sneezes. "Did you ever think you'd wind up here?"

"Where? In Maverick Miller's living room holding his baby? No fucking way."

"Yeah, that." Her fingers dip lower, to the collar of my shirt. "But also with twenty guys who look up to you. A team who respects you."

"I'll tell you a secret." I glance over at the dining room table filling with people. Laughter, jokes. Someone passing the butter and Ethan tossing an almond in the air and catching it in his mouth. "If I had a chance to do it all over again, I'd pick them every time."

"It's nice to see you open up. Spending time with the people you love is important."

"Yeah." My attention moves to her. I give her knee a squeeze with my free hand, not letting myself linger for too long, but this next part is for her. "It is."

Hannah inhales softly, and I hope she understood my message.

Professing my love for her in front of my players—including her brother—is not what I have planned, but I do want her to know I think she's special. I do want her to know she has a place here—with me, with the team.

"Do you want me to grab you a plate?" she asks, changing gears. "Since your hands are full."

"I'm going to get up here in a second." Murphy holds a fistful of my shirt while she sleeps. "Do you want to hold her?"

"I'm terrified I'll hurt her. And you look so attractive right now, it's nice to look at you."

A throat clears, and we spring apart. My hand falls from her knee. She scoots away so there's distance between us. Riley's eyes move from Hannah to me, pausing to look at her leg.

"Sorry to interrupt," he says.

"You're not interrupting anything." Hannah tosses her hair over her shoulder. "I'm going to get some food. Good to see you, Brody."

"You too," I offer, staring at the floor instead of her ass while she walks away.

"That was interesting." Riley takes a seat on the couch. He adjusts his prosthetic leg and looks at me. "Anything you want to talk about?"

"You didn't see anything," I warn him. "And if you did, do I *look* like I want to talk about it?"

"No." He taps his fingers on his thigh. "I'm going to be honest with you, Coach. I don't remember a lot of the days after my accident. The first couple of months are a blur, between the pain, the medications, and the general feeling of not wanting to exist anymore."

"Are you feeling that way again?" My eyes cut over to him. "I'm here for you if you are. No judgment."

"No. I'm so fucking happy, man, I keep waiting for someone to wake me up. I don't remember a lot of my life after losing my leg, but I do remember the conversation you and I had. You told me I had to find something that makes me feel good. And… I found it. Through playing again. Through helping you coach. Through Lexi." He fixes his glasses and smiles. "Maybe you need to hear it for yourself."

"I do plenty of things that make me feel good."

"If, hypothetically, you were hanging out with someone's sister, he wouldn't care. I mean, he'd care at the beginning, because he doesn't like being left out of things, but after he cooled down, he wouldn't care. He's a lover." Riley shrugs. "He wants the people in his life to be happy."

"You think so?" I ask.

"As long as it's not Ethan."

I bark out a laugh. "I don't know what you saw, but I'd appreciate if you didn't say anything to anyone. Hypothetically speaking, certain people are very important to me. I'm not ashamed of them. I just want to get through the playoffs and let everything slow down before I figure out how to tell other interested parties what's going on."

"My lips are sealed," he says. "Do you love her?" When I don't answer, Riley nods. "I get it. We're so lucky, aren't we?"

With a hand on my shoulder, he finds a seat at the table with Lexi, smiling when she puts a grape in his mouth.

I stand, handing Murphy off to Liam, who shoves Hudson out of the way for a turn. I fix myself a plate then join the team, incapable of sitting anywhere else except with her.

Hannah beams when I fold my legs in the small chair to her left.

"Is Riley okay?" she asks.

"He knows about us. Hypothetically." I take a big bite of salad. "I kind of let it spill."

"Oh, shit. Do you want me to sit somewhere else?"

"No." I put a palm on her thigh under the table, desperate to touch her. "I want you to stay right here."

Because I love you so fucking much.

"Listen up," Maverick announces, from the head of the table. "We're heading into the playoffs tomorrow, and every sportscaster is predicting our loss in the first round. We've had our backs against the wall before, and we always come out on top. This next game is no different. Is the goal to win the Cup again? Of course. It always is, but despite everything we've been through the past couple of years, it'll be a goddamn honor to take the ice with you all tomorrow."

"I hate that I'm the only one who gets emotional at these things." Grant chugs his water. "I'm fighting for my life over here."

"Because you have a sensitive soul, G-Money." Ethan pats his head. "And that's why we love you."

"Protect my net, and we won't have any problems." Liam's eyes dart around the table. "Any questions?"

"We've worked hard for this," Hudson says. "We'll take it day by day and know we're all out there giving our best effort for sixty minutes."

"Is this how all your team dinners are?" Hannah whispers, leaning in close.

"Don't know. I never come to them."

"You should start." Her fingers touch my knee, and I'm glad for the tablecloth that covers my legs. "They're fun."

"I know we're going to your place tonight, but I have Liv the day after tomorrow." With everyone around us distracted by Murphy's crying, I decide to be a daredevil, playing with the ends of the ribbon tied in her hair. Bright pink, my favorite one of hers. "She told me to ask about doing dinner together next week at our place."

"That's a big step. First time hanging out with her off the ice since you broke the news to her about us. I hope I do okay."

"You're going to do great, sweetheart."

She gets pulled into conversation with Lexi and Piper across the table. I finish my food, my pinky linked with hers throughout the rest of the meal. When she grazes my arm when she stands, it feels like someone is watching me. Watching *us*, but when I survey the table, searching for any signs of who it could be, I can't for the life of me figure out who it is.

FORTY-TWO
HANNAH

"WHAT'S the name of the place we're going tonight?" Brody asks from my bathroom. He checks his reflection in the mirror and frowns, fixing his hair. "Prince?"

"Price," I say. "It's the new gay bar in town."

"I'm honored Tierney wants me at at her birthday celebration."

"She's very excited to officially meet you." I smile his way. "And I'm excited to see you dance."

"Don't get too excited. Those flowers in the kitchen? Those are for her," he says. "Birthday flowers, yeah, but also apology flowers for how poorly I move on a dance floor."

"You're not a fan of grinding?"

"There will be *no* grinding." Brody flips off the light and walks into my room, letting out a whistle. "God damn, Hannah. Look at you."

"Too much?" I pull on the hem of my short silver dress, hoping I didn't overdo it. "I have a black dress I can put on instead."

"Don't you dare." He rests a hand on my hip and moves my hair away from my neck, kissing me there. "What a lucky bastard am I that you're coming home with me after."

"That's determined by how well you dance." I giggle when he licks my throat, cupping my ass with both hands. "We need to get going. The Uber will be here any minute, and we're already behind schedule."

"In a minute," Brody mumbles, bunching my dress at my waist. He hisses when he finds my bare ass. "*No underwear?* Are you trying to kill me?"

"Don't think it was for you. The lines would ruin the outfit, and I want to look good for my best friend's big night! Unhand me, you strong man." I put a hand on his chest, not bothering to fight him off. "You look good too. This shirt? And your jeans?" I touch the collar of his light blue top. "You sure are stylish, BB."

"This is my first time at a gay bar. And I dressed okay? Too casual? I brought options."

"You're perfect." I kiss his cheek and grab my purse. "I can't tell you how much it means to me that you're giving up one of your free nights during the playoffs to spend time with my best friend."

"Is there going to be a test?" he asks.

"No. Tierney isn't like that." We file out of my apartment, hand in hand. Brody keeps the bouquet he bought for her close to his chest. "As long as her friends are happy, she's happy."

In the elevator, he crowds my space. He runs his hand up my leg, stopping at the top of my thigh. "It's a shame you don't live on a higher floor so I could get you off on the way to the lobby." He pushes a single finger inside me, covering my mouth when I try to moan. "Guess I have to settle for teasing you."

Nobody else joins us in the elevator, but the ride down goes far too fast. I'm panting by the time the doors open, heat rolling through me Brody carefully pulls his finger out of me and licks it clean as we step outside.

"You're a menace," I say, climbing into the backseat of the Uber. "And a tease."

"You like it," he murmurs in my ear, pressing a kiss to my forehead.

No, I want to say. *I love it.*

I love you.

I almost let it slip yesterday when he handed me a pancake for breakfast, but I chugged my glass of orange juice instead. I think he's almost said it too though. Last week, he looked at me across the couch. Started to say something, then grabbed his phone, mumbling about lineup changes under his breath.

His shyness made me fall in love with him a little bit more.

The club is loud when we get there, and I thank the bouncer when he lets us in. We find Tierney in a VIP section toward the back of the room, and she squeals when she spots us.

"There you are!" She springs to her feet, giving me hug. "You look gorgeous, Han."

"So do you, birthday girl. Gold is your color." I squeeze her hand. "This is Brody, my—"

"Boyfriend," he finishes for me, and my grin threatens to break free when he holds out the flowers to Tierney. "These are for you. It's nice to meet you."

"Look who's out here raising the standard." She accepts the gift and pulls him in for a hug too. "I normally think men are shit, but I'll make an exception for you after you found a way to make it to Hannah's competition."

"I'd do anything to make her happy." His arm slides around my waist, so easy and natural. I lean against his chest. "And I'm going to do my best not to let you down."

"Drinks are free, courtesy of Jamal paying for the open bar." She gestures in the direction of her brother who is chatting with a girl in the booth. "Help yourself to whatever you want! We're going to do cake a later, but I need to do some dancing first."

"We're going to grab a drink and meet you out there," I tell her, kissing her cheek. "You're not allowed to lift a finger tonight unless it's to drink a glass of champagne."

"I wish it could be my birthday every day."

With the shake of her hips, she makes her way to the dance floor, finding a pretty girl with dark hair to slide up next to.

"What do you want to drink?" I yell over the music, leading Brody over to the bar. He folds himself behind me, hands on my hips. "I'm going to do a whiskey and ginger ale."

"I'll have one of those too, but make it a double. My tolerance for clubs is low."

"Funny how we've been to two clubs together." I get the bartender's attention and place our order. I spin in his hold while we wait, draping my arms around his neck. "We don't have to stay long. I appreciate you being here, even if it's only for half an hour."

"We'll stay as long as you want. Do you want to know why?" He leans in close, mouth right near my ear. His breath is warm, his hands are roaming, and the pulsing bass of the music makes the moment sexier. "I have earplugs in my pocket."

"Oh my god." I giggle. "That's *hot*, Brody."

"Bought them on the way home from practice today. Problem solved."

I love you, I love you, I love you.

Those three words threaten to come out again. I grip his collar, desperate to bring him closer. I kiss him, my tongue tangling with his. My mouth says the things that I can't, and Brody answers me with enthusiasm. I don't pull away until there's a tap on my shoulder and two drinks are being slid our way.

"Thank you," I say, and Brody drops a wad of cash in the tip jar.

We move over to the birthday girl's section, but the space

has filled up. Brody takes a seat on a long booth and pulls me into his lap, making sure his hand shields my ass from view.

"Comfortable?" he asks, and I nod.

"Very. Are *you* comfortable?"

"My knee has been acting up the last couple of days. I think it's because I've been hitting the ice hard with the guys during our playoff series. Besides that, I'm sipping a good drink. I have a beautiful girl in my lap. What the hell can I complain about?"

I pull out my phone, carefully balancing my drink so it doesn't spill. I flip the camera to selfie mode, pressing my cheek against his.

"Smile, Brody," I say, and he turns, kissing my neck instead. I sigh, content when he does it again. "What's your favorite flavor of cake?"

"Hm. Chocolate with vanilla frosting. What about you?"

"I like that too. We should take a slice home and find a new purpose for the frosting. I'd let you lick it off me."

He chugs his drink and helps me to my feet. Guiding me to the dance floor, he finds a dark, secluded spot and pulls my hips to his.

"Where would I lick it off of?" he asks. Back here, it's harder to make out where his hands are. It's more difficult to see, and I rely on my other senses. His knuckles, running along my hip. His heavy breathing and the jut of his cock through his jeans. "Maybe your ass? Your tits?"

"We can get creative." I lift my arms above my head, swaying my hips to the music. My dress is obscenely short, sitting right at the tops of my thighs, and I know I'm playing with fire. "You know I'd be a willing participant."

Brody and I move together, finding a rhythm. It's not very coordinated, but it's hot as hell to have him like this; a little clumsy. A little sweaty. Staring right at me. He holds my chin tight and kisses me roughly, fingers threading in my hair.

"Are you wet?" he whispers, even though no one else could hear him over the noise.

"I've been wet since you teased me in the elevator."

"Here." He nudges his thigh between my legs, crouching slightly. The friction of his jeans rubs against my pussy, and I gasp. "How does that feel, angel?"

"I think if you keep doing that, you could get me off," I admit.

"It's a good thing I wore dark denim so no one can see the stain you leave behind." Brody kisses my forehead, spinning us on the dance floor so my back is against a wall. He puts his hands on either side of my head, caging me in. "I feel so fucking reckless with you, Hannah."

I whine, desperate to quell the ache between my legs. My need for him grows, and I don't care that I'm panting. I don't care that we're both bending our bodies in awkward positions to make the angle work, because Brody is making me feel like I'm on top of the world.

Maybe it's the music or our closeness or the drink I had, but I want to tell him. I *need* to tell him how I feel, right this very second.

"*Brody*. I think—I lo—"

He cuts me off with another kiss but then pulls away when his leg almost gives out.

"Shit," he mumbles.

"Are you okay?" I swallow, trying to catch my breath. "Did I hurt you?"

"No. It wasn't you. Just my knee. It's sorer than I thought, and putting all that weight on it—" He grimaces and shakes his head. "I'm fine."

"Let's go sit down."

"But I didn't get you off. You were almost there."

"I can finish later and be perfectly happy." I lace our hands together, winding through the dance floor crowded with bodies. "Let's get you some water."

"I'm not dying Hannah," he says, stopping us in the middle of a walkway. "I'm sorry. I didn't mean to snap at you like that. I just… this injury happened years ago. Why the fuck am I still having phantom pain?"

"Because you've been pushing yourself these last couple of weeks. Because you're a great coach who doesn't know how to be anything but the best, so you work your players up to that mindset as well. Because you're a good man who goes to the club I drag him to and dances even though he's not very good at it." I touch his cheek when he winces again and grabs his knee. "A Tylenol and a day off your feet will do wonders."

"No time for that when we have games to win." Brody sighs, resting his forehead against mine. "This is embarrassing. And it's so loud in here."

"We can leave. Tierney is having so much fun, she won't notice we're gone."

"No. She's your best friend, and I don't want to make you suffer with my grouchy ass." He lets out a soft laugh. "Would you hate me if I went home?"

"Not one bit. Are you going to go to your place or mine?"

"Mine. I need to be up early for practice in the morning, and I don't want to disturb you while you're getting your beauty sleep."

"Are you sure?"

"I'll bring you a coffee when I drop Liv off for your lesson." Brody smiles. "Go have fun, sweetheart."

"Kiss me before you go?"

"Like you even need to ask." Brody smiles, bumping my nose with his. He hums against my mouth, and I melt into him. "Text me when you get home."

"I will," I say, but as I watch him disappear out into the crowd, my heart is pounding. My palms are sweating, and being here without him isn't nearly as fun.

FORTY-THREE
HANNAH

"YOU SEEM NERVOUS," Brody says. He closes his laptop and follows the path I'm pacing around the kitchen. "What are you stressed out about?"

"I've spent a lot of time with Liv. The three of us have spent time together, but this is the first night we're going to hang out as a—" I clamp my mouth shut. "Never mind."

"As a family?" he finishes for me, and I nod.

"That's weird. I'm sorry. Liv's not mine. I recognize that. I hope you don't think I'm trying to wedge myself into the Saunders' family tree or anything, but I—"

"Hey." He hops off the barstool and walks to me, cupping my cheeks with both hands. "I'm going to say the thing to you I know I'm never supposed to say to a woman, but I'm willing to pay the consequences."

"What's that?" I ask. "That I should smile more?"

"No." The low rumble of his chuckle relieves some of my tension. "That you need to calm down."

"I'd argue with you, but I'm pretty sure you're right." I stand on my toes so I can rest my forehead against his. "I'm just nervous."

"I can ask Kali to take Liv to her place. That wouldn't be

a burden on her," Brody says. "We'll do this another night. I'll pour you a glass of wine. I can run you a bath."

"I'm okay. Really." I give his arm a reassuring squeeze. "I want to take this next step with the two of you. I just know how much I care about you, and how much I care about Liv, and I want everything to go well."

"We'll treat it just like every other time we've been together. And if she starts asking us questions we don't want to answer about the future, I'll break out a water gun and cut her off."

"You have a *water gun?*" My shoulders loosen with a grin. "And you carry it around with you?"

"I did this thing with the guys the other day before our game instead of our usual practice. They were stressed. A long year and the start of the playoffs is catching up to them, so I had three dozen Super Soakers delivered to the arena. We had a massive water gun fight that somehow turned into a slip and slide across the ice. The next day, they went out and played their best game of the season." He shrugs. "I'm sure there's some science behind that, and I'm sure it can apply to nosy fourteen year olds too."

The front door to the apartment opens, then slams shut. Footsteps skip down the hall, and Brody rubs my shoulders when Liv appears around the corner.

"Dad. Don't be mad at me, but I got detention today," Liv says. Her backpack goes flying across the floor. "I had a good reason for it." She takes off her sweatshirt and brightens when she sees me. "Hannah! Hi! Are you eating dinner with us tonight?"

"I am." I lean my elbows on the island. "Your dad keeps talking about this soup you two like to make, and I was hoping to try it out for myself."

"I've been needing a new sous chef. Dad is way too particular about keeping things clean." She rolls her eyes. "A paper towel is out of place, and he's unhappy."

"Hang on." Brody moves away from me and folds his arms over his chest. "We need to go back to the detention part. What did you do?"

"Bruce Leeland said he could beat me in a race around the track because I'm a girl and *so much slower than him*, so I told him to give it a try. I kicked his ass, and after, I put up a sign in the cafeteria with a picture of his face on it."

"And?" Brody asks through clenched teeth.

"And… I might've written *lost to a girl* under it," she adds innocently. "It's not defamation. He *did* lose to a girl."

"Jesus Christ." He pinches the bridge of his nose. "You know what? We're going to table this discussion. Soup and brownies are on the agenda. I'm in a good mood, and that's a parenting conversation we'll have later when we don't have company over." He pauses to ruffle Liv's hair. "How much did you beat him by?"

"Five seconds," she tells us proudly, and Brody smirks.

"That's my girl."

"LIV. This is delicious. Have you always liked to cook?" I ask, taking another bite of the broccoli cheddar soup.

"Yeah. Dad taught me some of the nutritional impacts food has on athletic performance, and I've tried to be better about making meals at home instead of going out to eat with friends." She cuts her piece of cornbread in half. "I'm also working with my school cafeteria to make sure we have better food options at lunchtime. For some of my classmates, they only get two meals a day. Greasy pizza is delicious, but not four times a week. It's been fun to get people's opinions on what the kitchen should serve."

"Liv, I'm going to say this as a completely unbiased party." I scoot my chair closer to the table. Brody's leg presses into mine, and he rests a hand on my thigh. "I think you could rule the world one day."

"Thanks." She beams, proud of herself. "Thank my dad. He's always told me to kick ass and take names."

"And lectured you about your use of vulgarities, but I don't think it's sticking at this point." He sighs, thumb stroking over the curve of my knee. "I promise I don't walk around here spewing expletives," he tells me, and I laugh.

"I know you don't. Only occasionally," I say.

"I'm going to grab a beer. Do you want anything?" he asks.

"I'm good. Thank you."

"Liv?"

"I'm fine, Dad. Thanks."

He touches my shoulder before heading to the fridge, and Liv puts down her fork.

"My dad likes you so much," she says. "Has he given you all the gifts yet?"

"Gifts?" I frown. "What are you talking about?"

"I'm not sure what they are. He comes home from all his away games with this little bag, but he won't tell me what it is. Just that it's for you." She pops a crouton in her mouth. "Maybe it's for a surprise he's putting together."

"When I find out what it is, I'll let you know." I smile when she pumps her fist in the air. "Tierney is going to come to our session tomorrow, if that's okay. She wants to see your choreography for the Potomac Memorial, and I thought it would be good to get an outside pair of eyes on your program."

"*What?* What's her favorite color? I'll wear one of my new outfits so I can bribe her to give me compliments."

"Stop it." I swat at her arm. "You know you're a great skater. You don't need to bribe anyone."

"Do you really think that?" Liv asks.

"I do. Your dad already likes me enough," I joke. "I don't need to butter you up to win him over."

"True." Brody kisses the top of my head before sliding back in his seat. "Uh." He coughs and sips his beer, cheeks turning red. "Sorry for the PDA, Liv."

"Two adults who like each other kissing on the cheek?" She gasps. "The horror!"

"Okay, enough with the sarcasm, kid. This is new for me. For all of us. I'm trying to figure out how to act around you without making it uncomfortable for anyone."

"He's never brought a woman home," Liv says to me. "He's never had a date to any of the Stars' galas. He's never snuck someone out of the condo while he thought I was still sleeping." Her tone softens, and she looks at Brody. "Dad. You've spent fourteen years doing everything you can to make me happy, and now it's your turn to be happy. If kissing the woman you care about makes you happy, I hope you're not going to hold back for me."

"Olivia Elliot. When the heck did you get so mature?" Brody asks, and I swear I hear a tremor to his voice. "Thank you for your feedback."

"Bryant and Mom kiss all the time and I'm fine with it." She picks up our empty bowls and brings them to the sink. "Brownies next?"

Liv and I mix the batter while Brody does the dishes. An egg ends up on the floor and we burst out laughing when he scowls at us, grabbing a mop to clean up the mess. We add a bag of chocolate chips to the mixing bowl and Liv licks the spatula clean, flinging the leftovers at Brody and squealing when it lands on the wall.

While we wait for the brownies to cool, we head to the living room. Liv sits on the floor between my legs, her back to me while I separate her hair into sections for a French braid.

"Oddly enough, I don't know how to do a braid on myself," I tell her. Brody flips through the television channels to find something for us to watch, his free hand on my lower back. "When I was younger, all the girls at the events I was performing in would come to me and ask me to do their hair."

"Did you give them all the iconic Hannah Everett ribbon?" Liv asks, tipping her head back so I can get her part right.

"Nope. That's only reserved for special people in my life." I pause. "I have one for you. I was going to wait until tomorrow when Tierney was with us, but I'd like to give it to you tonight, if that's okay with you."

"*Really?*" Liv spins, forgetting about her hairstyle, and sits up on her knees. "You brought me a ribbon?"

"Yeah. I know I've been coaching you, but you've helped me so much too, Liv. I'm immensely proud of how far your skating has come, and I'm glad we've become friends." My smile is sly. "But don't expect me to start going easy on you just because we're making brownies together."

"I wouldn't dream of it." She flings her arms around my neck and I laugh, hugging her back. "I'm so glad you're in our lives, Hannah," she whispers, and it's the greatest compliment in the world.

AFTER LIV HEADS TO BED, Brody and I take a seat on the terrace off his bedroom. I drape a blanket over my shoulders, gaping at the city view.

"How is this the first time I've been out here?" I ask. "It's stunning."

"Given the first five months of our relationship happened when the weather was below fifty degrees, I didn't think to show you," he says from behind me, the two of us sharing a large chaise lounger. "Do you like it?"

"It's spectacular." I settle into his embrace, resting my cheek on his arm. "Tonight went well. Even with the detention Liv earned."

"Heaven help me. I'm praying to every deity out there she doesn't go through a rebellious stage at any point in her life. I'm not sure I'll be able to handle it." He kisses my cheek. "She loves you. I hope you know that."

"I do."

"Good. And now that we're alone again, I want to talk to you about what you said earlier."

"Which part?" I sit up, turning my body to face him. He's smiling at me, the light from the moon making him glow in shades of silver and gray. "Did I do something wrong?"

"Sweetheart, I don't think you could ever do something wrong," he murmurs. "When you talked about the three of us being a family, you were right. I do think of you as part of this family. You slot perfectly into the life Liv and I have. It might look different from the conventional definition, but it works, and I'm having so much damn fun with you."

Tell him, my brain screams.

Tell him how you feel.

"Brody?" I whisper.

"Yeah?"

"I want to tell you something, but I'm scared."

"What are you scared of?" he asks gently.

"What happens if things go wrong?"

"And what if they go right?" he says, and it makes me want to explode with glee. "I'll be here. Whenever you're ready."

"Even if it takes me years?" I ask.

"Even then. Look how great six months have been. Can you imagine six years?" He hooks his fingers around my chin, kissing me. "I'd say sixty, but I'll be dead by then."

My laugh starts as a giggle. It turns into full-blown hysteria, and soon, Brody is laughing too. I don't know how long we sit out there howling into the night, just that it's right.

FORTY-FOUR
BRODY

H.E.

I am so excited for you, baby.

Game seven!!!

ME

I've been in a dozen of these throughout my career, but I'm nervous as hell about tonight.

Liv and Kali will be here, but they're going back to her place after the game.

Come home with me?

H.E.

A win or a loss, I'll be there.

I'll find you in the tunnel after <3

ME

I'll be waiting with open arms, sweetheart.

"LISTEN UP, boys. It's game seven. We have the advantage of being on home ice, but that doesn't mean we're going to let up on our aggression," I say, addressing the locker room. "Our opponents have been coming out hot every single night, and we've consistently found ourselves down in the first period. I need sharper passes tonight. I need cleaner shots on goal. I need you to trust each other and know this group of guys has what it takes to go all the way." There's a murmur of agreement, and I nod. "Three minutes until we're going out there and proving every single person who has ever doubted us wrong. We're leaving it all out there, okay? Empty tanks, full fucking hearts. A win takes us to the next round. A loss sends us on a four-month vacation. How this plays out is entirely up to you."

"Hands in," Maverick yells, popping to his feet. His eyes meet mine, and I wonder if this will be the last time he's going to lead the team in a huddle. If tomorrow he's going to hang up his jersey and call it quits, going out bruised and defeated, but moving on to more important things. "Family on three. One. Two. Three."

"*Family*," everyone yells, and Grant jumps up and down. Ethan hits his stick against the wall and Liam yanks down his goalie mask, mumbling under his breath.

I feel the energy in the air too. It's clawing at me, and I bump their fists as they file out into the tunnel, giving each player a final piece of encouragement that I hope will motivate them for the next sixty minutes.

When the locker room empties out, I take a deep breath. I savor the quiet, the still calm that always happens right before pandemonium breaks loose. It's hard to believe this might be it for our season after how far we've gotten in the past, and when Parker and Mikal welcome me out to the hallway, I give them both a look.

"Ready?" I ask them, and they both grin.

"Wouldn't want to go to battle with anyone else," Parker says.

"It's been an honor." Mikal laughs. "This feels more intense than we played in the Stanley Cup game sevens. Different atmosphere. Different stakes."

"Because it might be the last time we see this lineup out there," I say. We make our way to the bench and the roaring crowd. I keep my focus on the ice instead of searching the crowd for Hannah. I can't see her, but I can *feel* her. She's somewhere up there, screaming as loud as she can. "Let's go out with a bang."

The first two periods are the most intense we've played all season, and I can barely track the puck with how fast the game is moving. It's impossible to yell out calls over the noise from the fans. The Atlanta Yellowjackets give up nothing, matching our aggressiveness from the very start.

Both teams shoot lights out, but neither are able to score. Penalties get handed out left and right, and it's like everyone in the building knows this might be a race to one. The first team to get the puck in the net is going to be the winner, and as we get ready to start the third, I stand in front of the guys in the locker room to give them their final pep talk.

"You all know I'm not usually one for words," I say.

"Please, Coach. You're the most eloquent guy here." Ethan laughs. "Give us a five minute soliloquy."

"I'm not doing anything like that. I want you to know you all are doing everything right tonight," I tell the group. "Our effort is there. Our defense is there. We're taking good shots on goal. *Great* shots on goal. I don't want anyone to get discouraged, okay? The last forty minutes didn't matter. Forget about them. The next twenty is where we're going to focus, and I want each of you to take a second and close your eyes. Reflect on why you're here. Who are you playing for? *What* are you playing for? When you have that answer, I want you to grab your equipment and head back out to the ice and know the men behind you have your back. No egos. No glory. You're all in this together, and no matter what happens out there, it's been a goddamn honor to stand alongside you all this season." I take a breath. A rare wave of emotion starts to rise inside me, but I do my best to clamp it down as I make eye contact with every guy. "I'll see you out there."

The room stays silent, and I watch each player get up, one by one, and file out with their heads held high. Maverick is the last one to stand, and his exhale is shaky.

"Let's get this done," he says, and I clasp his shoulder.

"You get a shot, you take the shot," I tell him. "I know you've put your hero complex away, but what a fitting end to the story that would be."

"Story? Coach, I'm living in a goddamn fairytale." He smiles. "Job's not done. And I'm not stopping until it is."

The third period starts out with the Yellowjackets on a power play, but Liam blocks their three shots on goal. He sacrifices his body, diving for each puck. Dropping into a split and reaching his blocker back, making the save of the year.

I blink and the first fifteen minutes of the period are gone, and during a timeout, I step off to the side with Parker, Mikal, and Riley while the guys grab a drink.

"What do you think?" I ask them. "I'm turning over head coaching duties to you all. What play are we running?"

"Grant's been our highest scorer this season," Parker says. "But I'd go with Maverick. Captain. Veteran. He has the experience under pressure and can find the goal."

"Same. If we could get him set up with a wrist shot near the crease, he could sink one," Mikal adds.

"Mitchell?" I ask, and he clears his throat.

"I disagree. I think you go with Richardson," he says.

"Why?"

"Because it's unexpected. Because he wants this win. Because Maverick and Grant look gassed, but Ethan looks like he's just getting warmed up."

I crane my neck, looking down the bench. Riley's right. Maverick and Grant have their heads between their legs, trying to catch their breath. Ethan's on his feet, staring at the ice then checking the tape on his stick.

"Ethan," I call out, and his gaze snaps to mine. "Come here."

"What's up?" he asks, sliding past Richie Davenport in his goalie gear.

"How are you feeling out there?"

"Uh." He's eyes bounce to each of the coaches. "Good, I think? Is there something I need to focus on during these last five?"

"Win the face-off, then I want you to try to get open in the slot. Miller," I call out, and he's slow to get to his feet. "I want you to try and set up a centering pass from the right wing to Richardson."

"Shit, yeah. Sounds good." He grins and bumps Ethan's knuckles. "Ready for the big leagues, man?"

"Shut up, Cap. I was born ready," Ethan says, and I glance at Riley.

"Good call, Mitchell," I say, and he pushes his glasses up his nose with a smile.

The play resumes, but we lose the face-off. The Yellow-jackets take it down the ice, their captain launching a stellar snap shot that Grant dives in front of, deflecting the puck to the left wing.

"Who has it?" I ask after a skirmish against the boards. "Fuck. Hayes does."

Hudson kicks the puck over to Maverick who looks over his shoulder instead of the open ice in front of him. Everyone knows he's the fastest player out there, but he lifts his chin and barks out an order I can't hear. Hudson drops back, switching sides with Grant while Ethan trails them down the middle. Just before Maverick reaches the goal, he sets up a drop pass, faking the goalie out and skating past the puck.

By the time the tender realizes his mistake, Ethan's scooping up the puck and charging forward. Right at the crease he rears back, the puck going in the net and the building erupting in screams.

"Holy shit!" Riley yells. "It fucking worked."

The five on the ice grab each other in celebration, but there's still three minutes on the clock. I urge the bench to settle down, and when Ethan skates past, accepting high-fives, I grab his jersey.

"I know you don't think you were a good student, but you are a fantastic listener," I say to him, my forehead pressing against his helmet. "You have so many skills outside of hockey that are essential to this team, Ethan, and I'm so fucking proud of you."

"Thanks, Coach." He grips me in a hug, his sweat soaking my suit. "Thank you for believing in me."

"Plenty of time left. Keep our composure, yeah?" I say, patting his chest, and he nods. "Let's go, boys. Gotta hang on to it."

The momentum is in our favor. The crowd is more alive than they've been all night, on their feet and physically rocking the building with how loud they are, but I've never been an optimist. I know anything can happen if there's time on the clock, so I keep my excitement down. I don't overreact to a missed slashing call. I keep my shifts the same amount of time, not wanting to get too frantic in case we have extra hockey ahead of us.

The Yellowjackets make a surge with twenty seconds left, winning a face-off and setting up a backhand shot. Liam anticipates their next move, and when he dives on the puck and an Atlanta player still tries to knock it in the goal, hell breaks loose as time expires. Gloves are thrown. Someone loses a helmet, and players are separated.

"No fucking goal," Parker yells, watching the replay on the

jumbotron. "Where's the fucking goalie interference? He's on top of Sullivan!"

The building waits while the referees figure out the official call, and when they deem it a no goal and the end regulation, our bench throws their gloves in the air.

"Second round, here we fucking come!" Grant screams, starting a dogpile on Ethan. "Easy fucking E is our hero!"

I pull each coach into a hug, finding Maverick in the mess of jerseys and yelling at him to get the guys lined up for the handshake line.

"Locker room straight after," I say, jogging off the ice.

I get stopped a half a dozen times by members of the media wanting a comment. I put on my best face and answer their questions, wanting to see my girl and celebrate with her.

By the time I break free, I see her lingering by the locker room in another one of my jerseys and ripped jeans. She lights up when she spots me, running and jumping into my arms.

"You did it," she says when I catch her, spinning her around and burying my face in her hair. "You *did it*, Brody."

"I can't believe it. What a comeback. What a shot by Ethan. We live to see another day." I kiss her temple. "I'm not sure I've ever been that stressed out before."

"Your shoulders were up by your ears." She giggles and I set her down, letting out my first breath in what feels like years when she wraps her arms around my neck. "I am so proud of you."

"Thanks for being here." I slip my palms in her back pockets. "I'm going to be a while. Interviews. Debrief with the guys. Checking the score from the other series to see who we're matched up against. Will you hate me if I make you wait an hour? You know what? Take my key and go to my place. I'll be there—"

"What the *hell* are you two doing?"

Hannah's eyes go wide. She peers over my shoulder, dropping me from her hold. I spin, finding myself face to face with Grant, who doesn't look like he did twenty minutes ago. His gaze is murderous as his eyes bounce from Hannah to me.

"Grant," I say, and he drops his stick and gloves.

"Are you touching my *sister*?" he asks, voice so low, I have to strain to hear him. "You can't be serious, Hannah."

"Hey," I snap, stepping in front of her. "You're not going to speak to her like that."

"Someone better tell me what the fuck is going on. Right fucking now."

"Brody." Hannah touches my arm. "It's okay."

"You're sleeping together," Grant whispers. "I fucking knew it. I thought I saw something between the two of you at the team dinner, but I blamed it on being tired."

"We're doing more than sleeping together," I say.

"Are you? I fucking respected you, Brody. I looked up to you. You've been my idol for years, but the whole time, you've been exactly like everyone else," he spits. "A goddamn fuck-boy. You have a kid and you're out here spending time with a twenty-five-year-old? Grow the fuck up and go out with someone your own age."

"A fuckboy? I *love* her," I seethe, my anger reaching a boiling point. "And you're not going to drag my daughter into a discussion where she doesn't belong."

"Why not?" He steps toward me, an arm pressing into my chest. "Hannah is young enough to make you a father of two."

"*Enough*," Hannah says, and we both go quiet. "How dare you talk about me like that when I'm right here?" She looks at her brother, and when I steal a glance at her, I see the hurt in her eyes. I want to reach out and comfort her, to hold her, but I don't want to make this any worse than it is. "You want to call out my age and say I'm your younger sister all while you sit here and act like a child. How dare you think this has anything to do with you, Grant?"

"Is Brody forcing you into this?" He swallows. "Does he have blackmail on you?"

"Forcing me into a relationship with another adult?" Hannah's laugh is fractured. "I'm not having this conversation with you." She turns to me. "I'll wait for you at your place. I don't want to be here."

"Of course." I fish out my keys from my pocket and take off the one to my condo. "I'll be there as soon as I can."

Hannah turns on her heel and leaves the two of us staring at each other.

"I trusted you," Grant says, wiping his nose and ignoring his teammates making their way to the locker room. "And now you're dead to me."

I don't offer him a rebuttal knowing this isn't my battle to fight. I sigh and brush past him, doing my goddamn best to fake my enthusiasm for the cameras while feeling like complete shit.

FORTY-FIVE

HANNAH

IT TAKES Brody two hours to get home. By the time he does, I'm in his bed. I'm wearing one of his big T-shirts and doing the crossword puzzle with his glasses on my face, squinting at the paper I'm holding in front of me.

"Hey, sweetheart," he says from the doorway.

"I'm getting a jumpstart on your crossword puzzle," I say, and he smiles.

"Can I join you?"

"Sure." I pat the mattress, propping the pillows behind me so I can look at him. "How were the celebrations?"

"Not as celebratory." Brody gently takes the crossword puzzle and pen out of my grasp, setting them on the bedside table. "Are you okay? There was a lot that just happened."

"Do you want me to be honest with you?"

"Always." His fingers make quick work of unknotting his tie. "You can tell me anything you want."

"I'm really upset by Grant's reaction. I know he's coming from a place of love, but it's my life. I'm an adult who is free to do whatever I want, however I want to do it. Hearing him insert himself into a conversation where he doesn't belong sucked," I say, watching Brody take off his suit jacket and

416

shirt. "And the things he said about you?" I shake my head. "That was inappropriate."

"I'm not saying that I'm on his side, but I see where he's coming from." Brody's shoes and slacks come off next, and when he's left in his briefs, he sits next to me on the bed. "He's a protector. He's protected you for most of his life, and now, there's someone else who is protecting you. And it doesn't help that it's a man fourteen years older than you who he's known for quite some time." He takes my hand and kisses my knuckles. "I know the difference in our age doesn't bother us, but to other people—especially your brother, who was completely caught off guard by our relationship tonight—it's jarring."

"This is my fault. Running into your arms like that with your players and cameras around? I didn't think of the consequences."

"Hey. It's no one's fault. We could just as easily say it's *my* fault, because I could have had a conversation with him in private where I told him how I felt about you," he says, and I sit upright. I yank his glasses off my face and shove them with the crossword puzzle. "What's wrong?"

"You told Grant that you love me," I whisper, and Brody's Adam's apple bobs. "Is that true?"

"I know what I told Grant, but I also know what I told you that night we spent with Liv. I said I'd be here whenever you were ready, and we don't have to talk about this if you're not—"

"I love you too," I blurt, and his jaw goes slack. "I love so many things about you, I could probably make a list. But I want you to know that I love you too."

The second the words leave my mouth, I'm instantly lighter. It's like I'm floating on the clouds, indescribable happiness hitting me in the dead center of my chest when Brody threads his fingers through my hair. When he brings my mouth to his, kissing me in a way that's so different from how he's done in the past, but still so achingly familiar.

"Say it again," he murmurs against my lips. "Tell me one more time, Hannah."

"I love you. I-I've felt this way for a while now, Brody, but I told you I'm scared. I'm so scared, because this started as something purely physical." I put my hands on his chest, his heart racing as fast as mine. "Because I have no clue what I'm doing. Because we don't care about the age difference, but I recognize that you've lived a whole life before me, and I worry I'm not going to be enough for you."

"Not enough for me?" His thumbs wipe away the tears I didn't know started to fall. "You don't know, do you, sweetheart?"

"Know what?" I ask, and Brody pulls away. Gives my hand a squeeze and stands. "Where are you going?"

"Give me a second." He disappears into his closet, and I hear boxes shifting around. The scrape of a hanger and something falling to the floor. When he returns, he's holding a notebook and a shoebox tight to his chest. "I want to show you something."

"Is it your sex toy collection?" I ask, making a joke because it feels like my feeble, fragile heart might crack in two.

"No, but let's come back to that down the road." His smile is magnificent; infinite blue skies. Cotton candy sunsets. "Do you remember when we talked about bucket lists?"

"Yes." I cross my legs. "You said you weren't sure what would be on yours."

"I figured it out." Brody hands over the notebook. "Take a look."

My hands shake as I open the front cover, finding my name on the lined paper. I flip to the next page, and it's more of the same. Over and over again, hundreds and hundreds of times, *Hannah Everett* is written in his tiny, compact scrawl. Blue pen, red pen. A couple pages of pink too.

"I don't understand." I trace the swoop of his letters. Run my fingers over every word. "It's my name."

"You don't think you're enough for me, Hannah? Baby, you're fucking *everything* to me. I don't want anything if you're not there. That's it."

My bottom lip trembles. Another tear falls, staining the paper and making the ink bleed. "You are such a romantic," I whisper, and his laugh is the sweetest sound.

"I'm not finished." He hands over the shoebox. "If there's ever a day where you're wondering if I'm thinking about you, I want you to look in here."

I set down the notebook and take the box, careful to work off the top. Inside are dozens of small plastic bags, each tied with a thin pink ribbon. I pick one up and find a keychain inside.

It's one from Nevada, *beam me up, Scotty* written under AREA 51. The next is one from Cleveland. I find one from Atlanta. Another from San Diego. Three from New York.

"Is this what Liv was talking about?" I sort through them, laughing at some of the unique ones. "The things you bring home with you?"

"From every road game since you told me you collected them. I went out in each city, trying to find the best ones." Brody laughs. "You are always on my mind."

"Brody." I set the keychains down and scoot the box out of the way. "You are the most perfect man."

"And you are the most perfect woman. I know how Grant reacted wasn't ideal, and if you need some time apart to process it, I get it."

"No. *No.* I don't want any time apart." I reach for him, greedy when he leans against the pillows. When he gathers me in his arms and sets me in his lap, his mouth on my neck. "I think it's best if Grant and I cool off for a bit. What you said was right. I know he does mean well, but it's going to take time for us to tackle this."

"I have to be honest with you, Ilan. If he talks to me like that in front of the team, I'm going to have to bench him. I'd do the same with any of the guys, but I've built a locker room based on respect, and that—"

"Wasn't respectful," I finish for him. "I know. And I'm sorry he made that comment about being a father to two daughters. That was out of line."

"Before you and I hooked up the first time, that was one of the reasons why I told myself we couldn't be together. You were too young. The fucking joke is on me because you're mature, levelheaded, and way more articulate than me."

"You wrote my name in a notebook, Brody. We know who the more articulate one is." I take a beat, trying to process the last three hours. The enormity of what Brody and I shared with each other and how *hurt* I feel by Grant's words. "Will you get in trouble with the team after tonight?"

"For, what? Dating someone's sister? Please. The league wouldn't fucking dare to punish me when some of the pieces of shit out there who have sexual assault allegations against them are still playing." Brody brushes a piece of hair away from my face., tucking it behind my ear. "God, Hannah." He kisses my shoulder, my collarbone. "I love you so fucking much."

His phone rings from somewhere on the floor, and I pat his hand. "Go answer it," I say.

"Are you sure?" he asks. "Might be a call that takes up thirty minutes of my time."

"I'm sure. Tonight was a big night. Don't let what Grant said overshadow it."

Brody kisses me again and shifts out from behind me, swiping his phone off the ground. He joins me back on the bed, answering the call and hitting speakerphone.

"Maverick," he says.

"Hey, Coach. I, ah, heard about what happened with you and Grant. I just wanted to make sure you were good?"

"He told the team?" Brody groans. "Fucking Christ."

"No. *No.* When I saw him throwing his stick in his stall, I pulled him aside and got him to tell me what was going on. No one else knows." Maverick coughs. "Okay, Hudson knows. But only because I needed his advice. This is way out of my wheelhouse."

"I'm fine. This doesn't change anything going forward with the team unless Everett starts breaking our code of conduct."

"Understood. He was cooling off when he left the arena, and Ethan offered to drive him home."

"Good. Yeah. Thanks for checking in, Miller."

"Dude." Maverick laughs. "Are you happy or what?"

"I'm happy," Brody says. "Which is why I'm hanging up with you and putting my attention in other places."

"Totally fair. See you Monday?"

"Yup. Be good, Miller."

"Did you ever think you'd be the subject of locker room gossip at almost forty years old?" I ask, plucking the phone from Brody's grip and moving it out of the way. "It's kind of funny when you think about it."

"How in the world is it funny?"

"You went so many years flying under the radar, and now you're front and center with the drama." I smile. "But I still love you."

"Fuck," he growls, yanking my shirt over my head. "Say that again, Hannah."

"I love you," I repeat when he kisses my neck.

"I love you," I say when he pins my arms over my head.

"I love you," I whisper when he fucks me nice and slow, our own celebration for the night.

"I love you too," he answers when I drift off to sleep after a shower, and I dream of my name written in his notebook a thousand times.

FORTY-SIX
HANNAH

TIERNEY

Any word from Grant?

ME

Nope.

Two weeks and counting.

TIERNEY

Shit.

Have you thought about reaching out to him?

ME

No. He's the one that needs to fix this.

TIERNEY

Agreed.

Do you think you'll forgive him?

ME

He's my brother. I don't have to always like
him, but I will always love him.

THE STARS ARE in the middle of a rough second round playoff series. They started down 0-2, but they've managed to claw their way back to tie the series at 2-2 with three days off before game five. I've watched from my apartment, not wanting to be near the locker room if it means I have to see my brother.

Petty?

Maybe.

But at twenty-six-years old, he needs to do some maturing before we talk again.

"Coming," I yell to the person knocking on my door, fixing my earring as I run down the hall. "Just a second!" I turn the knob and grin at Brody standing on the other side with a bouquet of roses in his hands. "This is a nice surprise."

"Hi." He bends to kiss me, putting a hand on my hip. "These are my apology flowers."

"Apology flowers?" I wrinkle my nose and take the roses from him. "What did you do?"

Brody clears his throat and looks to his right, waving his hand. Footsteps grow closer, and Grant appears at the threshold. Sunken cheeks, scruff on his jaw. His skin is pale and dry, and when he looks me, I find his eyes red-rimmed and bloodshot.

"I found someone who said he wanted to talk to us," Brody explains. "But I'm going to defer this conversation to you."

"Is he *drunk*?" I lean forward to sniff Grant's shirt. "You look like shit."

"Feel like shit too." He glances at Brody, then at me. "Can I come in?"

It would be easy to say no. To slam the door in his face and leave him out there with his thoughts, but my chest pinches tight at the sight of his hair looking longer than usual. At the way his shoulders curl in, and I sigh, stepping back.

"Yeah," I say. "You can come in."

"I'm sorry for springing this on you," Brody says as Grant drifts past me. "He's looked lifeless at practice and in our games, and when he came to me and asked if the three of us could have a conversation, I wasn't able to say no."

"It's time we got this over with. I'm not mad at you," I say.

"If he raises his voice, he's out," Brody warns. "I'll do it myself."

"And this is why I love you." I kiss his cheek and close the door, making a detour to the kitchen to put the flowers in a vase. I grab a glass of water and bring it to the living room where Grant is sitting in a leather chair, staring out the window. "In case you're thirsty," I say, setting the glass in front of him.

"Thank you," he says.

I take a seat on the couch, watching Brody hang out in the hallway. "I'm going to let you two talk first," he says when he catches my eye. "I'll check back in with you soon."

When we're alone, Grant takes a sip of the water then sets the glass back down. His exhale is long, stilted, and he finally acknowledges me.

"I'm sorry," he says, and I snort.

"Sorry for what, Grant? Embarrassing me? Saying hurtful, callous things to me and the man I love? Asking if I'm being blackmailed?"

"All of it. I was caught up in the moment and said things I regretted, because you're right, Hannah. You're an adult. You're the only one who can make decisions about your life, and my opinion shouldn't have any say in what you do or don't do." Grant sighs and rubs his forehead. "I wish you would've told me about what was going on before I saw you two. Kissing like that? Interacting like that? I didn't know what the hell was going on."

"I've been very intentional about what I share with you, Grant. You're a professional athlete who is constantly having microphones shoved in his face. Why should you have to answer questions about my personal relationships when they don't have anything to do with the sport you're playing?"

"Because I want to know these things. Because I want know you're okay and taken care of and fucking *happy*, Hannah. Because I love you, and hearing about it from you is less of a blow than stumbling into it after a game. I thought we told each other everything."

"Do you want me to be honest with you?"

"*Yes*," he pleads, and I roll my lips together.

"Brody and I have been seeing each other since the night of the gala. We also slept together the night Riley got hurt, but we didn't talk again until he reached out about coaching his daughter." The words are tumbling out of me now, things I've kept inside for weeks, months, *years*, finally rising to the surface. "It started out as a one-night stand, but then I went and fell in love with him because he's great and wonderful and so *not* the man you all think he is. I'm going to therapy twice a week to talk about my burnout and setting new goals for myself, and I think I'm going to announce my official retirement from skating soon because my heart still isn't in it anymore, and I know that's okay. And I'm bisexual," I add, and he falters. "I had a girlfriend when I was nineteen, but I also like men. There. That's me being honest."

"Y-you're bisexual?" Grant's shoulders fall away from his ears. "Why didn't you say anything? Did you think I would *judge you*?" He stares at me, aghast. "I would never—"

"I know you wouldn't, but, again, my personal life doesn't need to occupy a space in your professional life. I'm not embarrassed of who I am, but I'm *protective* over it. Over who gets to see these sides of me, and the only reason I didn't tell you is because your heart is so damn big, Grant. You'd donate to the LGBTQIA+ centers in the city. You'd make the Stars'

Pride Night a big deal, but you're a hockey player. *That* is your priority, and I'm okay with my relationships being left out of the limelight."

"Hannah." He buries his face in his hands. "Relationships, jobs, sports… all of those things come and go, but this? *This* is who you are. It's your identity, and it's something I *want* to know about even if there's a damn microphone in front of me." Grant slowly lowers his hand, revealing tear-stained cheeks. "I want to know about everything—including Coach… Brody… what the fuck am I supposed to call him now?—because I *love you*. And when you love someone, you get over yourself. You put your personal opinions aside, and you listen. Which is what I should've done originally. I'm so fucking sorry that I didn't."

I stand, moving to where he's sitting. I perch on the edge of the chair and put an arm around him, resting my head on his shoulder.

"I'm sorry for not telling you. We told Olivia, Brody's daughter, because she's the most important person in his life. You're the most important person in *my* life, and I should've been honest with you from the beginning," I say.

"I probably wouldn't have believed you," he mumbles. "It's *Coach*. And you hooked up with him the night Riley was hurt too? Wait a fucking minute." Grant sits up. "His shirt was on inside out that night. *You* did that?"

"Guilty." I laugh. "I"m not the only one who deserves an apology from you. Brody does too."

"Where is he?" Grant asks.

"BB," I call out. "Can you come in here?"

"What the hell does BB mean?"

"Broody Brody," I say.

"Ah. Okay. Yeah. That checks out."

The floor creaks, and Brody emerges from down the hall. He smiles at me, and I motion for him to join us.

"How's everything going in here?" he asks.

"Grant?" I say.

"I'm sorry for the things I said to you, Coach. I was caught up in the moment, but that doesn't excuse my actions. I was out of line, and while I'm still trying to process the two of you together, my behavior was inappropriate," Grant says.

"I get it. I would burn the world to ash for Liv, and if I saw something that caught me off guard like what you saw, I'd probably react the same way," Brody tells him. "But I need to know that you're not going to hold this against me. Away from the rink, you can think whatever you want about me. But when you're under my roof, wearing my team's name, you're going to have to show me some respect."

"I understand. And if you need to bench me, I know I deserve it."

"Let's consider today a fresh start. There's a lot of emotion, a lot of feelings. We can acknowledge that none of us are perfect, and we'll try to be better going forward," Brody offers.

Grant stands. He walks around the coffee table to Brody, holding out his hand. "Since we're away from the ice, I'll add this: if you hurt Hannah, I will not hold back on how I take care of you."

"That's fair, Everett. But I promise I won't." Brody looks over at me. "I'm in it for the long haul with her."

"Good. And, hey. Please no PDA when I'm around." Grant groans. "I'm not ready to see any of that yet."

"Fine, but only because you said you're really fucking sorry, and I felt every syllable of that apology." I throw a pillow at Grant's back. "Are we all good?"

"We're good. I appreciate you all listening to me." It's Grant's turn to glance my way. "Please don't hide any other parts of yourself from me, Han. Fifty years from now, I won't be hitting a puck, but you'll still be my sister. I don't want to not know who you are."

"I promise I won't." I swallow down the lump in my throat. "Thank you for coming by, G."

"I should go. Ethan mentioned something about a human Mario Kart game in his living room, and I'm concerned someone is going to wind up with a concussion." Grant sighs. "One day he'll grow up."

"See you at practice tomorrow, Everett," Brody says, shaking his hand. "Big game five coming up."

"Yeah. You two have a good rest of your day." He gives me a hug. "Text me, Han."

"I will." I smile and let him out, a weight lifted off my shoulders when I close the door. "That went well."

"I'm proud of you for accepting his apology." Brody pops to his feet and gives me a hug, swaying us back and forth. "Because I'm going to put him through hell at practice."

"Knowing Grant, he'll willingly suffer." I laugh and bury my face in his shirt. "Can you stay for a little bit?"

"Depends. What did you have in mind?"

"I was hoping you'd help me hang some of my new keychains on the wall," I say.

"Okay, but only if the penis one goes front and center," he says, and I sigh.

"I guess what they say is true. Men never grow up."

"We grow up. I just wanted to make you blush." Brody kisses my cheek. "I love you, sweetheart."

"I love you too, BB."

"Let's get dick-ssembling."

"Please never say that to me again," I tell him, squealing when he lifts me over his shoulder and carries me down the hall.

The keychains don't get put on the wall, but I'm not worried. We have so many more days to spend together.

FORTY-SEVEN
BRODY

"ARE you going to tell me why I'm blindfolded?" I ask Hannah.

"Because I have a surprise for you, obviously," she answers, guiding me forward. "And I don't want to ruin it."

"Sweetheart. I told you that you don't have to cheer me up. We lost in the Stanley Cup Final, but I'm not mad about it. We had a hell of a season and—*motherfucker*," I curse when my toe hits something solid. "What was that?"

"A stair. I'm sorry! Your legs are so goddamn long, it's hard to maneuver you around objects."

I smile at the apology in her voice and the hand she's keeping on my waist. She made me put on the silk blindfold twenty minutes ago, but I haven't been able to get any other details about where we're going out of her.

My girl knows how to keep a secret, and I'm impressed.

The rest of our season was something for the history books. We fought all the way to the championship, coming up just short to a young LA team, but none of the guys are disappointed. They gave everything they had, and on the night they had to lace up and take the ice, someone else had more to give.

Shit happens, and with the offseason in full swing, I get more time with Liv and Hannah, which means all of my days are great.

Maverick hasn't given me an answer about next season yet. Our governor has scheduled a few meetings about a possible trade, and from the guys he's eyeing, we're going to be the early favorites when we report to training camp.

"Are we playing another game of strip skating?"

"No, but we should try that again. It was fun, wasn't it?" she says.

"Very fun," I agree. "Are we almost there, Han?"

"Yeah. One more minute." A door opens, and I'm greeted by a cool rush of air out of the summer sun. It's eerily quiet, and I can hear my shoes echoing over the surface we're walking on. "I hope this is worth it."

"I'm sure I'm going to love it."

"What if it was a podcast recording?" she asks.

"Anything *but* that."

"Okay. Take your blindfold off, Brody."

I work the blindfold over my head, squinting into the dark room. "Are you abducting me, sweetheart?"

Lights flash on. Dozens of faces pop out of me. Someone blows a streamer, and I put a hand over my chest, scared fucking shitless.

"HAPPY BIRTHDAY!" everyone yells, and I reach for Hannah's arm.

"It's a surprise party," she says, and I see everyone from the team and their significant others. Kali and Bryant and Liv are here too. So is Tierney and her brother, and a couple other coaches I know. "For you."

"What in the world?" I look down at her. "This is all for me?"

"Yup." She smiles. "No gifts. No photo booths or anything like that. I know it's a lot of people in one place, but when I mentioned the idea to Grant, he told Ethan, who told Riley, and pretty soon *all* of the boys wanted to be here to celebrate you. I'm sorry if it's totally overwhelming."

"No." I shake my head. "It's perfect."

I make a lap around the banquet hall, stopping to say hello to everyone who came out. It *is* a lot of people, right near my threshold for socialization, but then Hannah brings me out a cake. Makes me blow out the candles the cuts a slice for everyone, the attention moving away from me to the delicious dessert instead.

"Happy birthday, Dad," Liv says, "Forty years old. How do you feel?"

"Like I'm eighty." I steal a bite of her cake and wipe a spoonful of frosting on her cheek when she complains. "Where are my earplugs?"

"Feels like it was just yesterday when we had Liv." Kali sighs, giving me a hug. "Now she's fifteen, and you're entering a new decade. Times are changing, folks."

Maverick, Emmy, and Murphy are here, and when I steal their little one and find a quiet area away from whatever board games everyone is playing, I relax.

"Should I cancel the clowns?" Hannah asks, joining me.

"Yes, but only because they are goddamn terrifying."

"Brody." She shakes her head. "Not in font of the baby."

"The baby who can't hold her head up, let alone spell? Noted, sweetheart." I lean over so I kiss Hannah's cheek. "Thank you for doing this for me. It's the perfect end to the season."

"I thought so too. We have Liv's competition in August, then that's it. Nothing to look forward to as we get another year older."

"I thought I was supposed to be the cynical one in this relationship?" I ask, and someone clears their throat behind us.

"Are we interrupting?" Maverick says, holding Emmy's hand.

"Not at all. Do you want your baby back?"

"I mean, *fine*. I guess I'll take my darling baby girl back from you and have her all to myself." Maverick puts his arms under mine, safely bringing Murphy to his chest. "Do you have a second?"

"I'm going to grab some food," Hannah says. "So you all can have some privacy."

I watch her walk away, still fucking mystified how that woman loves me like I love her. Maverick laughs and breaks me from my daydream of her waking up next to me every morning this summer.

"You're so down bad," Maverick says.

"So what if I am?" I challenge. "Is that a problem, Miller?"

"No. I just think it's fucking hysterical all it takes for grumpy, broody brutes like you and Liam to fold is a blonde woman who is basically sunshine fucking incarnate," he says, and Emmy hums in agreement.

"The grumpy men do have a type," she says.

"Okay, enough with the analyzation of my love life." I look between them. "What's up?"

"I wanted to let you know I made my decision about next season."

"You did? What is it?" I ask.

"Emmy and I are both going to play, her in Baltimore, me in DC."

"That's great you two. I'm hoping for a Stars and Sea Crabs Eastern Conference showdown."

"With one caveat," Maverick says. "This is my last ride. My farewell tour, and one final season. If at any point our travel schedule becomes too hard to manage with both of us in the league, I'm going to be the one to bow out. Emmy deserves her shot at winning the Cup, and I'm not going to stand in the way of that."

"I'm hoping our schedules work out so I can face off

against him and kick his ass," Emmy tells me. "I always was the better skater out of the two of us."

"You're so beautiful, but that's just not true. We can go settle this on the ice right now, if you want," he says, and I hold up my hands.

"Please don't flirt in front of me," I say. "It makes me sick. Did you tell the boys?"

"Not yet. Figured I'd save that for another day, and I wanted you to be the first to know," Maverick says.

"I appreciate the heads-up." I glance at Emmy. "If we can't win it all, I'd be happy with a Sea Crabs victory so I can cheer you on."

"Appreciate that, Coach." She looks down at Murphy in Maverick's arms. "We'll let you get back to your party."

"Are you going to have that seat at the bar for me?" Maverick asks, and I smile.

"Yeah, Miller. Open invitation, whenever you want to come by."

IT TAKES me ninety minutes to reach my socialization limit, and when Hannah and I head home with the rest of the cake, I glance over at her in the passenger seat.

"I've spent two out of my last three birthdays with you," I say.

"It could've been three in a row, except you weren't talking to me," she teases. "I"m glad we're past that."

"Me too." I rest a palm on her thigh. "Today was my big day, but tomorrow is yours. Are you ready to announce your retirement from figure skating?"

Hannah made the decision early last week, and I've been trying to be there for her however I can. I know her heart is heavy, but after some extended conversations with her therapist and Tierney, this is what she thinks is best for her future.

The door isn't locked, just closed, and from how she smiles when she steps on the ice when we skate every day, I have a feeling she's not leaving forever.

"Yeah. It's not a failure but a redirection, and I'm not any less than who I was before just because I'll never compete at a World Championship again." She rests her head against the seat. "And I'm happy with that."

"I only had one night with you when you were still training at that level, but you're much brighter now, Han," I tell her. "And I'm so proud of you."

"You helped! With Liv, with our sessions. With letting me just... *be* out there."

"And the time I let you win that race," I add, and she rolls her eyes.

"We can do a redo so you stop complaining. I'll even give you a five second head start. You're in a different age bracket now. You need the advantage."

"You're such a shit," I mumble, pinching her skin. "I was going to suggest we find some creative uses for that cake when we got home, but now it's just going in the fridge."

"Home," she repeats. "I like that you call it that now, and not your place."

"I know you mentioned not wanting to getting married, Hannah, and I promise I won't surprise you with a ring. But I'm in this for the long haul with you. If you want to find a new place for us to live together, we can do some browsing. If you want to stay in your apartment and keep your space, I'm all for that too. But my condo will always be open to you, whenever you want it. Even if I'm out of town, I'll give you a key."

"Think I might just sit in your closet and stare at all the times you wrote out my name," she says softly, folding her hand over mine. "I love you, Brody, and I'm so lucky to be a part of your family."

And to think I almost messed this all up by running away.

Hannah was the best birthday surprise two years ago, and I can't fucking wait to see where we are twelve months from now.

Wherever it is, with her by my side, I'm going to be on top of the fucking world.

FORTY-EIGHT
HANNAH

August

"BRODY," I say. "Do you want to sit down?"

"Hm? What?" He touches his jaw and looks at me. "No. I'm fine."

"You've been walking up and down the stairs for the last ten minutes."

"Because I need to get a workout in," he grumbles, and Kali laughs.

"You're pacing," she says. "Which means you're panicking."

"It's going to be okay, baby." I hold my hand. He takes it, threading our fingers together and kissing my knuckles. "Why are you panicking?"

"Liv's competed in events before, but this is the most important one of her life. I want her to do well." Brody sighs and finally sits next to me on the metal bench, tapping his foot. "I don't want her to get hurt or be disappointed in herself if something goes wrong."

"And if everything goes right?" I say, stealing his line and throwing it back to him. When he glances at me, I smile.

"What? You know I'm always going to be the optimist when you're being a pessimist."

"You're right. I know I can't always be there to catch her if she falls, but I really don't want her to fall."

"She's going to do great, Brody. And after, fall or no fall, we'll go get milkshakes. We'll go back to your condo, and life will go on." I see Liv waiting with a group of girls on the other side of the rink. Pride almost bursts from my chest with how excited she looks. "I'm proud of how far she's come."

"Still remember the first time I ever brought her on the ice." He drapes an arm around my shoulder, pulling me close. "I was an assistant coach in Chicago. We had the Winter Classic at Wrigley Field, and after the game, I put Liv in these tiny skates. She was so fucking small." He laughs and presses a kiss to my forehead. "Can't believe how much she's grown."

"She was so small, yet I had to yell at you because you were zipping around the rink with her like you didn't have a care in the world," Kali says. "That was precious cargo you were holding, and you were spinning like crazy."

"Okay, I did one spin, Kal. Nothing that brought harm to any parties." Brody sits up. "Is it her turn?"

"Yeah." I pat his thigh when Liv files onto the ice. She takes a minute to gather herself, dipping her chin to her chest and closing her eyes. I hope she's repeating the mantra I taught her. I hope the ribbon I tied in her hair earlier brings her luck, and I'm more nervous for her program than I've ever been for anything I've performed. "Think you're going to be able to get through this?"

"I need your hand," he mumbles. "So I don't start to panic."

"I'm right here," I say. "And I'm not going anywhere."

"Thank fuck for that." He takes my hand again and lets out a long sigh. "I love you so much, Hannah."

The offseason has been good to us, and with Liv out of school, the three of us have spent the summer making memories. We've visited almost all the Smithsonian museums and had picnics on the Mall. There was the trip to the Kenilworth Aquatic Gardens to see the water lilies in bloom and paddleboarding in the tidal basin. Bowling nights, movie nights, days where Liv and I hang out without Brody around, everything feels *right*.

And Brody?

He spends every minute of every day making sure I know how valued I am. He showed me where my keychain wall can go if and when I decide I'm ready to move in with him. We skate together every day, lap after lap around the rink where we talk about everything on our minds. He and Grant are starting to figure out their relationship away from the ice, and they're supposed to get dinner together tomorrow night.

"I love you too," I say, squealing as Liv's music begins. I pat Brody's knee. "Here we go."

I know Liv's program like the back of my hand, all six of the intermediate elements things we've practiced together for months on end. She starts off with a beautiful double axel, and she holds her camel spin perfectly with an outside edge. Her Salchow and toe loop jump combination go well, but the lift off from her flip jump is shaky. Brody stiffens beside me, but Liv cleans up the landing, and moves on to her spin combination. She goes for a bonus with triple toe loop, and I jump to my feet when the music ends.

"That was good, right?" Brody asks, clapping. "I'm still trying to figure out how to look for small errors."

"It was very good. She did all of her planned elements, and her presentation was beautiful. No time violation, and I didn't see anything else that could get her a deduction. She's in group B, which is definitely the more advanced group of girls." I crane my neck, waiting to see what the judges score her. "Oh my *god*. She got a 34.58!"

"I don't know what that means, Hannah."

"Sorry, sorry! I need to teach you the breakdown of how

programs are scored—there are so many components—but I think it's going to put her as the second skater in her category!"

"Second? *Second?* Out of, what? Fifty girls? That's fucking amazing," Brody says. He wipes his cheek and turns his back to the rink as Liv hops off the ice. "Sorry. Something in my eye."

"Emotional," Kali whispers to me, and I hold back my laughter. "Always is when Liv is involved."

"You are such a good dad," I say, kissing his shoulder. "She should be over here in just a—*Liv.* My girl. You were wonderful out there." I squeal and wrap my arms around her in a hug. "How are you feeling?"

"That was so scary." She laughs and hugs me back. "I thought I was about to bust my ass with that flip jump. A *flip jump*! One of the most boring moves out there."

"You recovered the landing perfectly! No falls. No deductions. What do you think about your double Axel?" I ask, vibrating with excited energy for her. "I'm being so obnoxious. I'm going to shut up."

"What?!" Liv gives me a gentle shove. "Don't you ever shut up. You're the reason I got here. You're the first coach who has ever made me feel like I could do the things I hadn't learned yet, and I'm so grateful for you." Her eyes move to her parents, and she smiles. "Hi, mama. *Dad?* Are you *crying?*"

"*No,*" Brody says firmly, but he sniffs. "Allergies. A fly. Don't make fun of me, kid."

"I love you too, Dad." Liv smiles. "What are we getting to eat?"

"Are you sure you want to hang out with the three of us?" I ask. "It looked like you were friendly with some of the other girls in your group."

"A lot of them are with Washington Figure Skating Club. They said I should come join them, but I told them I already had the best coach out there." She shifts on her feet. Lets out a sheepish laugh. "If you want to still coach me, that is."

"You're stuck with me, Liv. Next up: Eastern Sectionals in November!"

We all climb into Brody's SUV, reliving Liv's performance a second time. By the time we get to the diner where we're having lunch, she's recanted each element for a third and fourth time.

"Safe to say she's proud of herself," Kali says from next to me in the booth the sever seats us in. "And you did all of that as the tallest one out there too."

"That was pretty cool." Liv opens her menu, turning the page. "Thank you all for coming to watch me. I know it's been a long ten months with getting me to and from the rink, and if I don't say it enough, I want to make sure you all know I appreciate how much time and energy you put in to helping me succeed. Hang on. I made a list." Liv sets her small purse on the table, rifling through it for a folded piece of paper. "Mama, for sewing me this outfit and always having snacks in the car after my lessons."

"Kali, you *sewed* that? It's stunning." I gape at Liv's bedazzled costume and all the intricate details. "You could make a career out of selling them for local girls."

"Really? The stitching needs some work, and I underestimated how many sequins would be needed." She laughs. "Next time, we're doing double."

"People would pay a lot of money for something like that." I wave at Liv. "Sorry, kiddo. I interrupted you."

"It's okay. Mom's work deserves to be bragged about. Okay, next on my list is Dad, for coaching hockey and having the connections that were able to help us find Hannah." Liv clears her throat. "And for always making sure I get my homework done, even if I don't want to do it."

"So I'm only wanted for my connections?" Brody scowls

and folds his arms over his chest, sitting back in the booth. "Doesn't seem fair."

"Sorry, Pops. Until you can teach me a double Axel, I have to be grateful to Hannah for getting me here." Liv smiles at me. "I know it's cheesy, but you started off as my coach, and now you're my friend. Thank you for believing in me from the very beginning. I'm glad you're a part of our family."

I reach across the table for her hand, but I make sure I look at Brody as I say this next part. "Thank you for welcoming me into your family. It's been such a joy to spend time with you and watch you grow and believe in yourself. We're just getting started."

Later, after we drop off Kali and Liv at Kali's home, Brody and I climb into bed. He pulls out his crossword puzzle and I lean against him, opening a book and letting out a sigh, blissfully content how everything has turned out.

"Sometimes I wonder if all of this would be different if Riley hadn't gotten injured," I say, and Brody hums.

"How so?"

"That first night we were together, we would've had sex. You would've gone home in the morning, and, what? We would've been friends? Started dating? Never spoken to each other again?" I tilt my chin up to look at him. "Going sixteen months without talking to you sucked, but I'm not sure this would've worked out otherwise."

"Maybe it took knowing I'd never have you again to realize how lucky I was to have had you that first time." Brody kisses my nose. "And, you know, figure out how to *not* be the dick who left you and said to forget it never happened."

"I didn't let myself think about," I admit. "Not until you started getting more intentional with your touches."

"I thought about it all the time," he admits. "I dreamed about you. I fell asleep hoping you were having a good day. I was fucking haunted by the look on your face when I left, and

I'm so glad I found my way back to you. I love you very much, Ice Queen."

"I love you too, BB." I pat his chest. "I'll let you get back to your crossword puzzle."

"It's easy tonight. All hockey clues. One word, ten letters. 'An illegal penalty in hockey where a player hits an opponent with their stick held in both hands.'"

"Cross-check?" I guess, and he grins.

"Very good, Hannah. Ready for the next one?"

"Hit me with your best shot, Daddy."

Brody sputters out a breath and squeezes his eyes shut. "I need a goddamn warning before you say that. The spike in my heart rate could kill me."

"Whatever you say, Daddy."

His fingers twist the edges of the paper. "This next one is fitting, because it's where you're going to be if you aren't careful. Two words, six letters. 'Another name for the penalty box.'"

"Sin bin?" I answer.

"Perfect," he muses, tossing the paper to the side. He rolls on top of me with a smile. "Any last words before I punish you for driving me out of my mind, every second of every goddamn day?"

"Yeah." I touch his cheek where his smile begins. "I'm still a faster skater than you," I whisper.

"In your dreams, Everett," he whispers back,

"Pretty sure you are my dreams, Saunders."

"And what a lucky fucking guy am I."

EPILOGUE

Brody
Eighteen months later

"BRODY SAUNDERS." The reporter from NBC smiles at me. "Welcome to Italy for the Winter Olympic Games."

"Hey, Rebecca. Good to see you," I say into the microphone she holds my way. "It's an honor to be here representing our country."

"What kind of energy are you feeling as you head into the prelim round early next week? You're coaching a very talented hockey team from the United States."

"We're feeling good," I answer. "Our roster is full of guys who are excited to be here, and we're anxious to see how we perform in our first game. A lot of our players participated in the 4 Nations Face Off a few years back, but for some of them, this is their first time competing at an international level of this caliber. They're going to be shell-shocked in the best way."

"The field is deep this year with several talented teams. Who do you see as your biggest competition?" she asks.

"Canada will always be a powerhouse in the sport, but luckily for us, they're not in our group. Look. We could sit here and analyze statistics and numbers, but you never know what's going to happen until the puck drops. The last time the U.S. won a medal at the Games was back in 2010, and it was silver. You'd have to go back to 1980 for our most recent gold medal, and we all know that's when everyone started believing in miracles." I chuckle and put my hands in my coat, the cold air making my fingers numb. "We take it day by day. We're soaking up the atmosphere, getting in some good training sessions, and we'll be ready to get to work next week."

"Let's switch gears and talk about the women."

"Oh, let's. I could talk about women's hockey all day."

"You're the first NHL coach to sign a woman to his team. DC is getting a PWHL team next year. Amelia Green is the first female head coach in the NHL, and three more women were hired as assistant coaches throughout the league during the offseason. This surge of attention on women's sports is inspiring to see."

"It's about time professional sports league invested time and money into women's sports, and it's about time the world started paying attention. You can't mention USA women's hockey without shining a light on Emerson Hartwell. She's been a dynamic force, and her comeback has been a joy to watch." My lips twitch with a smile remembering Emmy's joy when Maverick delivered her the Olympic jersey she'd be wearing. He and Murphy had on matching ones too. "As far as other players? Genevieve Grayson out of West Bridge University is going to take the PWHL by storm next season. A projected number one draft pick who transferred to a dying NCAA program and breathed life back into the school? She'd have a field day out there playing with my guys."

"Last question before I let you go," Rebecca says. "You're in Italy. The weather is beautiful. What other events are you looking forward to spectating when you have some free time?"

"We had the chance to share the ice with the athletes on the speed skating team, and my guys are jazzed to go support them. They're like bullets out there. As for me, my other half is performing in the medal round of the free skate today." I check my watch. "In fact, I need to go. I don't want to be late."

"Thank you so much for your time, Brody. We appreciate you stopping by, and we're cheering you and the team on."

"Thanks for having me, Rebecca."

We exchange a handshake, and I accept her warm wishes to pass along to Hannah. The walk to the skating arena is short, but I take it in a jog. It might be my nerves. It might be my excitement. It might be my fear of being late and missing a second of Hannah's program, and I try to not panic when security gets backed up. Flashing my VIP badge helps, and by the time I find my seat, I let myself relax.

"Hey." Grant sits next to me and leans forward in his chair, elbows on his knees. "I was worried about you."

"Sorry. I was doing an interview with NBC." I shrug off my coat, the arena warm and full of people. "That media training class I did with Piper makes talking to reporters much more tolerable."

"Only took you, what? Seven years?" He snorts. "I saw Han and Tierney. They're both doing well, and I gave my sister the gift you had for her." His gaze cuts away from the ice and over to me. "Do I want to know what it was or will it make me throw up?"

"A ribbon." I smirk. Gold, to match her outfit and the medal I hope she brings home today. "Is that a problem with you?"

"Not at all, and I'm going to pretend it has a singular function of only going in her hair." Grant shivers. "Don't ruin hair accessories for me, man."

It's been a learning curve for Grant and I on how to navigate our relationship on and off the ice. I never want anyone on the team to think he's getting preferential treatment—he never will—but when we're away from the rink, we're good friends. Liv and I spent Christmas in Florida with him and Hannah, and he stops by my place to eat dinner with the two of us.

Every few months he gives me the same warning: break his sister's heart, and he'll break me.

It's funny the guy who is eight inches shorter and thirty pounds lighter than me thinks he can kick my ass, but I have to admire his determination. I'm glad Hannah has so many people in her life who care about her.

"How is she feeling?" I ask, wiping my sweaty palms on my joggers. "She doing okay?"

"Nervous, but ready, I think." He smiles. "She's been waiting for this for a while."

My girl, the fucking warrior.

Hannah spent six months in retirement, then got the itch to skate again. She kept things easy at first. No pressure, no goals, just focusing on her strength and conditioning before diving into the technical aspect of her program. I know she was hesitant, afraid those same feelings might start to claw back the more time she spent on the ice, but they never came. We had a conversation about how far she wanted to take her training, and when she said she wanted to fight for a spot on the Olympic team, I supported her every step of the way.

There was the Dallas Classic. The Cranberry Open and Eastern Sectional. Skate America and the Grand Prix Final.

They all lead us here: minutes away from her free skate after a beautiful short program two days ago allowed her to advance.

Hannah is the tenth woman to skate. She makes her way onto the ice, scanning the crowd. I lift my hand in a wave when she spots me, and a smile bursts across her face.

I can't believe I get to see her smile like that for the rest of my life.

Grant won't stop fidgeting when the music starts. He covers his eyes. Gasps when she lands a jump safely and squeezes my hand so tight, I'm fucking *certain* my fingers are broken.

Her blades touch the ice with precision, and I can see the steely glint of determination in her eyes, even from up here. Every move, every spin, every element is goddamn perfect. I count through the sections of her four-minute program I memorized months ago, on the edge of my seat every time she launches herself in the air.

"If she gets this quadruple Axel right, she'll only be the second skater to land one in competition," Grant whispers.

"Sh. I'm trying to channel her good energy," I whisper back, and she takes off. "Come on, baby."

Hannah moves into it, setting up the entry she's nailed perfectly before. I stop breathing when she lifts off the ice, counting each rotation until she lands. It's half a degree off, a slight bend in her knee, but she's upright, and Grant screams.

"*Oh my fucking god*. She did it. SHE DID IT," he whisper-shouts.

My eyes fill with tears, so fucking proud of how hard she's worked to get here. The second the music ends I'm on my feet, whistling and cheering with the rest of the crowd.

"What do you think?" I ask Grant.

"Has to be at least good enough for a bronze. No one else is going to try that move. I'll riot if she doesn't medal."

He doesn't have to, because Hannah's score puts her in position for a silver medal. It's still early, with fourteen skaters to go, but by the time we shove our way down to where she's waiting with Tierney, her chances are looking better and better.

"Hi," she says, running into my embrace when I get close. "I'm so glad you're here."

"You were beautiful out there. How's your ankle? Did you land on it wrong?" I ask.

"It's sore, but I'll be okay. The skater from Japan is phenomenal, isn't she? She's only seventeen, and I officially feel like a grandma." Hannah laughs. "Everyone is so young and talented."

"I'll make sure to sign you up for some AARP discounts," I murmur, kissing the top of her head and giving Tierney a hug. "I'm so proud of you, sweetheart. And I love you so much."

"I love you too." She throws an arm around my neck. "Do you have something with the team, or can you stick around?"

"Free until dinner. Liv wants us to FaceTime her when we know the results. My phone has been blowing up with texts from her, which means she's not paying attention in class." I laugh and touch the ribbon tied in Hannah's ponytail. The perfect bow, the perfect color. The perfect woman. "She also demanded we bring home a souvenir for her."

"Already have that covered. I got the girls competing today to sign an old pair of skates." She pauses to wave to someone from France. "I thought they would look great on that floating shelf in Liv's room. I can't wait until June to give it to her for her birthday, so it'll be an early present."

"Damn you, Tiny Everett," I grumble, a hand on her waist. "You're going to give her the better gift for the second year in a row."

"Suck it, Saunders," Hannah teases, reaching up to touch my cheek. "What a dream this is, huh? Both of us at the Olympics. Walking in the Opening Carmony together. We're so lucky."

"Okay, lovebirds. Can I say hi to my sister, please?" Grant asks, and Hannah bursts out laughing. "The room we used to share was *covered* in figure skating outfits. I deserve at least a hug."

"Sorry, G." She slides out of my hold to give her brother a squeeze. "The Everett siblings take on the Olympics. Is that better?"

"Much better. And I better see you near the glass during our first game next week, cheering us on," he says. "The woman sitting next to me in the stands asked if I was a figure skater, and when I said no, she said that checked out. Apparently, I don't look strong enough to lift a woman over my head? I'm *offended*."

"You'll survive." Hannah accepts a congratulations from another skater and tosses her ponytail over her shoulder. "I should get back to my coach while we wait for the last few skaters to perform. I'll find you all after?"

"Sounds good. Proud of you, sweetheart." I give her another kiss, and when I put a hand on Grant's shoulder, he's staring at his phone. "Everything okay, Everett?"

"Um." He looks up, the color gone from his face. "I think we have a problem."

"What's wrong, G?" Hannah asks, touching his wrist. "Did something happened?"

"Uh, you remember how I asked you about the CBA a while back, Coach?" Grant says, holding up his phone, and I squint at the screen.

"'Up and coming hockey heartthrob caught in steamy tryst with NHL coach?'" I read. "Why are you showing me a gossip website?"

"You know Amelia Green? The head coach for the Baltimore Sea Crabs?" he asks.

"Yes," I say slowly. "I had lunch with her last week. Do *you* know Amelia Green?"

"I guess you could say that?" Grant lets out a nervous laugh. "I'm, ah, kind of in a relationship with her. And I think I'm about to be in a shitload of trouble."

The DC Stars will be back with more stories soon!
Here's who else is getting a book:

Grant (off-limits woman, age gap where she's older, secret relationship)
Ethan (accidental pregnancy, forced proximity)

ACKNOWLEDGMENTS

I can't believe we've reached the end of another book, and we're one step closer to finishing the series that changed my life. I'm forever indebted to all the Bookstagram and BookTok content creators who took a chance on a girl who wanted to write a hockey romance series that was a little different from anything else out there, because you all have changed my life time and time again. It's a dream to call this *work*, and even on the hardest days where every single word and every single sentence is like pulling from a well that's run dry, I think of you all and the magic you create, and my inspiration never runs out.

Thank you to my beta readers for all your feedback. All your input is instrumental to each book's success, and I'm so appreciative of the time you give to me to make these books the best they can be.

To my lovely Hannah. I'm so proud of you for starting your business, and I'm even more proud that I get to work with you. Thank you for always putting up with my hectic schedules, and thank you for being my friend. Knowing we can walk into Waterstones in the very near future and see the books we worked on together sitting on a table in the romance section is an absolute joy.

Britt. The craftsmanship you have and the skills you possess are nothing short of magical. I know I've sent you half a dozen voice memos raving about how much I adore you at this point, but you are the best of the best. Thank you for your patience, your grace, and being so incredibly thorough while also being so incredibly kind.

To Chloe, for another wonderful cover! Your ability to create a masterpiece from my simple prompt of *can she be pulling on his whistle?????* to a cover that looks like THIS is mind blowing. It's always a delight working with you!

M&R, my favorite guys. I love you forever and always.

And to you, dear reader. Thank you for your support, your love, your endless enthusiasm. You all make the publishing world go round, and I'm so grateful for you.

ABOUT THE AUTHOR

Chelsea is a best-selling romance author who writes fun, fresh, and flirty love stories with plenty of spice. When she's not making fictional characters banter for twenty chapters before they finally kiss, you can find her trying to pet as many dogs as she can.

Stay up to date by signing up for her newsletter: https://authorchelseacurto.myflodesk.com/newsletter

instagram.com/authorchelseacurto

amazon.com/author/chelseacurto

tiktok.com/@chelseareadsandwrites

threads.com/@authorchelseacurto

ALSO BY CHELSEA CURTO

D.C. Stars series

Face Off

Power Play

Slap Shot

Hat Trick

Love Through a Lens series

Camera Chemistry

Caught on Camera

Behind the Camera

Off Camera

Other Books

Dashing All The Way

In The Dark

An Unexpected Paradise

The Companion Project

Road Trip to Forever

Booked for the Holidays

www.ingramcontent.com/pod-product-compliance
Lightning Source LLC
Chambersburg PA
CBHW022017300726

48970CB00003B/931